KELLY HOUSE

KELLY HOUSE

John K. Spitzberg

iUniverse, Inc.
Bloomington

KELLY HOUSE

iUniverse books may be ordered through booksellers or by contacting:

iUniverse
1663 Liberty Drive
Bloomington, IN 47403
www.iuniverse.com
1-800-Authors (1-800-288-4677)

ISBN: 978-1-4759-3068-9 (sc)
ISBN: 978-1-4759-3069-6 (hc)
ISBN: 978-1-4759-3071-9 (e)

Library of Congress Control Number: 2012909893

Printed in the United States of America

iUniverse rev. date: 12/19/2012

DEDICATED TO

JEFF
JERRY
ROYANNE
JEREMY
JORDAN
And
EMILY

ACKNOWLEDGEMENT

Thank you to Peter Olevnik, Peggy Rhodes, Nancy Sanders and Grace Shahrokh who gave me permission to use their work. Thanks to Howard Poteet who I knew in the last century and who was a gifted writer. For Robert Service, the great bard of the north and Gahlil Gibran gratitude for your genius and finally to Carol Thomas and Grace who helped me edit the book, a heart felt appreciation. To all of you I am indebted.

PART I

EMIGRATION

CHAPTER ONE

Aflood of sunlight embraced the sky on the day that Gerald Janokoski and Lee Lansing were due to be released from Greentree Rehabilitation and Nursing Home in Plantation, Florida. It was exactly the kind of weather that snow birds died for. Mancini music soothed the halls of Greentree as it made its way along the corridors and into the patients' rooms. A mellow seventy-seven degrees with a cool breeze, lazy billowing clouds clear of the heaviness of impending precipitation greeted Lee and Gerald as they walked out of the facility on their own without the support of walkers or any other device to keep them from losing their balance and falling.

Gerald walked with the shuffle and slowness expected of a gentleman who had fractured his hip and was exceedingly cautious as a result of that mishap, while Lee suffering from Parkinson's disease walked with the gait and awkwardness associated with her malady. On this day, though, the duo forgot their aging and infirmities and walked with purpose and determination. As they saw it, this was the beginning of a new lease on life.

Their departure was not typical because they were members of Greentree's famed writers' group which by now was highly touted at the rehabilitation center and throughout South Florida within the nursing home industry as a means of helping the elderly cope and even exceed their rehabilitation goals. Staff members, tears in their eyes, other patients and even administrative personnel lined the hallways to say goodbye and wish the two of them good luck as they embarked on their new adventure. They would be leaving soon for Asheville, North Carolina, and their new home, the writers' collective for disabled elderly, Kelly House.

Still to leave Greentree forever and join the pair were David Greenberg, Sadie Goldenblum, and Britt Manning, the remaining patients in the writers' group. They, too, were scheduled to make the exodus from Florida to the "promised land" of Western North Carolina and the beckoning Appalachians.

Unbeknown to the group was a reporter from the Sunshine Journal notified by his editor to find out about the commune and to do a story- if one even existed. The editor received a telephone call from a friend of a friend who worked at Greentree. She talked at length about the newly formed writers' commune made up of patients and volunteers adding with delight that there was a fresh buzz of excitement which seemed to surround the entire facility.

No one was ever able to figure out who called the press. It was only a matter of time anyway before the secret was out. Ben Zangwell, the founder of Kelly House, knew that eventually the press would become interested and want to know more the project. For many years Ben led a clandestine existence out of necessity and now things would change. He winced. It was no surprise that on the Friday that Lee and Gerald left, a reporter and photographer were present to take pictures and interview them about their future plans.

The reporter had several pictures taken and asked for a group shot of the writers with Pauline Baldwin and Ben, once fellow volunteers who had assisted them in their writing. Pauline was there to become a charter member of the new commune and would be leaving for the mountain antebellum home as a member of the commune. The reporter wanted to talk to the social worker, Jane Finestein, who started the writers' therapy group, and to get the full story. As far as the reporter knew, no commune had ever been born at a nursing and rehabilitation facility in Florida or anywhere else and no commune had ever been founded for such old people. That had to be newsworthy.

Gerald agreed to speak to the reporter about his part in the whole affair and readily gave his phone number to the reporter. He would call Gerald on Monday and pay him a visit in Coral Springs. As for Lee, he arranged to have a colleague pay her a visit in her room in Ft. Lauderdale. The reporter thought it would be a good idea to meet Lee and Pauline together since Pauline had assisted Lee in her writing. Pauline suggested that they might be a little more comfortable were they to meet in her condo in Oakland Park on A1A.

Pauline lived in opulence on the fourteenth floor of her rounded skyscraper condo with a magnificent view of the ocean and the comforts of never having to leave her building full of magnificent shopping opportunities and a mini mall on the first floor with a full gym, Versace clothing boutiques and high quality antique and collectible shops. A four star French restaurant, fine Italian dining, gourmet dining for any palate and a smorgasbord of international wine cellars provided the residents with ample reason never to leave the confines of the building. There were two such buildings connected together with a subterranean walkway and tram. For Pauline it was exactly due to this lifestyle that she felt smothered, useless and had to escape to become constructive and feel a sense of worthiness.

The weekend was a lonely and disconcerting one for David Greenberg who for the last six months or more had spent most of his waking hours with Gerald. Although he realized that they would soon be back together talking and writing, he sorely missed his pal. He spent the weekend writing notes to himself about the areas of his life that he had not covered thoroughly enough or not at all while in the writer's therapy group with Jane. These would be the first areas that he wished to examine in writing as soon as he got to the commune.

The other things that he wanted to attend to while remaining in the center were related to his rehabilitation. Stan Darling, his physical therapist, and one of the occupational therapists had fashioned a splint of sorts for David to use on his right hand. He still had no feeling on his right side including the hand, but the splint did allow him to use the right hand for gross motor activities by using the left hand to maneuver the right.

David wanted to do as much as he could so that when he moved he'd be able to use the right side a little more effectively. Everyone in rehab was amazed at his determination to make it work. They could remember the days when Mr. Greenberg had all but given up and preferred death to life. Now, when they encountered him, there was camaraderie and joined purpose which made them feel worthwhile and him grateful for their hard work. Now when staff encountered him, he was a new person in their eyes as well as his own.

David was scheduled to leave the center in a week and return to Whispering Pines Village. He, too, would keep his one bedroom apartment for a year as agreed upon by the others and Ben. The agreement was that for the first year Ben would handle all costs in North Carolina and David would take care of the condo bills in Florida, a win-win plan.

Each member would have a year to decide whether communal living was right for them or not. Each writer would have a place to return to if it didn't work for them. In actuality it would be no different than what they had now when they were first hospitalized and then sent to the rehabilitation program. David saw it as an agreement in which no one would lose the security of knowing that they had a home. David reflected on Jane's words. "There are no losers, only winners." He thought back on how he used to envy her youth and cheerfulness, albeit naivety with more than a little anger and caustic cynicism. Now he, too, had reason for a new spirit of joy and hopefulness. Former President Obama's book, *The Audacity of Hope* seemed so apropos now.

David wanted to talk to Ethan and Diana, his son and daughter-in-law. He wanted to ask them whether they would be willing to look in on the apartment and take care of anything that came up. David believed that once the mail system caught up he could probably handle most of his bills, taxes and important matters. He didn't consider his stroke and its aftermath to be a deterrent any longer, but rather a challenge.

Britt Manning and Sadie Goldenblum spent more time together now that Lee and Gerald were gone. Britt thought back to the time when she had made fun of Sadie and almost scorned her for her simple and child-like love of everyone. Sadie reminded Britt of Betty White who used to play Rose in the *Golden Girls* long ago. Britt mused to herself how from such a hateful and angry woman she had found love for her friends and a spark of something she couldn't put her finger on for Ben Zangwell.

For Britt there would be little to do. She had a room in Deerfield Beach in one of the small motels that lined AIA. Since she was willing to sign a yearly lease, she was given a room, bath and small kitchenette for $450 a month with a first and last month paid in advance. The owner, a retired steam fitter and his wife who also suffered from emphysema like Britt, took pity on the little old lady. Had Britt known that was his image of her, she would never have stayed there. He reduced the price significantly. It also meant that the room was paid for even in the off season, so everyone was happy.

Britt received $575 in Social Security and $20 to $25 a month from royalties on some of her pictures taken in Siberia when she taught English with the Peace Corps years ago and pictures taken in Alaska when she tried without success to become a teacher in the Bush, what Australians referred to as the Outback. She maintained a post office box and held it for some twenty years or more. That's how she was able to get her checks. Whenever she moved she'd send a forwarding address to the post office which would then send her mail to her.

It wasn't much to be sure, but it would have to do. The question which Britt posed to herself and discussed with Sadie was whether she should hold on to the apartment or let it go. That meant that she could pocket the social security and royalty checks for a year. That would give her over $6,000 if she decided that North Carolina or the commune was not for her.

"So what do you think, Sadie?"

"My husband, Morris, used to say that a bird in the hand is worth more than---I've forgotten the rest. Why don't you talk to Ben and see what he thinks. Men have a better mind for money than women, I think." She smiled benignly.

"Oh God, Sadie. There you go again with that 'men know more than women' stuff. I don't think so at all. Women have been taking care of money and families all by themselves without men to help for a long time now. And they didn't have men telling them what to do!" There was a time when Britt would have exploded at this simple woman, but now all she could feel was great love and caring for her. Things had really changed.

"I know you're right, but Morris, may he rest in peace, use to say that women are best when they don't have to trouble themselves about money matters. Of course when he was gone for all those years as a merchant marine, I did take care of a house full of people and children."

"See what I mean! You've been doing by yourself all along."

Sadie smiled innocently with no indication of understanding Britt's point.

"What are you going to do with your condo, Sadie? Come to think of it I don't remember you ever telling us anything about where you live or anything like that."

"Hmm, you're right. Britt, I didn't. I guess I forgot. Doing all that writing with Jean's help was mostly about my life before I came to Florida. Well, anyway I have a two bedroom condo in Hollywood off of Sheridan Rd. I'm not far from 441. It's in a senior community, but nothing like David's. That's a huge place. I used to have a girlfriend there, but she died, may she rest in peace. Mine is small, about four buildings. People are allowed to have small pets and for the most part they take care of them pretty good. I'm going to keep the condo. That's for sure. I have a neighbor who takes care of things for me when I'm not there, like now."

"That's good. I never owned anything of my own. In some ways I liked it that way. I could always move around without having to worry about reselling or anything like that. In other ways I always wanted to own something. Never did talk about that in group, but it's not such a big deal now. I was the proverbial rolling stone-never to be caught with my pants down." Britt laughed, "Unless I wanted to take them down, you know what I mean? Don't look at me that way."

Sadie didn't seem to catch the joke. Once again Britt thought of Rose Nyland from St. Olaf, Minnesota. She wondered whether Betty White was still alive. Bee Arthur and Estelle Getty were dead. What was the name of the character Blanche? Rue-something…. "I don't think that I could have ever been happy not owning my own house, Britt. It was the center of my world." Her eyes misted with memories and smells of her kitchen.

They sat in silence staring at the floor each with her own thoughts.

"How do they say it- 'Different strokes for different folks'," murmured Britt.

"I think I heard someone down in rehabilitation say that. I want to get out of here as soon as I can and move to North Carolina. I need to write letters to my son Sammy and my daughter, Elaine. I'm not sure where Sammy and Pat are now, probably still on that *goyisha* island in Georgia, Saint something or another. But Elaine and Josh are still in their house. I wonder how Sammy's going to feel about my writing about Messianic Judaism." Sadie scrunched her face in deep concern.

"Yes, you talked a lot about that in group. I don't know whether he'll like you knocking what he believes in, especially you being his mother," lamented Britt.

"True, but one thing I learned in these six months with Jane and all of you, especially David is that I shut my eyes too much just because he is my son and I love him. I shouldn't have gone along with everything he said. I should have really stopped supporting him the minute he tried to drive the devil out of my poor sick sister, Jennie. May she rest in peace? But, I didn't."

"No use crying over it now, Sadie. It's in the past. Maybe when you get to the commune and start writing, you can expose the group without exposing Sammy. You know, deal with their ideas, not the people who have them. Does that make sense?"

"I guess." Sadie's blank gaze made Britt doubt that she understood. "Well, I'm tired. I'll see you at dinner. I hope that we can eat with David. He must feel terribly lonely without Gerald."

With that the women parted and went to their rooms. They, too, would be leaving Greentree within two weeks for their new venture.

CHAPTER TWO

Benjamin Zachariah Zangwell sat in his apartment reflecting about the many things which would have to be done before anyone could move into Kelly House. His apartment was small, with a Lazy-boy chair in which he spent much, too much, time watching reruns of Stephen Segal movies and a few comedies. He loved Special Victims Unit out of the New York Police Department and loved the humor from NCIS. Primarily, he loved the characters in both of the shows and in SVU, the horrendous story lines. He also watched his girth grow as he munched on things which were bad for him, particularly with his diabetes.

When Ben first bought the old house in North Carolina, over twenty years ago, he never figured on the elderly angle. Ben's original idea was to bring together everyone interested in fighting the World Trade Organization, the amorphous titans of industry who maintained slave labor, women, and children in factories, mines and sweatshops throughout the world to bolster unimaginable fortunes for themselves to learn how to fight these giants. It didn't come to fruition as he planned.

One mission and then another never permitted the idea to take shape. And then 9-11 disrupted any idea of a school for dissidents. Many Americans bought into the idea that somehow anyone who didn't agree was a terrorist. The White House was entirely too paranoid to tolerate any underground, subversive school. Even under the Democrats, with a brilliant enlightened president, Ben couldn't organize the school, and then the right wing religious zealots made it impossible to rise up. Mediocre intelligence within congressional ranks, incredibly greedy money interests, and a massive grass roots program, spearheaded by people who couldn't adjust to the fact that a man of color was duly elected as President, disgusted Ben. So he spent a lot of time in foreign countries where there might be turmoil, but he couldn't understand the languages that well, and preferred to roam the globe rather than get involved. He saw himself as an ex-patriot until his health brought him home and to Florida.

Zangwell found himself living into his eighties in Southern Florida, and doing some volunteer work at Greentree Rehabilitation and Nursing Home. Still maintaining his six feet, two inches, but having gained over one hundred and fifty pounds over his perfect weight, bouts with diabetes and gout which he never completely controlled, some residual pain from his having been shot twice in Viet Nam and once stabbed as an operative with the Central Intelligence Agency, a few hemorrhoids and he was for all practical purposes in pretty good health. He often mused at the name given to the CIA. He saw the name as an oxymoron.

He knew that he wasn't going to live forever and he wanted to leave something for others. Kelly House became the way to do it. While volunteering at Greentree, he met Ted Kelly, a patient who came to the center with severe cardiac and respiratory problems and a significant history of pancreatic disease. Kelly was a patient who Zangwell chose to help put together an autobiography. But Ted died and Ben decided to name the commune after him. It wasn't quite that simple. Ben reflected on how it all started.

The social worker at Greentree, Jane Finestein, devised a plan to have her group write their personal life histories. Her idea was that writing, discussing their writings in group session and using the material to open doors to the past would help them to explore their depression and move on to happier and fulfilling lives. For Kelly it didn't come soon enough because at Greentree, he had to be re-hospitalized and died at Heart of Miami Hospital.

Ben used his resources to find out about Ted Kelly who on the surface was a cynical, sardonic, gruff union business agent. In fact, he was a true humanitarian who gave more than just money and his life blood to help those with less than he had. Ben had his friends check out Ted's past, and found that while he lived in Springfield he supported coal miners who were on strike in the coal fields, the same miners whose ancestors had been aided one hundred years before by Mother Jones. Kelly was famous for raising money and tossing in equal amounts of his own for food, clothing, household items for striking workers and their families. For years, Kelly found the down and out, America's marginalized, the people who others threw away and supported them with his own money, time and resources. People who didn't really know Kelly thought him sardonic, irascible and arrogant. Those who knew him, ushered him into their private worlds, loved him and knew him for what he really was, a real mensch.

Many a starving artist who portrayed the life of the working man and woman were aided by Kelly, and he had hundreds of their works, canvases which the Smithsonian in Washington D.C. wanted for their collection of Labor History and art. Kelly also was a collector of labor, revolutionary, and philosophical works which he bequeathed to the Illinois Labor History Society.

The group members were all people who were not progressing in their rehabilitation, but their autobiographies were instrumental in helping them gain insight into what kept them from getting well and getting on with their lives. Kelly, before his relapse, was well on his way to the recognition that he allowed his body to deteriorate partially because he recognized his weakness of always deferring to the union bosses who often did not have the welfare of the worker at heart. For more than thirty years, Kelly allowed this inconsistency to eat him alive and he internalized it until his death.

Ben thought about the others who were to join him in this new venture. He didn't pretend that he knew as much about the others as he did Kelly. But as an octogenarian he was tired of living alone, tired of finding causes to sponsor and tired of watching his back all the time. He smiled at the remembrance of a movie he'd seen on TV, *The Bucket List*. Hell, he'd done everything the two characters played by Jack Nicholson and, "what the hell was the other guy's name? A senior moment, I guess." did. And then he remembered, Morgan Freeman. Then his brain switched to a picture of Sadie Goldenblum.

Zangwell spoke to Jane and she shared limited information with him after checking with the patients because she didn't want to violate confidentiality. She gave him access to records. Jane told him that Sadie's children had embraced Messianic Judaism years ago and that her son made his living as a radio and television evangelist of sorts.

Was it a mother who he hardly remembered? Did he see Sadie in a babushka carrying a sack of potatoes in Russia? It was fuzzy, but something washed in his thoughts and it was pleasant and soothing. Yes, that was part of it. She was maternal and he didn't have to fear that he would nestle in her big and flabby arms. She was a sweetheart who probably wouldn't contribute a lot of writing and creative thought to the commune, but instead would encourage others and see the gold thread in the tapestry of negativity which was sure to pop up often when the others were sad, empty of ideas for creating or going through bad times physically or mentally. Sadie was a diabetic who lost a leg beneath the knee due to poor circulation. She still cheated on her rigorous diet. Constant monitoring her sugar was paramount for her to remain healthy.

It was a shame that when the group visited Asheville and Kelly House she immediately took delight in the kitchen and her ability to start cooking again for everyone. Ben knew that Jane's concern about Sadie was that she continued to mourn the death of her husband, Morris, to whom she was married for fifty years, and that she felt estranged from her children because they had chosen a different religious path than hers. Zangwell didn't have much use for religion of any kind seeing it and nationalism as the two most adored institutions and, yet, the two most responsible for more death and destruction than anything else known to mankind. He didn't pretend to be a great thinker, but he couldn't understand why the rest of the world didn't see the horrors of those two themes in the same way. "Religion and Nationalism- Forget it!" He'd take the happy Buddha any day. Buddhism was a way of life with no dogma, no insistence on suffering as a means to finding peace. He wasn't quite right about that, but what the hell. He didn't have to be, but he did think that he resembled the Buddha with a bit of happiness and sadness at the same time.

"Z," the name given to Ben Zangwell years ago by Langley associates at the "Company," and carried on for about forty years by friends and foe alike, did not like any religions. It seemed that a hundred years ago he could remember having been spared fundamentalism of any kind. True, his parents spoke of their Jewish roots in Russia, but spared him having to prepare for Bar Mitzvah or having to spend any time in a synagogue. He found himself profoundly moved while living in Israel and visiting the Wailing Wall, though. He preferred not to dwell on the reason for his emotional outburst.

He returned to Sadie. He knew that she was interested in looking into her son's work and writing about it. He assumed that she would have to learn to use the computer and do most of her research on the internet. Come to think of it he didn't know anything about Asheville's library system and what would be available to the commune members at the University of North Carolina in Asheville.

Gerald Janokoski, born into a Polish Catholic family, was probably the best educated of the writers. At least he talked as though he was well educated. A teacher for enough years to retire on full pension, the record revealed that he taught English and then went to work with kids who were potential high school drop-outs. Ben smiled when he read, in the patient records, the part about Gerald being a Viet Nam protestor. Back then, he visualized the young teacher and his friends marching with purity of heart while he and his friends were getting their asses shot off in the rice paddies in the jungle. "Z" never resented the protesters or the kids who went to Canada. He could never understand the vets who hated them so. Ben hated the cliché, "You do what you gotta do," but for this he understood its use. For Ben it was simple. He wanted to jump out of planes, climb mountains, learn to eat snake and live a rough life. The Marines did it for him, "Semper Fi." It wasn't patriotism so much as it was loads of testosterone and the family of fellow Marines.

Gerald was a widower whose wife taught in the same system that he did, and who was quite a spunky fighter for her colleagues. The two of them fought many battles against the administration and at times against the National Education Association's professionals who were supposed to be there to help the teachers. Gerald told Ben that one of the things he wanted to examine was a book written by Upton Sinclair in 1924, nearly one hundred years ago, *The Gosling*. Sinclair thought that the NEA was made up of stooges who worked for the textbook industry and local school boards. Janokoski wondered whether his literary hero was correct about the NEA and whether there was a lot of change now in the twenty-first century. It would make for interesting research.

Why Gerald was in the rehabilitation center and particularly the group was what Ben wanted to concentrate on now. Apparently, Gerald slipped in his kitchen while drying dishes and fractured his right hip. Additionally, he had a bad stomach problem which plagued him for years. There was reference to a "nervous stomach" whatever that was. Regardless, he would need a good gastroenterologist for sure and probably to continue physical therapy. Ben read that broken hips were usually the prelude to elderly dependency. Gerald had beaten the odds. He walked out of Greentree on his own. True, he shuffled and moved slowly, but possibly that would improve with time.

The other factor in Gerald's recovery was that he came to the group very depressed and still deeply mourning over his wife's death from complications brought on by cancer. The autobiographical work seemed to have helped him to cope with his depression, but Ben knew that Gerald hadn't been able to get through the grief of the loss of his wife and that he might require some counseling or whatever people did about prolonged grieving. Ben looked forward to getting to know Gerald better.

Britt Manning was about Ben's age and from the looks of things a woman with a steamy past to say the least. She was from New York, but had traveled all over the country as a photographer. She started out in the group a very angry and mean-spirited woman, and, according to Jane, her writing and bonding with the group, although painful for the group members at times, had changed that image significantly. She was particularly affected by Ted's death.

Britt had also been in the Peace Corps in Siberia, Russia for a year or more and had taken some pictures of her tundra experience which had sold well in the United States. She tried to live in Alaska and actually married a man there who held her in some sort of bondage. Britt told the writers that when she got to the new place she wanted to find a series of letters that she wrote and do some intensive writing about her sense of feeling enslaved in Seal Point, Alaska.

Ben also saw a reference to shell shock. He knew the term as post traumatic stress disorder. It was the same in all war. Apparently, Britt had gotten involved with a Korean War vet who came home a damaged man. Every war kept the Veterans Administration busy with men and recently women who physically, mentally or both were never the same again. A few years back they had to add traumatic brain disorders from the wars in Iraq and Afghanistan.

Britt had fallen for some mountain man who ran away from civilization to his own crevice in the earth. She seemed to specialize in finding lost souls like this Jason fellow. Ben felt good about Britt. He even thought he and she might do some traveling together and who knew what else. "Once a Marine, always a Marine." He laughed at himself and for a moment looked down at his torso and what once was. Gone were the flat, rippled muscles of a taut stomach. His tummy was in the way, and he groaned through clenched teeth.

Lee Lansing, the other patient who already was released from Greentree was in her late seventies. She suffered from Parkinson's disease and the aftermath of cancer of the breast. She was a widow who twice tried to kill herself. Luckily, the second try was here in Florida and she, herself, called 911. Overdoses of medication swallowed with wine made her a very sick and uncomfortable lady. She was admitted to the rehabilitation center because her niece worked there and was able to bend the rules to get her into the facility instead of a mental hospital.

Ben knew Lee to be a very creative person. In her youth, she had patented a baby carrier, several dress designs and owned her own successful business. Married three times with three grown children and some grandchildren, she had finally found a match with a husband who knew all about her Parkinson's and decided to do everything in his power to help her beat it. Nothing worked permanently. Then she had the bout with cancer for which the doctors had to remove part of a breast and several lymph nodes. This was the third year of remission and if she did not have another flare up within the next two or three years, she might be out of the woods. Ben figured that a good oncologist would have to be found in Asheville. He took a few notes for later reference.

However, the sudden death of her husband, Sandy, seemed to have broken her spirit and she tried to take her own life out west. Selma Richardson, the executive administrative assistant at Greentree, and Lee's niece went out, packed her aunt up and brought her to Florida. There were references to her coming there with anger because people wouldn't allow her to end it all. However, the record was clear that once she started writing about her past and after she met a woman who volunteered to help her write, her suicidal attempts stopped.

Ben thought about how fantastic Lee's story was. Raised by a lesbian mother with a woman she called Aunt Jean for the first ten years and then by her first name thereafter, Lee experienced a childhood of loneliness, being ostracized, and the realization that this kind of upbringing made a profound difference in the way she viewed herself. Her mother, being masculine, didn't know how to raise a daughter, and had little time for her partner and a daughter too. Lee had been married to two cold and impersonal men much like her mother, and then found the love she'd longed for in Sandy Lansing. She was well into her fifties when they met. Ben didn't know in which direction Lee's creativity would take her. He had no doubt that she would sooner or later contribute at the commune.

Pauline Baldwin, like him, was one of the four volunteers who became involved with the group. A stately woman, whose life as the wife of a Nobel Prize winner in chemistry, was oft times lonely. She blamed no one. It was a life she chose and her philosophy was that she had made her bed and would not complain about it.

But, it had a price. Her only daughter was remote, her grandchildren not warm and accepting of their grandmother. Pauline married a scientist, Max Baldwin, a quiet, scholarly man ten years her senior. She met Max while studying art and literature at Berkeley. He was not very articulate, but she could see that he was a genius in his area of expertise. A doctorate at twenty-three, a patent on three chemical adhesives which were used in the field as wound binders led to a professorial appointment at the University of California, Berkeley. He was granted tenure, younger than anyone in the Chemistry Department had ever been awarded it.

They met at a coffee house quite by accident. She was sitting there reading an assignment from her English Literature class and Max attempted to balance a coffee, croissant, and a scientific paper all at the same time. He sat down at her table without realizing that someone else was already sitting there. He begged forgiveness for intruding upon Pauline's space and was about to get up and leave.

Pauline, also shy and very reserved, nevertheless boldly suggested that he stay. They made small talk about the weather, the marches and the war progress in Viet Nam. Max was 4F, but felt that he was doing all he could for the war effort by patenting the chemical binders which he hoped would save lives. They shared some interests. Classical music, art galleries, some reading material and wandering the streets of San Francisco were held in common. Within a year they were engaged. Neither of them was religious and so they agreed to marry at the Unitarian seminary on the campus and a student was assigned to perform the ceremony.

Max's brother and mother came to the wedding from Cleveland and Pauline's mother and father flew in from China where he was doing medical missionary work near Mongolia. It was a small affair. Max's brother was the groom's ring man and Pauline asked a classmate to serve as her bride's maid. The couple honeymooned in Hawaii on Oahu, sitting on Waikiki Beach, and visiting the culture center on the north side of the island. Max felt some guilt because the island was crowded with servicemen, many of them on R&R from Viet Nam and many of them on leave from military hospitals. It was Pauline's first experience with so many disabled people.

They stayed at Berkeley for eight years. A daughter was born whom they loved very much. Little Jessica was treasured and yet destined to endure the same sense of loneliness that her mother had experienced. Pauline often thought of settling down, but Max was a rising star and needed her with him on all trips and for editing his papers.

The war ended and Max was well on his way to international acclaim for his work in medical engineering. First one invitation to lecture in Germany, and then another, and another made it clear that Max could no longer give full attention to a teaching schedule and pursue scholarly research duties at the same time. He seemed to become more introverted as he aged.

When Jessica was six it was time to think about stability and schooling for her. It was decided that Pauline would remain home with the child and Max would be free to make his appearances wherever he was asked to go. The Nobel Prize only served to make him more famous and more sought after. Soon Max was involved in the new and controversial sciences related to cloning, DNA and RNA studies. He was now involved with the political as well as scientific community.

Pauline, who as a small child traveled with her medical missionary family, was sent to boarding school in Luzerne, Switzerland, so that her mother and father could continue their work. They deluded themselves into thinking that it was not safe for Pauline to join them in the hinterlands of the world's third and fourth world countries. In fact, if they had been honest, they would have realized that they really had little room in their lives for a third person, albeit their own child who they loved deeply. But, Pauline knew it deep down in her heart and found boarding school friends who shared similar experiences with their famous and wealthy parents.

Although Pauline vowed not to ever send her children to boarding schools, when she married and realized her desire to be with Max, the Baldwins came to the same conclusion that a boarding school for Jessica was the answer so that Pauline could accompany her husband on his speaking missions. She realized that perhaps her upbringing had something to do with the man she chose to marry and this decision to place her daughter in a safe and excellent academy for young girls. She cried over her decision, but the die was cast long ago.

In truth, Max needed Pauline because he was not an articulate man and needed her help in writing his speeches. She earned her BA in English Literature while they were still at Berkeley and knew syntax, grammar and vocabulary usage well. She would be an excellent aide to him, not to mention his companion, she told herself. He was also very lonely on these trips because he was not an extrovert and often found himself alone and miserable.

Thirty years or more of world travel, a married daughter and two grandchildren that Pauline had met only once, a dead husband and a houseful of memories and trophies from her travel over six continents many times over was what Pauline brought with her to Oakland Park and the beautiful hi-rise condo with her view of the Atlantic, the Intra-Coastal and Ft. Lauderdale. On a clear night she could see the lights of the skyscrapers in Miami.

The only excitement in her life had been when her husband was approached by some people in Washington D.C. to report back to them on his impressions of the scientific advancements in medicine of certain countries he visited. Max didn't share this part of his work with Pauline, but she believed that he was probably hired to be a spy. There was always a sense of fear and excitement when he was speaking in the Middle East and Asia. But Max seemed to be nonchalant about the assignments as though he might simply be whetting his scientific curiosity.

The downside of her life was, of course, that here she was in her seventies, a widow with little contact with her only child and grandchildren. Once Jessica suggested that her mother's decision to board their only daughter was a mistake, one that Jessica did not intend to make. The cycle would stop with her. Pauline took the rebuff with dignity and knew that her daughter was correct. They saw each other at Max's funeral amidst all the pomp and ceremony and both felt a profound sadness and longing for something more than a perfunctory hug and cheek kiss. An occasional email, exchange of birthday cards and monetary gifts would have to suffice. But, neither Jessica nor Pauline took steps to restart a more loving and connected relationship.

Pauline spent a few years traveling, playing bridge and making a few friends who were in her age range in the condo, but one day she wandered up to Greentree and went in thinking that maybe they might need some volunteer help. The staff had orders to treat anyone who came and asked about volunteering as an honored guest and to quickly notify Aileen Rosen, the Activities Director. She was also the Volunteer Coordinator.

Pauline spent a year coming once a week for two hours and working in the activity room with patients. She read to them, played some cards and took around a library on wheels cart to the various wings. She tried to talk with some of those poor unfortunate people in the Alzheimer's wing, but found that nerve racking for her. In her second year she read a memo on the bulletin board about a special project concerning patients writing autobiographies, and decided to become involved.

The notice stated that any volunteer interested in helping with the project should inquire at the desk. She did. That was how she met Lee and the rest of the writers and worked for some six months or maybe it was seven, she could not remember. And now she was about to move to North Carolina and make a home with her new friends and that strange man, Ben Zangwell. She felt a sense of elation that she had not felt in years. She felt, what was it, like she did when Mommy and Daddy would take her to far off places before they put her in that school so many years ago.

The last of the charter members, David Greenberg was probably the most complicated of the group. He suffered from a right-sided stroke which meant that the left hemisphere of his brain was compromised. David also had problems with diabetes and had become overweight. His emotional conflicts, although ameliorated somewhat by the work he did on his autobiography and the group discussion, persisted. He had an up and down relationship with his older son, Julius, and his family and only a tentative one with his younger son, Ethan.

True, he saw a good deal more of Ethan because he lived in Florida, not far from Ft. Lauderdale. In his grand children's formative years, David spent a little more time with Justin and Essie, and so they loved their Uppah. Uppah was their name for him because he didn't want them confusing Diana's father and himself. Uppah was a Siberian Yupik Eskimo word for grandfather. David learned that when he lived with the Yupik Eskimo in Alaska.

He was able to put to rest his guilt at leaving Heidi and the children back in the seventies during the last century. The group and his writing did that much for him. But his feeling that he had to walk on eggshells with Ethan and his almost non-existent relationship with Julius and his family continued to bother him. What was it that Gerald had said to him? "You can choose your friends, not your family." How true! David spent many nights tearfully wishing that he had not left Heidi. Would that have made a difference in his relationships with his sons? His mind filled with doubt.

It was Adrian Sloane who helped him to write and get on the ball with delving into his problems. Adrian suggested that the relationship David had with Ethan might be fine as it was. Many fathers and sons had loving relationships without being pals or buddies. She questioned whether it was the norm for fathers and sons to have a lot in common. David thought about that and was coming to the conclusion that maybe what they had was as good as it was ever going to be, if not perfect. He could live with that even if the relationship felt less than perfect.

Adrian was one of the two volunteers who decided that she did not want to live with other people in a communal lifestyle. She loved the writers and particularly David with whom she spent many hours, but she treasured her privacy more than anything else. With a tinge of sadness, she decided to return to her home in upstate New York and try to make a go of the cold and abusive weather. She could always continue as a snow bird and visit the commune in winter.

David wrote a good deal about his life and had always done things the hard way as he saw it, but in fact big chunks of his past were not put on paper or tape recorder. He spent ten years in uniform and had stories to tell about experiences which would make for interesting and sometimes shocking tales, and fifteen or more years in a school system working with emotionally disturbed children who broke the hearts of so many people. His life in Alaska and as a civilian in Viet Nam after the conflict were not discussed and yet provided him with episodes often not mentioned in the travel logs of interested vacationers. His days living in Florida, especially the short time in a condo as a condo commando, were both humorous and sad. David would have lots to write about once he settled down in Asheville.

His first job was to get out of Greentree and that meant hard work in rehab. The new splint fashioned for him was a major help. Stan Darling and the staff were reaching the point where they felt that they had done everything they could do to help him live independently. The truth was that they felt certain that he would always need some help, maybe a nurse's assistant to help him with every day chores and bathing. Ben realized this and was concerned whether those services existed in Asheville.

Jane Finestein, MSW, was 57 years old. The way she and her husband, Seymour, saw it she would continue to work at Greentree for another five years until she could march over to the Social Security office on Sample Road and draw her allotment. She didn't see herself working until 67 or was it 68 years old. Each year dooms day predictions of the ruin and demise of Social Security were sounded. Yet, the program was securely fixed in the American psyche. Even the Tea Party fanatics of the first and second decade of the current century didn't want to see Social Security perish. Too many of the members were elderly and counted on their monthly benefit. That was about the only thing Jane agreed with them on politically. She shuddered at the thought of elderly gun toting and bible thumping people walking around with little tea bags hanging from their three pointed Minute Man hats.

Jane spoke to David about his needs when he would leave the facility. She arranged to have an agency send a nursing assistant into the apartment at Whispering Pines Village. Were it not for the fact that David would soon be leaving for the commune, an assisted living home would have been in order. Ethan and Diana did not offer to house David or that might have been a possibility. American children in their milieu rarely saw it as their role to make a home for their parents for more than a short visit. David understood that and didn't feel neglected or abandoned. It is what it is. He believed that it might have something to do with the past and he accepted their silence without rancor.

David was scheduled to leave Greentree in one week, as was Britt who decided to return to her studio on A1A until it was time to leave for North Carolina. She, too, was doing all she could to exercise the remaining lung capacity in order to better care for herself. Britt, forever the independent spirit, saw no reason at eighty-one or was it eighty-two, to change. Jane called for oxygen canisters to be delivered at the motel and for a nursing assistant to give her three days a week. This way the woman would be able to take Britt shopping on Hillsboro in the Cove Shopping Center and drive her to doctor appointments.

CHAPTER THREE

On Monday, Gerald received a call from the reporter from the Sunshine Journal. They arranged to meet the next day for an interview. The journalist, a young cub reporter from the University of Missouri, was on his first full time job. He was interested in Gerald's history, his life in Florida and how he made the decision to attempt to live in a communal setting, especially at his age. The part about his age was left out of the conversation. A snow-white haired, well-dressed older gentleman wearing a cashmere light weight sweater with leather elbow patches greeted the youngster. The young reporter had a wistful thought upon meeting Gerald, that he might look this way some day. It saddened him briefly.

Gerald filled him in on his teaching career, his life with his beautiful and inspiring wife, Claire, who died of cancer. He told the young reporter, who dutifully took notes, about his decision as a younger senior citizen to come to Florida, the difficulty at finding anyone to share his life, and then his fall in his kitchen, and the hospitalization and rehabilitation. What Gerald left out was his intense loneliness, grief, and despair which had eventually led him to the writers' group.

The young man couldn't help but compare Gerald to his own grandfather. Gramps came to visit back at the farm in Kansas and just never left. He lived with his son and daughter-in-law for at least twenty years and then died. Gramps had always been a part of the household. Sure

Mom had more work, more laundry to do and had to struggle through the old guy's forgetfulness, embarrassment over his open fly and wet spots on his pants, things like that, but that was life back on the farm. No one would ever think of their home without Gramps. Things were really different down here in Florida.

The part about the commune would have to be supplemented with a follow-up interview with Ben. The reporter decided to seek him out after he finished his interview with Gerald. He might even ask his editor for funds to visit the commune itself so that he could expand the story. He was right. The concept of a writers' commune for disabled elderly had the potential to become a major piece of interest. Having no background with unions or teachers' problems, the young journalist found it difficult to focus on Gerald's discussion about wanting to do some writing on Upton Sinclair's exposé of the National Education Association back almost a century ago. The young, eager cub reporter's name was Bobby Tubbs.

A Jamaican, who went to Florida International University and studied journalism, was assigned to interview the women. Mary Smith called Pauline and arranged for an interview with the two ladies. She came to the same conclusion as her colleague from Kansas that white people here in South Florida were very different from her kin. She remembered sharing a room in her village with her grandmother until an additional room could be constructed onto the home so that Grandmother would have her own space. No one ever thought about an assisted living facility or nurse's aide. It was never discussed. Grandparents took care of themselves, and then when they couldn't, the children did. That was the tradition. It was not questioned and wealth or lack of it played no part in the decision. It didn't matter whether there were good feelings about the grandparents or whether the elders were kindly. It was the way it was.

Some of her friends in the Haitian Catholic Church were caregivers here and just shook their heads at the White folks. They told her that if the children liked their elderly parents, they visited more regularly. If not, then seldom were they seen. As memory faded and other brain disorders manifested, often it was the black women who became like their children, their spouses, and the center of their lives. In every facility and nursing home it was the same. Had she talked to Tubbs, she would have seen that this was an urban phenomena and not a racial difference.

The Jamaican reporter knew that thousands of her people and many more from Haiti, the Dominican Republic, and all the islands in the Caribbean, were in the business of taking care of elderly citizens here in Florida and elsewhere. She wondered whether they questioned the same things that she did. What did they think about caring for other people's parents? It was their bread and butter, but she wondered whether it would be a good story and whether she could convince them to talk candidly about their experiences with the families and patients, anonymously of course. Even as young as she was, she realized how sensitive these issues were down here, and she wondered whether any of the White children felt guilty about leaving their parents in the hands of others.

There were rumors that this was a Jewish thing. But these two women were not Jewish, and of the people going to North Carolina only two out of the six were. But in the condo developments, nursing homes, private homes and other places many were Jewish, Italian, and Russian and had roots in all of Europe. Once in a while she'd heard that an American Black woman or man had a nurse's aide from the Islands. But that was a rarity as far as she knew.

Mary Smith determined to pursue this matter, and maybe write a story about it. She didn't think that the Journal would be interested because they had a large Jewish readership. She hoped it wouldn't offend anyone, or even worse, be considered anti-Semitic to look at this sociological phenomenon. For sure, she didn't want to offend her Jewish readers, and people hinted that the Jews were easily offended. Well, so were the American Blacks, men and women alike. This much she knew just by watching her fellow Africans. Not so in Jamaica. Why should there be any thin skins? She escaped overt prejudice and discrimination in her young life, and could only imagine what that was like here in the South. In her courses at school, she'd read of this country's prejudices, racial inequality and the terrible battles to acquire civil liberties. Martin Luther King was as much a hero to her as to those born in America.

Pauline and Lee answered Mary's questions which were pretty much along the five "W"s and "How" line. Straight reporting was the way the Journal liked it, but Mary wanted to somehow humanize the story. She wrote about Lee's children, her love and devotion to Sandy, her husband who died suddenly. Lee was open about her suicide attempts and her anger at being denied the right to kill herself, an idea she still clung to even now that she was feeling better about herself since joining the writers' therapy group.

A person should have the right to end their lives or have medical help in doing so. She saw this as an intrusion of religious influence and another instance of religion determining law. Her hero was Jack Kevorkian, the doctor who spent time in prison, and vowed to continue his fight for the prerogative of human beings to have help in ending their own lives. She smiled proudly at being a member of the World Federation of Right to Choice.

Other civilized nations had already crossed the Right to Choice bridge and now had very humane laws concerning self-euthanasia. She saw it rather ironic that the United States still had the death penalty whereas other civilized nations did not, but here people could not determine whether they wanted to live or die. Mary did not know whether her newspaper would permit her to raise this issue, but she knew that somehow she wanted this in her article. As for Pauline, the cub reporter found her to be a woman still searching for her place in the new experiment.

She talked about her life and her distant relationship with her own daughter and grandchildren. It occurred to Mary that having money brings with it a lot of problems which poverty eliminates. She laughed at herself. Was she making a case for being poor? She doubted it.

Back at the Journal, Tubbs and the Jamaican shared information for the story. They would write his together for joint by-lines. By-lines were even more important to young reporters than money. They served to go into portfolios for better jobs later in their careers. It was interesting to find that they shared the same questions about living arrangements for the elderly down here in Florida, but Bobby wanted to meet with Ben before they began to write the story. He was certain that he would get a different perspective on life from the huge man.

He called Ben from the Journal office and got him on the first ring. "No problem, son. Where do you want to meet? Sure, I know the diner. I eat in it three or four times a week. Eleven Wednesday morning. OK. See ya there. Have a good day."

Meanwhile, Ben had work to do. He reread the preamble that he shared with the writers a month ago and studied it to see if there were any changes he wanted to make.

> *Kelly House shall be a home for any person over the age of sixty-five wishing to devote his/her life to creating written prose or poetry that serves to liberate the mind of the writer.*

Ben thought aloud, "What about painters, sculptors, other forms of art. Those people would need a place to work, a studio. What about playwrights. They'd need some place to put on their works. So many forms of art. I wonder if photographers would need their own dark room. I can leave all that up to the charter members of the commune." He wondered whether any Cherokees would show up with a desire to do bead work or basket weaving, and then tossed the idea as just a stereotypical way of viewing Native Americans in general. What about street orators who wished to take around their own soap boxes like in the old days of the Wobblies. Was that an art form of some sort? He doubted it. Some of the members might have different ideas about that.

> *All rules governing the management of **Kelly House** will be made by democratic process with consensus being the goal. Each month a new house director who is capable of managing the daily, weekly, monthly routines of managing a home will be elected with no one being able to hold this office for more than two months in a row. Anyone who wishes to hold the office will be given the opportunity to do so.*
>
> *It shall be a standing rule that the only way that anyone who meets the criteria of wishing to create prose or poetry, but who is not admitted into **Kelly House,** will have to be denied entry by all members of the household including Benjamin Zachariah Zangwell.*

*All deliberate attempts to ostracize any person shall not be acceptable
to the body.*

Ben knew his history of social living experiments which fell apart
because one person became a god. "I don't want any dictators or demigods
running the place," he thought. He'd seen too many of them.

1. Anyone who is presently a writer or volunteer helping writers at
    Greentree will be given the opportunity to see Kelly House in
    Asheville, North Carolina. All arrangements will be handled by
    Ben.
2. If anyone is interested in the concept of living in a commune after
    seeing the house and discussion, Ben will finance the moving
    and relocation for anyone who wishes to begin their lives at Kelly
    House.
3. Ben Zangwell will agree to finance all costs associated with this
    project and requests that any commercial value derived by those
    in the commune who are successful in publishing their works or
    selling their art shall be split between him and the artist, 50/50.

The writing still made sense to him. He wrote it, but Ben realized that
it might be wise to call a meeting of the group before they left to discuss
several of the points and get ideas from the others concerning things he
may have left out. They already accomplished number one. That was moot.
He decided to bring the preamble, for lack of a better word, with him on
Wednesday to the interview by Tubbs.

Ben placed a call to the contractor in Asheville to find out how the
work was going on the house. He had already committed to $100,000 for
the needed changes. He had no idea whether this would suffice or not, but
he was prepared to spend more if needed.

The outdoor ramp was up and already used during the visit over the
weekend. Bathroom fixtures with railing and a new type of slip-proof
flooring were installed. There was a problem with the water supply because
the well had not been used for a period of twenty years or more. People had

to come out and clean it out and make sure that the piping to the house was in good order. New ordinances dealing with lead and other health issues were discussed and it was decided to do testing on the water and total system. Another $5,000 was needed for this. It was worth the money.

The elevators were being installed as they spoke, and that meant some major renovation of the two floors to make room for the lift. The contractors believed that the work on the elevator would be completed within three weeks. He also was very happy with the kitchen renovation and told Ben that he, himself, had picked out the new appliances and felt sure that Ben would be very pleased. Ben thanked him and called Maria.

Maria and Juan Morales were really employees, but more than employees, they were Ben's best friends. The Morales, originally from Mexico, a town just south of the capital, migrated to Texas and found Texas to be a difficult place to raise their children. They chose San Antonio, the home of the Alamo as their home. Juan joined the Marine Corps and spent two of his four years in Viet Nam. He met Ben, a captain, on his first tour in Special Operations and served under him. Juan's relationship with Ben flourished as they struggled day by day to get through to the next. When the captain was injured and sent back to the States, Juan had six months to go on his second tour, managed to live through it, and shipped back to San Diego. Ben and Juan met again at the depot while the couple were reunited and renewed their friendship.

Maria was pregnant with their second child, and asked Juan to return to San Antonio to be a father to his children. After three and a half years in uniform and highly decorated, he was given his honorable discharge and released to return to civilian life and return to school on the GI Bill. He took a Bachelor's Degree in elementary education at St. Mary's University and spent the next ten years teaching in an elementary school in the barrio along Commercial. Maria worked part time as a cook in one of the schools and was able to be with the children when they were not in school.

Throughout the years somehow Ben Zangwell and Juan kept in touch. Ben visited once or twice and the children always called him Tio Ben. Juan marveled at the man's ability to escape the jaws of death in Viet Nam and then later when Ben was recruited by the "Company" his uncanny agility in making fools of the drug cartels. Juan laughed with Maria in bed while they talked of his friend. "I think the captain must have used up at least eight of his lives already." They both loved him and the children adored their Tio Ben.

Juan didn't understand all of it, but something Ben was involved with left "Z" with more money than anyone could have envisioned in their wildest imagination. Zangwell was already a legend in the Corps, but it was while working for Langley that he acquired the moniker "Z" and was known to the entire spying world, both friend and foe alike, as the dangerous and enigmatic "Z".

The story that Ben told Juan and Maria was that he was assigned the duty of working with the DEA on a sting operation against the Colombians, Jamaicans, Vietnamese and Chinese. They were in the process of cutting up the world distribution of cocaine and heroin. There was distrust and mayhem between the factions. Money, lots of it, was to be transferred to banks around the world, laundered and re-distributed in such a way that it would be available when needed by the drug lords. Someone scammed them and stole millions. The newspapers worldwide received tips about the scam and printed stories that seventy million dollars was somehow lost by the cartels. As for the cartels, they blamed each other and were sure that one of them, or maybe two of them, had stolen the money. "Was there no honor among thieves?"

According to Ben the newspapers were way off the mark about the amount of money, what had happened, and who was responsible for the scam. He swore Juan and Maria to silence and told them the story. He had a purpose and they were the only ones to whom he confided. He needed to do so because he decided that having the money without a plan as to what to do with it was useless. He needed them to tell him he was crazy or to join him, and by this time he had come to love and trust them. The children were older and near graduation from high school. Juan and Maria decided that they would make themselves available to work for or with Ben wherever and whenever he needed them.

It went back to Viet Nam. While he and others were killing Viet Cong who had determined that they wanted another form of government other than the French colonialism and American style democracy, he came to the conclusion that all armies were puppets of people who rarely dirtied their own hands. He killed women and children who played no part in the intrigues of the warlords, and who wouldn't have recognized Lyndon Johnson if paid. He watched his boys die one after the other for ideals they barely understood and for the glory of the Corps. Dying for the glory of the Corps was not the issue. Dying for politician's political testosterone was. The proof of that was that now the Communist government in Viet Nam was fully recognized and Washington dealt with it as an equal. The enemy was now fanatical Islam and boys and girls were dying and being maimed the same as in Viet Nam. The rich were richer, the poor were the lambs for slaughter on both sides. Nothing changed.

Viet Nam was the first of many questionable operations that Ben found himself engaged in for the United States. He watched closely and tried not to become a doomsday philosophical dissident. He preferred to remember the U.S. of World War II fame because he saw that war as being the last morally correct action taken in the name of humanity. He could even find reason to have used the most horrible weapon known to man against the enemy on the grounds that fewer Americans and allies would die in the long run.

After WWII, he had to struggle to give the politicians their due for every action taken after that. One that he admired was Harry Truman for the Berlin Airlift, but Korea and the action there, he wasn't convinced of that wisdom. The Gulf War was also a difficult call. Ben wondered whether the moneyed interests were behind that, or whether perhaps there were some moral reasons to defend the Kuwaiti government. He was willing to give the benefit of the doubt to the government. One thing Ben was certain of was that Capitalism served the rich much more than it did the poor, and that he wanted to use his money to support activities which benefited the overwhelming majority of the world's population against the one or two percent with most of the wealth in the world.

For a while the focus of Ben's attention was the World Trade Organization, the IMF, and World Bank. He saw these organizations as a conglomerate of business and political interests without a soul. He wasn't sure that he believed in a soul, but he couldn't come up with a better word to define what he meant. Distaste for NAFTA was a part of his sense of despair, and although he admired Bill Clinton, he distrusted him as well. It was difficult for Ben to conclude that the leadership, both donkeys and elephants, could be in on such heinous and malevolent skullduggery. He didn't mean this in a religious sense, but more or less in a moral one. The monolithic WTO had taken on a gigantic proportion that was now joined by the defunct Communist world in Europe and the current Asian governments as well. There was profit beyond words to be made and they all wanted a piece of the action. Later he was to hate the idea of corporate person- hood as well and fight against the behemoth businesses that destroyed everything in their path.

Thousands of people, young and old, throughout the world with interests of their own, were slowly forming to fight the monsters. But, without funds and know-how, they could only manage small skirmishes when the WTO met in such places as Seattle, Quebec, and Genoa to plan and coordinate their efforts. These meetings had to be held in person because the security over the internet, telephones and coding systems were compromised by whiz kids who could hack into their communications. The titans of the WTO were like the dictators of old who met to finalize their deals with a handshake.

"Z" saw the police using their powers to protect the leaders of the world in their treachery. They used their armored cars and tanks to destroy children and the elderly who deigned to try to stop these unholy alliances from taking place. For Ben and others, this was no different than the use of Wells Fargo and other security firms who beat and murdered women and children in the coal fields or in front of factories in the labor wars of the 19th and 20th centuries. This was no different than when unarmed zealous students and idealists marched against the Chinese regime in Tienanmen Square in Beijing only to be mowed down by troops and destroyed. It was the same in the Occupy movements the world over. Police became the apparatus that wealthy men used to defeat the masses. Ben didn't exactly consider himself a Marxist, but the man made sense in so many ways to him.

One day while browsing in the Swap Shop on Sunrise Boulevard in Ft.

Lauderdale, he happened upon a cap and hat salesman, a Pakistani who at one time was a biologist in his country. Ben could get anyone to share their lives with him. He saw a cap with "Question Authority" embroidered on the front. The cap cost him $3.50. He scooped it up. It was to become his constant companion where ever he went. He was amused as he thought about the effect the words had on his neighbors and especially the condo commando president.

The president was certain that Ben wore it especially to upset him and his stomach ulcers acted up every time he crossed paths with that "awful man." The little gentleman kept his distance and grimaced in silence, but Ben saw his demeanor and always found it amusing. Others in the condo didn't know the significance of the words, but always found their neighbor to be helpful, if not a bit of an enigma in the community.

Juan and Maria's kids were grown and on their own. When Ben decided that he was going to go into semi-retirement, he asked them to come to Florida and live. Juan would do odd jobs such as drive the Mercedes, and Maria could help out with projects as yet undetermined.

Ben hated to drive, found it aggravating. He had grown to such proportions that he could not drive the car that he wanted, a two-seater sports car. He couldn't fit into it. He preferred the three wheel tricycle which he found at a thrift shop. He assumed that he could always claim that he was getting his exercise by riding around on the tricycle. Juan kept the car and was always in cell phone contact with the "Jefe," the boss. Maria turned out to be helpful by going to Asheville to arrange for the writers to see the house and the surroundings before they decided if it was for them or not. Ben had not begun to think about whether the Morales would want to relocate again for him and this time to a community where few spoke any Spanish. At least in Florida there were other Mexican people near them and the language was spoken by most of their neighbors although most of them were from Cuba and refugees from the days of Fidel Castro who was dead. But most only entertained dreams of returning to their Island to resume their lives. They had long ago become Americans and grew to love their lives. Ben thought about the fact that so many of the Cubans embraced conservative and anti-Castro sentiments. It saddened him.

A telephone call to Maria asking her to go back to Asheville to oversee the work on the house was what Ben had in mind. He wanted to be certain that he was not taking advantage of her good nature. Clearly, if he would have asked them, they would have said emphatically that whatever he wanted of them was their desire to do. Juan and Maria adored Ben. He made their lives, if not extravagant, one of total comfort and ease.

They talked it over at Ben's insistence. He did not want them to feel that Maria had to do this for him. Juan decided that he wanted to see this house, too. He would drive her to Asheville to get accustomed to the drive, leave their personal car there for her to get around in, and then fly back commercially. They left two days after speaking to Ben. Juan decided to take the turnpike north to Interstate 75 and continue to Atlanta. They found a motel on the outskirts of Atlanta in a little town, Hoschton, Georgia, and then were on the road again on Interstate 85 through South Carolina to Spartanburg until the road met Interstate 26. From there it was a straight shot northwest to Asheville nestled in the Appalachians. Juan lifted his chin slightly and looked around, his eyes taking in the grandeur of the mountains, beckoning everyone that drove the lovely Interstate 26 to come, to enter their world. They marveled at the fact that the further they got from Florida, the more enchanting the scenery became, not to mention the coolness and diminished humidity.

Maria suggested that they stay in the same motel that the writers and she had stayed before. The owners and help were happy to see her again and asked about all of the guests that she brought before. "In all likelihood we may need to stay with you again for a week, or even two, if the house isn't ready for us."

The owners, an Indian couple with two little children, smiled contently. "For you and your employer, we will be happy to entertain you here at Namaste." The word meant welcome and was used freely in their homeland.

They would all be at Namaste in three weeks. It was not necessary to leave a credit card number or any amount of money as a security deposit. How could they forget the generosity of that great man, Ben Zangwell?

Juan toured around the city while Maria went about her work. He loved the old house, and saw exactly why "Z" loved it so. The builders were everywhere. The day that the couple arrived at the house new appliances for the kitchen were to arrive, and the old wood-burning stove was being disassembled. Juan had the feeling that Ben would like it to remain on the grounds and he asked whether they could find a place for it somewhere. It was decided that they would lug it downstairs to the basement which could easily accommodate it and anything else worth saving. Maria took a look at the equipment invoices and was satisfied that the new refrigerator, stove, sinks and shelves would be acceptable to the group.

The elevator had taken some doing, as did the installation of a new bathroom on the first floor. Architectural plans had to be drawn and the code enforcement division of the local government was required to pass their approval before construction or installation could begin. There was a question about whether Kelly House was to be considered a nursing home or assisted living facility. If so, the requirements were very different than if the house was used as a private residence. Ben assured the bureaucrats that the commune was not a business, not a facility, but was in fact a home for people who happened to be senior citizens and who had some physical disabilities, but in no way, a rehabilitation center or anything like it. Ben had his legal counsel and let the people at the bank handle these matters with the enforcement people.

Ben retained Slavin, Springler and Jones, Inc. in Asheville to represent him and Kelly House in all legal matters. A call to them took care of the potential problems. Another concern that Joe Slavin raised with Ben was whether the home would be considered a legal entity. He pointed out that in all likelihood there would be no legal issues with the commune members, but should anything happen out of the ordinary, Ben might want to consider incorporating the commune. If a lawsuit was ever filed against Ben, he would be protected. He wanted advice from another firm which he had used to deal with some of his holdings and the firm in New York agreed with Slavin.

Would the commune become a business? If the writers did sell their material and begin to receive financial reward from it, how would that affect Ben? He did have the clause about a 50/50 split on earnings. But, what would this mean legally for Kelly House?

His CPA and the law firm were not only in favor of the advice given by the lawyers, but were adamant that Ben take their advice. His attorney promised to consult the law firm in Asheville.

Ben met Bobby Tubbs at his favorite diner as prearranged. He wanted to give a good story, but not discuss anything about his finances because he didn't want the cartel to come looking for him. He knew that they wouldn't just look for him. The writers were in danger, too. Ben ate his favorite cheeseburger with three different cheeses, cottage cheese because he thought he should cut out the greasy fried potatoes, and he devoured his sugar-free Jello. The reporter was not allowed to accept any free lunches from anyone. It was the Journal's policy. So he had coffee and a bagel toasted well with cream cheese. In Kansas he didn't know whether bagels were sold anywhere, but thought maybe in Kansas City, Kansas, and Manhattan where he went to school.

"Where do you want to start, Bobby?"

"Mr. Zangwell, why don't you just begin where you want to, and I'll stop you when I have questions." The reporter had been raised to call all older persons by their surname, but Ben quickly put that rule aside. It put Bobby at ease.

"Fair enough. I came down to Florida because I was beginning to feel my old age. Arthritis, diabetes, a few other pains and aches. I guess you don't know about those things yet, kid." Ben smiled and laughed. "I thought it might be interesting to do some volunteer work with people my own age." Bobby noticed Ben's body language especially his belly laughter, bright eyes and bright red nose.

Bobby stopped him. "What made you go to Greentree?"

"Greentree was close to where I live. I could get there without too much trouble on my tricycle. When I went in they were enthusiastic about volunteers. I figured it would be an interesting way to pass time. I didn't go every week, but I started going a lot more when I got involved with the group and met Ted Kelly."

"I take it Kelly House is named after him. Why?"

"What do you know about Ted?" Without waiting for an answer, Ben continued, "He was a union business agent who led sort of a double life. He didn't make that much money on the job, but almost everything he had went to helping others one way or another. Food, mortgage payments, rent, school supplies for the kids, things like that. He was a real humanitarian without the big bucks. A lot of those guys give money away to make their taxes less burdensome, you know a tax write-off. Not Kelly."

"Did he tell you all about his financial help?"

"Hell no, no way. He was a cynical, closemouthed bastard. I had to do some digging on my own to find out all that stuff." Ben smiled to himself as he used "bastard" to describe his departed friend. He saw surprise on Tubb's demeanor when he uttered it. Bobby was furiously taking notes as Ben spoke.

"What happened to Mr. Kelly?"

"He died during the time he was at Greentree of a massive heart attack or stroke. I don't know which. He was in terrible shape. He was one of those people who give everything to their job. He gave a hell of a lot more than a pound of flesh. That's for sure! Came down here to see a friend, retire, and get his health back. Not much of a retirement."

"So this idea to start a commune for elderly people, where did that come from?"

Ben told him the story of how he bought the place in Asheville, wanted to use it as a training school for civil disobedience, and never got around to doing so. He spoke about the idea to the group and they liked it.

"I told them that my only requirement was that the commune not become a closed affinity group."

Puzzled, Bobby asked, "How do you plan to prevent that from happening, Ben, and what do you mean by affinity group?"

"An affinity group is a group of people who fall in love with themselves and close others out. I hope that as long as I'm alive my preaching about the nature of groups to become inbred will get them to focus on the problem and to spot the tendency before it happens. Maybe it's pie in the sky. I hope not."

The reporter wasn't sure that he understood all this heavy duty sociological jargon. He planned to talk to his colleague about it. The rest of the interview centered on how Ben planned to get the people to the new home, the logistics more or less. Ben told him that he had advised the people to hang on to their current dwellings so that they would have some place to return to if they didn't like communal living.

Bobby was interested in the idea of publishing the writers' works. A rumor had spread that Ben was a publisher. "I don't know a damn thing about publishing books or anything else."

All the rumors about him being in the newspaper business were just that, hoopla. He knew very little about it. During his time with the CIA he had short training courses about misinformation propaganda, and how to plant ideas that the agency wanted people to believe, but he, himself, had not been as effective in that area as other operatives.

"I guess there are literary agents who might be willing to tackle new writers. They'd probably want a ton of money to take a chance on someone new." He was right, of course. Rarely were budding writers successful at selling their material and rejection slips were the norm.

"Of course, we might publish ourselves, you know, self-publish and sell at book fairs. That sort of thing."

The reporter felt that he had enough material about the commune, but not much on the man, himself. "I have a good story about the commune, the writers, but not much on you. It would help us a lot if you would tell us something about yourself."

This was what Ben feared most. In some ways, he was much more comfortable not sharing anything about his personal life, but he liked the young man and wanted to cooperate as much as possible. He thought about what he could say without divulging anything about the money.

"I was born in Kiev, Russia about eighty years ago. I don't like to tell anyone my exact age. Probably vanity. I spent the war in Russia, but then my parents emigrated to Israel for about three years and then to Colombia, South America for four years. I learned to speak fluent Hebrew and Spanish. I'm not sure why they moved to the good ol' USA, but we had relatives in Zanesville, Ohio. That's where I went to school and learned to speak English. School was boring and the teaching for the most part was just plain inadequate. So, I joined the Marine Corps and stayed through the Viet Nam War." Ben winced when he talked about war and especially Viet Nam.

"They liked my ability to speak Russian and I learned to talk Vietnamese. I did some work for the government as a language consultant." He didn't want to discuss his work with the CIA. He left that out.

Bobby began to see that there were gaps in Ben's story and decided not to probe too deeply although he saw a big time story and maybe even a movie about the man. "That's about the extent of it. I got out of the service and was involved in business and some other things I'd rather not go into."

"What about marriage, children, grandchildren?"

"No children that I know of, and no marriages. I guess I moved around too much for thinking about settling down and finding someone who'd tolerate me. Maybe, if I could have married a girl from Viet Nam or Laos, I would have, but back then it was too difficult to consider it. But, I'll tell ya, Bobby those women were the best. Beautiful beyond belief and dedicated to the pure pleasure of their man- what can I say? I had a fiancée once, but she died in Hong Kong and is buried up at the commune on a hillside overlooking the mountains." Ben choked on his words. Tubbs was sure that he saw tears in the old man's eyes and heard a wistfulness he hadn't heard before.

They spent two solid hours on the interview, and when they both looked at their watches were surprised at how much time they had been together. They bid each other farewell and Bobby promised to call Ben and go over the story before sending it to his editor.

On Friday the week following Gerald and Lee's departure from Greentree, the group met in the dining hall. Britt, David and Sadie were to leave in one week. Lee and Pauline arrived before anyone else. They were anxious to say hello to everyone. Lee wanted everyone to know that she received a phone call from her niece Selma, who had insisted that she come to Florida after Sandy's death, saying that she was in Calgary with Roger, her new 'friend', and that she found Calgary fascinating. Selma confided to her aunt that she had sex for the first time in her life. She was fifty-three years old. Her voice was lighthearted, almost dreamy, and she giggled as she talked about things she would never have dreamed possible just six months ago.

Ben thought it wise to meet with the entire group once at the rehabilitation center to discuss when they were going to leave for Asheville as a group and how it would be done. He thought that if his new friends were going to take a lot of their personal possessions, possibly some pieces of furniture, whatever, this meeting would be a good place to raise these issues, try to nail down some specifics.

Jane and Aileen popped in to say hello and to be as supportive as they could. Jane finished her research paper and spent two half days with Dr. P, the statistical guru at Florida International University in North Miami. She was the director of the Ph.D. program in Social Work research. The doctor crunched numbers for Jane using Jane's assessment sheets, and concluded that there were tremendous gains for the writer population, although there were only five left after Ted Kelly died.

For the control group using the same formulas, she concluded that the validity and reliability factors were adhered to and that the control group did not show any significant improvement using a cognitive/behavioral approach in therapy. She pointed out that the factors related to the writers getting better might be attributed to the commune and the fact that the group had an opportunity to relocate and not return to the same environment from which they came.

Jane was honest in her research design and pointed out in the conclusion that this might be the one flaw in her research. She could never have anticipated the commune when she started. Her conclusions were that depression, lethargy and procrastination in working toward returning to an independent lifestyle had definitely been affected by the autobiographies. Writing about one's life and using the writing in a group therapeutic environment was without a doubt helpful in recovery. Her paper was submitted and accepted by the International Journal of Geriatric Rehabilitation.

The editors sent back proofs for some revisions, questioned some of the research methodology and wanted some questions answered relating to the statistical formulas used by Dr. P. Jane was asked to do a small autobiography and to do a page thanking anyone she deemed important in making the paper successful.

She asked and received permission to use the patients' names, volunteers', Selma's and Mr. Cohen's, the CEO at Greentree. He was stunned that she wanted to thank him publicly, and Jane detected a crack in his armor as the tough-nosed businessman who had little patience for the human side of the business.

Ben began the meeting by giving the writers a rundown on the progress made so far at the house. There were a few questions, but mainly people were concerned about how they were going to get there and when.

"I think that we should discuss the fine points of the stuff I gave you the last time we met. Does anyone have any questions about the ideas concerning affinity groups?" Ben almost said rule, but he didn't want to convey the idea that he had established rules. The group would define their behavior and their way to reach consensus together.

"I think that we need to talk about your expectations for our writing. I mean what happens if we get there and our creative juices fail us?"

"Good point, Gerald. What do the rest of you think?"

"Does it mean that we have to leave just because we aren't writing," asked Sadie?

"I'm not really one of you anyway" said Pauline looking somewhat anxiously from one face to another. "I just helped Lee. But, I do have some ideas that I'd like to experiment with."

"Well, we need that for sure, Pauline. But, we also need some ideas about getting published. It's one thing to create, another altogether to sell."

"You are quite correct, Ben. When I tried to sell some of my poetry a hundred years ago, I found that out. I couldn't sell anything."

"Gerald, I bet that you could do it now, though. You're more mature, and there may be a market out there for senior moments of poetic inspiration."

"That sounds good, David. I will have to remember that for a title for my work." The others shook their heads in agreement.

"One of the things that I want to do first, just as soon as we get to Asheville, is to find those letters of mine from my stay in Seal Point with my mountain man husband." Britt smiled at the others.

"Does that mean that you'll have to do some traveling?" asked Sadie.

"I don't know whether I can or not. That's a problem. What do you think, Ben?"

"I suppose that depends on how much energy you have, Britt, and what you'd have to do to find them." Britt had a fleeting thought about Ben and her traveling together to find the letters. She thought they might be in New York at her nephew's home.

"Well, it doesn't look like you guys want to talk about the affinity angle of this commune. Am I reading you correctly?"

Everyone looked around at each other. They all seemed to agree. "OK, but at some point it may become a factor. And no, Sadie, once a commune member, always a part of the family whether you write or not." Ben looked around the room for affirmation. Again everyone agreed.

"When do you think we'll be making the move," asked David?

"Jane tells me that you, Sadie, and Britt, will be out of here in one week. How long after that would you be ready to go?"

"I need to give my notice. I know you said we should hang on to our places, but I thought about it and for me, if I stay a year in Asheville, I can save $6,000. That will be more than I've had in years," said Britt.

"I understand that, but if you don't like it and want to move, will $6,000 be enough to find a new place? With the problems that you have, will it be enough to find what you need?"

"I don't know, Pauline. But, all I have now is a studio on AIA in Deerfield. I don't think it would be wise to hang on to it and spend all that money when I'm not there."

"I see Britt's point, but I have so much stuff in my one bedroom and I own it. I think I'd be better off keeping it like Ben suggested and not have to be bothered with asking my son, Ethan, and the grand kids to move me out. I'd have to get a storage room somewhere." David had made up his mind.

The writers were all thinking about the move now. Pauline, Gerald,

David, and Sadie agreed that they wanted to hold on to their homes. But Lee and Britt came to the conclusion that they had nothing to hold on to, had no furniture or need to return to the places where they lived now. Pauline offered Lee the use of one of her bedrooms to store anything that she needed to keep safe. Barring any unforeseen problems, it was agreed that moving day would be set for April 1, a Monday. Ben hoped that April Fool's Day was not an omen of things to come.

CHAPTER FOUR

David, Britt, and Sadie left Greentree on Friday, March 15, with much fanfare. By now the articles concerning their move to the commune had been printed, and TV stations had made announcements on community news of the elderly commune founded at Greentree. Sid Cohen couldn't believe how much good publicity he was receiving as a result of the work that Jane Finestein, the social worker, and the writers had done. When he thought back at the amount of trouble he and the former physiatrist had thrown at Jane, Ben, and the project, he shuddered. "What a schmuck," were the only words he could find to describe his own behavior.

Sid was beginning to be recognized in the industry as a leader and promoter of innovative and experimental ideas. No longer did he consider himself just a businessman who wanted to make a huge profit without thinking about scruples. He smiled a great deal more than in the years past, spent more time at Greentree, but perhaps the biggest difference was that he listened to his staff and became a major supporter of new ways to benefit clients and patients. His cynicism and hatred of the State of Florida's Department of Children and Family's watchdog role diminished, but did not completely evaporate. He still bristled when they arrived, but no longer was certain that they were there on some personal vendetta against him. It would take a long time for him to accept their banal bureaucracy.

David returned to his one bedroom condominium at Whispering Pines Village. He had a full time nursing assistant who worked a twelve hour shift with someone else coming in for an eight hour period. His stroke made it impossible for him to live alone. Jane and Ethan met on two occasions to discuss the living arrangements for David's returning to his apartment. David did not want to go to Ethan's home even though it would only be for two weeks until the move to the commune. In the past, friends marveled at what they perceived as David's lack of selfishness. They believed that he was worried that his family would have to care for him, but, in fact, David didn't want to be disturbed by them. He didn't want his routines disturbed. He wanted his life on his terms, not anyone's dictates. He wondered whether communal life would interfere with his independent way of life.

An agency was contacted who made the assignments to private homes. They understood that the aides would only be there for a short period of time while David prepared for his trip. These agencies, and there are many in South Florida, were, in David's opinion, greedy and what he hated about Capitalism. They made a lot of money, but the actual help made close to minimum wage. It was despicable as far as he was concerned, and he took great pains to educate the workers who would listen. The government was just as much at fault in its duplicity.

A private non-medical van picked up David with all his belongings, a wheelchair and a walker that had been given him by Mr. Cohen. Rehabilitation services were contacted and arrangements made for David to have two visits a week until the move. The new physiatrist on staff, Dr. Ruth McNichols, wrote plans for the new facility and coordinated the transition. She, too, explained why it would only be for one or two sessions. She also called Asheville Rehabilitation Association and alerted them to the opening of the commune, and the likelihood that they would soon be working with a few new patients from Florida. The medical director in Asheville seemed pleased and promised to work closely with Ruth on a smooth transition.

So David's return to Whispering Pines went well. Ethan, Diana, and the children were on hand when he arrived. David was introduced to George, his new nursing assistant, who hailed from Trinidad in the Caribbean. He was new to the States.

George, too, wondered about the fortune that his people and others had in having so much work which in his country would automatically belong to the family. No elderly person would ever be taken care of by strangers. In his mind it was really different here, and he was happy about that because he didn't want to run a fruit stand in a flea market, or do dishes in a restaurant just to get a foot in the door. The United States was a country where fortunes were being made, even if it meant starting at $9.28 an hour. "It's better than Trinidad and that's no lie". He didn't say that out loud. George was a likeable man who told David about his family back in Trinidad. He hoped to be able to bring them to the United States as quickly as possible. He was a deeply religious man who somehow combined the animism from his African roots with his Christianity. He helped David get ready for his trip.

Britt was fitted with a portable oxygen tank, a number of nasal plugs, and big tanks were arranged to be sent to the little apartment on AIA. That, too, was part of Jane's duties - to arrange for any medical supplies which would be needed. When Britt arrived, her landlord and his wife were out of town visiting their son and daughter-in-law in Jacksonville. New people were living in the studios on either side of Britt. She had the Meals on Wheels lady again who came every day with a hot meal and a ready smile. It turned out to be the same woman Britt met before her hospitalization and rehabilitation. Delores felt warmth, a joy and, yes, a sense of gratitude. She never experienced a friendly, warm, personable Britt before. The Britt she remembered was not a person to look forward to seeing again. Actually, it was a major shock to find a warm, loving, caring and friendly person who greeted her at the door. What happened to the old woman with the biting sarcastic and mean-spirited tongue?

As for Britt, she noticed Delores for the first time and appreciated her volunteering. Britt invited Dolores to come in, offered to make her a cup of coffee, and inquired about her health and the health of her family. "Honey, if you don't mind me saying so, you look great and much happier than I've ever seen you before." Britt beamed.

For the last six and a half months, Britt had become part of a loving family and once again she was alone. She had everyone's telephone number and even Ben's private beeper number, should she become despondent, lonely or just want to talk to someone. It was still cool enough to sit outside and watch the world go by. Her little beach chair was still there where she left it almost three quarters of a year ago. The new neighbor, with beer in hand, told her that the owner was due back next week. Britt would give notice then.

Sadie Goldenblum returned to her condo on 441 in Hollywood by non-medical van. She took her writing, clothes, a walker and crutches with her. Everyone at Greentree wept a bit when Sadie left because staff, the patients and, of course, her new family loved her so. People felt so comfortable with her and everyone, black or white, young or old, male or female somehow saw a piece of himself or herself leaving. Sadie seemed to dig into people's goodness no matter how buried it might be. She didn't do it intentionally; it was a gift.

Meals-on-Wheels operated in Hollywood, and Jane arranged for them to begin their work as soon as Sadie returned. Jane also arranged for the Alert Program to call Sadie every morning for the next two weeks until she departed. It was a wonderful program operated by the Crisis Hotline in Broward County. The purpose was to check in with some elderly people every morning to let them know that someone cared and to be sure that they were alive. If they didn't answer their phone, a kindly police office would be dispatched to call on them at home to be sure everything was fine. The Concern Line was manned by volunteers,themselves elderly folks, who had a desire to be helpful and useful.

Sadie's diabetic supplies were also arranged for, and the medical supply store would bring the syringes and insulin to her. At Greentree she learned to take her blood minimally once a day. She hated this chore and was squeamish about seeing her own blood, but seemed to link her writing, moving to North Carolina, and her health together. She began to take the monitoring of her sugar levels seriously.

When Sadie arrived home, she found letters from her son and daughter. Both were upset that she was going to share their firm beliefs with the world and especially in a critical manner. Both were eager to see their mother and suggested that she didn't need to go to the commune. In fact, Elaine offered Sadie a room of her own and total care if she would like to come back to the East and live with her and Josh, Sadie's son-in-law. She was very happy that Elaine made the offer, but now she saw her place with her new friends. For a brief moment, she wondered why Elaine wanted her to move in with her now after all these years. She never did before.

Returning to her apartment was a bit bewildering to Sadie. When she left, she was transported in an ambulance. She and her neighbor, Dilly Mandel, had exchanged keys just in case of an emergency, and Dilly found her on the floor.

Sadie may have been unconscious for a day or two when her friend, Dilly Mandel found her. Dilly called 911 immediately. It was scary for her, but she was a part of a community volunteer emergency management team pledged to go into action if a hurricane or some other sort of catastrophic incident should happen. She knew first aid, how to triage, and was part of the team which would help people relocate if necessary. This was the first time that she was called upon to use her new skills. It both scared and excited her. She hadn't done anything important in a long while or she thought maybe never before.

She knew that her friend, Sadie Goldenblum, was a diabetic and was supposed to use insulin daily. She also knew that Sadie often forgot to take her insulin or indulged in forbidden foods. So finding her in a diabetic ketoacidosis state was anticipated at some point. For years Sadie had fought off unhealed wounds and gangrene. But after the hospital emergency room was able to stabilize her, they sent her up to the medical ward and there her doctor found major wounds on her left leg and foot. Specialists were called in and her children notified by the hospital.

They responded immediately to their mother's bedside and signed papers allowing the surgeons to remove her leg below the knee. It was impossible to save the leg. The children stayed for a week and then returned to their families. Sadie remained in the hospital for about a month because it was difficult to get the sugar under control. Once it was controlled and remained so, the social worker made a call to Greentree for her admittance for rehabilitation services. In all, Sadie was gone from her condo in Hollywood for nine months. Diabetes took so much from so many and particularly in the poorest of neighborhoods.

It was good to be back. Dilly made dinner for her on her first night, and was thrilled to hear about her stay in Greentree. Dilly made hospital calls but did not visit at the center. This was definitely a new Sadie, and she had never seen such positive energy in her before. They discussed what Sadie wanted to take with her to North Carolina. "I want to take my bedroom set. It means so much to me. Morris would have loved it, may he rest in peace."

When she came to Florida, she went to some thrift stores on Hallandale Boulevard and Miramar Parkway which supported Jewish philanthropic organizations. Their merchandise was a better quality than some of the other thrift stores had, but the prices were higher too. She bought a beautiful bedroom set with a queen size Serta mattress. She wondered whether Ben would allow her to bring the entire set.

Additionally, she brought all her kitchenware with her from Baltimore. She wanted to bring it for her new kitchen and her new mission in life. Packing it up was the problem. This, too, she'd discuss with Ben. The rest of the furniture could stay in Hollywood.

Gerald determined that he'd keep his condo in Coral Springs. That was a given. He saw himself probably staying in Asheville for a year, no more; he was sure that he did not wish to remain forever. As he looked around the apartment and thought about what he wanted moved, he focused on his books. There were at least five hundred of them which would make for the beginning of a library. He had all of Clair's literature books because she had spent twenty-five years teaching Advanced Literature to high school advanced teenagers. She was on every book dealer's preferred list for complimentary copies. Of course, their desire was that she would change textbooks to theirs and this would mean thousands of dollars to them. Gerald remembered what Upton Sinclair said about the book companies running the education system and especially the National Education Association.

Gerald had loads of workbooks in every imaginable subject dealing with remedial work for the children that he worked with when he taught potential high school dropouts. Almost every author and publisher with a new idea on how to keep children in school and promote interest in learning sent Gerald a copy of their book. Adding Claire's books and volumes that they had collected together during their wonderful marriage amounted to a small but significant education collection.

He'd try to box them up for pick-up by the van. As for anything else, he decided that he would take a Lazy-boy chair that he loved, although he often regretted sitting in it because he almost always fell asleep while reading. Maybe he would bring his bedroom set, and, of course, his clothes. He doubted that he had enough warm clothing in his wardrobe. It was a given that the mountain air would chill at night and that in the winter he would need some heavy sweaters, galoshes for snowy or rainy days, and heavy corduroy pants.

David's arrival at Whispering Pines Village and his apartment was a gala affair. The community newspapers ran the article written about the commune and the writers. He found messages posted by neighbors on his door welcoming him home. There was always some sweet older lady wanting to entertain him with a home-cooked meal. He left there with everyone fearing the worse. Too many residents went away in an ambulance and never returned. Already three or four of his neighbors passed away or left for a nursing home never to be seen again. It was that way in every building in the senior citizens' village.

David speculated that in some ways the people who ran the place were responsible for some of the problems. He thought about research which showed that many elderly people were lonely, depressed, and a small pet like a dog or cat often provided them with the company needed to help them defeat their despondency. The condo Don, an Italian who everyone spoke of with too much reverence for David's taste, was always surrounded by his lieutenants who ran the individual buildings. It would have been easy to choose a few buildings far away from the center of activities to have as pet-friendly buildings, but they wouldn't hear of it. Sometimes it drove David to muttering about their stupidity.

His intent before the stroke was to leave the village some day and find a place where he could have a small dog and a cat. He traveled so much back in those days that he was almost happy that he didn't have a pet. It would have meant kenneling. Years ago Ethan and Diana had taken care of his calico cat for him, but they were never happy with that arrangement.

David, like his pal Gerald, had many books and wanted to take them with him to Kelly House. His library consisted of an assortment of fiction and non-fiction. He had many textbooks from his studies in education, paramedics and social work. Most of them were terribly outdated. An amazing amount of research in emergency medicine had taken place since David went to Broward Community College to study for a year. He imagined that the textbooks had changed five or six times since he studied. He smile at the thought of Jim Reed, a cocky instructor who favored the words "cretin medic" to show his displeasure at some of the work done by his contemporaries when he was an active medic. David decided this was a good time to throw out or donate to a library most of his textbooks. Sadly, he knew that he would never need them again. As for his Social Work books, they had always been wasted paper as far as he was concerned. In the short time that he practiced, he never needed to refer back to any of them for advice or research.

David did not necessarily begrudge his time spent in the two year social work program. It had been entertaining, and he did well enough to be elected to the honor society, a feat that he didn't think was such a big deal considering that the work was laborious although not mentally challenging for the most part. He liked most of his instructors. They were well-meaning people and that was important in David's mind. Some of the other students, though, were people David wondered about. He laughed to himself, "They probably wondered about me, too". He thought them to be mundane, blatantly boring people and wondered whether their clients would experience them in the same way.

While at school, he worked for the Department of Social Services as a family services worker. Clients were mainly young people who didn't know how to parent because they had never been parented effectively themselves. Some, too many, either were in trouble with the law, mentally ill, addicts or a combination of all three. David's own addiction was over-eating and he understood the dynamics of addiction. He wondered how much addiction had to do with genetic markers, wiring and environment and, for that matter, whether resilience was simply guided by wiring as well.

He didn't see the genetics as an excuse, but he knew that those who saw addictions as easily controllable, a matter of will, and the help of the Lord were just minimizing a very powerful and destructive force in the lives of so many. While at school, he attended an AA meeting or two for a paper he was writing. These were meetings that seemed to be very helpful to the alcoholics and their families, but he wondered whether AA alone could really get at the root problems of the alcoholics.

As David was going through the books to be discarded, he remembered that he had gone to some meetings of Overeaters Anonymous. One group met at a hospital on Sunday mornings. He used to spend Saturday nights at the firehouse as a volunteer emergency medical technician and then he'd go over to the meeting. He called the international office and they suggested the hospital. They called it a breakfast meeting. That surprised David and he asked what the members of the group ate. The lady at the other end of the telephone said, "Nothing."

The meeting was an all male group and most of the men had tipped the scales at well over 350 pounds before they found OA. David thought back about the group and the stories these men told- over and over again. So having gone to about six or seven meetings he quit. He couldn't identify with any of these men or their lives. It seemed that all of them had been raised to be couch potatoes and were obese as children. These were men who fell into the category of the millions of children who were allowed to snack constantly, watched too much television, and rarely ventured outside to play or participate in sports. Some, on the other hand, were sexually abused as children or emotionally harmed by unthinking parents.

No so for David. He rarely watched TV and was an athlete. Over the years as an adult, his weight crept up on him and finally culminated in helping him to become a diabetic, type II. The doctors continuously harangued him, "Lose weight, fifty pounds, and you won't have the problem of diabetes any longer." David tried OA again, once. This group was a male and female group, but he was turned off by the call for Jesus' help and the preponderance of stories told over and over again. He quit that group, too.

He looked down at himself, the paunch which was always his companion, and felt his handlebars. He fingered his jowls and looked at a mirror on the wall.

"Well, I know this is stupid rationalization, but maybe carrying an extra seventy pounds will be good for me some day if I ever get stomach cancer. At least I'll have some fat for the cancer to eat off of before it attacks my organs."

Even as he said this he was saddened by his lack of willpower and ability to do what the doctors told him.

"Maybe in the mountains things will be different and I'll make another effort to do something about this weight."

The last thing he remembered before falling asleep was wondering how many people told themselves the same sort of thing. Twice he had lost at least forty to fifty pounds. The first time was when he was an officer in the National Guard. But, in his mind's eye he saw himself as a teddy bear, and this new, slimmer image he noticed every morning upon waking and looking in the mirror was not him, so he gained the weight back plus some for good measure.

The second weight loss was due to a bacterial or viral menace that attacked his stomach lining after he returned from Southeast Asia. A month of drinking beer, coca-cola, and bottled water didn't protect him from finally picking up the horrendous bowel-cramping little warrior. David lost about forty pounds over that fiasco, but regained it all back within a year.

David went back to thinking about his time with the State of Florida. He couldn't remember a lot and cursed his loss of memory. That was about twenty-five years ago as far as he could recollect. The department was under a lot of pressure then to take more responsibility for the foster care program. Every now and again a story would appear in the paper about some foster parent taking advantage of children, sexually, physically, or mentally abusing them. All of his colleagues were overworked including himself. One of the judges from the county was taken to Tallahassee by a new Republican governor and put in charge of the entire department. Her answer to the problem was to place the work load in the hands of private agencies which would provide the monitoring of the foster care system. Although the governor approved the plan, he finally dumped her as a political embarrassment because the privatization didn't change anything.

The department still had major problems and under her administration did not get any better. As David thought about it over the years, private companies didn't have to offer competitive salaries or provide worthy benefits that were comparable to those paid by the State. He smiled, "That was one time when you got what you paid for."

"Hell, that was a long time ago. We still have kids who have lousy parents, drugs and alcohol. What can you do? I guess everyone is doing the best they can." Then David thought about Ted and Ben and realized that Ben would probably knock the hell out of that argument. "Maybe when we get to Asheville, I'll get involved there some way. I'll become a guardian ad litum, if they'll take me." With that, David felt sleepy and went into his bedroom for a nap. He was sleeping more since he returned from Greentree.

CHAPTER FIVE

Jane looked out her window onto the small courtyard in the middle of the garden. It was a beautiful, warm, and green day in the middle of March. The weather gave signs of returning to the humidity and heat that Southeast Florida was known to experience for at least nine months of the year. But today the remnants of a cool spring day were still lingering. As she lazily looked upon the greenery, her phone rang. The call was from a professor of geriatrics in the School of Social Work.

"Mrs. Finestein, this is Jay Thommey at Dade University. I teach a course in geriatric interventions in our school of social work. I read an interesting article in the paper about your experiment and I'd like to invite you to speak to my class about the group and the commune."

Jane didn't hesitate. "I'd be delighted to do that, Dr. Thommey. When would that be?"

"The class meets on Saturdays in the morning. How would this Saturday be for you?"

"Fine, I think." As she thought about going, an idea struck her. What if she could bring some of the writers and volunteers to share their experiences with the class.

"I wonder whether you'd like some of the writers to come along too. It occurs to me that the students might like sharing some insights with them instead of just listening to me go over what happened."

"I never thought about the possibility of them joining you. A great idea, Mrs. Finestein, really great. Do you have enough time to coordinate that?"

"I don't know. Let's see, it's Tuesday morning. I might have enough time to see if anyone is interested. Could I let you know by Thursday?"

"I don't see a problem," said Thommey. "I'll fax over the directions to the building and room number. What's your fax number at Greentree? When you get here the building shouldn't be hard to find if you do bring over some of the writers."

"OK, then fax the information over and we'll talk on Thursday, and thanks for the invitation."

Jane was overjoyed to know that the group experience had found an audience and that some of the patients would get a chance to share some of their experiences with others. She decided to call Ben first and tell him about the call. He was cautious about using up his writers' energy knowing that in a couple of weeks they would be making a trip of some 800 miles by bus. But, he realized that what they had accomplished would sooner or later have to be shared with others, too. When Jane asked if he would come to the class, he wasn't sure that he wanted to share any of himself with students, but his curiosity was aroused. He agreed to come.

Next Jane called all the writers and told them of the invitation for Saturday. David was the only one who couldn't go because he was spending the entire day with his family. The others agreed, and Jane made the arrangements for the transportation. She'd call them back with the details. Mr. Cohen was happy to make the Greentree vans available and Jane once again thought about people being able to change regardless of age or stage of life.

On Saturday at 7:30 in the morning the van drivers began to collect the writers and Jane. Ben and Jane met the van at the facility and then one of the vans went south to pick up Lee, Pauline and Sadie while the other to the north to collect a very excited Gerald and Britt. It was agreed that all would meet at 9:30 at the classroom which was in the south of Miami, just off Route One. Everyone dressed nicely for the occasion and wore light weight clothing. Ben even wore long pants, but did not leave his cap at home.

Pauline and Lee wore the same elegant dresses that they had worn when they visited Ted Kelly at the hospital before he died. Sadie decided to wear one of her pants suits over her prosthesis. Onlookers were surprised to see so many 'old timers', and such a crew at that, going into Willis Hall.

Dr. Thommey's classroom was able to accommodate his class of twenty-two students and his visitors. He had given Jane a rundown of the composition of the class. It was a graduate level elective for master's and doctoral students. Most were working full-time and going to school part-time to earn their degrees or continuing education units needed in order to maintain their credentials as licensed clinical social workers.

Some of the students actually worked with the elderly either for the State or in private nursing homes. These students were particularly interested in hearing about the writers, and the others were happy to break the routine of Dr. Thommey's lecture and discussion. One or two of the students looked to be around the age of Pauline who was the youngest of the soon-to-be communal residents. But for the most part, the students ranged from upper twenties to mid-forties and early fifties.

The instructor introduced Jane, and she in turn introduced each of the patients and volunteers to the group. She spent about twenty minutes reviewing the experiment and discussing her belief that these patients were either clinically depressed or experiencing enough depression, anxiety and malaise to keep them from moving forward on their rehabilitation regimes. Quickly, she reviewed the theory behind the writing of autobiographies and how they could open doors for the patients into their past which would shed light on the present. Jane admitted that she wasn't sure whether the writing or the fact that her group was moving into a commune in the Western North Carolina Appalachians was the catalyst that drove them to want to achieve both physical and mental health. She concluded her remarks by pointing out that it could be both. She admitted that the commune could, in fact, have significantly tainted the research design.

Next Ben, somewhat embarrassed because he had barely finished high school much less college courses, rose and presented a brief capsule on his motivation to open Kelly House. Being unaccustomed to speaking publicly, he gave the impression of gruffness and impatience with the process.

However, the older students saw through his exterior and found themselves intrigued by this human walrus with the handle-bar mustache.

Each of the writers and Pauline were given a chance to add any additional thoughts and then the floor was open to questions and comments. The first was from the instructor.

"If not for the commune, where do you believe you'd be now or going to once you left Greentree?" It was addressed to all the writers.

Britt let out a sigh heard by all. "I was a miserable woman, hated everyone and myself. I can't begin to think of all the times I wanted to die. A lot of people feel so isolated and useless. I think that it was the writing for me that helped me to see that it didn't have to be that way. I also learned to love my friends here and poor Ted, the man who died, the one Ben talked about."

"But Ms. Manning," pressed Thommey, "what would you have done if, for instance, you were part of the control group which Jane talked about?"

"I don't know, really. Probably back to the room in Deerfield Beach or maybe my emphysema would have killed me. I mean it will never go away and I'll always cough and have trouble breathing, but who knows, maybe I would have just shriveled up and died there." Britt began to cough and her breathing became uneasy.

With effort she squeezed out, "The writing did help me, though, to become more tolerant of others and to feel love for them. Maybe, I don't know, maybe I would have been okay in Deerfield anyway." She shook her head in doubt.

Gerald broke in. "I know that I would never have been able to put my past behind me in any meaningful way without the writing. For me, going to Asheville is a plus and a new beginning, a chance to do some things that I would not have been able to do if I went back to my condo.

Maybe I would eventually have met some friendly, understanding woman. Maybe- but I doubt it. Now, everything is different. I will never stop loving my dear wife and remembering all the wonderful years we had, but the future is not nearly as dim as it was before." Gerald took Sadie's hand and squeezed it while smiling lovingly at the others.

A hand from the middle of the room rose. It belonged to a young woman who appeared to be in her early thirties. "My name is Amy, and I feel a lump in my throat listening to all of you. I think of my grandmother who is in her late eighties and seems to be sitting alone hoping that she'll die soon. She's in a nursing home and they treat her well and all that, but she's so lonely, I think. What can I do? My parents are in their sixties, and they don't want her to live with them."

"It's a fine line, I think." Lee seemed to be talking to herself and everyone could see that she was having trouble with her Parkinson's disease. The students bent forward to listen.

"I wanted to die too, just like Britt for many of the same reasons. I tried to kill myself twice, but a nursing home is not the place to find meaning and purpose. Somehow, I wish that all of my friends who are in their later years could do what we are about to do. I mean not everyone wants to write, some like to paint, garden, walk, play with dogs and cats- anything is better than languishing in a chair in a hallway of a nursing home somewhere."

"I'll let you in on a secret." Sadie smiled mischievously and said, "I'm not really much of a writer. My friends can tell you that, but I will have a big kitchen in Asheville at the commune and no one will ever go hungry without at least soup and a sandwich to munch on." Everyone laughed with her.

"Look, the truth is that there are few elderly people who go through this life without aches and pains and a lot worse. I think it was Kahlil Gibran who said it best, though. May I?" Pauline turned to Dr. Thommey for permission. He nodded.

> *Your joy is your sorrow unmasked. And the selfsame well from which your laughter rises was oftentimes filled with your tears. And how else can it be? The deeper that sorrow carves into your being, the more joy you can contain.*
>
> *Is not the cup that holds your wine the very cup that was burned in the potter's oven? And is not the lute that soothes your spirit, the very wood that was hollowed with knives?*

When you are joyous, look deep into your heart and you shall find it only that which has given your sorrow that is giving you joy. When you are sorrowful, look again in your heart, and you shall see that in truth you are weeping for that which has been your delight.

Blushing Pauline said, "That was from *The Prophet,* and I memorized it when I was a school girl so many years ago. I never forgot it. I think it applies to us and to you as well. Most of our contemporaries are dead and buried and many elderly people have memories and histories which are complicated by sadness. But, the issue is to find meaning, live life, do what you want to do until-----."

Everyone shook their head in agreement with Pauline. She was becoming recognized by the group as a very profound and thoughtful woman.

Another hand rose belonging to a young man in the back of the room.

He tilted his head and asked, "Okay, so how can we social workers and people in this class be useful? We're getting some very useful information and seeing some great films and all that, but what can we bring to our work with people who have fifty or more years on us?"

"Do not discount us and do not assume that we cannot hear you or that we have lost our faculties," Gerald said and told the group about Ted being called a 'lizard' by the paramedic, and how David became irate at the medic for using that word to describe elderly people. No one laughed and most thought about their parents or grandparents and what it would be like for someone to call them a lizard.

"If you decide to work with a geriatric population and I guess some of you do now, look at our age group as you would your own. We represent a cohort of sorts with experiences and backgrounds just like you have. Tap into that if possible. Look for those areas which interest your patients, clients, whatever you call them. Find those qualities which got them to this point in the first place and help your elders to reflect upon their pasts. For whatever it's worth, listen to them with eager ears. Never, never talk down to them."

Everyone listened intently to Gerald although some did not fully understand what he was saying or the reason for the demonstrative tone in his voice. Dr. Thommey and Jane sensed that Gerald may not be getting through to some.

Jane began, "There's a lot of resilience in many of your patients. Age plays a role, but it isn't the major element. The major idea, in my opinion, is to find those pieces remaining that offer hope and a reason for getting out of bed in the morning. That's what the writing did for these people. Not all of the elderly will be offered what Ben here is offering, but that doesn't mean that there aren't other ideas out there somewhere. I think that my role as a social worker is to convey that hope and that excitement about what tomorrow may bring and to be a conduit for channeling good mental health."

Thommey smiled and said, "Amen." He looked at his watch and found that the time had slipped away. The class seemed to have barely begun and was now over. The students stood in unison and clapped heartily. For many, new ideas for ways to get involved with their own family members and in their professions were before them. Some seemed eager to get to it. For others the questions were yet to form in their minds. They would wait until the next session for discussion.

CHAPTER SIX

On the way back to their homes and Greentree, the writers were clearly worn out and yet satisfied with themselves. Ben noticed their weariness and sitting next to Jane mentioned that he was concerned that some of them might have trouble with the trip to Asheville. The introductory weekend had been a flight in a private Lear, but in a week they would be going by bus about eight hundred miles. Even though the plan was to stop near the cut off to I-26 in South Carolina, it was still a long haul and the fatigue factor was something with which to be concerned.

Jane didn't think that there would be much of a problem so long as bathroom breaks were considered and medication regimes were adhered to properly. The first van dropped off the writers living in the south of Broward County and Pauline stayed for a few minutes to make sure that Lee was comfortable.

Ben promised to call each of the writers and Pauline. He decided that he would consider Pauline a writer and not have to signal her out each time he thought of the group. April 1 was just ten days away. He, too, was happy to have been a part of the group's first formal recognition of their achievements while at Rehab. He thought that there would be many more such occasions.

The next ten days were spent in a whirlwind of preparations. Still to be done was hiring the charter bus line which would furnish a bus for the group and jury rig some sort of means of transporting most of the goods that the writers wished to bring with them. Ben thought this a better way to move everyone to Asheville. He could have flown them again, but then their goods would have not accompanied them, and he wanted to encourage the writers to begin to take responsibility for their furniture and clothing; really to become self-sufficient again to the extent possible. He discussed this with Jane and she wholeheartedly agreed.

The home in North Carolina was being worked on and the contractor felt reasonably certain that everything would be in order. An elevator had successfully been erected in the house to reach from the ground floor to the second and instead of continuing it to the basement, a railing and lift had been placed on the stairwell which could accommodate a wheelchair. That way if the members decided that they wanted to make the basement into a sort of workroom for their writing and anything else, everyone would be able to use it.

A bathroom with a stall big enough for a wheelchair had been constructed on the first floor. Unfortunately, the bathroom took the place of the servant's room which must have gone back to before Civil War days. But after the city inspectors finished their routine and declared the room fit for the disabled, there was no room to reconstruct the old servants' room with the pot-bellied stove.

The ramps which were hastily arranged for the weekend jaunt were redone to be permanent and secured with railings for anyone able to ambulate but might need something to hold on to.

The second floor bathroom fixtures had been replaced as had all the appliances in the kitchen, a new hot water heater, central air conditioning unit installed for the first time in the mansion, and new carpet and safety tile added. The architect had done a great job.

The writers decided that they would like to live two to a room. Lee and Pauline and David and Gerald were a given. Surprisingly, Britt asked Sadie to consider joining her to which Sadie beamed and hugged Britt with a wet and generous kiss on her cheek. Of course, Britt held her breath, fearing rejection. Old tapes are hard to erase- the notion that she was not worthy of affection or love from anyone except men who she still saw as wanting one thing. Sometime Britt had dreams about Sadie being her mother or was that a wish? She didn't know, but she did think that if she could somehow have a mother again Sadie would be ideal.

So it was decided that the six would share rooms and that would leave a room for Ben when he was there. Still there was the consideration that new writers would probably join the commune and that eventually new bedrooms would have to be constructed somewhere to fit new members into the house. Actually, there were still four rooms available. Whether they would be big enough for doubling up was a concern for the future, not now.

Ben became a little more nervous each day as they grew closer to the move. His diabetes was beginning to cause him some trouble and he found himself getting up four or five times a night to urinate. On the rare occasions when he took his blood counts, the figures were usually in the 200 range. As big a man as he was, he was afraid of needles and feared having to give himself insulin shots. So when he realized that he was beginning to have a serious problem, he doubled up on his Metformin and Glyburide. This he knew was a mistake and often resulted in his sugar levels plummeting to the 50 range and bouts of diarrhea from the Metformin. When his sugar plummeted, he would require instant dozes of sugar, candy, anything which would feed his brain the sugar it needed. Carrying little bags of sugar helped, but sometimes he forgot and when that happened, it was bad. Eyesight would go, sweats would stain his shirts, and he would experience an altered mental status until he could satisfy his brain cells craving for sugar.

This time Ben went off to the Oakland Park VA clinic where he went for his routine medical care. It was a badge of honor for him to use the VA although he could have easily afforded a private physician or been seen by any of his medical friends that he knew from his days in Special Ops or the "Company." Ben loved the VA because it was the closest that the United States would come to socialized medicine. Veterans could go there, be seen and taken care of with prescriptions and every service imaginable for a few pennies, and then only if they could afford the small costs. Sure, the lines were long, waiting for appointments sometimes a couple of months or more, but it was the one area that neither the Democrats nor Republicans tried to get rid of. Tamper with, yes, but destroy, no. Even the Congress' clumsy attempt at health reform didn't hold a candle to the VA's medical system. That was Ben's opinion and the Tea Party could go to hell as far as he was concerned.

So Ben went in without an appointment and was seen after a two hour wait. He saw a physician's assistant he had known for a few years. Once she was juggling a failing marriage, a seat on a community council, a rebellious son who had some brushes with the law, and an eight hour day at the outpatient clinic. He often marveled at her ability to do it all and always have a cheerful smile on her face. At the same time, he thought about why he'd never married.

She didn't bullshit Ben. When he went over his numbers with her, she was visibly displeased. Without a fasting blood workup, she could not be sure what was going on, but clearly he needed to get his blood levels under control and pronto.

She was particularly interested in his project with the group and thought Ben to be a total enigma, just as everyone else did. But like almost everyone else, she loved the big bear of a man. The PA decided to increase his meds and advised him to make an appointment at the clinic in Asheville as soon as he could. She suggested that he take his records with him so that he wouldn't have to wait for the normal government snafu to be seen. This he did before he left. The records clerk made copies of his chart and Ben left with new meds, his records, and an admonition to watch his weight, diet, and take his medications as directed.

Meanwhile, Maria Morales was wrapping up her meeting with the contractor concerning last minute changes and additions to the house. The four bedrooms which were to become the living quarters for the new occupants were completed and Maria wanted to make sure that they would be suitable for the double occupancy. Each of the rooms was fitted with a state of the art closet organizer which would double the amount of space so that two people would have room for their clothing. Maria was still concerned that there would not be enough room for each person's belongings. But, the group decided that they wanted to wait until they got to Asheville to do furniture shopping.

The motel owner was overjoyed and not only for business reasons to know that her writers would once again be staying at Namaste for at least a week when they arrived. The new van that Maria purchased for the commune would be standing by for her to take the group shopping for their new furniture and to buy whatever was needed to get started. She had the names of furniture and bedding stores and directions to them.

Already Maria had purchased living room furniture, a 56 inch television and arranged for cable and telephone service to be installed the day that the group was to arrive in Asheville which would be on Tuesday, April 2. Kitchen appliances were installed and the water pressure increased significantly. Sadie would be happy. Even extra lines were placed for the purpose of computer links to e-mail, fax, whatever the writers might need. Of course this was the modern era and some of them carried their own cell phones.

The city inspectors met Maria and Charles Linquist, the architect, at the house and went over the electrical, plumbing, and construction work. They were satisfied with the work and proclaimed Kelly House ready for occupancy. Maria was the first to ride the elevator to the second floor and held her breath after crossing herself and asking her patron saint to take her hand. The lift worked perfectly, thanks to her saint, and Maria smiled with this knowledge. It didn't matter that the engineers might have different ideas.

Having no wheelchair, she was unable to ride the chair lift to the basement, but Linquist assured her that it worked. She went down the stairs and was amazed to find that the subterranean area was clean, dry walled and painted. Lighting fixtures were placed throughout and the big area was constructed for work, play or whatever the group would want. Another room in the back of the basement could be used as a storage area. A door to the backyard was constructed which complied with housing regulations to have an entrance and exit in case of emergency.

Maria would have liked to buy curtains and make the living room, dining area and downstairs bathroom a beautiful and charming design, but she realized that the men and women coming might have very different ideas about the décor. so she refrained from doing what came natural to her.

On Thursday, Maria and Ben concluded their telephone conversation with a most emphatic and heartfelt thank you from Ben. "I think you've just about thought of everything, Maria. I can't begin to thank you enough. If you want to come home, please do. Fly, whatever."

"Why don't you see whether Juan can be of help to you on the trip. I can wait for him here and the two of us might do some traveling around before we go back to Florida."

"Great idea. Have you talked to him about it?"

"No, just thought of it this minute, Ben. But I'll bet he's going to want to come. Sort of like taking his children to college the first time, only it's a commune and they're older than he is." They both laughed at the idea.

"I'll call him and see if he wants to join us for the trip on Monday."

"Bueno, mi amigo. Hasta luego."

Ben called Juan and he was happy to be included in the move. He saw no conflicts with time or his substitute teaching that he did once in a while in North Miami and all over Broward County. He'd be at Ben's apartment at six on Monday to pick him up.

Ben had an idea to share with Jane and Sid Cohen. He thought it might be appropriate for the bus to leave Greentree. Maybe if they wanted to call the newspaper kids to see whether they wanted a picture of the writers leaving Greentree for Asheville, it might make for an interesting picture and a good story. He smiled to himself and thought about his original reluctance to getting involved with the press, but now things were different. He wasn't quite sure how, but he felt so lighthearted and pleased with himself, the group, even the world. Not only were the writers changed. So was he!

He got Jane on the first ring and she liked the idea. She'd discuss it with the CEO and she'd get back to Ben.

Ben arranged for a couple of vans to pick up David's, Gerald's, Pauline's and Sadie's things that they wanted to take with them. The vans would gather up the goods, store them until Monday and bring them to wherever the bus was to leave from. Had he thought of everything? Probably not.

He suggested that telephones not be disconnected until Monday morning in case he needed to be in contact. A call was placed to each member to get a definitive list of the items they were going to bring and he tried to visualize whether everything would go into the bus and the two vans.

Both David and Gerald had boxes brought to their apartments so that their books could be packed. With help from George, his nursing assistant, David packed four book boxes, making sure that they wouldn't be too heavy. Clothing was packed into three canvas bags. He decided that he didn't want to bring a suit, just work pants, sweaters which he rarely wore in Florida, but had saved from his days in the north.

He threw in a lot of CDs that he loved. His opera was definitely going as was much of the folk music. Broadway shows needed to go also. Knowing that he was going to share a room with Gerald made David a little uncertain about bringing his radio, cassette and CD player because he didn't know whether Gerald would like his music at all. That was one area they had not discussed yet. He'd find out for sure though. David had a fleeting thought. "It's like getting married. It's not a lot different than '*Getting to know you.*'" David laughed out loud and it startled George.

Furniture would be left because David would continue to maintain the apartment at least for a year. Again he mused to himself, "It's like a contractual marriage with an out-clause if I don't like it." It reminded him of two of his marriages which were contractual in his mind. "This is the best of all possible worlds. But, if I could only take my Lazy-boy chair." It was a relief when Ben agreed that somehow it would be included.

Gerald, moving ever so slowly, also had some boxes for his books and he wanted to bring those writings which meant a great deal to him. "I definitely want to bring the paintings." He had one done by a student who was so disturbed but discovered a love for painting which was to become his profession years later. The painting was of the streets of Washington, a portrait of two angry and hostile young black males leaning against a wall full of bullet holes and pocked like chicken pox scars on a baby's face. The youths bore the anger and frustration of a generation of lost black males whose lives would most certainly end in prison or slabs in the morgue. The artist painted from personal experience and reflected his own possible downward spiraling life were it not for his creative genius.

Another painting was of a young black male holding his son, a baby. It was painted in blues and had been done, he was told, by a black artist who had deformed hands without fingers. His hands looked like claws instead. The picture was shockingly beautiful and the pride in the face of the father was incredibly powerful.

His neighbor helped Gerald pack the pictures and his clothes. Like David, he had three canvas suitcases which were light weight and could hold everything he wanted. Gerald felt no need to bring any furniture with him and was happy to leave everything in place until his return.

For everyone each new day was full of anticipation and excitement, and by Monday no one had slept more than a couple of hours a night. Each dreamed all sorts of weird dreams shrouded in fantasy and difficult to remember upon awakening. Britt's dreams were perhaps the most disturbing because she thought that she remembered being lost and very vulnerable.

Gerald's stomach ailments intensified and he was forever on the toilet with diarrhea and a lot of gas. He believed this to be related to the move and was not worried about it although it was painful. The worse of it was the lower bowel cramping that no amount of medicine would assuage.

David, Sadie, and Lee knew that their difficulties in sleeping and waiting through the days until Monday were normal for them. They stayed as busy as possible and dealt with the nervousness and excitement more or less in stride. For them, it was more a question of whether Monday would ever come. Meanwhile Sadie's children called three or four times and tried to persuade her to change her mind and to live with Elaine and her family, but her mind was made up and that was that!

On Sunday, two moving vans arrived and the drivers collected all the furniture, boxes and suitcases from each of the travelers. Pauline decided to bring her bed with her and so spent the last night with Lee in her niece's apartment in Margate. The two women shared Selma's queen size bed and Pauline cried for the sister that she never had and the years as a child when she wished desperately for the camaraderie of a sister with whom she could have shared her loneliness.

Ben lived sparsely, almost rustically. His clothes, a couple of books, and his one CD player were the only items he was bringing to Asheville. He kept his condo also because he anticipated that he'd be back in the area for business and whatever other needs he had. At the last minute, as the van pulled up to his apartment, he decided that he'd bring his favorite chair with him. It was huge and he felt small in it.

For some time he had been thinking of selling his place, but like the others, he didn't know whether the mountains would be the answer. It was not the communal living. It was more the idea that he was a wanderer, had a lust for the unknown, and even at eighty-two years old, it never left him. It was a constant companion driving him. Secretly, many of his friends wondered over the years whether he was running away from something, whether there was a psychological reason buried in their friend which drove him to meander through the world. But, in fact, he was just one of those rare people who truly made his home where his hat was at any moment. And then there was the expatriate thing as well. Maybe he would write about his dislike of the "American Way."

On Sunday night he made one last call to each of his flock to be sure that everything was in order. It was, and in less than twelve hours, they would be starting out on an unimaginable journey and a new life. For Ben, though, it was another operation and he was responsible for his team members.

CHAPTER SEVEN

It seemed very appropriate that the group should leave for North Carolina from Greentree Rehabilitation Center in the heart of South Florida. That was where it all began. Monday morning, April 1, was a warm, sunny day. The sun made its appearance over the ocean in all its brilliance and strength. Britt was the first to see it and waited patiently in her chair outside her little room for three hours to watch the sun rise. She couldn't sleep. She made coffee, parked herself on her little porch and lazily, yet excitedly, waited for her sun to say, "Good Morning, sunshine." She used to do this every day before she got sick.

The others, more or less, did the same and in the same fashion. Even Ben was itching to go and reflected back on his days in the Corps and 'Company' on the day of a major ops or deployment. Nothing changed. This was the day, and he was on edge. Heralding his flock to Asheville was his mission. He hoped it would be no April fools mine field.

It was the same for the staff at Greentree. Bobby, from the newspaper arranged for a photographer and decided that a follow-up story was in order which would feature the writers getting on the bus and departing for the adventure. His editor liked the idea and laid a youngster on the job. When the photo guy arrived at Greentree, he couldn't figure out what all the hoopla was all about, but everyone seemed to be bustling with great excitement.

The two vans with the furniture and the rest of the belongings were at the facility by 5:30 in the morning. The drivers waited for the bus to arrive. All the suitcases and boxes were placed and secured into the bus without trouble. Ben paid the van drivers with a generous tip for their care with the goods. He waited for the writers to arrive.

He knew that he had somehow begun to think of the senior writers as his children, well not exactly his children, but something akin to that. "Juan, do you think I'm being too possessive or overprotective. I don't want to smother them."

Juan understood this walrus of a man and knew him better than anyone, even himself. Juan knew that Benjamin Zachariah Zangwell was a man who felt very deeply about responsibility and loyalty. These people were under his care now, and he would protect them against the world. If necessary, "Z" would die for them. This was the man, the spirit, the gestalt of a complicated and tortured man who had lost the only woman he loved in Hong Kong and had buried her on the hillside overlooking the panorama of the city of Asheville just behind the big house.

This was a man whose years of retirement had been spent in giving of himself and his money without hesitation to quiet his guilt for deeds done in the name of his beloved country. While so many of his comrades spent their lives in veterans' hospitals or on the streets and bars, he spent his in trying to right the wrongs he felt he'd contributed to for the security of a nation. Now, finally, he could rest and really think of relaxing and enjoying his last moments on earth. Juan believed in a heaven and knew that his jefe would be going there. He never told that to Ben because he knew that Ben had no god or gods to bow down to and worship. That was their one big difference.

The vans carrying the group arrived at the same time. David, Gerald and Britt were the first to come down the ramp. The photographer shot pictures of them and wondered what the big deal was. He'd talk to the reporter later to understand why this was so important and so early on a Monday morning. Pauline, Lee and Sadie came next. Sadie was proud of herself because she wore her new prosthesis and proudly descended the ramp without the help of the driver. She was still in pain, but today she would smile and not let anyone know it. Her face reflected her bravery.

Jane, the early morning staff, and a few ambulatory patients who were friends of the writers were on hand, and hugs and kisses were shared. Even Ben hugged them and was happy to see the staff show up for the departure.

Pictures of the writers getting on the chartered bus were taken and at 7:20 the bus began its 800 mile journey to the mountains of Western North Carolina. There was not a dry eye except for the young photographer's. Jane's eyes misted and she thought back to the beginning of it all. Who would have ever dreamed that this would be the culmination of the therapy group?

"I feel like I'm off to camp," laughed David.

"Me, too," chimed in Britt, "But I've never been to camp. This must be what it feels like."

"One hundred bottles of beer on the wall, one hundred bottles of beer. If one of them should happen to fall, ninety-nine bottles of beer on the wall."

"Sadie dear, where did you learn that song," cried Pauline, laughing almost hysterically.

"I don't know. It just came out of my mouth. I must have learned it as a little girl or maybe my children taught it to me."

Everyone laughed. Juan began to sing a song in Spanish. It was lyrical and everyone knew that he, too, was caught up in the moment of excitement of taking a long trip as though he were a little boy.

For about the first half hour everyone talked at once without really listening to each other. Later David and Britt pressed their noses against the window as they had when traveling on the Greyhounds and moments of nostalgia crossed their minds.

For David it was the first time that he ran away as a youth of fifteen and let a young woman of nineteen from Oklahoma nestle on his shoulder while she allowed his hands to caress her breasts through her sweater. The poor girl was returning from New York where she tried to break into show biz only to find that people were only too eager to lie to her to get her into their bed. No one had told her of the nights that she would spend cold, hungry, and disheartened in the Big Apple. Pregnant, depressed, and disillusioned, she was returning to face her parents who were waiting in anticipation for their only daughter. She didn't tell them about the pregnancy fearing that they wouldn't be able to cope with it. The rest of the sad tale was what would she tell her high school boy friend? David never knew her name and they parted company in Chicago in the cavernous station below the Loop on Randolph Street.

Britt also was young the first time on the dog bus. It was during the Viet Nam War and he was a young marine covered with ribbons, scars, and horrors deep within him. His name was Jimmy Tennet, and he was returning to the front after convalescent leave. She held him tenderly while he cried and tried to tell her the horrid tale of the village that they destroyed and the death of families caught in the tragedy of civil war. They made love on the back seat of the bus under a blanket and for Britt it was the first time that she didn't submit to gain some advantage. She willingly gave of herself in order that someone else might gain some peace of mind and sense of wholeness. It made her feel worthy, too. She remembered going to the Viet Nam Memorial Wall in Washington D.C. with her only son, and finding James Tennet, Corporal, the young marine's name there on the wall. Even now tears flowed silently.

The others sank into light naps while Ben and Juan talked quietly. "Thanks for bringing me along, Jefe. Maria tells me that spring is beginning in the mountains. It must be magnifico."

"I hope so. I want them to have good memories of their first days in the house. Funny, who would have thought that the old house would be used this way? I mean I really thought that I'd make it into a school for shit-kickers who hated the establishment like me or a folk school like Horton did in Tennessee. Dreams work out in strange ways. Right?"

"Si, maybe this is better. No telling what will come out of these guys and maybe some others who we don't even know yet. I might decide to do some writing myself about Mexico, my childhood, you know."

"Sorry, you're too young to join this group, but maybe in twenty or thirty years." They both laughed and fell silent, each thinking. The driver, a middle aged Haitian turned to Ben and announced that they would be in Ft. Pierce soon. People were beginning to stir and Ben turned to the group.

"How about a rest stop here? Pierre can use a break and I could use some coffee. How about you?"

All seemed contented to stop and made ready to get off the bus at Fort Pierce. Sadie strapped on her prosthesis which she had removed. The bus pulled into a parking lot and the crew got off. There were people everywhere on their way north and south. Snowbirds were going home. At least three or four Greyhounds were parked up on the hill and hundreds of eighteen wheeler trucks plastered the parking lots and truck stops. It seemed that everyone turned and looked at the writers as they sauntered into the fast food restaurant. It wasn't really true that they were the center of attention, but they were beginning to see themselves as special. Ben noticed that and wondered whether this would be a problem later.

The men headed for the bath room and women got in a long line for the ladies' room. The women didn't rejoin the group for at least twenty minutes. Coffee, egg McMuffins, and juice were the order of the day. Pierre, the driver, smoked and sat off in the smoking section and pondered the ways of the crazy Americans, and wondered at the exuberance and bravery of these old people leaving the warm weather and normalcy of the tropics for parts unknown. He, too, like so many of his countrymen wondered at the independence and vitality of these people. In Haiti, if a person lived as long as these, they weren't going anywhere.

The trip from Fort Pierce to Jacksonville took another four to five hours. Twice the bus stopped at rest stops even though there was a bathroom on the bus. Sadie and Lee felt that they needed Pauline to give them a hand. David needed help to relieve himself. Ben thought he could help on the trip, but he needed Juan to give him a hand. A nursing assistant was already hired and waiting in Asheville to take over from George.

The passengers stopped for lunch in Jacksonville at a service plaza on Interstate 95. David required a wheelchair which Pierre retrieved from the bottom of the vehicle. Sadie could have asked for one, but instead used her walker as did Lee. In all the excitement Britt felt the need to wear her nasal piece attached to a small canister of oxygen and set at two liters. Her Chronic Obstructive Lung Disease, which the professionals referred to as COPD, was aggravated by the stress of the move and smog created by the traffic.

Ben, Juan, and Pierre took orders for those who couldn't stand in the long lines while they held the two tables side by side. Gerald and Pauline decided to get their own food and waited patiently while thirty or forty people ordered in front of them.

Lunch went well and lasted a bit longer than Ben had planned. Days before he had arranged for a motel just south of the intersection of I-95 and I-26. There was no concern for the rooms being held for them, but the dining room attached to the motel closed at 8:00 pm. He was just a little fearful that they might be moving too slowly with the stops they made to arrive in time to settle in and get to the restaurant for dinner. He had a back-up plan of course. He always did. It would be Chinese take-out that he and Juan would get.

The trip through the southeast corner of Georgia, past Brunswick and Savannah, took a little more than two hours without anyone calling for a rest stop. By the time they arrived in St. George, South Carolina, and the Restful Haven Motel, an AAA recommended tourist convenience, everyone was exhausted from the trip. Pierre roomed alone and was too tired to join the group for dinner. He had some chicken jerky that he bought in Ft. Lauderdale the day before. He ate the chicken, showered, and fell into a deep sleep.

The others had about fifteen minutes to freshen up and meet in the restaurant. David, in his wheelchair, was pushed by Gerald who slowly and somewhat laboriously took his responsibility very seriously. Britt and Sadie were both fatigued, but buoyant. Juan and Ben joined the group as did Pauline and Lee ready for dinner, a little talk, and a night of rest.

Ben wondered whether he was putting the writers through too much stress and whether he should have flown them to Asheville instead. He fell asleep and dreamed about Viet Nam and the jungle. Sending his men into the tunnels to root out "Charlie" was a recurrent and disturbing part of his dreams. He woke in a sweat and relieved himself. Snoring in the other bed was Juan oblivious to his boss's worries.

At six the phones in each of the rooms rang and it was time to rise and shine for the final day of travel. It was probably hardest for Gerald who had to help his friend, David, out of bed and into his clothes. He did his best, but finally had to ring for Juan to come and help David out of bed and into his chair. His catheter bag was emptied and medications given before 6:45. Sleepy, but excited, the crew assembled for their breakfast and departure. Suitcases were loaded and final last minute checks of the rooms were made. Pierre looked at the mileage and realized that he had about another five hours to go until their arrival. He was excited about seeing the beauty and splendor that everyone talked about.

As the bus plodded its way along I-26 west and rose into the mountains, the excitement which the passengers had the day before paled in contrast to this day's. In the distance could be seen the beginning of the Appalachian Mountains and the birth of spring. The colors were just beginning to change and all pressed their noses against the cold glass panes. In actuality, they could only see the hills begin to usher in the mountains, but it would be awhile before they could really see peaks.

Each of the riders, including Ben, marveled at the beauty of the trees and especially Gerald and Britt sat transfixed and basked in the beauty that Nature bestowed upon her elderly children. Gerald's poetry and Britt's photography often captured the beauty of nature, but neither of them had done any of their work here in the Appalachians.

Pierre sensed a need to find a rest stop for the writers. The bathroom on the bus was too small to accommodate David's or Sadie's wheelchairs and too petite for Ben. A sign appeared for a rest stop two miles up the road and soon they were there. David's wheelchair was pulled off the bus and he was pushed by his friend, Gerald. The Americans with Disabilities Act and the good will of the State of South Carolina saw to it that at least one commode area was tailored for the disabled. Not only could the wheelchair fit into it, but there was a sink and mirror installed in the area for taking care of toiletries and washing up. The same was true in the ladies' room for Sadie who also used a wheelchair.

A half hour later and with resolve to make it to lunch in Columbia, the state capital and the home of Ft. Jackson Army Base where Ben had completed his basic training, the group was off. The highway was noticeably more crowded as if the whole world were going to Asheville. Behind them the sun was warm and rising quickly in the east, assuring the writers that their moving day was to be beautiful and full of the serenity that spring brings with it. The new leaves on the trees seemed to beckon to them to come and be a part of their newness and rebirth.

They could see little children playing in fields by the highway, and there was a dog or two walking along the road seeming oblivious to all the traffic.

"Do you think we'll be able to get a dog or two for the house," asked David of no one particular.

"You say something, David?" It was Juan who was sitting in the seat just behind David.

"I was just thinking about my dog, Maxwell, who was a lab mix. That's all. I saw a dog along the highway and wondered whether we'll want to have some pets in the house."

"Me, too. I always had dogs in Mexico. More like coyote, I think. They were wild, not like the pets we have in this country. No one could afford a pet back there. Seems like there were hundreds of them. Everyone would make fun of us Mexicans and say that we ate our dogs. No way, Mano. I never ate a dog, not even in Nam. But I heard a story that the Thais have a dog-eating festival once a year in some villages. Not a safe place for a pet, even a coyote." Juan laughed and David joined in. He knew that in fact some Vietnamese ate dog in an offshoot Buddhist tradition once a month to bring people luck. David never knowingly joined in.

Around two in the afternoon, Pierre grabbed his microphone on his console and announced that Asheville was about twenty miles further. Rock formations and peaks seemed to be everywhere. This announcement brought a surge of talking over each other and craning necks to be the first to see the city. They didn't realize that the only way that they would see beautiful downtown Asheville would be if they would take I-240 into town. That wasn't on the agenda for this afternoon.

The bus pulled into the familiar motel driveway with the multicolored sign 'Namaste' to greet them. Maria and the couple whom they met the first time were there. "Namaste, Namaste, welcome, my friends, to the city of the Homeward Angels." Their rich brown faces beamed. Maria was in tears and silently offered a prayer of thanks to her patron saint.

CHAPTER EIGHT

Ben knew that the group, and for that matter, he also needed to rest, and decided that on Wednesday and Thursday nothing was as important as building strength for the move to the house. The weather was cooperative with temperatures in the seventies and low eighties. Across the street was a fair diner with senior citizen dinners if people wished to eat there.

Pierre was the only one who had duties, and on Wednesday, Juan, Maria, and he took the bus to the commune to empty its contents. She knew that the writers were going to double up, but she didn't know which room would go to whom. She had the suitcases and book boxes taken to the second floor using the elevator for which they were thankful. Clothing, book boxes, and all the personal items would be sorted out on the weekend.

David and Gerald decided to find some place where they could talk privately about their experiences so far. They found a small park with a bench or two and some playground equipment. Kids were probably in school and no mothers with babies or small fry were out.

"Well, now it's put up or shut up."

"What do you mean, David?"

"I mean that we will have to earn our keep at the commune and get busy writing. I hope that I don't run into writer's block or something else which will keep me from creating something worthwhile."

Gerald smiled and patted his friend on the shoulder as he continued, "I really do not think that you, of all people, have to worry. Do you remember all the things you talked about in our therapy sessions at Greentree, but you never wrote about? Let's see, there was your work as a social worker, some of your trials and tribulations with the Children and Family Services in three states, your travels throughout Asia, your time in Montana with that homeless shelter, and so many other experiences."

"I know, but I worry that nothing that I have to say will be of any commercial value to Ben. I mean, look at all the money and time he is giving us and what if nothing any of us write about can find an audience that has any interest. Let's face it, Gerald, we're just old folks with a lucky break."

"Not really, my dear friend. You sell yourself short. It really does not matter whether our creations are marketable or not. Certainly, I have a moral obligation to do the best that I can, for myself primarily and to Ben secondarily. I am absolutely certain that he would agree."

"Perhaps, but I fear that something may get in the way." David couldn't shake the premonition as he thought about his new friends and the obstacles that they faced. "And what about you, what do you plan to write about first?"

"Well, do you remember that I, like you, talked about spending time in a school for severely emotionally disturbed children when I taught? I have been thinking that I may wish to explore some of those years at greater length and in much greater depth. There were so many experiences there that I can write about and I think would be of interest to some people, perhaps special education teachers if no one else.

"Oh yes, and the work that Claire and I did on behalf of other teachers as members of the, for lack of a better word, union." Gerald grimaced and shook his head as he spoke about the Association.

"I have these books by Upton Sinclair which exposed the National Education Association as a front for book sellers. I think that book sellers are no longer involved with the NEA, but I would be most surprised to find out that the Association did all it could for the concerns that unions are tasked with, like pay, hours, and working conditions. I would also say that is particularly true in those 'right to work' states in the South. They still admit administrators into their ranks. It is a total abomination in my opinion."

"Gerald, you still have the fiery rhetoric of the free speech movement of the early 1900's". David beamed. "Did I ever tell you that I used to volunteer for the Iditarod race in Alaska a few years ago? I might write about it."

"No, David. This is something new from you. I knew that you and Britt spent time there independent of one another, but I do not believe that you ever mentioned the Iditarod to anyone."

"Well, back in the last century and even early part of this one, I went up to work for the race as one of a thousand or more other volunteers. I might write a short story about the race or some of the mushers." David smiled just thinking about the times in Anchorage in the middle of March. A chill enveloped his body and he shivered. Even now it was hard to forget the bitter cold and ice. "I wonder whether we'll get much snow up here in winter."

"I missed snow and cold in Florida, really. I love being somewhere with four distinct seasons. Florida was so, how should I say it, one dimensional. Of course, we did have hurricanes, didn't we? Were you ever exposed to one there?"

"Actually, no- not really, Gerald. I missed Andrew back in 1992 by one day. I flew to Chicago to attend my friend's wife's funeral and returned to horrendous devastation. It was like a war zone after bombing."

The two friends had been talking for about two hours and David was beginning to feel the need for a nap. So Gerald rose slowly and pushed David in his wheelchair back to Namaste.

While David and Gerald were gone, Pauline, Sadie, Lee and Britt also were engaged in their own conversation. Interestingly, they also talked about the future. But the women were not as concerned about their writing as where they would put their things and how they might chose to decorate their rooms. "We'll probably want to frequent yard sales, thrift stores and Goodwill to find what we need."

Pauline smiled. It would be a first for her to make pilgrimages to second hand stores. "Sadie, I've never been in a Goodwill store before. My husband wouldn't hear of it. He was something of a snob about such things and I went along with it."

"No me! I could live in thrift stores and go to a hundred yard sales without a blink of the eye."

"Really Sadie, you're kidding. I hate to shop, always have and usually buy the first thing I see," lamented Britt who often had little money to spend.

"Before the Parkinson's disease and cancer I used to own a shop in Washington in a little town not far from Yakima. I designed mood dresses and even had a patent on a baby carrier which sold well. I tried to adopt some of the designs which the Yakima Indians wore. They were so colorful and rich in design.

"I think that I want to write more about the Native Americans that I met in the west. My heart went out to them. They would bring beautiful bead work and quilting and sell them to me for next to nothing to get alcohol for their men." Lee grimaced.

"I met a lot of women in Alaska who were the same way or needed money for their own drinking or drugs," said Britt. "I would give them some money if they'd let me take pictures of them and their beautiful children. I know that was wrong because it meant that they would drink it away or give it away. Too many of them had it stolen by the men they lived with. Damn shame really."

Sadie and Pauline listened intently. They had never experienced anything like what Lee and Britt were talking about.

"The only alcohol I ever drank was some Shabbat wine or some on Passover when we drank a little wine at the Seder," Sadie offered.

"What's a Seder?" Britt asked inquisitively.

Sadie beamed, "In Judaism, the women make a wonderful Jewish dinner which everyone comes to in their finest clothes. Morris, my dear husband, may he rest in peace, used to sit at the head of the table and everyone would read the Haggada. That's the story of the exodus from Egypt. You remember Moses, right? He led the children of Israel out of the land of the Pharaohs into the Promise land."

"I never heard that story. The only one I remember is that the first drunk was Noah and he had sex with his daughters. That's in the Bible. They got him drunk and then slept with him, but I think they called it knowing them. I don't think I'd want to know my father in that way," said Lee.

Sadie looked perturbed. "I think that you mean Lot, not Noah. Lot slept with his daughters."

"Lot, Noah, what does it matter? We weren't there," said Britt.

All of the women thought about that image and shuddered.

"So if you had such a strong Jewish upbringing, why are you so upset about your son and daughter being so committed as Jews, Sadie?" asked Britt.

"Because they're really Christians, not Jews. They believe in Jesus as the savior and they speak in tongues. Morris, may he rest in peace, was so crushed by his son and daughter, not to mention the grandchildren being raised that way. It killed him."

"Well, dear. You are going to do more research on these, what did you call them, Messianic Jews, and find a way to write about it. I will help you all that I can. Maybe doing research will be the way that I will be useful to the commune," said Pauline.

Sadie wiped away her tears, blew her nose and smiled at Pauline with gratitude.

The women heard the men returning from their walk and agreed to rest a little before dinner. Pauline and Lee returned to their room while Sadie and Britt lay down to rest and maybe catch a nap.

Ben thought that a quick trip to the house on Thursday might be a good idea. The actual move into the commune would begin on Saturday morning and perhaps the first night spent at the commune would be Sunday night. The group seemed to have recovered from the long bus ride and was so excited that it was put to a vote.

"Are you kidding? I'm ready to move there now, this minute. I mean I love the folks here at the motel, but I'm just itching to get started," said David.

"I'm also ready to begin my new life as quickly as is possible. We have so much to do." Everyone chimed in to piggyback on what Gerald was saying.

"OK, it seems that everyone is ready to move. That's what I call consensus. Let's take a ride then and make notes about what we still need and maybe we can make a stop at the Moose Café for lunch."

Sadie's face lit up like the night sky full of stars. "I loved it there. Real southern food and so much of it. What a beautiful landscape with such beautiful rolling hills and that gorgeous hotel in the distance."

"I loved their fried chicken and fried green tomatoes," Britt replied.

"The meatloaf was great, Britt. Maybe I'll try the chicken or chicken fried steak if they have it for lunch," said David. Everyone but Gerald salivated just thinking of the cuisine. Poor Gerald still had to watch his diet lest his ulcers return and cause him trouble.

A white van which could seat a small army arrived with *Kelly House Senior Commune* stenciled on both sides of the vehicle. It was big enough for two wheelchairs, had comfortable chairs and could seat three people comfortably in the front. Juan was driving and had just picked the van up from the company which sold it to Ben. The van would have cost a small fortune, but the manager gave Maria a huge discount when she explained what was needed and why. His own mother was wheelchair bound and needed constant care from a certified nursing assistant. It was a tax write-off, but that alone wasn't the reason that he was so accommodating.

Ben hadn't seen the van before and let out a low whistle of approval. The seats were even big enough to allow him to sit without discomfort. The back had a lift to raise wheelchairs in, and there was ample room for seven or eight passengers. He realized that he'd have to hire a full time driver and valet for the commune. "Just another small expense. It's worth it so that Juan and Maria won't have to feel obligated to be here all the time," Ben said to himself.

This was the first day that everyone would drive into the city. Again, weather cooperated with a warm sun, giving the mountains surrounding Asheville a beautiful light green tinge. Traffic had smoothed down from the onslaught of rush hour and the early morning congestion around I-26 and I-240.

The van moved easily through the street, passing the Western Carolina Rescue Mission. Homeless men and women lined the streets, many with dazed looks, and then passed the park where the writers had seen homeless folk sitting on park benches and a few kids with dogs sitting on the knoll strumming their guitars. Today, some two months later, there were more people outside. David noticed a group of men standing at stone inlaid chess boards studying their moves with great attention. He decided that he would go there and challenge some of the players, but he figured them for hustlers out to make a few bucks.

Ahead were Pack Square and the Vance Monument obelisk where marches and vigils were held when people wanted to express themselves against or for any burning issues. Once in a while, Ben joined Veterans for Peace who rallied against the politicians responsible for the wars in Iraq and Afghanistan. When he purchased the old house he often saw another group, Women in Black, on Friday nights, silently bearing witness to lost loved ones and the horrors of war. They were not a friendly bunch and would ignore him and any other males who might wish to engage them in some conversation. From his point of view, some of them were simply male-phobic who joined with their sisters in this effort. For some, he had no proof other than his gut reaction, and he was sure they were lesbian women who simply wanted no part of men, even if they were in political agreement.

The van continued past the court house and the municipal government buildings, through the tunnel, up the hill, past the small Greyhound Bus station and then turned right heading for the house and their new home. Family homes gave way to what used to be farmland and remained open fields of alfalfa and thick grasses. A horse or two munched on the luscious grasses. Perched on a gentle hill stood Kelly House.

They drove along the driveway until they could see the inviting front porch and there, hanging from the porch pillars, a big white banner with words painted in rainbow colors: **WELCOME HOME TO KELLY HOUSE!!**

Not a dry eye in the van, everyone lost for words, so happy and pleased was each of the occupants of the vehicle. Those sitting next to each other held hands, and even Ben was caught up in the emotion of the first moment that all eyes fell on their grand home. Their new beginning was finally their reality.

CHAPTER NINE

Standing on the veranda, the architect and Maria beamed proudly, inviting everyone to come in. Introductions were made and Maria had arranged to have coffee, cookies and cake available. It was a gala affair. In most circles wine and even harder liquor would have been served on such an auspicious occasion but it was not appropriate for this population. Nonetheless, Maria had thought of everything. She brought out three bottles of bubbly Champagne with such a small percentage of alcohol that she thought would not affect anyone. Blue glazed plastic champagne glasses were passed around and she poured each a glass of the fizzy liquid.

"I want to make a toast." All heads turned to Gerald. "To Ben, to Ted Kelly, to Jane Finestein, to Juan and Maria and to all of us, let us drink from these goblets in appreciation for everything you have done for us, and may our first day here be the beginning of the rest of our lives."

"Hear, hear." The entire entourage spoke as one.

"I would like to say a prayer in Hebrew. We say it when we drink wine. Champagne is near enough I think," offered Sadie.

"Sadie, I remember you used to say two prayers on Friday nights when we ate together," said Britt.

"Yes. When drinking wine we say: 'Baruk ata Adonoi, Eloheinu, melekh ha-olam bore pri ha gafen. Blessed are you, Lord our God, king of the Universe who creates the fruit of the vine.' This is a sacred time for all of us, and I just felt that we should bless God for bringing us here." Maria and Juan crossed themselves and their eyes watered as they nodded their heads in agreement.

David, who had more or less abandoned his Jewish religious beliefs, always recognized his roots, and found himself whispering the Shema, the prayer recognizing the monotheism of the Jewish people. David toyed with secularism, Unitarianism, and had an abiding interest in figuring out what, if anything, he really believed.

For Ben, all of this was touching, and he realized that Sadie and the Morales needed this religious stuff, but he had little toleration for it. Were it not that he loved Juan and Maria and was feeling emotionally bonded with Sadie, he might have scoffed at their religious sentiments. He hid his skepticism. He would have rather just drank the Champagne or something a good deal stronger and gotten on with life.

"So, where do we start?" Britt was becoming impatient with all the pomp and ceremony. "Let's see our rooms first." She looked to Sadie for confirmation.

"I want to see the kitchen, Maria. Then, I want to see our room," said Sadie while the others began to look around the living room and peer into the dining area.

Ben, desiring some order, suggested that the group break into pairs with people who would room together going to the bedrooms together to figure out what they would need. Maria grabbed a clipboard and agreed to show the writers around upstairs. Juan and Ben remained downstairs.

Sadie smiled benignly and figured that the kitchen was more important than rushing to see the bedroom. Britt was slightly annoyed, but wheeled Sadie into the kitchen anyway. For a moment Britt remembered how she might have handled the situation in the past and was happy with her acquiescing.

Sadie couldn't contain herself when she saw all the new, shiny, stainless steel appliances and storage area. There were more shelves than she'd ever seen in her own home, a dishwasher, garbage disposal, and electric stove. She made little gleeful noises which were not missed by Maria and Britt. Following them were Lee and Pauline who also were impressed by all the modern and beautiful appliances. They, too, although not like Sadie, saw themselves doing a lot of the cooking and spending time in this room. Maria asked whether there were any suggestions for improvements as she showed them the utensils and plates, glassware and other dishes which she had purchased for the group. No one could think of anything to add to the kitchen. Ben stood in the doorway out of sight and was pleased by the reception, so far.

David and Gerald roamed around upstairs. They took the elevator to the second floor and then peered into each room. They chose one that had a skylight and a huge walk-in closet. They asked Juan to help them measure the dimensions of the room so that they could determine what size beds and chests would be appropriate. There was enough room for night stands for each and a desk for writing if they wanted to stay in their room for some work.

Next, they went to the bathroom on the floor and David was pleased to see hand rails, plenty of space for his wheelchair and towel racks for each member. It was a huge room and he hoped that some day he could be out of his wheelchair and actually walk into the room – with help, of course.

Gerald asked Juan about hanging his paintings, book shelves and a place for a comfortable chair. "I think there is enough room for it all, but perhaps you can wait until you all meet together to discuss all these issues." Gerald smiled, and continued to look at the closet.

After they satisfied their curiosity and peered into every room and closet on the floor, they descended in the elevator and Juan made sure that they knew how to run it, or in emergency, to call for help.

Maria decided to go upstairs with the ladies, and she took Lee and Pauline first. The elevator was not big enough for all participants to ride in it at once, particularly if one person was in a wheelchair. She showed them how to work the lift and handle any emergency should they have one.

Next to go up were Britt and Sadie and they joined the other women. The men hoped that the women would not be offended that they had picked out their room already. As it turned out Britt and Sadie liked a room at the end of the hall which had windows with a view of mountains and apple orchards. It had a walk-in closet, enough space for beds, vanities, night stands and maybe a desk in the middle of the room.

That left Lee and Pauline with little choice but to pick the last room, except for a small room which Ben would have for himself should he be at the commune. Lee especially liked the fact that the room was the closest to the bathroom which she appreciated. Had Gerald and David thought about their bladder issues, they might have picked that room, but they didn't, so Lee and Pauline claimed it. It had a walk-in closet and ample space for Pauline's bedroom set which Ben graciously accepted to have moved up from Florida. They looked at the bathroom, liked the tub which they preferred to the shower stall which the men seemed to like better than a tub. The women were quite satisfied with their new quarters and went downstairs for a discussion session.

Maria had already purchased a dining table which could seat all the commune members and had room for as many as five or six more people if needed. The dining room would serve as the meeting room for administering the needs of the commune.

Ben was the first to speak, "Well, are there any questions before we begin our first meeting here in our new commune?"

"Yes, I have a question." All eyes turned to Pauline. "How did you do all this? This must have cost a fortune, Ben. I feel guilty accepting everything you've done without paying you something." Everyone nodded their agreement.

"Well, look, if we make any money on the work you produce, that will be enough for me. Don't forget I owned this house long before I met any of you, so the only costs were in getting it ready for you guys. Don't worry, I won't go hungry." Everyone laughed, including Ben.

"So, I take it you are satisfied with the rooms you've chosen."

"Well, Ben, probably Gerald and I ought to have chosen the bedroom closest to the bathroom, but I think we'll be OK with the one we have." David looked to Gerald for confirmation. Gerald shook his head in agreement.

"What about getting furniture and the like?" asked Britt.

"Good question, that's next. Maria, Juan and I thought we can start by going to some furniture stores, mattress outlets and for those who want Goodwill, Salvation Army stores, you know,whatever. I've made lists of what we need to get started so that we can move in on Saturday," said Ben

Maria chimed in, "Hopefully, we can finish our shopping tomorrow, and if things can't be delivered right away, we can rent a van and drivers to pick the stuff up, deliver it and set things up. We'll have to buy bed linens, I guess. The more I think of it, maybe Saturday is unrealistic for the move. Maybe we should wait until Monday."

"Maria, you have a point. I don't want to wear anyone out or push too hard to get out of the motel too soon," said Ben.

"Any thoughts about the move and buying what we need?" The group had none.

"OK. Anyone need to use the john before we go?" Pauline wasn't sure what Ben meant by 'john' and turned to Lee with a quizzical look. Lee laughed, "It's a guy word for bathroom. In the military they call it latrine, I think in Australia, it's a loo."

"Oh, my do I have a lot to learn."

When the members and staff were ready to leave, the writers were reluctant to leave their new home, but they were excited about shopping and going to the Moose Café for lunch.

Lunch was wonderful as it was the first time they'd been there. The waitress was the same woman who'd waited on them on their first foray. She couldn't forget this bunch and was happy to see them. Ben found her attractive and somewhat seductive, or so he hoped. She told him she'd been working at the café for years and had grand kids. He was surprised and told her he thought she might be in her thirties. She was delighted by the banter and gave him a bigger piece of rhubarb pie and ice cream.

Britt was dying to go to Goodwill on Patton Avenue. Ben told her that she didn't have to worry about costs this year. He quipped that he'd make his money back somehow and she giggled with delight while batting her eyelashes at him. The others roared with laughter at the two of them flirting.

They couldn't find any mattresses, but vanities and other needed items were found, and Maria arranged to pick them up the next day. When it was all said and done, most of the needed items were found. Next they went to Mattress Heaven on Biltmore Avenue and finished their work by purchasing enough twin sized beds for all who needed them. Bed linens were purchased at Sears in Asheville Mall.

"I'm so tired out and my oxygen is getting low," said Britt.

"Me too, I think that I need a long nap." Everyone wagged their heads in agreement with Gerald. He pushed David's wheelchair the entire day and wouldn't allow Juan or anyone else to help him. But, it took a toll. His hip wasn't completely healed yet.

Back at Namaste Motel everyone dispersed and went to their rooms for their well-deserved rest. Ben was satisfied with the day's activities and appreciative of the fact that the writers wanted to save him money. "If they only knew how much I could have spent without feeling it in the slightest. I bet they still would have wanted to go to Goodwill." He was talking to himself. It only made him feel more love and devotion to them.

On Friday, Juan and Maria went to Goodwill, picked up the items saved for the writers and Maria bought some more items for the kitchen and bookshelves for the living room and Ben's smaller bedroom.

The beds were due for delivery in the afternoon and the delivery men would set up them up so they would be ready for the bedding. So far, everything was going like clockwork. But something bothered Maria, and she wanted to discuss it with Ben and Juan. "I think that after yesterday and their getting so tired out, it's going to be a long time before they can stand on their own. You know what I mean, Juan?"

"Si, they were pretty wiped out. Gerald did too much pushing David around and he was a hurting puppy. Britt's tank was almost empty, and yet she kept going, huffing and puffing, but she wouldn't give in. Sadie's new leg bothered her and she wouldn't let us get out the wheelchair. I don't know."

"Thank God for Pauline. She babies Lee like her own daughter, even though Lee is older than Pauline." Maria shook her head in wonderment.

"Do you think that Ben may have to hire a housekeeper and cook? It would drive Sadie nuts not having charge of the kitchen, but I'm not so sure she can handle all that work. What do you think, sweetheart?"

"Maybe, that's the first hurdle the group we'll have to discuss, Juan. I mean I would feel horrible if we were to leave, and Ben might be called out for something and just one nursing assistant be there for David. I doubt the others could manage on their own- at least not for a while."

The couple worried about the problem while they waited at Kelly House for the guys from the mattress company to arrive. When they pulled up in their truck, worries were forgotten and work began. Maria showed the guys where each bed would go, and then Maria and Juan made beds, placed furniture in the places they would have wanted it to go if they were moving in. The writers could rearrange everything later if they wanted to do so.

On Friday night it was decided that the move would be the next day. "Why don't we take the van and go down to the park for the drumming and dancing circle?"

"Great idea, Britt. It's a pretty night and I bet there'll be a huge crowd there," said David. In his youth he used to own three or four drums and try to drum during drum circles in Ottawa, Canada. Well, actually that was the first drum circle he ever saw, and he determined to buy his own drum. Sometimes, his memory failed him. Later, while watching the drummers in the park, he remembered that he didn't really drum in Canada. The first time was in Alaska in Anchorage at the Viet Nam Memorial park on 6th Street in the 1980's.

They piled into the van and drove to Doc Chey's Noodle House on Biltmore. Lines were short, the wait about ten or twenty minutes. The writers were getting used to people trying to avoid staring at them, but the stares were generally accompanied by smiles and gentle nods of the head as a mode of communicating a greeting.

The food was scrumptious and plentiful. The second adjective was more important than the first in Ben's mind. The tangy Thai cuisine, so rich in secret sauces made everyone's mouth water. Again, poor Gerald stuck to a bland diet. For Ben, Pad-Thai was a no-brainer choice. He was introduced to the noodle dish in Thailand during the war. Often he'd slip through the Ho Chi Minh Trail lines and into and out of Laos to the east of Thailand. The Mekong River was jealously guarded by the Thai Army, and Americans were always welcomed.

The others decided to order Chinese, Thai, Japanese, and assorted dishes and shared them at a large table set up for them. Britt taught Sadie how to use chopsticks. Everyone seemed to talk at once, and joy floated through the air.

"Do you want to walk to the park?"

"Can you make it, Gerald? It's about three or four blocks but they're up a slight hill. Asheville streets are kind of like the mountains, hermano." Juan had never called any of the men "brother" before. It was an honor bestowed upon people he felt close to.

"I can try. We'll just have to go slowly and methodically."

They walked to College and turned left. They heard the drums before they saw the drummers. It was still light outside, but in the east darkness was descending upon the city. David was the first to spot the three chess boards made of black and white marble squares. One board was taken by a young white boy, his father watching from the sideline, the opponent a black man who kept licking his lips and humming nonsensical notes. The boy smiled and peered at his dad frequently. David thought of the movie, *Looking for Bobby Fisher,* and young Joel Benjamin, chess prodigy.

About fifty or more drummers were sitting on the cold stone steps while bongos, Djembes, Ibos, Brazilian pandeiros, talking drums of all sizes and shapes were being beaten by young men with dreadlocks standing at the bottom and leading the rhythms of the chant. There was an excitement born by the cacophony of the drums, the cadence of the sounds. On the steps were men and women, some in their fifties and sixties, sitting next to young hippies, and all were pounding and trying to keep up. The smell of marijuana permeated the park, but police personnel, clearly uncomfortable, kept their vigil without stepping in.

Standing on the top of the amphitheater were tourists looking down upon the scene in wonderment. At the bottom were young girls with babies in their arms, older men and women, dancing, swirling, and gyrating, some in rhythm with the drums, others not. Homeless individuals mingled among the tourists being careful not to let the police see them ask for money. Young children ran around and rolled down the hills under the watchful eyes of their parents. Dogs on leashes tried to get at each other to play, but were held tightly. Here and there someone with a dog being held by a makeshift leash of rope sat with glazed eyes looking at no one in particular. Everywhere were happy, free souls living life to its fullest- for the evening.

"Oh my god, oh my god, it's like San Francisco in the sixties," yelled Britt over the din. "I love it."

"It takes me back to Oak Park, Illinois and the kids in the park. People were so free." David, too, was lost in the past. "You know, I used to teach there."

"Let's see if we can't find a place where we won't be trampled," said Ben. He looked for a place where his brood wouldn't be in harm's way. Both Sadie and David were in their wheelchairs and could sit comfortably on the top landing. With Ben standing next to them, no one approached for money. Britt, Lee, and Pauline opted to sit down on the steps. A young man offered Pauline an African Djembe drum. She shook her head and thanked him over the noise, but he insisted and she finally overcame her shyness and took the drum.

Pauline had never held a drum, much less played one. She gingerly hit the tight skin of the instrument. She seemed to be surprised when she heard the noise emanating from it. She listened to the cadence and rhythm of the drummers and tried to copy it. Slowly, she began to pick up a beat and worked out a cadence of her own which she thought matched what she was hearing. Pauline liked it.

"I feel like dancing with those youngsters below." Britt was having a little trouble with her breathing, but had her oxygen on and felt the rhythm run through her body. She got up, went to Ben and grabbed his hand. "Come on big man, let's go down there and show those kids a thing or two."

"Are you kidding me? I can't do that. Take Juan and Maria down there if you want to shake a leg."

"No, I want you!" She was laughing and wouldn't stop pestering him.

Ben, never to say "Never" to a good looking woman, gave Juan a look to watch the group and taking Britt's hand, walked down the steps, past the drummers on the stairs, the young boys with the bongos and onto the floor of the amphitheater. He caught the swaying of the dancers, the freedom of it all and began to sway and weave with Britt. She had her little canister of oxygen in a pouch on her side, and began to do a belly dance imitation, moving her eighty something hips and head along with everyone else. Within a minute or two they were winded but totally engrossed in the drumming and forgot everyone else around them. Neither felt self-conscious, nor did they realize that all the dancers had stopped and were making a circle around them and clapping wildly. The leading drummers sensed that something was going on with the dancers. They moved to see what was up. A huge man, hair flying in a cool breeze, walrus gigantic head with a belly reminiscent of Old Saint Nick, was dancing with a little white haired old lady, and they both were in a world reserved for youth. The drummers instinctively slowed the frenzy of their rhythm and watched in amazement for a good two or three minutes.

Ben began to feel faint, held up a shaky hand and motioned Britt to stop gyrating. He whispered in her ear, "Let's go back to the group. I think these kids need their dance floor back."

Britt felt something for the man, not Ben the philanthropist, but this man and something stirred in her loins. She turned and walked toward the group to the cheers and applause of drummers and tourists alike. What was she experiencing? "Women my age don't have these thoughts," she muttered to herself, but tell that to her body.

It was dark and the group grew tired. "I'll go get the van from the parking lot and bring it here."

"Gracias, mi amigo. I'm bushed. I must be getting old," laughed Ben. Darkness had enveloped the park and the police began to disperse the drum circle gently.

In the van Ben spoke to Juan. "They had a great evening, we all did, but I think it's time we got this ball rolling. What do you think about moving to the house tomorrow after a slow morning and some group talk at the diner after breakfast?"

"They're ready for the house and the house is ready for them. At least they have beds now and with our help for a couple of days, they should be OK," Juan answered.

Ben thought a bit more and listened to the soft snoring in the back and said, "Maria told me that you both thought I should hire someone to be with them on a consistent basis. I agree with that. They're not ready to run things on their own yet, maybe never will be. I don't know. Let's put it to them tomorrow."

Juan agreed.

Everyone slept soundly and when they finally were ready to go to the diner it was 10:30. The waitress looked forward to the group's presence because it always meant a great tip. Waitresses throughout the country made such terrible wages and hoped for tips to make it all worthwhile.

The group made idle chatter while they ate and drank their coffee and tea. Ben asked for their attention and said, "Well, what do ya think. Are we ready to move to Kelly House?"

"It's really here. I mean, I guess I just thought I was on a vacation, you know the motel, the great dinners and lunches, all the shopping. I guess this is it." Britt didn't look at Ben for fear that she'd let on that she was also thinking of last night and her silly feelings. He blushed too, and Britt feared that he could read her thoughts.

"I, for one, am ready to embark on the next phase of our odyssey. My creative juices are craving to be expressed in rich and tantalizing prose." No one quite knew what Gerald was saying, but it sounded good. He drank his tea with a little smile on his face.

"Have we bought any food for the first evening meal?" Sadie smiled benignly.

Maria was the first to answer. "No, I didn't even think of that. I'll go to the store and stock the kitchen. Maybe we'll make our first meal Mexican, if that's OK with everybody."

"Only if I can help you shop, Maria," said Sadie.

Maria had anticipated that Sadie would want to go with her for grocery shopping.

Pauline spoke up, "If you wait for Lee and me to set up our room and our toiletries in the area provided for us, I'd like to go with you both. I want to know where the nearest grocery stores are located, anyway."

"I mean no offense, Maria, but I do not think that my intestinal fortitude will handle very hot sauces. Would you mind something on the milder side, please?"

"Of course, Gerald. No problem. I don't cook so much hot food anymore. Juan has trouble, too, if I really spice it up. You know what I mean. Toot,toot."

Juan gave her a dirty look and turned away sheepishly.

"Anyone have anything to say about moving today?"

"I'm ready as I'll ever be," said Britt, and the rest of the group agreed.

"It's done then. Today, what day is it? April 6th is the first day of the opening of Kelly House." Everyone clapped and got up to begin their new life.

PART II

COMMUNAL LIVING

CHAPTER TEN

The banner was still up, and welcomed the new occupants to the house. Gone was the sense of glee and frivolity of the previous evening at the drumming, a feeling that had been so prevalent among the writers. There was a strong sense of purpose and resolve to get on with the move and begin to write.

Not all the writers felt the same determination, but David, Gerald, Britt, and even Sadie were ready to begin to do the work they had talked about so many times at Greentree Rehabilitation and Nursing Home. Lee and Pauline were not as focused on their projects, but assumed that eventually something would fall into place and that they, too, would be caught up in the spirit of the purpose of the commune. However, Sadie's main focus was on the kitchen and nourishing the friends she had grown to love and cherish so much that she thought of them as her writers.

The entire weekend was spent in rearranging furniture, unpacking their suitcases and working together to make their living space attractive, convenient and to their taste. David and Gerald were gratified to have David's Lazy-boy chair in the bedroom where they could use it for reading, snoozing, listening to music or whatever. David brought several paintings of Alaskan scenery. One was a dark blue view of a cabin in the wilderness with the northern lights playing overhead. Another bigger work was a print by Jon Van Zyle, the Iditarod artist of a musher, his sled, and dogs on the trail covered with ice and snow. It spoke to David with great compassion and yearning.

Gerald had two paintings as well. He hoped that the group would vote to have them downstairs in the living room or common room where they could be seen by everyone. They were the pictures of a black father and his son and the other of black teens in Washington D.C. standing next to bullet hole pocked marked buildings. "I think that the Van Zyle ought to be seen downstairs too, David. That way everyone could love it as much as you do."

"Maybe, you think they'd really like it. I mean, I guess Britt would, but the others?"

"Why don't we suggest a meeting to decide which art work will be placed on the walls in the communal areas where everyone congregates? That way everyone will have a voice in our house."

"Good idea, Gerald."

Gerald did most of the work because David was unable to hold anything and ambulate at the same time. Already they were beginning to have a sense of interdependence, but David realized that it was more his dependence upon Gerald. He hoped that would change soon. It never occurred to Gerald that David was abusing his help or friendship.

At the same time, Pauline and Lee were working in their room. Pauline's bedroom suite which Ben had encouraged her to bring from Florida, since it would make her feel more comfortable, took a lot of room, but Lee's twin bed fit neatly into the opposite corner next to a small bed table with a reading light. The room was painted an aqua green which blended nicely with the furniture and the painting of lilies in a vase which Pauline owned. Lee brought two pictures of her three children when they were young and a picture of her deceased husband, Sandy, when he must have been in his sixties. He'd been a handsome, dignified and thoughtful man. One could see that his eyes absorbed all. Those eyes also spoke volumes of compassion and kindness.

Pauline hoped that there would be a place for flowers. She placed a picture of Max on the table. Next to the picture was a five by eight inch snapshot of a young woman and a little girl. Pauline's hands lingered on the picture as she caressed it, and her eyes misted. Her eye makeup smeared as she dabbed her eyes with a small handkerchief. Lee watched Pauline and knew whose picture it was. She wanted to comfort and console Pauline, but couldn't find words. Pauline smiled weakly, straightened her back, and continued her work.

In the bathroom on the floor were four medicine cabinets and plenty of shelving for medicines. The group had discussed how they would separate their medicines which were probably fifty or more bottles because each of the communal members had their share of prescriptions and herbal remedies. It looked like a shelf in CVS. Pauline gathered up Lee's state of the art medicines. They were the drugs for her Parkinson's, more bottles for depression, and multiple vitamins. She thanked God that she was spared these problems. Her own bottles were just over the counter items like aspirin, vitamins, and little packs of Emergen-C, a powder that she took every day with cold water. It was supposed to ward off colds and the like. Maybe it worked. She hadn't had a cold in years.

Pauline shared a cabinet with Lee and placed their toothbrushes in a holder. She placed a five by eight card under the dental materials with their names on it. Pauline wondered whether the men would object to some dainty pictures on the bathroom walls or would they want something more manly. That would also be a subject for the first meeting of the commune to be held the next day.

Britt and Sadie surveyed their room. Twin beds were placed side by side with a table between. A lamp had been placed on the table. A chest of drawers with two sides, one for Sadie, the other for Britt was on the opposite wall. The house painters had painted the walls an egg-shell blue, and this appealed to the women. Britt unpacked her two valises filled with her lingerie. For a brief moment she considered whether she should pay a visit to a Victoria Secret's clothing shop to buy some alluring negligees. She laughed out loud.

"What's funny, Britt?"

"Oh, nothing, Sadie. I was just having a fantasy."

"About what?"

"Oh nothing really, Sadie. Just an old woman's moment or something like that." Time was when Britt would never have admitted that she was *old*.

"Are you sure?"

"Let me help you put your clothes in the closet. These organizers make everything so easy, Sadie. Which side do you want?"

"The one you don't." Sadie laughed at her own joke.

"How would you feel about me putting some of my photography up on the walls?"

"I'd love it. I just brought a picture of Morris, may he rest in peace, to put on my side of the chest of drawers."

Britt looked at her photographs, all of them eight by ten. She fingered one of a handsome young man with dark, curly hair, in a t-shirt which served to emphasize bulging biceps. He had an easy smile and a twinkle in his eye. Under the photo was a handwritten message, "I love you Mom. Micky."

"That's your son?"

"Sure is, Sadie. He must have been about twenty-five or thirty when this was taken. We don't talk a lot. He's an actor, but you know how hard that is. He's out in California and has been in a couple of movies- bit parts, but he's got so much talent. Some day he'll make it big, I just know he will."

"You never talked about him in group, Britt. Is he married? Does he have a family? Will we ever get to meet him?"

"Maybe, and no and no. He's gay, Sadie. I think he's got a partner, but for some reason he thinks I don't approve of his lifestyle, but that's not true. It's in his head, not mine. I love him anyway he is."

"I don't think I know any gay people. My son, the one I want to write about, says being that way is an abomination. I told him he was wrong. God loves all his children, but he wouldn't change his mind."

"That's why I love you so much, Sadie. You're so fair minded. Micky was always such a sweet little boy, but he never was comfortable with girls. I think from the very beginning he knew something was different about him, but he tried. Lord knows the girls were all over him, but-----"

"He's very handsome Britt "said Sadie. "The photo tells it all! And spirited too! I like the spark in his eyes. It's easy to see that he's kind and loving, like his mother."

"I used to think that it was because I didn't have a husband to help raise him, but there are plenty of men who were raised by women who aren't gay, and a lot in a traditional family with moms and dads who are. So who knows? I just think that we are wired to be straight or gay or both. Love is love and I've always thought we can love both men and women. The Greeks were bisexual. I read that somewhere."

"Don't beat yourself over it, Britt. We all do the best we can. I can't say I ever heard that a person was gay from bad parenting, or just because they come from single parent families."

Sadie shook her head, but Britt misunderstood the movement. "Don't worry, Sadie. I love you like a sister." They laughed and continued their unpacking.

"I wonder if Ben will let me place a mezuzah on the side of our bedroom door. It's got the Shema in it and brings good luck to whoever lives in the room. I have one here in my suitcase."

"I've seen them on the door frames at the homes of my Jewish friends. I asked one once what it was and he told me that it was from the Bible, I mean the prayer inside of the little stick."

"That's right, Britt. It comes from the fifth book of the Torah, Deuteronomy. God commanded the Jews to put a mezuzah on their doors so that everyone would know the home belonged to a Jewish family."

Ben wandered around. He unpacked a few of his things in his small room off the kitchen. It was more like a gigantic broom closet. He had a fortified extra wide twin bed, table with lamp and a small chest of drawers. His medicines were placed on the chest along with a couple of magazines. He loved *The Nation* which he read religiously. Considering his wealth, Ben lived frugally.

In the afternoon Maria, Sadie, and Pauline took the van to the grocery store to stock up for a couple of days. They found an Ingles nearby. The store had motorized carts with baskets, and Sadie suggested she would be happy to use one so Maria and Pauline could go on without her. She wanted to explore the store. When they finished, they went to a Latino grocery which had all the spices and ingredients which Maria would use for her Mexican dinner. Pauline wished that they could have gone to a natural food store, but the others weren't enthusiastic.

The men napped while the women were shopping. It was a beautiful day and Juan took out a blanket from one of the rooms, placed it on the hill under a billowing oak tree and fell asleep.

Dinner was a great success and even Gerald ate a mild burrito, two tacos and some mild dip with avocado and sour cream. He ate a lot for a guy whose stomach was going to hell in a hand basket. The others tried to eat more than Ben and Sadie who devoured the Mexican dishes with gusto. Red wine accompanied the meals and the pastries bought at the Mercado were fabulous. Sadie tried unsuccessfully to eat one.

"No, you don't, not while I'm around," commanded Britt.

"Oh, Britt, just a little one – please," Sadie said. She and the others had to laugh at her sounding like a little girl begging for a treat.

"Here, I've cut a small piece for you. Eat it slowly and count to ten between each bite and it'll last longer," replied Britt in consolation.

Sadie gave her a contrite look; she was happy that Britt cared.

Gerald offered to help with the dishes as he had done so often when Claire was alive. He realized that he hadn't been in a position to offer his services since she died. Maria suggested that he could clear the table, and she would stick the dishes and utensils in the new dishwasher. Everyone agreed that the first dinner at Kelly House was a huge success.

Well fed and wined, they sat around lazily, discussing the day's activities, their bedrooms, and the beauty of the Appalachians. When Ben looked at his watch, it was past eleven. He bade everyone a good night. Juan and Maria went to one of the empty rooms for which they had also bought beds and linens, and fell immediately into a pleasant and deep sleep. Maria didn't hear her husband's snoring that evening.

Slowly, the six remaining commune members made their way to the elevator and then to their rooms for their first three hundred and sixty nights of rest.

CHAPTER ELEVEN

Sunday morning was cool, and the writers needed sweaters if they wished to go outdoors for early morning air. Florida seldom saw this pleasant breeze without humidity. Breakfast was simple, not like the evening before. Gerald got some cereal and fruit out for himself and David, while Pauline did the same for Lee. A huge coffee urn was percolating and the teapot began to whistle. Cups were set out for the latecomers. Sadie and Britt were still asleep, and Ben wondered whether they would be late risers regularly.

Maria and Juan asked the group whether anyone cared to join them for church because they were going to try to make Mass at the Basilica in town. Everyone begged off; no one seemed to have any desire to go to any other religious service. So Maria and Juan took the van and promised to pick up a Citizens Times newspaper on their way home.

Ben asked the writers whether they would be ready for their first communal meeting and they all agreed to hold it that afternoon around three or four depending on what was going on.

The first lunch was informal with lunch meats, Maruchan and Ramen instant noodle soups available for microwave or top of the stove cooking. David and Britt were delighted because both swore they pretty much lived on these cheap and yet filling chicken, beef, shrimp, hot and spicy soups. It was the first time that Pauline and Gerald tried one, and they found them tolerable.

David thought to himself that you really get to know someone when you live with them. True, he'd eaten with Gerald at Greentree many times, but then the kitchen staff did the cooking and even the lunches were full meals. David began to see that Gerald was finicky, at least about food.

David went up to the room to nap and turned on his single CD player. He decided that he wanted to listen to some opera and chose Puccini's *Greatest Love Duets* to listen to while he sat in the chair with a book to read. He was soon fast asleep.

At 3:30 everyone was seated around the long dining room table. Sadie and David, in their wheelchairs, sat at the opposite ends of the table so that they would have room to maneuver and no one would trip over them.

Ben welcomed everyone to the first meeting of the commune, and briefly ran over the guidelines which they already knew about. He suggested that good notes should be kept at each meeting so reference could be made to shared decisions, that votes would result in consensus, but if not possible, then majority rule.

He explained, "If it's impossible to come to one hundred percent agreement, then as a second means of enacting business, majority rule will have to suffice."

Ben made no bones about it; he preferred consensus. He asked whether anyone would be willing to chair the first meeting and act as a note-taker.

Pauline raised her hand, "I would be happy to take notes, but I am not ready to assume leadership."

"I would like to suggest that this first meeting be chaired by you, Ben. You brought us here. You are responsible for our resuming our lives. What do the rest of you say?" asked Gerald.

"I agree with Gerald and make a motion that Ben be elected to chair the first meeting," said David.

All hands rose in support of David's motion except for Ben's. He blushed slightly, and felt honored to have this first meeting under his chairmanship.

"Well, there was no consensus here. I would have voted 'No'. But thank you for this honor. Shall we start?"

"When I was condo president and president of Parents without Partners, we adopted a shortened version of Robert's Rules of Order in order to conduct business," said David. "I move that we use Colonel Robert's order of business and rules to conduct our business."

"I second the motion," said Britt.

"All in favor say 'aye' or raise your hand." Ben saw that Sadie and Lee were unsure of what was happening, or maybe he was going too fast for them. "Sadie, Lee, do you have any questions about this motion before we take the vote?"

"No, but don't we need a parliamentarian in order to use Robert's," asked Lee. She understood more than he'd given her credit for.

"What do the rest of you think?" Ben asked.

"I was a parliamentarian at union meetings when I taught school." Gerald spoke up. "It would be like old times for me. but I wouldn't want it to be my only role at these meetings."

"Without objection then, if we vote to use Robert's Rules of Order, Gerald has volunteered to see to it that we follow the rules." Again heads nodded up and down showing support.

"OK, let's vote. It appears that everyone is behind using Robert's. Gerald, you are the designated parliamentarian by acclamation."

Ben's thorough planning for this first meeting was paying off. The writers adopted a system to use and someone to watch over the proper use of that system.

"OK, this being the first meeting of the commune, there is no old business, no committee reports, no treasurers report or secretaries minutes to approve." Ben surveyed the table and found no dissension. "So, let's talk about new business, shall we?"

Britt spoke, "I remember reading the material you gave us. It said that there would be a house manager elected every two months. Is that person the same as the chairperson for these meetings?"

"Any discussion? Usually, according to Robert's there must be a motion on the floor before discussion, but we're just getting started, and I feel like this is administrative management of the house and that includes these meetings. What do the rest of you think about Britt's question?" queried Ben.

"I, for one, suggest that they be one and the same person. Otherwise, it may become too cumbersome to keep all the duties and roles uncomplicated," said Gerald. "Oh, one more thing while we are discussing management and chairing the meeting. The meeting chair would also be for a two month period to build a little continuity into the system. We could try it and see how it works."

"Everyone understand what Gerald is saying? House manager and Chair two months. Am I correct?"

"Precisely, Ben."

"Any questions?" Ben looked around the table and hearing none said, "Remember folks, anything can be revisited if it isn't working. Let's vote."

Again all hands rose in support of Gerald's motion. Ben smiled once again. He loved it when people could reach consensus. He hated dictatorship even if it were benevolent. The temptation for benevolence to give way to tyranny was just too great in his mind.

"Any nominations for house manager and Chair?"

"I move that Pauline be elected." Lee, in a weak voice, tried to speak with more volume. She was having trouble and her head weaved from side to side. The excitement of the moment made her Parkinson's more pronounced.

"I second the motion," said David and added, "But who will be our secretary if Pauline is house manager? Maybe you, Sadie?"

"Any more nominations?" The group seemed to ponder for a moment.

"I nominate David," said Gerald.

"But I just seconded Pauline's nomination," David countered.

"That is perfectly legal in Robert's rules."

"I don't think that I'm up to all the work," David grimaced. "For the welfare of the commune I should probably decline."

"Are you sure, David?" asked Ben.

David shook his head in affirmation. He had trouble doing the simplest things for himself, and although he was gaining strength every day, he wondered if he would have even survived the trip from Florida to Asheville without Gerald's help. How in the world would he ever run the operations of an entire house?

"Anymore nominations?" asked Ben.

"How about you, Ben? I mean you brought us here and this is your nickel. Don't you want to just see that things go well for two months or so?" Britt cooed.

Ben smiled at Britt and for a brief moment thought about her perkiness and beauty. "Thank you, Britt, and I mean that from my heart, but this is really your commune, and I may or may not be here for two months. I never know. So we'd better get used to you all running things."

After about five or six minutes of talking and contemplation, Gerald said, "I make a motion that we accept Pauline as the first house manager and chairperson of Kelly House for the next two months beginning tomorrow morning."

All hands rose again and an overwhelmed Pauline sat stunned. She did not raise her hand.

"I take it that this is a consensual vote even though Pauline didn't support it." Ben announced.

Pauline was just too modest to vote for herself, at least in a hand vote.

"Well, thank you all. I have not the faintest idea what to do, but I know that you will be with me and support my dumb decisions, no, I mean challenge them."

Everyone laughed and blew kisses at her. Juan and Maria bowed to her in jest.

"Well then, is there any other business to deal with?" Ben looked around the table.

"David and I were wondering about some of the art we brought with us. Is a vote necessary to decide which paintings remain in our room and which will be hung here or in the living room?"

"Why can't that be something that the house committee deals with when it gets formed?" Ben hoped for confirmation. He handed Pauline a list of committees which he thought might be useful to handle day to day operations of the commune. She took the list intending to put it in the first minutes and then to work with it as the first house manager. She calculated that she was in the hot seat until June 8th.

"When can we begin to get busy with our writing?" asked David.

Maria responded, "Just as soon as you feel ready. You haven't been down in the writing room downstairs. You might want to be the first to ride the seat elevator to see it. We bought some computers, paper for printers, three or four file cabinets, and computer desks. Maybe all of you should see the room tonight or tomorrow morning."

It was the first time that Maria spoke in the meeting.

"Come to think of it, I haven't been down there yet. Forgot all about it with everything else we were doing," said Ben.

"Do I hear a motion to adjourn?"

"I move that we adjourn," Britt called back. She was already heading for the stairwell to the basement.

"OK, if no one has anything else, this first meeting of Kelly House is over."

Those who could took the stairs, while David and Sadie learned how to use the rail elevator. The platform for the wheelchair was just big enough for one chair and controlled by a hand held remote system for up and down motion. It was controlled by whoever was in the chair. It worked without a problem although painfully slowly. Sadie vowed that the day would come when she could walk up and down stairs with her new limb.

The writers were duly impressed by their new workroom. Lights had been installed using halogen lights which were supposed save electricity and met the standards of the Greenies. Two computers were laptops, three desktop models. In the corner was a Mac for those who wanted to use it. The filing cabinets were stationed, each between two computers for the writers to store their materials. Two printers, one a HP, the other a house brand were set up so that the participants could use either one. They would need computer instruction.

A door led to a gazebo which Ben built years ago and a small garden with a tiny cross near a knoll nearby. This was where he'd buried his fiancée many years ago. The writers could go outside for sunlight and rest. Ben thought that they might like to do some serious thinking about what they were creating under the pergola. He also thought that meetings, group discussions, whatever, would be enjoyable out there. Of course, this was no school for rebels.

Almost immediately, each of the group members chose their computer and their filing cabinet. Pauline wondered whether that would be a problem in the future. She was already beginning to think like a house manager.

When everyone was gathered back in the living room area, Maria and Juan made an announcement. "We're going to be leaving on Tuesday morning to return to Florida. Our work here is done for the time being."

Maria with a tear in her eyes said, "This is your home really, not ours, and if we stay longer, we might not want to leave. We love you like our family, but it would not be right for you to become dependent on Juan and me. Do you know what I mean?"

It was a painful moment. For the writers, too. They were saddened but realized that Juan and Maria needed to get on with their lives as well. Hugs, tears and handshakes ended the night. It was as close to a group hug as possible with two in wheelchairs, Ben hovering over all with his 350 pounds of bulk.

CHAPTER TWELVE

T he next week was spent getting bedrooms, the bathrooms, kitchen and workroom squared away. These were Ben's words, but the women in particular saw it as beautifying and making the house a home.

It rained on Tuesday, the day that Juan and Maria left Asheville. They took the Mercedes, and decided to drive through Charleston and Savannah on the way home. Juan was fascinated by the Slave Quarters in Charleston. Maria marveled at the huge mansions on the ocean. Everywhere they turned, there were federal government signs designating homes as national treasures. Hurricane posters were abundant with signs for evacuation. This they recognized from Florida.

In Savannah they searched for Mrs.Wilk's Boarding House. It was touted as a family experience in Southern down home folks cooking. The line was nearly around the block, but the wait was warranted. Once in the restaurant, the Morales were placed with ten other people who also were tourists. The table was long and bowls of heaping mashed potatoes, greens, corn, fried chicken, ham, turkey, roast beef, succotash and foods which neither of them knew the names were served and passed around.

It was a meal from heaven and definitely one that Ben and Sadie would absolutely die for. Introductions between mouthfuls, small talk, and camaraderie made the experience memorable. The finish were dishes filled with blueberry and cherry pie covered by vanilla ice cream. No one would want to look at food again- at least for a couple of hours.

Juan and Maria found the car and drove to Pirates Alley where artists painted, sculpted, and poets read their poetry from soap box stands. It was a glorious afternoon. The rest of the trip was tedious because they drove the I-95 corridor which they did frequently.

"What about a stop in St. Augustine before we head for home?" Juan asked.

"If you want, mi amor." Maria was getting sleepy from all the food and walking around Pirate's Alley.

Pauline accepted her duties seriously and spent all of Monday, Tuesday, and Wednesday familiarizing herself with her house manager role. Ben suggested that a diary would be a good idea, but he wasn't sure whether this noble experiment should be chronicled.

Pauline would have done it anyway. She still saved many diaries over the years in her travels with Max. Somewhere buried deep within her boxes which she left in Florida were pictures, diaries, clippings of her husband's interviews with journalists and TV commentators. She didn't keep them with any intention of writing a book, but because she wanted to have them for her daughter, grand-daughters, and for Max to enjoy in his retirement.

"Strange, how all those memorabilia that I have saved for my family came to naught."

"Did you say something, Pauline?" Ben asked.

She shrugged and sighed, "I was just saying that Max is dead and my daughter doesn't have any interest in his past. I wonder how many families have had similar experiences. Writers whose children never read a word that their fathers or mothers have written, artists whose kin don't want their art when they die, poetry which is never passed on from generation to generation because …"

Ben remembered the class at Dade University to which the writers and he went, and the poem that Pauline recited to the students. He saw such a profound sadness in her and a lump in his throat seemed to grow.

"Things can change, Pauline. Your daughter may come around some day. You should let her know that you're living with us now in a commune. Maybe she'll have a change of heart."

"Perhaps."

"I think you should assist me in hiring the housekeeper for the house. She'll be working for the house manager, not me really. Do you think we should advertise for someone to live in or out of the house?"

"Let me think about it, Ben."

They had already discussed finances. Ben made it clear to Pauline that a simple phone call would assure enough money would be placed in the bank. On Wednesday, they took the van and went to a local credit union and opened two accounts. One was for daily expenses, the other for unforeseen problems. As house manager, Pauline's signature as co-signatory was used. Every two months the new house manager would have to sign on, a bit tedious but part of the plan.

Gerald offered to help with the kitchen chores and cooking for which Sadie was pleased. Duty rosters were drawn up for cleaning communal areas. Pauline thought that bedrooms should be the responsibility of the occupants. Bathrooms had to be cleaned and another roster was composed for that detail. A lawn service would be hired for mowing the grass and keeping the driveway clear of snow during the winter. Had Pauline and Ben thought of everything? Probably not.

Everything that they did would be brought to the group on Sunday afternoon for consensus and vote. Even the house manager was constrained to having agreement by the entire commune. This was part of the agreement Ben wrote.

Pauline and Ben placed an advertisement for a housekeeper/health aide in the Mountain Express and another in the Citizen Times. The Mountain Express touted itself as being independent, but in fact had to make their money by selling advertising. This meant that they had to please their customers like any other paper. But, unlike the Citizen Times, the Mountain Express appealed to the younger generation and older, hippy-like people. At least this is what Ben told himself. He hoped that the ad would attract people who were interested in working in this environment.

Phones were in place with two on the second floor within easy access, two on the first floor, and two in the workroom. Two days after the classified ads came out in the Citizen Times a barrage of telephone calls flooded the commune. Several of the inquiries were from people who either wanted to do housework and some kitchen duties, but no direct service to the writers, or were people who were certified nurse's aides with no interest in any household chores.

Pauline and Ben agreed that they would interview all who wished to come for an interview. While they were going about finding help, the writers were busy completing their bedrooms and beginning to set up their space in the workroom.

A deluge of calls came in from people with interest in geriatric work. Ben and Pauline screened the callers for expertise, interest, and personality. Three warranted interviews.

By Friday, Pauline was a little tired because she seemed to spend most of her time cooking and running to the store with Ben. She was now driving the van and had a pretty good idea of where stores, pharmacies, the nearest post office, and dollar stores were located. Gerald helped as much as he could in the kitchen and with those jobs which the others could not do for themselves. Even Britt pitched in where she could and seemed to enjoy her role of mothering Sadie- the quintessential mother of all souls.

The interviews went well. Many of the certified nursing assistants were from Asheville, Buncombe County Technical School, AB Tech for short. They had completed a six week course which when licensed gave them the ability to care for the sick and disabled. Some of the applicants were middle aged women who wanted to supplement their family income. Others were young women who saw their CNA status as a stepping stone to registered or practical nursing. None of them wanted to live in the commune as a family member.

"Well, this may be more difficult than I thought," said Ben. "Maybe we need help in finding what we're looking for."

"I liked Hazel and Dorothy the best. But, you're right. Finding someone who wants to do both health aide and housework may be impossible. What do you think about splitting the jobs? The cleaning and cooking could be a day job. I think that we could get along on the weekends by ourselves, just have someone in Mondays through Fridays, perhaps from eleven in the morning through dinner. They could clean up, prepare light lunches and prepare a regular meal for us."

"A good point to consider," Ben replied.

"The nurse could be the one to live-in and be available for David, Lee, and Sadie. They need it the most, I think," Pauline continued. "I believe that there are companies here just like in Florida where they could send someone out for the days that the health aide was not working. What do you think, Ben?"

"You may be right, Pauline. It isn't like 2-in-1 oil. What would you say to the health aide being a male for David? Do you think that Lee and Sadie would object to a man helping them bathe, dress, you know the things you women do?"

Pauline laughed and punched Ben lightly in the arm. "You have such a way with words, Ben. No wonder that Britt likes you." As soon as she let the cat out of the bag, she blushed and berated herself for saying anything. "I mean we all love your wittiness and use of the English language."

Ben was slightly taken aback at the mention of Britt and that she might have an interest in him. He thought to himself that he might score yet. Once a Marine, always a Marine.

"Why don't we call a meeting and ask the group about your idea, Pauline. Let them vote on it. It's their commune, not ours alone. Anyway, I don't want to bring Rock Hudson into the house and have the women angry with me." They both laughed.

Pauline asked the group whether they could break away from what they were doing for a short, impromptu meeting, and they were agreeable.

"So, here's the question," Pauline said and reviewed her idea.

Ben told them of the problem with trying to hire someone to do it all. They listened and thought about the idea.

"So you would like a man to live with us and provide care when needed," asked Gerald.

"At Greentree there were many men who worked there as nursing assistants. They even gave us baths and washed our hair. At first I was worried about a strange man washing my private parts and what have you, but I got used to it, and they were gentle and had good natures. Always helpful."

"I agree with Lee. At first I felt awkward and suspicious, but that went away," said Britt. "No problem from my point of view."

Sadie seemed a bit preoccupied and Ben saw her consternation. "Sadie, what's up?"

"I was thinking that Morris, my husband, may he rest in peace, was the only man that ever saw me- you know what I mean. I still have that feeling of being shy around any other man. I mean no offense to anyone of you, but the Bible says that women should be seen by only their husbands."

"Show me that in the Bible when you get a chance, Sadie. I should have read that a long time ago." Britt had a twinkle in her eye, and she stole a glance at Ben. He averted his eyes and blushed too.

"Well, any more discussion?" Pauline was now the chairperson. "Are we ready to vote? All those in favor of giving Ben and me authority to hire two people as outlined, raise your hand."

All raised their hands and tentatively Sadie joined in. "Let's do it," Ben said.

The focus changed. Now they were looking for two people. Pauline suggested that they call Dorothy and Hazel back in for another interview if they were interested in the housekeeper/cook work. They did, but Dorothy had already accepted another position. Hazel was delighted to hear back from the commune members and agreed to come in the next day.

Two different advertisements had to be placed in the papers. The first was for the health aide, the second for a housekeeper/cook. This meant another week of everyone pitching in and the people with the greatest abilities helping those who were more limited. In some ways Ben thought this a good idea because it encouraged a different type of bonding and responsibility. Those who could help built their confidence, and for the others, determination to once again become more self-sufficient.

Hazel came in for the second interview. She was a tall, black woman who bore her posture with dignity and assertiveness. She'd been through AB Tech's culinary school and at the same time raised three children by herself. She explained that she was a widow, her husband having died in the Gulf War in a freak accident.

When asked about her interests, she replied, "I am a Baha'i."

"I've seen some of the Baha'i buildings in Haifa, Israel, but tell me more," said Ben.

"I am a Baha'i which means I have faith and love for Baha'u'llah. He was a messenger from God for his time."

Ben bristled. He thought to himself but did not say, "Oh shit, another fanatical religious nut."

"We believe in the oneness of mankind and that all people should think of themselves as citizens of the world. We have members in at least six continents, almost every country on the planet. We are all brothers and sisters with a deep and abiding love for God and his manifestations."

"I had many Baha'i friends in my lifetime, Hazel," Pauline said. "I met them in India and Viet Nam, wherever my husband took me. I believe they were the most gentle and compassionate people I have ever met." Ben saw a radiance when he looked into Pauline's eyes.

"So, do you mind doing housework along with your cooking?"

"Not at all, Ben. May I call you both by your first names?"

"Sure, we all use first names here. What more should we know about you?"

"I cared for my children after their father died, without help. Lord knows I could have used some, but I live frugally and spent it all on the kids. All three went to college and one is just now beginning a pioneering experience as a doctor in Ghana in a Baha'i hospital. He's so excited."

Pauline asked, "Obviously you drive, dear. Do you mind learning to drive our van so that you can go to the grocery and take commune members to their doctor's appointments once in a while?"

"No, Pauline. I can multi-task along with the best of them." Hazel laughed heartily, and Pauline and Ben loved her spirit. Her chocolate skin fairly shined.

Ben turned to Pauline and asked, "Anything else you want to ask, Pauline?" She shook her head, and asked Hazel if she had any further questions. They didn't have an application form yet, but asked for references. It was agreed that they would call her back within two days and simultaneously asked her to hold on before looking for any other jobs.

Ben laughed and said, "We want to check your references. You know make sure that you're not an ax murderer or something like that."

"I would like to show you around our new home, dear." Pauline couldn't conceal her fondness for Hazel. Hazel also had a good feeling about these two, and thought that she'd found a new job. She was happy to see the house and especially the kitchen and grounds.

The references were called and each spoke highly of Hazel. They were older people for whom she'd cleaned house and in one case cooked as well. All three of the references were families who moved around a great deal, some being snow birds who split their time between Asheville and cities in the Midwest or East. Two of the references told Pauline that they'd lived in parts of Florida and found the state too hot, too humid, and too congested. Hazel wasn't needed when they were not in Asheville. On Tuesday afternoon, Pauline called Hazel Wright and offered her the job at $12.00 dollars an hour with a forty hour work week. Social Security, hospitalization and benefits would be paid. Ben would have nothing to do with poor wages or working conditions which were substandard. Hazel accepted the position immediately.

Finding the health aide was a little more difficult, but four calls seemed promising. The prospects were invited out to the commune for initial interviews, and Pauline asked Gerald to sit in on the interviews. Three of the interviewees showed up at the appointed times.

One was a woman who'd worked at a nursing home for several years in nearby South Carolina and moved to Asheville to be closer to her grandchildren. She loved the geriatric population, but wasn't sure that she really wanted to live in the institution where she worked. She commented that the equipment that she'd used in the nursing home was not here at the commune, and asked if sling lifts to lift the writers would be provided. Pauline and Gerald looked at each other and knew that this was not the woman for them.

The other two were men, one an older gentleman who'd been a CNA for the Veteran's Administration in Houston and came to Asheville to retire. He found that he could not live on his retirement and wanted to augment it by working in his field. He was a pleasant fellow, obviously in good shape for a man sixty-two years old, but all three of the interviewers felt something missing. Later in discussion they had the same uneasy sense that this wasn't the man for Kelly House.

The last interview for the day was done with Stephen Two Springs. Stephen, a young man and graduate from the Cherokee Community College, was a practical nurse who wanted to work with the elderly. Raised by his grandmother and grandfather on the reservation in Cherokee, North Carolina, he had a deep and abiding sense of the wisdom of the elders and this job was a natural in his opinion.

Two Springs, a name given him by his grandfather was his Native name, but he told the interviewers that some people whom he met in the "White world" called him Stephen Sampson because his biological father used that name. The LPN made it clear that he wanted to be called by his native name.

"You know your qualifications are above the level that we need, at least for now, Stephen." Gerald was concerned that he might simply be looking for a job until something better came along.

"I understand what you mean, but I don't like just pushing medications. I mean I don't want to be a supervisor like in a nursing home or in a childcare center. I like hands on involvement. Here in Asheville that's what LPN's and RN's do. I want to be more involved in the lives of my patients, be there for them."

"You realize that four of the writers are women, only two men at this time. Do you have any qualms with helping older women bathe, dress if necessary, assist them when we need it?" Pauline spoke for her sisters.

"No, not at all. It's part of the job. I did my rounds in our reservation nursing home for the elderly and enjoyed it immensely. You know I was a CNA for a year before I went on for the LPN certification. In the hospital I had to work alongside the nursing assistants and RN's helping wherever I was needed. Oh ya, I even worked in a clinic on the res when I was in high school."

"What about part of your salary being living here with room and board?"

Stephen turned to Ben. "That was part of the reason that I answered the advertisement. It would give me a chance to pay off some loans, the car, and maybe even send some money to my grandmother back home. Social Security and a little money from the casino fund isn't much."

Ben was satisfied with this answer and had a good feeling about this young man with the long braid and jet black hair. Stephen looked fit and trim, and Ben sensed that he could lift any of the members without any machines or help from anyone else. His concern was cultural differences and whether any of those would get in the way. He'd served with Sioux, Nez Perce, Apache and Black Feet in Nam. They were great Marines until they went out on liberty and tanked up. Then they were hell on wheels and usually spent time in the brig. He couldn't remember how many stripes he'd taken, but they always earned them back quickly.

"OK, let me ask you another question. Level with me. Do you have any problems with alcohol, drugs, women?"

Pauline and Gerald appeared uneasy and embarrassed by Ben's line of questioning. Gerald was incredibly sensitive to discrimination of any sort and could remember Polish jokes, negative comments about Catholicism, off-color comments about women, gay and lesbian colleagues, Jews. It was all the same to him- prejudice and bigotry. He abhorred any of it and would not tolerate any students in his classroom using language aimed at putting people down for who they were.

Pauline's sensibilities were affected by what she perceived to be direct questions which could imply elitism and racism. This she had learned from her missionary parents and Max, her deceased husband.

Stephen thought about his answer before he spoke. "Alcohol kills a lot of my people in one way or another. My parents were killed in a car crash after an 'all nighter'. That's why my grandparents raised us kids. I know there's a genetic predisposition in all of the Nations for alcoholism and I have stayed away from drugs and booze for just that reason. As for women, I wish!" Stephen laughed and went on "I fell in love once with a girl in high school, but I wouldn't --- you know, so she found some guys who partied. One night she and a bunch of 'braves' drowned in the river after their car went in. She was pregnant." Stephen's eyes misted and he fell silent.

Ben and the others sensed his pain and recognized that Stephen was still in mourning about something which had happened twenty or more years before. Some experiences transcended cultural differences and background.

Pauline asked Stephen for some references. He asked if teachers at the Cherokee college were OK. She nodded approval. He gave her names of two. For the third he gave the name a charge nurse at the hospital that he'd done rounds in and the telephone numbers for all three individuals. As she'd done with Hazel, she offered a tour of the commune for which Stephen was grateful. She also showed him the small but adequate bedroom which would be his, should he be hired. He'd have to use the bathroom on the first floor.

Ben suggested that he would pay a fixed rate salary and not an hourly wage because Stephen or whoever they hired would be living in, and hours would be variable. This seemed fair to Stephen. Again as with Hazel, they asked that they be given two days to check references before he looked for another position and he agreed.

"So what do you think?" Ben looked at the others.

"I like him. I think he will be a tremendous help to us and such a rich life and culture to bring to the commune." Pauline was obviously sold on Stephen.

"I agree totally. How long we may be able to use his services is an issue. If he wants to return to school for his registered nurse's degree and perhaps his bachelor's degree may mean that he leaves us, but then perhaps he could get it in one of those on-line schools and continue to work here."

Gerald, too, gave his seal of approval.

"I'll call the references and see what they say."

Ben already had the cell phone in his hand. The two instructors were unavailable and Ben had to leave messages to return his calls. He mentioned that the reason he called was for references for a Stephen Two Springs.

The nurse was at work, and picked up the phone. When Ben explained the purpose of the call, she let out a low cry of excitement. "You've got to be kidding. Stephen is incredible. I never saw such empathy and caring from any of the students like Stephen's. Old, young, it didn't make a difference. Everyone loved him here. I would have hired him in a minute if there wasn't a freeze on. He'll be a tremendous asset to your commune."

Ben asked about his skills, and received the same vote of confidence. "Anything else you can tell me about him?"

"Hire him. You won't regret it." He thanked her and hung up.

"I gather it went well," said Gerald.

"She was pleased as punch," Ben smiled. Pauline laughed as she hadn't heard that phrase in a long time.

"Do we want to wait a day for the teachers to call?"

"I guess it's the right thing to do, but I don't want to wait too long. We might lose him."

As they were talking Ben's phone rang. It was one of the instructors from the college returning the call. Ben told him about the commune and the job. He received the same reception that he'd gotten from the nurse. Ben thanked him and hung up.

"I think we should call Stephen, and offer him the chance to come out one more time to meet the others. Let him evaluate what is needed here, and then if he's still interested, offer the job."

Gerald and Pauline enthusiastically agreed. Ben called, and left a message for Stephen to call. He did about thirty minutes later, and quickly accepted the invitation to come for lunch the next day. In the morning, Ben received a call from the other instructor who had glowing things to say about Mr. Two Springs.

Lunch the next day consisted of soup and salad which Gerald helped prepare. Stephen was introduced by Pauline. He readily answered questions thrown at him by the writers. They seemed to be interested in his background, and asked questions about the Cherokee, his grandparents, and growing up on a reservation. Only David, having taught in the Bush in Alaska, knew anything about Native Americans. Britt knew little of the Native villages having lived in a primarily white village. She knew some Natives, but the majority of the people in her small town were Caucasians. Both she and David had been through the *Intensive Introduction to Native Village Life* course at the University of Alaska in Fairbanks although at different times. It didn't begin to touch the experiences that they would encounter when they actually got to their villages.

Stephen was a hit. He fit in so well that the women who were concerned about their modesty and being seen by a male, a young one at that, forgot all about their worries. After lunch, Pauline, Gerald, and Ben showed

Stephen the bedrooms, the large bathroom upstairs, and the rest of the house.

He had no questions, no doubts, and said, "I really want this job if you'll give me a chance."

Handshakes between the men, a hug from Pauline, and it was decided that Stephen would move in the next day. He had few clothes, a few books, and brought a drum which he used in powwows held by his people. The drum was a huge, kettle-like instrument which he explained was made for him by his paternal great uncle. It was his pride and joy.

After settling into his room, putting his jeans, shirts, underwear, and socks away, Stephen found the restroom on the first floor, and put his toiletries under the sink in a basket. It was time to wander around, and begin his talks with the individual members. Sadie welcomed him in her kitchen. She talked about her diabetes, the loss of her leg, and some pain associated with the new prosthesis. Stephen took notes in a notebook.

David and Gerald were in the workroom huddled over a chess board. Stephen realized that chess players experienced their passions for the game seriously, and he didn't want to disturb them. He'd learned the moves in school, played a few games, but became bored with the deliberations.

After about ten minutes and a gasp from Gerald because he'd gotten caught in a queen pin which was a certain road to death, he resigned.

"How do you always manage to do that to me, David?"

"I am sorry, my friend. You'll beat me next time. I'm sure of it. Your game is improving every time we play."

David was always self-conscious about his lack of skills on the chessboard. He spent many years calling himself the best mediocre chess player in Florida. Beneath it all, he knew that he would never amount to anything in the game of kings. In truth, though, he won about seventy percent of his games.

"So, what can we tell you, Stephen? My hip is improving, I think. Now my hip is my weather forecaster. Have you read the records which our social worker in Florida sent up with Ben?" inquired Gerald.

"Yes, I have, Gerald, but I'm as interested in everyone's mental outlook as I am their physical prognosis." Stephen was hoping that Gerald would talk about his depression a bit.

"You know from the record that I was married to the most wonderful woman in the world. For a long time, I believed that I could not exist without her. But now I realize that I have to go on with my life, and my friends here have become my family. I still talk to Claire's son once in a while, and we are friends, but he has his own family, and his biological father is close to him and his grandchildren. So step-parents lose more than a wife or husband when the marriage ends for whatever reason in most cases, I think. I feel the loss, but I understand."

Gerald's demeanor sank somewhat, and Stephen picked up on it.

"Well, we have to connect with the occupational and physical therapists. Your rehabilitation record stated that you needed a few more appointments before they would clear you for good. I'll contact the place that does that work, and make an appointment if it's OK with you."

Gerald nodded his head in agreement.

"David, tell me about yourself. I've read your record also, and am surprised to see how well the splint is helping your gross motor activity."

"I think that I'm getting stronger each day. Like you said, gross motor, not fine motor skills yet. But, I'm optimistic. Someday I'll be back to normal. That's the plan, and I'm stickin' to it."

Stephen immediately liked David's attitude about his stroke and the aftermath. David was as upbeat as Gerald. Stephen recognized that first impressions were not always predictors of reality. David would need to remain on his medications, and be watched for possible recurrences of strokes, transient ischemic accidents, or even cardiac issues. He would need more sessions with the occupational and physical therapists. Stephen made some notes in his sheet on David, and looked for any signs of emotional difficulties. He found none at this time.

Lee and Pauline were in their bedroom reading quietly. The door was closed, so Stephen knocked softly. "Come in please." Pauline was so polite.

"I just wanted to come by and chat a bit. Do you have a minute?"

He looked at both women compassionately, but realized that Pauline was not one of the patients at Greentree and somehow she was his supervisor now, but would not be in another month or two. He didn't quite understand the business about house manager and consensus decision making, but the consensus thing sounded sort of familiar. He believed that his tribal chief held meetings with the elders, and used a similar concept in tribal gatherings and decision making.

"Lee, how are you feeling?"

"Better than I have in a long, long time, Stephen. I probably will always have these tremors, unsteadiness, difficulty swallowing at times, but I'm so much better now than when I went to the rehabilitation center. Thanks to all my friends- really my family here."

Stephen determined that he would read up on Parkinson's disease, and be ready should a need arise to take emergency action. He had read about Lee's attempts to commit suicide, and was saddened by the record. Too many of his friends and family had taken their own lives. For him, it was a terrible tragedy.

"How do you see me being of help to you, Lee?" Stephen believed that his patients ought to be consulted on matters pertaining to their own well-being.

Lee looked at Pauline, and seemed to be asking her to answer for her. Pauline wisely kept her own counsel.

"I guess I need people to watch for signs of depression. I mean, I don't know when the Parkinson's will get worse, change, whatever. There's no cure, and the prognosis isn't good, but I've found hope here amongst these wonderful and loving friends. I feel upbeat most of the time. Maybe I'm experiencing acceptance about my husband's death. I don't know."

Stephen had read *On Death and Dying* by Elizabeth Kubler Ross, and recognized acceptance as the final stage in the stages of grief.

"Well, your doctor at the rehabilitation center made arrangements for you to be followed up on a regular basis. I'm practicing driving that big van, and will take you to the doc. How does that sound to you?"

Lee smiled at the young man, and thought of her three children out on the Pacific coast before giving her answer.

"Oh yes, I don't want Pauline to have to bathe me, and always worry about me in the bathroom. I would hope that you have no problems with helping me once in a while."

"No problem there, Lee. That's what I'm here for. See you ladies later."

The last person on his list was Britt. She was in the garden sitting in the gazebo. Stephen approached her from the rear and startled her. He was apologetic, and determined to be more mindful of how he would move toward Britt in the future.

"So, how are things going, Britt?" He watched for any flashes of anger or a caustic remark about his entrance into her space. He'd read the social workers notes carefully.

Britt smiled up at him benignly. "I'm as happy as a lark. I love it here. The mountain air is so fresh and clean. Not like in Deerfield Beach. This place is so peaceful, and I love it."

Stephen was relieved that she didn't take his head off for startling her.

"How's the oxygen working? Is it helping with your breathing? We need to keep an eye on it. The company already brought a couple of canisters out for you. Any problems?"

"No, dear, not at all. I think this mountain air is good for me. Maybe better than the ocean air was. I might even try exercising a bit, and maybe the COPD will go away." For some reason she thought of Ben just then, and smiled up at Stephen.

Stephen was pleasantly surprised by the reception. He offered to do vital signs on her, and had his stethoscope and cuff handy. He wanted to make sure that her respiration and heart rate in particular were within normal limits. He also realized that up to now chronic obstructive lung disease had no cure, just containment with proper care. He pledged to make sure she received that.

"May I take your blood pressure and oxygen saturation levels?"

Britt extended her arm and finger. She was used to vitals. Used to be that she'd throw an empty bed pan at any nurse who threatened to attend to her. No longer. "Thank God for small favors." was all Stephen could manage to think.

Hazel's first day on the job would be the next day. The men were looking forward to her expertise in cleaning the rooms and hoped for a bit more variety than Sadie was capable of producing in the kitchen.

Ben announced, "Well, Pauline, you have your staff now. It's all yours. If you need any help from me, I'm happy to do what I can. Hazel and you can plan out the meals if you think that would be the best thing, or you can ask the gang what they want to eat. It's all up to the house manager to decide how he or she wants to run things. I don't think that every little detail must be voted on, but even that's up to you for the next two months."

Ben began to twirl his mustache. When he was concentrating his bushy eyebrows appeared to lift as though they were in synchronization with the furrows in his forehead. The twinkle was still in his eyes, especially when Britt entered the room, but Pauline realized that he was more subdued than when they had moved in. It was hard to believe that the commune had been up and running for three weeks already.

CHAPTER THIRTEEN

Pauline asked the members whether, in fairness to Hazel and Stephen, the weekly meetings ought to be changed to a day when both were available to attend, and whether the writers desired that the two be voting members. The meetings were changed to Tuesday afternoons. Pauline was just taking a straw poll. It would be brought up in the next meeting.

"Welcome to our fourth commune," said Pauline.

The secretarial duties were in the hands of Gerald for the time being. He believed that he could handle them along with the parliamentarian activity when needed. After the minutes were read, old business attended to and general discussion concerning minutia, it was time for new business.

"I move that Hazel and Stephen be formally accepted as voting members of the commune."

"Is there a second to Britt's motion?"

"I second."

"Thank you, David."

"Discussion"

"If Hazel and Stephen are to feel that they belong, not just work here, they ought to be voting members, and be able to make their points as strongly as the rest of us. That's it."

"I agree with Britt. Even if Hazel and Stephen should move on, I think that the positions demand equality and parity," said David.

"What about the fact that they are employees and not actual members?"

"True, Gerald. That could be a problem if there is disagreement about some part of their job duties or something else similar, but we are a different sort of employer than many. We treasure everyone's opinion and are willing to take the time to discuss, convince and consult," Ben said as he felt strongly about this.

"Is there any more discussion?" Pauline looked around the table, not wanting to rush this vote as it would be an important change to Ben's original set of guidelines when he created Kelly House. "OK, all those in favor of the question, raise your hand or say aye."

Everyone voted in the affirmative.

"Let's call Stephen and Hazel in and tell them the news," said Sadie. She was smiling radiantly.

As they came into the dining room, applause greeted them. They knew that their involvement in the community was being discussed and sat together in the kitchen having a cup of tea. Sadie couldn't keep a secret.

"So any more new business?"

"I move that we inquire about a communal membership in the College for Seniors at the University. Furthermore, I think that Ben should not pay for this. We all have some money and could pitch in."

"Is there a second to Pauline's motion?" Gerald took over to allow Pauline to make a motion.

"Second," said Lee.

"Discussion."

"I think that the program and courses at the senior college would be a good diversion from our commitment to writing and whatever creative work we do. Also, I read in the Mountain Express newspaper that there are classes on writing, art, sculpture and everything else we might be interested in. As for our paying for it, I believe that we ought to carry some of the financial burden here. Ben has been very kind and more than generous, but he should not be expected to do it all."

"I agree with Pauline. I would love to attend some classes on music appreciation and learn to play bridge." Britt was intense.

"Wait a minute, the agreement was that I would pick up the tab for a year. I appreciate the intent that you pay for yourself, but that was not our agreement." Ben was adamant.

"I think that we ought to separate the vote." David knew something about Robert's Rules of Order also.

"What do you all think?" Gerald asked the group, and they agreed to separate, although Sadie, Stephen, Hazel, and Lee looked perplexed.

Gerald explained. "What this means is that we would vote on whether to seek a communal membership separately from the question of who pays for it."

The four relaxed and shook their heads in understanding.

"Anymore discussion? Seeing none, I put the question before you. All those in favor, raise your hands or say aye." Gerald counted the hands.

Stephen and Hazel didn't vote. Everyone else voted in favor. "The motion is passed."

"Now for the part about payment. Any discussion? Seeing none, the vote is whether we should pay for the membership, or ask Ben for the money. A vote for the motion means we want to pay for it ourselves. All those in favor say aye or raise your hand."

This time all supported the vote, and it was counted as unanimous. Ben frowned, hiding his pleasure.

Pauline resumed the chairperson role. "Does anyone have any more new business to bring up? Seeing none, shall we go into good and welfare?"

Good and welfare was a chance to bring up whatever anyone wanted to discuss without vote or motions.

"I've been here three weeks, and haven't begun to write or even think about it much. I think that we ought to discuss a format or something similar to work on our purpose for being here." David took his responsibilities seriously.

"I agree with David. I think it's time for me to get busy finding those letters from my life in the village with my Korean War veteran who went nuts. I may have to go to New York and find them." Britt looked at Ben with a pensive gaze.

"Well, I told you that if you needed to go to New York we'd get you there some way. Those letters are important." Ben considered whether he ought to take Britt there and what that would mean in the eyes of the others.

Hazel, who hadn't so much as uttered a word until now, said, "I think that it's time that we have some way of exercising and getting outside of the house. I'd be willing to lead a nature hike, or have some sort of a work-out session right here in the house somewhere."

"Wow, sounds great. I never thought about that before," exclaimed Lee.

"I'd like a walking path or something like that so that we could keep our weight in check." Gerald said as he sneaked a look at Ben, and wished that he hadn't said anything about weight.

Ben confirmed, "When I'm here, I'd be happy to have some exercise. I need it big time, and we all know it. Don't worry about me, Gerald. I've never been so heavy and it's getting a bit uncomfortable."

"OK, who wants to look into this with Hazel?" Pauline believed in getting things done, not just talking about them.

"I would be happy to work on it with Hazel and Gerald or anyone else," said Stephen. "From a medical standpoint anything I can do to help everyone become healthier and more independent is great."

"Fine, as house parent, I mean house manager, I declare you a committee. Be ready to make a report next week or the next." Everyone laughed at Pauline's slip of the tongue.

It was nearly 4:30 when the meeting closed. People lingered around the dining room table for a while, and discussed their writing and duties on committees.

"So where are the letters, Britt?" Ben tried to be business-like, but his skin was hot and his face slightly red.

"Like I said before, I have a post office box and room in my cousin's house where I keep some things like the letters. I'd have to call him and ask if it's OK for me to come for a day or two to get some things. I could take the Greyhound up."

"Maybe I'll go with you to keep you company, if you'd like. I can take care of business while you're at your cousin's house. I can stay at the Army/Navy Hotel on Lexington while you're with your family," Ben offered.

"I'll call him and see when would be a good time for him to have me come."

"Let me know. I have a Veteran's Advantage card, and we could go up to the Big Apple. Maybe take in a Broadway show and a steak dinner at Tads or something." He hoped she would say "Yes."

Ben felt an excitement he hadn't felt in years. So did Britt. They agreed to check bus schedules, talk to her cousin about a good time to go. It would be the first time that Ben left the commune since it opened.

He called the Greyhound office and found out there was a night bus which would arrive the next morning and a return at night also. A re-run was on Broadway about a GI falling in love with a Vietnamese girl and having a baby. *Miss Saigon* always made Ben weep when the young girl killed herself. He knew that *Miss Saigon* was similar to a Puccini opera, *Madame Butterfly*. They both concerned young women who slept with a GI, fell in love, and got pregnant, only to be left when the soldier returned to America. The young women committed suicide. It was an all too familiar story with dire consequences. Ben found an outlet for his emotions in Puccini opera and some Broadway shows.

Britt used her cell phone to contact her cousin who was happy to hear from his long-lost relative. She filled him in on the commune, her illness, and her decision to write about her life. He knew exactly where the boxes were stored, and asked her to hold the line while he checked to make sure that they were still there. They were, and of course, she could come to New York for them. He also offered to mail the letters to her, but she declined. She wanted to get away with Ben, and see what sparks might fly.

Ben and Britt met again two days later and decided to go up to New York on Monday next for two days. They'd have a night on the town. Was this a date? What were they getting into? What did they expect of each other? Both felt apprehensive and a bit scared but that wouldn't stop either one. For Ben it was the old adage, "Once a Marine, always a Marine- Semper Fi."

David and Gerald met in the garden. It was a beautiful late April afternoon. David was still in his wheelchair and looked a bit tired. He'd spent the morning in the workroom beginning to gather his thoughts about writing his memoirs about his days in Alaska. He felt certain that he had stories rich in color and character which would interest anyone who'd ever considered teaching in the Bush. He wanted to chronicle some twenty years of trying to live in the Last Frontier as a Bush teacher. Ben suggested that he use a tape recorder. The tapes could then be transcribed into the written word. Unfortunately, David didn't have Adrian, his volunteer from Greentree Rehabilitation Center, to help him.

She was one of the original volunteers who took part in the experiment with the six patients. She'd chosen David to work with, and succeeded in helping him to let go of his guilt for having divorced his sons' mother and having a poor relationship with so many other women. Adrian was invited to come to Asheville, but declined, preferring to return to her family in northern New York.

"I think I'm ready to continue my writing. I think the move and excitement made me have a little writer's block or something like it."

"I agree with you, David. I think a new environment required me to adjust, but I am ready to begin again. I have not decided whether I want to do something which requires research or create something in fiction. I want a genre which is new, yet would interest readers."

"Gerald, have you considered doing both. For instance couldn't you create something in fiction which requires a certain amount of research? James Michener did that in almost all of his books. I read his *Alaska* and the characters were fictional but his history, geopolitical and sociological study was prodigious. The same went for his book, *The Source*. Lots of great writers fabricate a story built on historical evidence, I think."

"True, my dear friend. You know, I also have written poetry, and I may wish to publish some of my better works. Some of them were well received by colleagues and students alike." Gerald said and seemed pleased with himself.

"You see, you have so much to offer, Gerald. I have never been able to write poetry, although come to think of it, I did write a love poem to a young girl in college. She was studying English, read my poem, and red-lined all the mistakes. I guess she didn't see the love or lust or whatever it was in the poem. That was the last poem I ever wrote." They laughed.

"Ah, the bard miserably rejected. What a pity. David, you simply must allow your creative, poetic juices to flow forth again. I am quite certain that Pauline, Lee, Britt, and Sadie would *never* red-line your creative genius."

David and Gerald broke out laughing. "A little gossip if you don't mind." David looked around the gazebo to make sure he wasn't being heard. "Have you noticed anything interesting about Ben and Britt?"

Gerald shook his head, his mane of white hair and angular body belying his age of 76. Many mistook him for being in his late sixties. "I do not know what you are talking about, David. I try not to gossip, but I shall make an exception for you, dear friend."

David wasn't interested in Gerald's snobbery. "I think that they are interested in each other. Did you hear that they're going away on Tuesday to New York? New York, can you imagine that?"

Gerald cocked his right eye in doubt. "David, David- My good man, they're past that, I am sure. I mean how can it be that two people in their eighties would – you know?" Gerald was lost for words.

"Sadie told me that she heard them talking about going to New York for Britt's letters- *together.*"

"And so, what does that mean? Together, what is the significance of together? Anyway, it is their life and their business. We should not be interfering in their lives."

"Oh Gerald, we're a family. Families show interest in what each member is doing. Right?

"Well, if it is true, let us wish them well and a safe journey."

"Amen, Gerald."

The two decided to return to the house. Gerald pushed David's chair before him and smiled. He was smiling at the image in his mind of Ben and Britt making love. He thought of Claire and sighed.

While the men were gossiping, Hazel and Sadie were in the kitchen. Sadie sat on a stool, her prosthesis posted next to the wall. Sadie began the conversation. "Hazel, tell me about the Baha'i religion. I never heard of it until you came here. Do you believe in the same God I do?"

Hazel, smiled benignly, "Sadie, of course I do. There is only one God and he loves us all and protects us. Baha'u'llah was our founder in the

1860's. He came from a Muslim background in Persia. When he was a young man he sensed that the Muslim religion was not treating people correctly, especially women and he started a new faith."

"What did he think about Jesus?"

"Baha'u'llah believed that all the prophets of all the major faiths were holy and contributed greatly to understanding and were Messengers from God. He believed that he was sent by God to spread the idea that all human beings were really citizens of one world. We Baha'is believe that the day will come that all humankind love and live together as one people."

"What do Baha'is think of Jewish people?"

Hazel thought about this question for a full minute before she answered. "In my opinion, there are two parts to your question, Sadie. First were it not for the Israeli government and the Jews in Israel, the Baha'i wouldn't have a place to call home. Haifa is where our House of Justice is located. We Baha'is have been terribly persecuted just like you Jewish people. We share that with you, but Israel has offered us sanctuary and protected us from our enemies."

"What enemies?"

"Our religion was born in Iran where our leader, Baha'u'llah, was born. He was born a Muslim, but spoke against the leadership and their corruption. So the Muslims imprisoned him and many believers were martyred. Finally the Muslims exiled Baha'u'llah first to Baghdad in Iraq, then to Turkey, and then finally to the Holy land which at that time was called Palestine. That's where he died. The Palestinians sold land to the Baha'is much as they did to the Jews from Europe. When the Jews declared Israel a nation, we remained in Haifa and built our international center." Hazel radiated compassion as she tried to explain to Sadie the tragic story of what happened.

"Sounds a lot like what happened to us. People have been exiling Jews for centuries. I don't know why. And then Hitler. Why did he hate us so and kill so many of us?" Sadie had tears in her eyes as she thought about her people and her husband, Morris, who'd lost his whole family in Polish concentration camps. "I guess we're a lot alike, Hazel."

"Perhaps, dear Sadie, perhaps." Hazel thought about the teachings of the faith. All the prophets were loved by the Baha'i including Jesus of Nazareth. She doubted that Sadie would agree to that. Baha'u'llah even praised Mohammad as a man of God. It wasn't easy being a Baha'i and love your enemies as you did yourself.

"You know my son and daughter believe in Jesus as the Messiah, and my son is the leader of a lot of Messianic Jews. My husband, Morris, may he rest in peace, probably died because they believed in Jesus. Jews don't believe in Jesus, Hazel. We can't. I tried when I thought that I wanted to make it right with my children. Now I really want to write about what they believe in. But it's hard going against your children. Are your children in your religion, Hazel?"

"Two are and one isn't. It's up to your children to make their own decisions, to live their own lives, and that means religion as well. That's what we believe. We're told to seek truth and follow it wherever it may lead us."

"Hazel, I know you're busy with all the work looking after us and all that, but do you think that when I start to write again, you might look at some of what I write- you know sort of give me your opinion, help me with my grammar, spelling?"

"Of course, Sadie. I'd be happy to look at it and give you any thoughts I have. We could work out a deal of sorts. You help me here in the kitchen; I help you on your writing." She knew that Sadie wanted to be useful and felt that the kitchen was her domain anyway. They hugged and Sadie decided to nap for an hour.

Pauline had an idea. She decided that she wanted to have a car and be able to drive around Asheville, and maybe see a little of Tennessee. She heard that Chattanooga was lovely, and there were places in West Virginia that Max used to talk about when he was alive. He wanted to find Matewan, West Virginia, where he'd heard there was some interesting history to be learned. Something about miners and unions, she couldn't quite remember. She'd ask Gerald about it. He knew so much about the labor movement. If only Ted Kelly were alive, he'd probably want to go with her to see it and collect memorabilia about the union wars. What were their names who feuded? "Oh, yes, I remember now. The McCoys and Hatfields. They were from Matewan, too."

Pauline had money of her own, lots of it. In Florida, she'd driven a leased car which she returned to the company when she decided to join the commune. The van was necessary for David and Sadie in particular, but she thought a nice sedan would be useful to the commune and not terribly expensive. Maybe another lease for a year was in order.

Ben and Pauline met frequently to discuss routine house manager issues and go over business items for the weekly meetings. "Ben, I've decided to buy or lease a car while I am here at the commune. It will be useful to have two vehicles here at all times."

Ben laughed. "Fine, we can come up with money for that. I don't see a problem."

"You are not hearing what I am saying, Ben. I am going to buy or lease the car, not you. I have enough money to pay for one outright without having to take a loan and I do not, I repeat, do not want your money involved in this. It is my contribution to the commune." Pauline sat erect and experienced a heightened sense of well-being in being so assertive with the huge man.

"Well, well, if you insist, I understand. What do you want to buy? Do you need a North Carolina driver's license? I guess you do."

"I am going to ask Stephen to take me to some car dealerships and to the motor vehicle administration. I think I saw it when I went to the grocery store.

"Okay, Pauline, but remember if you need help- you know financial assistance, let me know." He smiled at her with pride in her independence. She, on the other hand, frowned up at him, but it was a playful and loving frown.

Within the week, Pauline took the driver's test and passed it the first time, bought automobile insurance, and owned outright a Subaru light blue small station wagon with enough rear space for at least one wheelchair. She felt a sense of freedom at not having to be locked into the use of the van and someone else doing the driving. She began to see her role differently now. She could help the writers more and assist Hazel and Stephen. As an afterthought, Pauline realized that she could go to some of the classes at the Reuter Center for seniors at the University of North Carolina, Asheville Campus. She was excited about taking some of the hands-on art classes.

Meanwhile, Stephen was beginning to feel comfortable in his new role and began to make the appointments with the physiatrist who would monitor and prescribe the modalities which would be needed for David, Sadie, and Gerald. A pulmonologist was contacted who would see Britt and make arrangements for the oxygen tanks and other items she might need. The new pulmonologist was contacted by the physiatrist at Greentree. As the two discussed the case in detail, they agreed that Britt was definitely in need of a watchful eye. The last patient was Lee whose Parkinson's disease demanded a neurologist familiar with the new treatments and procedures which seemed to come in spurts. The National Institute of Health was interested in the disease and Lee had been a patient of theirs for experimental surgery and participation in trials of new medicines, but then protocols changed and she lost her rights at NIH.

Stephen found a huge calendar which he kept on the wall in the kitchen so that everyone could read it and know when their appointments would be. Ben's diabetes and other aches and pains would continue to be watched carefully at the Veterans Administration Hospital on Tunnel Road, that is if Ben cooperated. The calendar was also used for other events which took place such as House Meetings, and whatever else Pauline felt needed to be posted.

Ben considered asking his provider for a 'script' for Viagra or maybe even long acting Cialis. He wanted to "be ready when the time was right." They still ran that advertisement on TV. He considered it an invasion of privacy, but if actors and actresses were willing to make a few bucks pretending that they needed the stuff, he'd turn his head. "Z" called VA and asked for the nurse, explained his request and she said that she'd speak to the physician's assistant. A call an hour later confirmed that he could pick it up in the pharmacy whenever he wanted to do so.

Four weeks into the life of the commune, the honeymoon was over. Pauline made a list of the grievances to address in the next group sit-down. She called Ben into the dining room while the others were busy doing other things.

"I think the use of the bathroom is the primary issue that the group has been concerned with and especially during the early morning and night."

Ben's head wagged up and down. "I've heard mumbling. I guess the honeymoon is over." He laughed and Pauline joined him with a chuckle "Any ideas, Pauline?"

"Perhaps, we could set up a system where each room would have the wash room for a half hour each morning and in the evening. Of course the use of the facility during the night would still be a problem. David and Gerald seem to need to use the toilet more than the rest of us."

"They may have prostate problems. I know I do at times." He whispered these last words under his breath. "Let's ask Stephen what he thinks is going on. Probably should have put in two 'heads' upstairs."

Pauline didn't know what a head was and Ben had to explain the word to her. Sometimes Marine jargon was hard to escape.

"I think that we also need to establish some sort of system to make certain that the writers will write. It was built into their program at Greentree. They knew that they would have to read their material at the group therapy session. So they prepared, perhaps like reciting in a classroom," Pauline said to start a new subject.

Ben had been wondering the same thing. He knew that it took a certain amount of time to adjust to the new surroundings, to feel at home, and do whatever it took to settle in, but there had been little writing, or even discussion about it. Pauline was right.

"What do you think we should do about it, Pauline?"

"Well, I think that we ought to bring it up to the group on Tuesday. I know you and Britt will be away for two days, but I still think that the group can begin to discuss what they will do and how."

Ben watched Pauline carefully to see whether she was chiding him in going to New York with Britt, but he saw no signs of her making fun of them. She was genuinely concerned about the writers beginning to do what they came to do.

"Why don't you see what they recommend and table it until Britt and I return from our trip to get her letters." This seemed to settle the question for the house manager.

"Anything else before the next meeting?" Ben wanted to discuss the bathroom issue with Stephen. There was no problem between him and the nurse because they shared the downstairs 'head' at night. True, he had to go more than Stephen, but they never ran into each other.

Over the weekend, Ben invited the group to a drive on the Blue Ridge Parkway. They did about fifty miles and marveled at the greenery and budding of the trees and flowers. Every once in a while they saw a fawn or doe on the side of the road. The gentle mountains were gorgeous and tantalizingly peaceful.

Weekend meals were prepared by Sadie and anyone else who chose to help. Hazel got into the habit of leaving two or three meals in the refrigerator that just needed to be warmed up for consumption.

On Sunday, Gerald asked Pauline whether she would be willing to take him to the Unitarian/Universalist Congregation in town. He offered to pay her for gas. She refused, but suggested that he could take her for lunch if he'd like after the services. After she'd spoken, she was chagrined that she'd been so bold as to tell Gerald that he could take her to lunch. Sadie would have called it chutzpah.

David spent Sunday morning in the workroom thinking about the writing ahead of him. He decided that he wanted to do a memoir about his twenty or more years of trying to make the Alaskan wilderness his home. He considered himself a failure at this effort, but continued to have a love-hate relationship with the Last Frontier.

He remembered that back at the rehabilitation center he spent loads of time with Adrian and Gerald talking about what he would write. David wondered whether Gerald would be available to him for fine tuning, thinking out loud and editing. He struggled with his new tape recorder and managed with the splint on his right hand and the use of his left to turn the instrument on. He fumbled a bit with the controls, and uttered a few nonsense words into the machine. Holding it fast with his right hand, he switched the machine to rewind, punched in and listened to his own voice. It was comprehensible which was anticipated, and would serve nicely to make his writing a go. The question was: how or who would transcribe his words so that he could re-read the work he'd completed? He wondered whether a typist could be hired to do the transcriptions. He figured that he could afford hiring one, perhaps a student to come in twice or three times a week to do it. He felt uncomfortable with Ben picking up all costs.

David began to think about a chronology for his memoirs. He knew that whatever it was going to be, now that the commune and Ben were involved, he'd have to give serious thought to who would wish to read it. Prior to meeting the group, his stroke, and his hospitalization, he didn't care whether anyone would read his 'stuff'. His kids, grandchildren and other family members didn't read it, had a disinterested attitude about anything he'd ever done. No one said it was bad writing, just not interesting to them. But now things were different. He had expectations placed upon him to try to market his writings. He had absolutely no idea how to begin.

He turned on the recorder, erased his experimentation, and began.

"Alaska, the Last Frontier, grabs men and doesn't let go. I know. I still cry myself to sleep wishing that I could have made it work. The 'It' is successfully living in the Bush as a Bush teacher. But I never had the personality to make it work. I didn't fit in with the lifestyle of the Athabascan or the Inuit. As a male it was important to fish, hunt, and construct your own house, repair snow mobiles or four wheelers, something manly. I couldn't do any of it. So when not in the classroom, I was relegated to playing chess with the kids or taking pictures, writing, something not really man's work."

He turned off the machine and rewound it to listen to what he said. It sounded about right, but he still needed someone else to edit it and transcribe it for him. At least he had started and felt energized to continue.

"I don't remember ever reading about Alaska as a child, but in the 11th grade I had an English teacher, a sourdough, the name given to an Alaskan bred and born there. She was raw-boned, freckled, had wild reddish hair, slender and yet sturdy. She'd grown up in Fairbanks and told us about temperatures 70 below zero and lower in the winter. Our blood froze with her tales of the winters in the great northwest.

"Her husband was a territorial representative before statehood in 1959. Of course, I graduated in 1956 when he still represented the territory and had no vote in the Congress. He was one of Franklin Roosevelt's cronies during the war, and was instrumental in seeing the Alaska Highway built to keep the Japanese from invading the mainland of North America, after their incursion onto one of the Aleutian Islands.

"The 11th grade was where I learned about Robert Service, the bard of the Yukon, and feasted on the madness of the men and women of gold rush days. I'll never forget some of those poems."

David pulled out a copy of *The Shooting of Dan McGraw* and began reading into his recorder.

Next he looked for a text of *The Cremation of Sam McGee* and recorded it, also. David Greenberg was so immersed in his recording and flash backs of his days in the great frontier that he didn't hear footsteps behind him.

"David, I've been watching you for about ten minutes. It reminded me of our time at Greentree when you would be so mesmerized by your memories that I feared you had perhaps had another stroke." Gerald patted David's shoulder.

David laughed, "I really want to contribute something special for my first work here at Kelly House. I never thought that I'd have the chance to do it, though. You know what I mean- our lives have a way of playing some weird tricks on us."

David sighed, "I want people to know Alaska as I knew it, but I don't have the vocabulary or skill to paint the picture as beautifully or as vividly as Service did in his poetry, so I thought that I'd borrow some of the richness he produced. Here's one."

The Cremation of Sam McGee
by Robert W. Service

There are strange things done in the midnight sun By the men who moil for gold; The Arctic trails have their secret tales That would make your blood run cold; The Northern Lights have seen queer sights, But the queerest they ever did see Was that night on the marge of Lake Lebarge I cremated Sam McGee. Now Sam McGee was from Tennessee Where the cotton blooms and blows. Why he left his home in the South to roam 'Round the Pole, God only knows.

He was always cold, but the land of gold Seemed to hold him like a spell; Though he'd often say in his homely way That he'd "sooner live in hell". On a Christmas Day we were mushing our way Over the Dawson trail. Talk of your cold! through the parka's fold It stabbed like a driven nail. If our eyes we'd close, then the lashes froze Till sometimes we couldn't see; It wasn't much fun, but the only one To whimper was Sam McGee. And that very night, as we lay packed tight In our robes beneath the snow, And the dogs were fed, and the stars o'erhead Were dancing heel and toe, He turned to me, and "Cap," says he, "I'll cash in this trip, I guess; And if I do, I'm asking that you Won't refuse my last request." Well, he seemed so low that I couldn't say no; Then he says with a sort of moan: "It's the cursed cold, and it's got right hold Till I'm chilled clean through to the bone. Yet 'tain't being dead -- it's my awful dread Of the icy grave that pains; So I want you to swear that, foul or fair, You'll cremate my last remains." A pal's last need is a thing to heed, So I swore I would not fail; And we started on at the streak of dawn; But God! he looked ghastly pale. He crouched on the sleigh, and he raved all day Of his home in Tennessee; And before nightfall a corpse was all T hat was left of Sam McGee. There wasn't a breath in that land of death, And I hurried, horror-driven, With a corpse half hid that I couldn't get rid, Because of a promise given; It was lashed to the sleigh, and it seemed to say: "You may tax your brawn and brains, But you promised true, and it's up to you To cremate those last remains." Now a promise made is a debt unpaid, And the trail has its own stern code. In the days to come, though my lips were dumb, In my heart how I cursed that load. In the long, long night, by the lone firelight, While the huskies, round in a ring, Howled out their woes to the homeless snows -- O God! how I loathed the thing. And every day that quiet clay Seemed to heavy and heavier grow; And on I went, though the dogs were spent And the grub was getting low; The trail was bad, and I felt half mad, But I swore I would not give in; And I'd often sing to the hateful thing, And it hearkened with a grin. Till I came to the marge of Lake Lebarge, And a derelict there lay; It was jammed in the ice, but I saw in a trice It was called the "Alice May". And I looked at it, and I thought a bit, And I looked at my frozen chum; Then "Here," said I, with a sudden cry, "Is my cre-ma-tor-eum." Some planks I tore from the cabin floor, And I lit the boiler fire; Some coal I found that was lying around, And I heaped the fuel higher; The flames just soared, and the furnace roared -- Such a blaze you seldom see; I burrowed a hole in the glowing coal, And I stuffed in Sam McGee. Then I made a hike, for I didn't like To hear him sizzle so; And the heavens scowled, and the huskies howled, And the wind began to blow. It was icy cold, but the hot sweat rolled Down my cheeks, and I don't know why; And the greasy smoke in an inky cloak Went streaking down the sky. I do not know how long in the snow I wrestled with grisly fear; But the stars came out and they danced about Ere again I ventured near; I was sick with dread, but I bravely said: "I'll just take a peep inside. I guess he's cooked, and it's time I looked"; . . . Then the door I opened wide. And there sat Sam, looking cool and calm, In the heart of the furnace roar; And he wore a smile you could see a mile, And he said: "Please close that door. It's fine in here, but I greatly fear You'll let in the cold and storm -- Since I left Plumtree, down in Tennessee, It's the first time I've been warm." There are strange things done in the midnight sun By the men who moil for gold; The Arctic trails have their secret tales That would make your blood run cold; The Northern Lights have seen queer sights, But the queerest they ever did see Was that night on the marge of Lake Lebarge I cremated Sam McGee

David finished reading the poem into his microphone, turned it off, and smiled at Gerald. "I have one more. Do you want to hear it?"

"Maybe later. I am happy to see that you are giving the great Scottish bard his due though. No plagiarism, my friend."

Gerald laughed and said, "Well, I have just returned with Pauline from the Unitarian/Universalist services in Asheville. A most beautiful and inviting service, not to mention the splendid building that houses the congregation. They are a friendly group of people. We felt welcomed."

"Where did you go for lunch, Gerald?"

"We stopped at a café on Merriman Avenue which had a Sunday brunch which was not bad at all and not costly either. So, I am happy that you are feeling the urge to write again. I suppose that you are settling in to the routines enough to allow your creative juices to find voice." Gerald winked at David.

"Gerald, I want desperately to convince my readers- maybe myself -that

I gave it all I had to stay in the Bush and succeed as a teacher. I've told you before that I lived all over the State of Alaska with Indians, Eskimos and just never fit in. I was terribly lonely." David's head drooped and his eyes misted.

"David, do you mind if I change the subject for a moment? I do not mean to cut you off, but I think that we need to discuss something before the next meeting."

David's interest peeked. He encouraged Gerald to go on. "I think that we need to have a process for sharing our writing and commentaries similarly to what we did when we met in group at Greentree. But, since this will not be Jane's therapy group, but more of a writer's collective, we need a different structure. Do you see what I am saying?"

"Yes, I think so. We need structure to produce and to be held accountable for our work. Are you proposing a format where the group members will act as quasi-editors or critics of sorts?"

"Perhaps, David. I suspect that the group will have to decide what it is to look like, but I am quite certain that the time is ripe for us to bring it up this Tuesday, and I thought that we, you and I, might present a format as a way of getting the discussion moving."

"OK. I agree with you. What about two people per week sharing new material of say two or three pages, maybe more? The others could receive advanced copies to look over in their spare time and make recommendations and the like on the work."

"A sterling idea, David. I believe that I once heard of a writers' collective which used a format similar to the one you propose. Of course, if a person has some other form of art to contribute such as painting or sculpture, we might need to find another paradigm for them to involve the group in their output."

Gerald felt satisfied that he had covered the issues he wished to address with the commune members on Tuesday.

"I think that you were speaking of your sadness at not fitting in to Bush living before we began to talk about process. Perhaps you might wish to consider an outline of some sort so that you can follow it as you create your narrative. If your memory is anything like mine, you will need to have some sort of mechanism to use which will keep the memoir moving in a direction and will make sense to you. Did you take any pictures when you lived in Alaska?"

"Yes, lots. I think that I still have thousands of them. I hope I can remember where I put them. Are you suggesting that I might want to embed them within the narrative?"

"Oh, yes, definitely! I think that the old adage 'A picture is worth a thousand words,' applies here." Gerald imagined that some of David's pictures would have major appeal to readers.

"Enough about me, Gerald. What are you planning on working on? Are you still interested in some historical novel about the teachers' union? You spoke about Sinclair Lewis so often."

"You mean Upton Sinclair, David. People often confuse Upton and Sinclair. Sinclair Lewis was a satirist and novelist while Upton Sinclair was a muckraker of the highest caliber."

"Sorry, I got confused."

"I will gather my books, thoughts, quills, and parchment and begin my diatribe against the National Education Association. Perhaps there are still people interested in the ramblings of an old reprobate and rapscallion somewhere."

David laughed so hard that he began to drool and cough. Gerald became alarmed and vowed not to exacerbate David's precarious condition again. But, soon David's state bettered and they were once again at ease in their conversation.

"So, did you get to know Pauline a little better, buddy?"

"What do you mean 'get to know' David?"

"You know, is something up between you two?"

"Something up?"

"Come on Gerald, don't be coy."

"She is a fine and decent woman with whom I find certain similarities to my own condition in life. We have both lost our spouses, have little involvement with our families outside of the commune and share some interests. But, no, dear friend, Nothing is, how did you put it, - *up?*"

"OK, OK, don't be sensitive. I only meant are you two like Ben and Britt, I mean – you know, involved?"

"Gentlemen do not discuss their involvements with the opposite sex, David. I may be from the old school, but I believe that there is room for some traditional code of conduct."

"Wow, OK, OK, Sorry. No more questions, Gerald." Gerald laughed heartily and the brief moment of discomfort faded. They were once again best pals.

Pauline and Lee had a similar conversation. Lee queried Pauline about her outing with Gerald and politely asked whether there was anything she should know about Pauline's feelings for Gerald. Not wanting to intrude upon Pauline's privacy, Lee was vague and quickly left the subject when she felt reluctance on Pauline's part to delve into her feelings. It may have been a male/female subtlety or perhaps the nature of the particular people. Sociologists have an interest in the differences between men and women as well as anthropologists on a global level.

They, too, discussed what they wanted to do to begin their creative work. Lee thought that she might like to write about what it was like to have been raised by two lesbian women back in the middle of the twentieth century. She told Pauline that she never had any feelings about her sexual identity being anything but heterosexual and that she adored the company of men, albeit Sandy, her deceased husband, was the best of the lot.

"I think that I can be very subjective about my situation, and with help I might find books or articles on being raised by homosexual parents. I don't believe that I could hurt anyone. Mom and her lover, Aunt Elizabeth are dead and buried. There are no relatives that I know of, and I've told my children all about Grandma and her complicated life style. Do you think this would be of interest to anyone else, Pauline?"

Lee seemed to want to say more. "She wasn't really my aunt, Pauline. Mom made me call her Aunt or Aunty. Maybe she sensed that neighbors would talk or something like that."

"I do not know what others would find interesting, but I would read it with keen interest. Why not others? What about living with Parkinson's disease? Do you think that you might wish to research that subject and write something about it? I am quite certain that journals or magazines concerned with the elderly and Parkinson's would be interested in your thoughts on the subject."

"True, I never thought about that. What about your interests, Pauline? Are you interested in writing or doing something else with your creativity?"

"Possibly taking some classes at the Reuter Center in fine art appreciation and drawing classes- perhaps sculpture classes if they have them. I ordered a catalog and it came in the mail two days ago. They are truly incredible. I counted over one hundred and fifty courses. History, philosophy, religion, exercise, bridge, science- all subjects. I think that the senior population here is very lucky to have a school for themselves on the University of North Carolina, Lee."

"I'd like to see the catalog, if you don't mind, at your convenience, of course. Now that we have the membership, we ought to take classes and whatever else they have."

"We can look at it together, my dear Lee." A funny thought crossed Pauline's mind, and she broke out laughing.

"What are you laughing at, Pauline?"

"I just had this crazy thought and picture in my mind of our dressing as young co-eds with pig tails and tight sweaters to attract the boys- our boys, of course, and parading around the campus with signs advertising the senior center." Pauline blushed and all the blood ran to her head. They broke out laughing and didn't stop for a full minute.

"We must get hold of ourselves or the others will call the ambulance to take us to a mental ward," said Lee. She'd been in quite a few wards herself and shuddered at the thought while at the same time snickering about the tight sweaters and flirting with Ben, David and Gerald. Then she thought about Stephen and blushed. She was intrigued with his brown, angular face, and pony tail of black shiny hair. His hair was so black and shiny that it was almost purple.

Ben and Britt made ready to go to New York. Britt picked out a flowered see-through night gown. She rarely wore it in Florida, but her body fairly tingled when she ran her hands over the material.

"What a silly child, I am," she giggled.

She'd discussed carrying her oxygen canisters with Ben and he saw no problem in putting two of them in his duffel bag.

On Tuesday night Stephen drove them down to the bus station an hour before departure, and they bought their tickets, using their senior discount. Walter, the station manager, recognized the 'Walrus' and had a warm smile on his face. Walter had to be somewhat careful about the station because, like all Greyhound stations, the homeless, down-and-outers, tramps, hobos, all sorts of men and women liked to hang out there and sometimes caused a ruckus. Of course, usually alcohol or drugs were involved when that happened.

Stephen waited until the bus arrived from Knoxville and bid his employer and new friends good luck and threw in a "God be by your side on your travels."

Ben silently winced, but said nothing to the lad of the Cherokee Nation.

On Wednesday afternoon Pauline held her fifth house meeting in the afternoon. This time was different because for the first time Ben was not there to offer guidance. There were many issues to be dealt with, and she would struggle through the meeting with the help of Gerald as parliamentarian. Hazel and Stephen were there in the roles of employees but with a vote of their own.

Old business was dispensed with quickly. A new and improved system for mail call was put into place and each of the house members now had their own cubby holes much like a post office box without a locked door. Privacy was on the honor system, and it seemed to be working well.

The bathroom situation was brought up without a motion as part of new business. The discussion bore out that this was indeed a difficult problem, particularly at night. It was also pointed out that there was no lavatory in the workroom or on the basement floor at all. For David and Sadie, this could be a problem were they not able to get to the first floor commode on time. This was really knotty, gritty stuff for the group to deal with.

Were Ben present he might have hoped that those who presented the problem also had solutions in mind. In the Marine Corps a rule of thumb was that one didn't present a problem without at least two or three solutions for the commanders to choose one to implement. Ben often wondered whether that system was promulgated because the commanders were too damned lazy to come up with their own solutions or too incompetent. He often thought of the book by Lauren Peter, *The Peter Principle,* which stated that all people are promoted to their level of incompetency. He agreed with Peter, at least in his experience in the Corp.

After much discussion, it was decided to table the issue until the next meeting when Ben would hopefully be present.

The next issue was not as knotty. Gerald motioned that each week the communal members meet for two hours in a writers' group to listen and critique positively material written the week before by two people per week. David seconded.

The discussion went well, and there was general agreement that something to promote the intent of the commune had to be done. Pauline asked about her involvement, and whether people who chose not to write, but to paint or sculpt or do origami for instance. How would they fit into the scheme of a writers' group?

Gerald had not thought about this angle, and asked that the question be divided. He wanted some sort of closure on the writers' portion, and to find another means of bringing people whose art form did not fit into a writers' group into the mind-set of producing.

The group agreed to division and continued the discussion about the main motion. Sadie was concerned that she might not produce enough and not be ready to read. Gerald reminded her that she had the same concern at Greentree and that she would not be punished or chastised for not being ready. She seemed unsure in spite of his answer.

After about a twenty minute discussion, Lee suggested that without Britt to vote it was not fair to her to be bound by a decision in which she had no part. Lee moved that the subject be tabled until the next meeting. Gerald reluctantly saw the wisdom in this, and agreed without debate to tabling his motion.

The meeting ended without a single motion being voted on, but the subjects were out there for thinking about and resolution in the near future. As far as Pauline was concerned, she was somewhat disappointed that her first solo meeting had not produced immediate results, but she also saw the wisdom in waiting.

New York was glorious, and although Ben and Britt were dog-tired from the seventeen hour bus ride with changes in Charlotte, North Carolina, and Washington D.C., they both felt alive and overwhelmingly excited for many reasons. Britt used the mountain of a man as a pillow on the bus and he felt stirrings he'd thought impossible at his age. Youngsters looked with pity upon the old folks and mumbled that they would never get that old. Once in a while a Marine would pass them, and Ben would give a 'Semper-Fi' to the young man which would invariably surprise the strapping young person. Instinctively, the Marine would straighten from his fatigue and snap a 'Semper-Fi' back with a recognition that somewhere beneath this old guy was a fellow leatherneck. It was palpable.

They took a cab from Port Authority to Lexington and the Army, Navy, Air Force and Marine Hotel. A young Puerto Rican woman checked them in, and Britt was politely asked whether she would like to use the rail chair to the second floor. She accepted with grace.

In the room was a queen-sized bed, a small cot, a table, chair, and small closet. The washroom was in the hallway and shared by a few other rooms nearby. Tuckered out and needing a rest, Ben offered the bed to Britt and made ready to lie down on the cot. Britt gently took his rough, gnarled hand, and led him to the bed. She gently pushed him down without a word, and joined him for a rest. His heart rate increased with anticipation, and she sensed that his manhood was being tested.

"Let's just sleep a while and then go get something to eat. Our appointment with my cousin isn't until tomorrow morning so we have the night to ourselves." Ben didn't see the mischievous twinkle in Britt's eye. He was already asleep.

Britt smiled and thought about so many men who'd fallen asleep on her when she was whispering sweet nothings into their ears just like Ben but after far more of a workout than he'd had. "Oh well, this is the price of aging."

"I know this great deli about two or three blocks from here. You up for some grub?" Ben was smiling, feeling so much more rested. He'd eaten in the deli every time he'd been to the hotel.

"Tell you what, you go to the bathroom. I'll change my clothes and then I can go to the head. He stole a quick glance at Britt. She was smiling angelically.

The walk up Lexington was a little taxing for Britt, but she was breathing without a great deal of effort with her two liters of oxygen to help her with the COPD. Two older waitresses greeted Ben, eyed Britt, and seated them toward the rear of the establishment. Pictures of local politicians, a governor or two, and some well-known actors and actresses adorned the walls. Of course, Yankees and Mets ballplayers smiled down at the customers.

"Ben, it's good to see ya again. How long has it been? Who's your lady friend?"

"Nell, you get younger year after year. Must be the great chicken soup here. This is Britt. Britt meet Nell."

The women eyed each other, and nodded comfortably. The menus were handed to each.

"Ben, let's see," Nell cocked her eye, "Matzo ball soup, chicken liver sandwich and blueberry pie. Right?"

"You never forget, old girl!"

"Who you callin' old?" She laughed. Her Bronx accent was unmistakable.

"And you, Britt, What'll it be?

"I would like some of the chicken soup with the half turkey on toasted rye. I like lettuce and tomato on it and maybe some fries. I'll have a diet Pepsi, if you don't mind."

"Your lady friend knows what she wants. Be careful Ben." Nell's lipstick seemed to smear as she said, "Be careful." She was only half joking. Britt caught the innuendo.

They ate heartily and made light banter. Ben had ordered advanced tickets to the Broadway show. *Miss Saigon* would start at 8:10, just in time to take a taxi to the show. As usual, Ben tipped Nell well and she gave him a peck on the cheek in appreciation. Britt was a little miffed, but did not show it. She knew that Ben had a way with women; for that matter, with everyone.

Ben and Britt had sixth row seats in the mezzanine. The seats were a little uncomfortable for Ben, but he managed to use a chair tucked away from the aisle, a chair brought up especially for him by the management. This was Britt's first time to see *Miss Saigon*. She took Ben's hand in hers, and wept as he did when particular arias were sung. She knew Puccini's *Madame Butterfly* and recognized the similarities.

Perhaps it was a mingling of her memories of her own pregnancy, alone, clearly helpless, because her lover had left her without ever knowing that he would be a father. Whatever the reasons, she wept at "Why God, Why?" and "I'd give my life for you," and laughed with Ben when the procurer sang, "The American Dream". The production was flawless and the whirring of the helicopter taking the last Americans out of Saigon poignant.

After the show, Ben took Britt to a nearby watering hole where signed autographed pictures adorned the walls, casts, dignitaries, and locals mingled to discuss the shows, politics of the day, and whatever came up. They each had a glass of Zinfandel white which went to their heads quickly. Another glass and they were mushy and a bit in love.

For both of them similar experiences were always followed by torrid nights of passion- but that was thirty or more years ago. When they finally returned to the military hotel and were in their room, the torrid night resolved in a quick rush to the bathroom and a kiss with as much passion as they could muster before they both fell into a blissful and noisy sleep.

In the morning Ben crept out of bed and looked at his sleeping beauty. He was moved by her gray hair over her face and her smile. Briefly, he reflected upon his fiancée who lay buried upon a hill overlooking Kelly House, and Ben stifled a lump in his throat. Could there be another chance for him?

He went to the bathroom, showered, and dressed for the day. They would see the cousin, take a tour of New York, if time permitted, and be back on the bus for the trip home. He tiptoed into the room and Britt was beginning to stir.

"Good morning, Sunshine." She smiled up at him and took his fingers and kissed them slowly while purring softly.

"Ben, did we, did we, you know- do anything last night?"

"What do you think? I'm a Marine." He had a broad smile and twirled his mustache in a rakish manner.

"Oh God, was it good for you?"

"The best, my love. But you don't remember?" Ben knew that he'd have to level with Britt, but for the moment he was having fun and loving her for allowing him to dream.

"It was a glorious night, wasn't it, my sweet." Britt thought of Celine Dion and her beautiful ballads so totally sensual and full of amorous love. Celine was an old woman now, a widow because she'd married an older man, but her music remained for the centuries. "I know we didn't make love, but I loved whatever we did and for me it was the same."

"Our little secret between us then, my sweet." Ben thought of the writers and knew that there would be questions and gossip. He wanted them to feel that he treated each alike, but perhaps that was impossible.

"Why don't you get showered, dressed, packed. Do you want me to go downstairs and get you some coffee and a roll or something?"

"Coffee with milk and one sugar substitute would be great. If they have any Danish that would be nice too." Britt sat up in bed.

In a burlesque like movement, Ben bowed, pretended to head for the window to jump out, turned, and saluted as he left the room. Britt laughed and nearly choked on her cough. She rose, took the bedroom key, and went to the woman's bathroom to shower and dress. She couldn't remember the last time she'd felt so happy and contented.

Cousin Danny met the two at the New York Public Library. It was a warm, soon to be muggy, and hot Big Apple day. He suggested that they meet downtown rather than take a taxi out to Staten Island where he had a small apartment with his three cats and sixteen homing pigeons which he kept in a loft on the roof.

Small talk about their lives over the last ten years or more, some youthful memories,and a few occasions when Britt had come to New York with her son, and the subject turned to her letters.

Danny reached into a leather briefcase, pulled out a packet tied neatly with a blue ribbon. Britt took them and without opening the packet sat silently, deep in thought. She seemed to be considering whether to open them or not. Ben watched her closely. What was she experiencing? What had she been through?

She opened the packet, took out one of the handwritten pages, and peered at it. They were written to someone, but she couldn't remember who. If it hadn't been for the first words, "Dear Joe," she wouldn't know to whom she wrote.

"Ben, I don't even remember anything about Joe. It's like going back and reading history without a reference point."

She had the originals. She must have sent him copies.

"It'll come back with time, Britt. We'll help you at home."

"I know you will, Ben. What if these letters are dumb, or worse, of no interest to anyone?"

"They're part of who you are, or were. It doesn't matter what others think."

Danny seemed to be a good chap and Ben liked him. They'd been at the library for two hours. Ben looked around and saw that many of the readers appeared to be homeless people reading the newspapers or writing on dirty tablets of lined paper. By their feet were garbage bags full of clothes and their worldly possessions.

Backpacks were checked at the entrance, but the garbage bags were left to the owners to care for them. Some of the patrons wore fine clothes. What juxtaposition to these poor unfortunates. Ben marveled at the fine sculptures and paintings on the walls. The building seemed to be dedicated to the finest minds in history.

Danny insisted that he take the two octogenarians to lunch, and had already picked out the restaurant where he ate whenever he took the ferry into town. He talked about his life. He was in his late sixties, divorced, with a daughter with whom he kept in touch. He worked for the City as a city planner and had a comfortable retirement, but worried about Social Security being solvent when he finally qualified for it. Congress had pushed the minimum age to seventy and Medicare to sixty-seven. He belonged to the Ethical Culture Society which was founded in 1876 by Felix Adler, a rabbi in New York, and attended functions regularly.

Ben queried him about the pigeons. Danny was delighted that anyone asked about them. He spoke glowingly of their superior ability to find their way home from such distances as Albany, Vermont, and other far off places. Ben was amazed that the pigeon owners were organized with their own web pages, associations, meetings, and gatherings. Danny boasted that he'd even had a couple affairs with other pigeon owners that he'd met online. The pigeons were their children and the women spoke of them as their little ones. When they looked at their watches, it was time to go sightseeing before the bus would be leaving. Britt kissed her cousin after promising to stay in touch. Ben allowed Danny to give him a bear hug and returned the hug. It was an emotional departure.

At 7:30 pm, tired, fully fed after their steak dinners at Tad's Restaurant near the Port Authority, the bus pulled out to return the duo to Asheville. It wasn't all they hoped for, but they had never before felt closer to one another.

"OK, so we didn't get it on, but I never had a better time, and it was all because of you, Britt."

"I feel the same, Ben. You showed me a great time, and I will always appreciate it no matter what happens now." Britt was used to men coming and going in her life and old tapes are hard to erase.

Pauline called Ben into the dining room after he returned and had taken a short nap. She told him about the meeting and the two issues which were tabled until he and Britt could return and become involved in problem solving.

"The men, that is David and Gerald, were the most adamant that something had to be done about the use of the bathroom particularly at night," Pauline said as she suspected that it might be more of a critical issue for the men than for the females. She decided to do some research on the internet before the next meeting, and discovered some interesting facts about honey buckets:

"A honey bucket is a bucket that is used in place of a flush toilet in communities that lack a water-borne sewage system. The honey bucket sits under a wooden frame affixed with a toilet lid. The honey bucket gets its name from the actual five gallon buckets which were once used as containers for honey. Honey buckets are common in many rural villages in the state of Alaska, such as those in the Bethel area of the Yukon–Kuskokwim Delta in Alaska, and are found throughout the rural regions of the state. Honey buckets are used especially where permafrost makes the installation of septic systems or outhouses impractical. They were also relatively common in the Yukon, but by now have mostly been replaced with indoor plumbing and sewage pump-out tanks."

This was the old Pauline who loved doing research. She'd helped Max prepare for his speeches throughout the world for so many years. She couldn't begin to count the number of times her tedious and sometimes laborious searching for sources, little known facts, and the like had found their way into the news-papers, journals and papers which Max gave before the scientific community. Her nose twitched. She'd never researched anything on honey buckets before.

Next she turned to the possibility of advanced environmental sanitation used in composting toilets. The Green Movement had made much advancement over the years, and this was another example of their dedication to making the Earth a safe and desirable place to live.

Of course, another possibility to bring to the group was to contact the American Red Cross off Merrimon Avenue and see whether they had any commodes for the disabled, to rent or buy. She discussed the options with Hazel, because someone would have to remove waste and dispose of it correctly. Hazel, although not exactly ecstatic about the duty, felt that her job included cleaning up after the writers. With research and solutions in hand, Pauline sat down with Ben.

"I realize that there is more cost involved, but we have to do something about the problem before it becomes a potential catastrophe."

"So basically, one head is not enough upstairs, and you believe that we need something in the workroom also?"

"Yes, definitely. We have six people upstairs presently, and we desperately need to find a way not to run over each other in a rush to use the facilities."

Pauline blushed because she was not accustomed to speaking about such things, particularly not to a man, but this was a part of her duties as house manager.

"OK, so you've done your homework. What's you recommendation?"

"There's a company called Envirolet which sells waterless remote composting toilet systems. They are part of the Green Movement and the computer information, which I have for you, makes them sound like a company we might wish to investigate. I think that the workshop downstairs might have space for such a contraption, but for upstairs I would be calling the Red Cross or going to one of the medical supply companies near Mission Hospital to see what a portable seat with rails would cost, or if it could be rented. We could put one in David's room and maybe one in Sadie's. Both rooms have the space and a little alcove where it would be unobtrusive and yet handy."

"I like your ideas, Pauline. Before Tuesday, could you telephone a couple of the stores and maybe the Red Cross to see what they've got to help us?"

She agreed and said that she would be happy to drive over and see what's available. The next issue was the need for some more formal means of getting the writing going, and holding the writers to some sort of easy, yet viable schedule. Ben listened and said that he was not as concerned about this issue as the first one.

The rest of the week was a blur of appointments to the various therapies and doctors' offices. Stephen seemed to be perpetually hurrying people not to be late and keep the doctors and occupational/physical therapists waiting. Those who had no appointments were busy at work in the writing room or reading. Walks in the gardens became more frequent. The early birds in the house loved the freshness of the morning mist and dew that cloaked the hillside. On the front porch were three rockers and an outdoor couch which swung back and forth. The front porch at Kelly House was an ideal environment for gathering one's thoughts for the day.

The weekend was restful. Once again Pauline asked Gerald if he would like to go over to the UU Congregation on Edwin. He agreed, and they ate a lunch with new people they met. It was at a pizza/movie restaurant with a buffet. They immediately felt comfortable with the man, a retired librarian, and his wife, an artist involved in basket weaving.

At home, Britt and Ben spent some time together, but both were sensitive to the fact that they didn't want their friendship to appear more than it was. Ben wanted to be sure that everyone felt comfortable with him, and that he wasn't appearing to play favorites. Britt understood and did not wish to take advantage of her special relationship with Ben.

On Tuesday afternoon the group met as scheduled. Again, Stephen and Hazel were an integral part of the proceedings. Pauline asked Gerald to call roll for a quorum, to read the minutes of the previous meeting, and then proceed with old business.

"Do I hear any motions? We tabled two items last week so Ben and Britt could be here. Gerald, would you read the first order of business? "

Gerald responded, "We tabled the issue of the need for more toilets on the second floor and workshop."

All eyes turned to Ben since he had control of the purse stings, and would ultimately be involved in the solution to the problem. He looked to Pauline and she continued.

"We all seem to agree that we have a problem. I have taken the liberty to do some research about how we might solve the issue. I prepared a paper and have made enough copies for all of you."

She passed out a three-page synopsis of her research on the potential solutions, and ended the paper with her opinion as to the best solution.

"Wow, this is great. You are so thorough, Pauline."

"Thank you, Britt. Let's hope that we can dispose of this material quickly."

Gerald laughed at what he thought was a pun. Pauline did not mean it as such, but caught it immediately. After everyone read the paper, Pauline turned to Ben.

"Ben, I think that you need to start the discussion because ultimately it is you who will be concerned with the financial obligations, whatever we do."

"Thanks, Pauline. I'm happy that you did so much homework on this. So that the rest of you know, Pauline and I met last week after Britt and I returned from New York. We talked about this, and of course, decided that no decision would be made by just the two of us. This is your commune, and I knew that problems would arise just like anywhere else where more than one person lives."

"So, Pauline, you are suggesting that a chair-commode be placed in each room upstairs so that essentially no one would have to go outside their room to use the toilet?" asked Ben.

"Yes, it's the most economical and the best way to assure that no one runs into each other at night when they have the urge. David's and Gerald's room has an alcove, and some sort of divider or curtain could be constructed to provide some privacy. Britt and Sadie have the same sort of space in their room and the same could be provided. As for Lee and I, thank God, I do not think that I have to worry about nature's unwanted calling in the middle of the night, but if I do, I can wait until I arrive at the bathroom. Lee, what do you think"

"It hasn't been a problem so far. I've been able to take care of my needs before I retire for the night."

David said, "I like the material about the composting toilets. I was not aware that technology has advanced so far. I used to live in a place where we used a honey bucket just like the article you quoted. You believe that we should think about one for the workroom, if it's feasible. Is that right, Pauline?"

"Yes, David. When I read the article about Alaska and the honey bucket, I thought of you and wondered whether you'd ever had such an experience."

Pauline suddenly had an epiphany. She realized that her English usage was changing as she used more and more contractions. At the boarding schools, the headmistresses would always remind the young ladies that contractions were the lazy way of speaking, and that young women of worthy upbringings did not use contractions except in rare circumstances.

Ben interjected, "Look folks, I think that I'm partially responsible for the problem here. When Maria was negotiating with the architect and the contractors, it never occurred to us that we'd need more bathrooms. No one thought of it. Stupid us! So if you want, we can call in the contractors again, find out what it would take to install another two or more toilets, et cetera. I want everyone to be comfortable and not feel that they have to wait in line, or excuse me, ladies, piss in their pants."

All three of the elderly men had experiences with poor bladder control, finding their pants wet, and cursing their aging. Medicines didn't seem to work very well, and surgical alternatives had less than desirable potential effects.

It was one of the first signs of returning to childhood as far as David was concerned. Every since his stroke, he often found himself damp or even wet and had to wear a diaper like a pair of shorts. The doctors suggested that as he improved he might need the diaper less and hopefully not at all in the future. He waited impatiently for that to happen.

Ben's problem was sometimes forgetting to zip up his fly and the ensuing embarrassment. Another problem was running to the men's room and missing the "wo" in the word "women" and finding himself begging forgiveness for barging in on some poor unsuspecting lady or ladies. It didn't happen often, but when it did, he just knew that someday he'd be arrested for indecent exposure or worse. It was a nightmare. He wondered why he never saw a woman barge into a men's room. Well, actually, when he was a Marine, he remembered getting it on with a Japanese girl in a stall in the men's room. But that was different.

"I like the idea of not having to go out into the hall at night. I have to use my crutches because it takes too long to put on my leg," Sadie said, and looked at Britt for assurance. Britt smiled at her and winked agreement.

The conversation went on for about twenty minutes. Hazel was asked what she thought. Candidly, she admitted that it wouldn't be a favorite part of her work to empty the waste, but she understood the problem and was willing to add this to her duties.

"Wait a minute. Why can't we do it ourselves?" All head shifted in Britt's direction.

"Of course, why not?" Lee responded to Britt's input and smiled at

Hazel. "It's our mess, not yours, to clean up, Hazel. Each room should be responsible for emptying their bed pan, or whatever you call it, washing it out in the tub and replacing it for the next night."

All of the participants except Hazel, Ben, and Stephen, shook their heads in agreement, and Hazel was especially delighted with the turn of events.

"Let's vote." David was ready to move on.

Pauline smiled and said, "All those in favor of this proposal say aye or raise your hand." Everyone raised their hand and the issue was settled. She continued, "I will purchase four of the units tomorrow, and if all goes well, they'll be in our rooms by tomorrow night."

She looked to Ben, who beamed. He would not have to spend a fortune for another bathroom, but more because the decision was made by consensus.

"I like the idea of helping the environment. Pauline. Why don't you call in Envirolet, and see what they recommend for the workshop area?"

She shook her head in agreement and continued, "Next business item tabled last week was some sort of means by which we can assure that we will write and try to fulfill our agreement with Ben. Do I hear a motion?"

"Yes, I move that we start a writers' group which will meet every Thursday morning at 10:00. Each week two members will present three to four pages of their work for critique and evaluation by the other members."

"Is there a second to David's motion?"

"I second it," Lee said.

"Discussion?"

"When we were at Greentree," David offered, "we had an informal presentation but for very different reasons. Now we must discipline ourselves so that we can produce our works. I would volunteer to be the first to read three or four pages of my new memoir, I mean play the beginning which I have dictated onto cassette tape to the group tomorrow if this is voted for."

Britt stated, "I have my letters now, and I want to get started, too. Strangely, David and I will be writing about Alaska at the same time. It'll be interesting to compare and contrast our experiences. Oh, I might not do a full three pages, but I volunteer to read second if we vote for this motion."

PART III

CREATIONS

CHAPTER FOURTEEN

Dav^id pulled out the manuscript from which he would read at the group's meeting later that week. He hired a student from the local college to transcribe from his tape recording about his days in Alaska. He turned on the tape recorder to compare it with the typewritten manuscript.

"Hitchhiking into Alaska from Canada over the mountain pass called 'Top of the World' just out of Dawson City was where it began. It was a late June day, and I had been trying for three or four hours to get some RV family to give me a lift into Tok on the Alaska Highway.

"The sun didn't set at that time of the year, and even though it was late June the temperatures were in the thirties when I finally managed to get a ride from a nice, elderly couple from Michigan in their gigantic motor home. Gas prices were high in the Yukon and Alaska, but nothing compared to what they are today.

"Going over the 'Top of the World' was more spectacular than anything I'd ever done before. The road was made of gravel, potholed, dangerous and almost a treacherous foot path. Looking on either side of the rocky pass one could look down thousands of feet on each side. One avalanche, one head-on and it would have been the end of the road for anyone caught trying to make it over.

About two or three in the morning, the sun still shining, we limped into Tetlin Junction, just twelve miles from Tok and a Greyhound bus which would take me to Anchorage. I thanked the couple profusely for taking a chance on a hitchhiker. I guess they were relieved that all had gone well."

David turned off the machine and sat thinking. Balding, with a crown of gray hair, light brown eyes obscured by trifocals glasses, David was about five feet, eight inches with shoes on. At one time, he'd been muscular and a sprinter in high school. Not concealing a paunch well, he still had a worthy physique for a seventy-nine year old, slightly stooped stroke victim with a right-sided weakness and fine motor skill disability.

He was lucky that he'd been found by the paramedics. They'd administered clot-busting drugs in the ambulance on the way to North Broward Hospital. The young men did a good job, but his frame of mind was shot. He felt that everything was over, that he could no longer travel, dance, and wander the streets of Pompano Beach as before. He worried about a weak relationship with his children and grandchildren, felt unwanted, and had no one to turn to for sympathy. That is, until now.

He turned on the machine again. "I was terrified, standing on this desolate highway called the ALCAN for Alaska/Canadian joint ownership. I had no idea then that I would drive the monster road seven times and in all seasons. Here I was at two or three in the morning. I could have read a newspaper without a flashlight. No one, no traffic, nothing. I think I stood on the road for about a half hour hoping to flag down a car going to Tok. But no one came along. The old couple had pulled their RV up to a closed gas station and fallen fast asleep. They needed the sleep after that extremely dangerous road.

So, there I was with my full-sized green backpack full of clothes, reading materials, a flashlight, radio, and toiletries. It probably weighed about thirty pounds. Not wanting to miss the bus to Anchorage, I decided to walk the twelve miles to Tok Junction where the Glenallen Highway intersects with the ALCAN. Go straight and you get to Fairbanks, go left- Anchorage. It's about three hundred miles to Anchorage through mountain passes, valleys and over rivers.

I didn't know any of this, then. All I knew was that I was going to try to hike the twelve miles. I began trudging along the side of the road.

Trees, millions of them, streams with tiny bridges, and always my brain playing tricks on me. I imagined that I heard bears, moose or elk on the other side of the trees and that surely I would be confronted and eaten by a bear. The noise seemed to get louder and then die out to the sound of water meandering through the frozen permafrost.

Still no cars, no one, and by the time I did see someone, I had walked six miles, and was determined to finish the hike without being picked up by anyone. I was on a mission! I sang, screamed, yelled, made maddening sounds, farted – anything to ward off the sudden confrontation that I knew would be my fate were I to stop the crazy behavior. I read somewhere that one should let bears know you're near. They would have had to be deaf not to hear me.

Six miles into my walk, my left leg began to ache and throb. Each time my ankle twisted on a piece of rock, or the muscles cramped, only made it more difficult to continue. It was like my personal odyssey. Around eight-thirty or nine in the morning, I finally reached Tok and an open restaurant. By that time I was limping visibly, and my leg was crying for some sort of medication. I took two aspirins, ate breakfast, and found a big chair to wait for the bus. Peaceful sleep overtook me.

One thing that I forgot to mention was that when I crossed into Alaska from the Yukon Territory in Canada, I fell upon my knees, kissed the ground like I'd seen so many veterans do upon their return to the United States from Viet Nam or other countries during the Cold War. I don't know what came over me, but whatever it was, it was powerful. On this lonely outpost, with one agent dressed in semi-winter gear and sitting in a shack, I had the most memorable, stupendous sense that I had come home. The kids call it getting high on life, I think."

David stopped the recorder and checked to see how much more tape he had. With more tape, he'd be able to say more. He wondered whether anyone would like what he'd recorded or even find it interesting. His student assistant would finish the transcription.

Pauline offered, "David, look, I am not writing as the rest of you are doing, or are going to do. I would be pleased indeed if I could do some of the things that Adrian did for you. For instance, if you allow me to listen to the tapes, I could easily transcribe onto Microsoft and print out copies for everyone to read. You don't really need a student. I'd be honored to do this work for you."

"Thanks Pauline. When the student isn't available, I'll call on you for help."

When she returned David gave her his recorder and tapes and promised to buy a transcription machine for the next time. Pauline listened to three or four sentences, flipped the machine off, and transcribed what she heard. It took about an hour to finish, and then she made enough copies for all the writers.

While the two worked on David's material, Britt began to organize her letters, and to decide how to begin her contribution. Everything had taken place so long ago when she was in her late thirties. She sat at a desk in the workroom which gave her a window with a view of the hill where Ben's fiancée rested in peace.

Britt reflected upon that time of her life when she'd gone to Alaska to find a teaching job and take pictures of a Bush village and the people living there. She had had hopes of a documentary, maybe with National Geographic or one of the many Alaskan magazines which tried to attract tourists to the rough life of village living.

Back then there were no digital cameras, no state of the art instant photography, allowing one to see exactly what was captured instantly. Everything was film and multiple lenses with heavy camera bodies. Britt remembered her Canon AE-1 or was it 2. She couldn't remember. Once she'd owned a German-made Leica and even a Roloflex. She'd majored in Photography and Anthropology, and saw herself as working for National Geographic or Smithsonian Magazine. A few tears rolled down her cheeks as she thought of missed opportunities and broken dreams.

She started to type on the Toshiba laptop. "It's so fuzzy, but as I look back at my professional life, I dimly remember that I found my way to Alaska after receiving my Master's Degree in Anthropology. I was going to be a Bush teacher. I took the Alaska Marine ferry up from Seattle to Juneau.

On the ferry, I slept in a tent on the fantail of the ship and ate cheaply.

I had almost no money, no credit cards, nothing. It seemed that the boat was crowded with young hippies going to spend the summer working in the fishing industry in one capacity or another. Some of them brought sluice boxes and pans with the hopes of striking it rich in streams along the Bering Sea. I was old enough to be their mom, but we all had our dreams. I guess we weren't much different than the pioneers who'd come with horses and mules. A few years later, that's all.

Juneau's the state capital and the only way to get there is by air or sea. No roads connect it to anywhere else. In town, every building seems stacked upon one another because the mountains surround everything, and there isn't much space available except outside the town. The Board of Education was in one of those stacked buildings next to the capital and the State Court House. The governor's mansion is the highest building perched high up on the mountain. I've been there in the winter when all the Christmas lights were on at the governor's mansion. Pitch black outside with the mansion silhouetted in Christmas lights. Just beautiful.

The only certification I could get was for Social Studies because Anthropology was considered a subject in that area. Problem was that so many Bush teachers had degrees in history, geography, and economics. The school systems needed science and math teachers, and if someone was a special education teacher back then, the human resource directors drooled over you. I'll bet that's still the way it is in Alaska.

My photography degree didn't help much. Some of the districts were interested, but only if I had something else that they could use. I didn't.

When I finally got to Fairbanks, it was July 1st and a course was being offered for graduate credit. I think it was called something like 'The Bush Experience'. The guy who ran the course was a Bush teacher, had a PhD, and hired other Bush teachers, Natives, guest speakers, and people familiar with Native ways, philosophy and psychology. There were about forty of us in the course, and we were allowed to live in the dormitories since the University of Alaska was on summer break. We ate at the school cafeteria, and it was the first time in a long time that I'd eaten three nutritious meals a day.

I met two or three guys there, and of course they all wanted to go to bed with me. That's about all I had to offer then. I picked one, and we spent the entire summer making love, sometimes three or four times a day. He had a car, I remember that. We went all over Fairbanks, and I took pictures everywhere. There was a street near the river which had pawn shops, a drugstore, lots of run down bars and loads of drunken Indians roaming around the streets. I saw a lot of fights at night. It was easy to see because it never got dark the whole time we were there.

I used to go to the Quakers' meeting house when I was in California. Joe and I found a couple who were Quakers. They were really nice to us, and invited us to their house a lot. She was an expert on some sort of sea life, and he was a computer geek. The biggest thing I remember about them was that they lived in a geodesic dome and grew lots of marijuana plants. He smoked a lot of his product. I did too, but Joe didn't get high. It made me more amorous when we got back to the dorms.

They were a strange couple. Both were in their forties, childless, and I don't think that I ever met a woman who was so homely. He was no Adonis either. A few years later, after twenty or more years of marriage, she became pregnant with a daughter. She must have been the most beautiful child I ever saw, and grew into a beauty. It was the ugly duckling in reverse. The child was a gift from God.

The birth of Darlene, I think that's what they called her, changed their lives. They gave up marijuana, partying, and the easy-go-lucky life they had before her birth. None of us who remained in Alaska were invited to their home, and they moved out of the forest into a suburban house. What a change!

Years later I happened to be back in Fairbanks, and ran into the mom and her daughter. I think Darlene was fifteen or sixteen. She was a raving beauty. I could not take my eyes off her. Her blond hair was twisted into a beautiful ponytail, and her body was what most of us girls would die for. I could see the pride in her mom's eyes. We only talked for a few minutes. She was being home schooled by Alice, her mother. George was working in a computer company, and had been there for several years. Mom's protective eye watched everything, and she obviously felt uncomfortable talking to me on the street. So we said our goodbyes, and promised to talk again. We never did."

Britt reread her memoir and made changes. She thought about Darlene and wondered whether she'd married and had children. Britt figured that she'd be about thirty-five or older by now. That would mean her parents would be in their seventies or early eighties. She mused, "Life is strange. Who would ever have guessed that George and Alice would ever have borne such a lovely and sensuous daughter?"

Britt started to type again. "Joe had a friend from Trenton, or some place in New Jersey, who'd taught science and math in the inner city. He was in our class, and wanted to go to the Bush to teach. Fascinating guy, really. He'd taught chess to the kids in his school, and took them to the elementary school chess tournament in Chicago. They won or were close to the top. Joe used to say that the guy wasn't much of a chess player himself, but had a knack for teaching kids to play and win.

Anyway, at the end of the course, this guy, I think his name was Josh, got a job in the Lower Kuskokwim School District teaching science. He had all these green plants he wanted to take. He opened a suitcase, pulled his plants out of the dirt, stuck them in the suitcase with his underwear, and we drove him to Anchorage to catch a plane to Bethel. Strange guy, quiet, introspective, self-contained. He was already beginning to bald, and he was only in his late twenties. Joe got a call from Josh thanking him for driving him all the way to Anchorage. I remember that Joe asked him about the plants. They were fine and took well to village life.

Joe and I were moving toward saying our goodbyes. He needed to go home, and teach in his school district somewhere out East. He promised to come back, and I believed him. He was so in love with Alaska.

For me, the fun and games continued. There were other men and women who hadn't been hired yet, and the summer was coming to an end. We were all despondent and felt unworthy. You could always tell, though, when someone connected with a job. We had parties, drinking, and a lot of hugging. But most of it was wait, wait, wait. I tried to forget Joe and our nights of passion, and concentrate on getting a teaching job, but fewer and fewer human resources people came in. It was their summer,too, and they had families to visit and vacations to complete.

One day I was at the school cafeteria with about three other teachers, just hanging out. The place was empty except for us and a couple of grad students. The cashier came over and told me that a man was calling me from the job center up at the dorm. I ran over to the phone with my heart in my throat."

Britt stopped typing and tried to recollect the events as they unfolded. David and Pauline were finishing their work, getting ready for tomorrow's meeting.

"Are you doing well, Britt?"

"Why do you ask, Pauline?"

"You seem so lost in thought, my dear."

"I was just trying to remember. It's so hard sometimes. I guess I'm getting old or senile."

David smiled, and wagged his head up and down in agreement, "I know what you mean, Britt. I have the same problem. I don't know if it's so important that all the facts be exactly accurate. I mean who's going to hire an investigator to check our facts?"

He laughed, and the women joined in the laughter.

Thursday's meeting was the first formal gathering of all the writers. Ben and the staff decided to go about their business, and did not join the group.

David and Gerald brought in their coffee mugs filled to the brim with a Kenyan medium strength brewed in a large coffee maker. The women preferred tea, and had mugs of green and black tea. Only Sadie drank diet Pepsi and had crackers.

"I think we ought to remember today, and say a few words of appreciation to Ted Kelly for giving his name to our enterprise, so here is to Ted, our brother."

Gerald spoke so eloquently and added, "Let us also say a few words in silence, if you like, to our benefactor, Ben."

"All of the great artists, writers, sculptors, playwrights, and men and women of letters had patrons in the golden age of the Renaissance and during the Enlightenment," Pauline spoke quietly, and everyone bent forward a little to hear her.

"Well then, I believe that David is the first to share his work with us. Or is it you, Britt?" Gerald asked.

"No, no, it's David."

"OK, you've all read the start of the memoir. I'm open for any criticism anyone would like to offer, only please don't use a sledgehammer." David appeared anxious.

Pauline was the first to speak, "I am intrigued with your travels, the use of the poetry by Service, and the general way that the writing moves along the path to somewhere. But, I'm not sure where."

David's face reddened, and he felt the need to defend his ego.

Pauline continued, "Before you speak, David, may I suggest that the writers listen, take notes, whatever. When all the writers have spoken, then the person being critiqued could make any comments he or she wants. Does that sound fair, and will it be useful?"

Pauline had obviously been thinking of the format that could be followed.

"I agree with Pauline. We can all take what we deem useful from the group, and discard that which is not going to work for us," said Gerald, from his experience in writers' groups before Greentree and coming to Kelly House.

David felt slightly offended, but licked his wounds and listened.

"Well, I like it just the way it is. I loved his poems, and the description of his teacher, and his hike along the road to Tok."

Sadie smiled, and was again the peace-maker. It made David feel better.

"Perhaps, were David to be a little more descriptive, and get to the reasons why he felt that he didn't succeed in the Bush living, perhaps some examples in the villages. I find myself anticipating, looking for movement, too," Lee commented and struggled with her words a bit. She thought that the Parkinson's might be responsible.

After about forty-five minutes of discussion, it seemed that everything was said that needed to be said, and all heads turned to David.

"This was my first draft, and I thank you all for your comments. I am sorry that I became defensive. That won't happen again. I'm going to re-read it and try to incorporate some of your comments. I think that I will move the narrative along, and get to the actual stories which made me sure that I was not doing well in the villages."

"Britt, we've read your pages, and we're ready to talk about them. Is it OK with you to listen until we're finished, and then jump in?" asked David.

"OK, I'm ready. David, it's your turn to knock me down a peg or two." Everyone laughed, including David, and the ice was broken.

Lee was the first to speak, "Britt's story is so compelling. I feel like I was there with her, suffering."

The others seemed to be in agreement, and were temporarily at a loss for words.

"What a life she's led! I can't get over her sense of feeling so vulnerable," said Pauline, but inwardly she felt so very torn by the notion of selling one's body for the use of a car and a man's money. Yet, she did not look down upon Britt.

Pauline continued, "I think that she might wish to be more specific about the characters she talks about. I was a little confused by all the names. Let's see there was a Joe, Josh, and some others. I found myself having to go back to be sure who she was talking about."

"True, Pauline. I had the same problem, but like you, I found the characters compelling and fascinating. One thing I would like to see is more description of the people who were drunk on the streets. She missed some opportunities to be colorful and expressive. Just a thought," Gerald seemed to be reaching for some way to show support and give gentle criticism at the same time.

"I never had a life like Britt's. I could never have been so brave. Going all by herself all the way to the ends of the Earth." Sadie shook her head in amazement. "My husband, may he rest in peace, would never have allowed me to do that in a million years." Britt moaned after hearing that.

"What about her characters and her torrid sexual affair, Sadie?" David was playing with Sadie, and he knew it.

Sadie blushed at the mention of the word, **sex**. "I don't know about that part, but I loved Darlene, and the description of her parents. I want to know more."

"That's what it's all about, Sadie. If someone wants to read on, the book, the memoir, whatever, it is a success. That's what I think, anyway."

Britt listened to David. She'd kept her peace, listening and absorbing what was being said.

"Thank you all for your remarks. I agree with everything said, and I'll go into description of the nights in Fairbanks, and all the fights and mayhem. And I'll make sure that the reader knows who I'm talking about, too. These are important and worthwhile issues for me."

"So who feels that they'll be ready for next week?" queried Pauline.

Gerald and Sadie agreed to bring two or three pages of their material to the meeting. The meeting adjourned although no one was in a hurry to leave. Hazel appeared with a full coffee pot, tea, and sugar-free cookies. Everyone was pleased to enjoy a moment of socializing about nothing in particular.

CHAPTER FIFTEEN

Sadie went into the kitchen. "Oh boy, Hazel I'm on the hot seat!"
"What do you mean 'hot seat', Sadie?"

"I've got to present something next Thursday. I guess I better get busy finding out more about Messianic Judaism, and what my son is doing."

"It must be difficult for you, my dear. I mean you love your children, of course, but some things may be more valuable than love alone."

"I love my kids, but not their ideas. I want to be gentle and yet truthful. Can that be done, Hazel?"

"I think so. Baha'u'llah stressed searching for our own truth and that's what you seem to be doing. He also stressed kindness and gentleness."

"I guess I have a lot of studying to do before I begin to write."

Hazel smiled at Sadie and said, "Sadie, if you ever want to come to the Baha'i Center, let me know. You might find it interesting, and you'd meet some very beautiful people."

Sadie didn't answer, but mumbled a thank you as she was moving toward the rail elevator to go to the workroom.

The first thing she did was to find her writing that she'd done at the rehabilitation center and look it over. In it she discovered that she'd been pretty thorough in discussing her family, her lies to Morris about her involvement in her son's religious movement. She shook her head in disbelief, still finding it difficult to believe that she'd actually joined the 'movement' without telling Morris. "What I did was wrong, but he's my son and a mother's duty is to her children, or is it to her husband first?" Sadie spoke aloud to no one in particular.

She wasn't as familiar with the computer having worked for the government as a typist in a typing pool years ago. In the past, she had a Royal or Underwood with a ribbon and whiteout if she needed it. David and Gerald looked over her shoulder back at Greentree, and taught her some of the tricks of the Microsoft program, so Sadie didn't feel quite as intimidated by the new technology.

She began to type. "It's all so confusing to me. When I was a child growing up with my brothers and sisters, we lived in a Jewish neighborhood, ate kosher foods, celebrated Rosh Hashanah, Yom Kippur, Shavuot, Hanukah and always lit the candles on the Shabbat. Our world was the same world that our parents had in the old country. We walked to Shule, prayed before each meal, and talked to God. Sometimes he was happy with us, and sometimes so angry that he did terrible things to teach us to be good. Each house had a mezuzah on the door-post. We knew who we were.

Some families were Conservative Jews. Sometimes my father would say they weren't Jews at all because they didn't follow the Torah exactly. Of course, back then I didn't know any Reform Jews. I didn't even know there was such a thing as a Reform Jew. He wouldn't have thought they were Jews at all.

My parents were from Russia or Poland. I could never be sure where because the boundaries changed so often. The only thing I knew for sure was that wherever they came from, they were hated- just because they were Jews."

Sadie stopped typing and sat quietly for a minute. "Why was that? Why did everyone hate us?" She realized that question was asked by so many people without a good answer. She returned to the keyboard.

"Dad peddled anything he could buy cheaply and Mom took in boarders. That's how we lived, but we didn't know that we were poor because everyone for a three or four block radius was in the same boat. I remember that we weren't really the most Orthodox Jews. There were some who wore religious clothes all the time, lived like the Torah told them to.

They probably despised us, just like Dad did the Conservative Jews. It was one big hierarchy of who could be more Jewish. It was so confusing.

We had our share of tragedy too, just like everyone else. My sister, may she rest in peace, had mental problems and was always being sent off to a sanitarium or hospital for horrible shock treatment. The family loved her so much and tried to keep her condition a secret from the outside world, but everyone knew. Sometimes she would take her clothes off and run outside screaming bad words. I couldn't bring my friends into the house for fear that Jennie would attack them or cuss at them. I don't know where she learned those words. She never heard them at home."

Sadie sat and thought about her sister. Jennie always had a home with her and Morris, may he rest in peace. He was always kind to her and provided her a room in the house. She began to type again.

"Finally we had to take her to a place in Washington D.C. St. Elizabeth's, I guess she was the saint for mentally ill people, had some of the best psychiatrists in the country at the time. They diagnosed Jennie with schizophrenia. As new medicines became available, they gave them to her. They helped a lot. But she was always like a zombie. Thank God, they finally stopped that horrible shock therapy.

When she got older Jennie never left the house except to go to appointments. We had to remind her to bathe, to keep herself clean, and when she became a woman, I had to make sure she did the sanitary things expected of a young woman. Once in a while we'd take her to socials at the hospital or day center, but we were always afraid that she'd do something with a boy, a mentally ill boy like herself. I don't think she ever did, but that was what we were afraid of, anyway.

During the war, my brother, Kenny, was a navigator and was lost over France in a bombing raid. That nearly killed Dad. He sat Shiva, but that didn't help much. He was never quite the same. My parents wanted the boys to go to college, and Kenny was the only one who did, but then he died. War makes for so much grief. My heart goes out to all mothers and fathers who lose their children, even America's enemies."

Sadie stopped typing again and began to cry. So many years ago, but thinking about it made it seem like yesterday. The years had been kind to Sadie. Her round, pink face, ample bosom, blond curly hair which surrounded her small dainty ears, and round innocent blue/gray eyes made her a comely woman even at her age of seventy-nine. Weight from overeating and eating the wrong foods placed folds in her skin where they should not be, but except for her nagging and debilitating insidious disease, diabetes, she was basically in good health. For some men, she would be termed a 'softig', desirable woman, and Morris loved her mightily. In old Europe, her double chin would have made others assume that she was prosperous. That wasn't true anymore, but that's the way it was back then.

Here in America, the culture was different and she joined the vast majority of overweight, over-indulgent women who were constantly being barraged by television advertising to lose weight, to become more appealing to men by being slim and trim. Morris, may he rest in peace, called all those women twiggy as he caressed his Sadie. She smiled when she thought of his grabbing her back side and blushed at her love of his hands. She returned to the computer.

"Before the war my parents decided to go to Atlantic City, and buy a big house about three blocks from the Atlantic Ocean. It wasn't too far from the Steel Pier, or maybe the Million Dollar Pier. They opened a boarding house and people from all over the East Coast would come for a week or two to get away from the heat and humidity. Atlantic City was hot too, but the breeze from the ocean made it bearable. I remember all sorts of people would come with their children and we'd go to the beach and bake. No one knew that the sun would be so dangerous.

I used to get so sunburned because I am so light skinned. It must come from my Russian or Polish roots. I'd burn and suffer for two weeks, but finally after a lot of calamine lotion, I'd tan a little. When I was in my thirties, I was diagnosed with skin cancer and had a few removed from my head and nose. We just didn't know how serious the sun could be. I always envied Sephardic Jewish people because they were so dark-skinned and tanned so easily. We Ashkenazim Jews were from Europe and couldn't get a tan for anything. I knew a few people who actually got sun poisoning from staying on the beach too long. The kids, they're the ones who suffered the most. Now, thank God, they have all those skin protection ointments for protection. There wouldn't be so much skin cancer if we had had it back then."

Sadie stopped typing, and looked at her arms, and felt her face for bumps and scars from her minor surgery. She felt the indention on the skin on her nose, and remembered how painful it was when the dermatologist took off the basal cell cancer on the tip of the nose. The shots to numb the pain of cutting were so painful that she vowed that she'd never let anyone cut on her nose again, no matter what. The dent reminded her of the small pox inoculation on her arm. She returned to the computer.

"I met Morris in Washington D.C. He was an electrician with the Merchant Marines, and before the war he'd go on those ships carrying stuff to England, France, and Russia. It was called Lend Lease. I was so young when we met at the Jewish Community Center on 16th Street and Q. The building looked like a Greek temple, or something like that.

They had dances on the roof when it didn't rain, and that lasted for a lot of years. So many romances were started there between soldiers, sailors, and the young Jewish girls who migrated to Washington to work for the various government agencies. We came from everywhere, not just Rochester where I was born. I remember that I became friends with a woman from Chicago who was a typist for an agency which supplied synthetic rubber to the Army and Navy.

We went to the dances together to meet Jewish boys who our parents would approve of for marriage. She fell for a great dancer with curly brown hair, Yankle, but they called him Jamie or Jimmy, I can't remember which. He'd been in the Conservation Corps and his muscles were hard as a rock from cutting down trees somewhere out west. Morris, my husband-to-be, loved Yankle and his stories about the lumber camps, his life in Philadelphia growing up the son of a store keeper in a *goyisha* neighborhood. They were young and oh-so-good-looking.

I married Morris after two months of dancing and romancing."

Sadie laughed out loud when she reread 'dancing and romancing.' She began to type again.

"Morris came from Poland and was a village Jew, but he escaped the poverty and the Nazis with a friend or two. His whole family was wiped out except for a brother, Aaron, who went to Israel. Back then it was called Palestine. He died in the War for Independence in 1948, and Morris got a medal from the new Israeli government. It stayed on our mantle wherever we lived, and I buried it with him when he died.

Sadie wept silently for Aaron as she typed. She never met him, but he lived with them in spirit, and Morris always said *Kaddish* on the day he was reported to have been killed.

I became pregnant within two years with my son, and my friend, Edie, from Chicago, married Yankle, and they were pregnant with a son, too. We did everything together. The boys went to the Jewish Community Center, played basketball and poker while the girls took care of the home, worked, and nursed our kids. Funny thing was that even our parents became friends.

My mother loved Edie's mother, Gertrude, who lived with Edie and Yankle. She and her husband, may he rest in peace, moved in with them until he died just after their baby was born. They came down to Atlantic City for a couple of weeks in the summer, and helped each other when their husbands, my dad and Edie's Dad died. That was the way it was for years until my mom and Edie's mom died. Morris and Yankle always flirted with the girls at the "J". Edie and I knew it, but we were so in love we ignored a lot back then." Sadie turned off the computer and figured she had written enough for her presentation next Thursday. There was a lot more to write, but in three pages she couldn't fit everything in. And then she remembered something that stirred and aroused her. Morris told her that at the Jewish Community Center men swam in the nude. It was something about the Jews in the time of the Greek civilization and men swimming in the nude. What did Morris tell her? Oh yes, the Greeks idolized the male figure, and the Jews went along with it. Women wore bathing suits, though. Women and men, separately, used the pool at different times.

While Sadie was doing her writing, Gerald was at work deciding how he was going to present his research on Upton Sinclair's condemnation of the National Education Association back in the 1920's. Years ago while browsing through a collector's bookstore he came across two of the muckraker's books, *The Goslings* written in 1923 and *The Goose-Step* written in 1924. For a long time Gerald and Claire, his beloved wife, had chafed under the Association's sorry record as a union.

He believed that the National Education Association's leadership was much too cozy with school superintendents and boards of education. The NEA seemed to have a need to allow the paternalism which traditionally surrounded school systems to continue its grip, particularly in the South, with the horrendous Right to Work laws. Gerald began to write.

"Our county schools were considered the best in our state, and ranked high at one time, nationally. We looked good from the outside, but our teachers had to find additional work at night and during the summers to exist, or they had to live outside of the county to make ends meet. The Association spent more time talking about the needs of the students than the needs of the members. School principals were members of the same association. It was a terrible conflict of interest. The principals could hire and fire while the Association did precious little to support the teachers.

Strikes were unheard of, and any consideration of an action against the system would be automatically compromised because the principals intervened, and demanded that the teachers cease and desist. I remember a year that the pay raise offered was so minimal that teachers would not receive any new benefits for the first year and a half, and only one percent for the second and third year.

So, some of us who were angered and frustrated by the offer wished to work to the rule. All that meant was that we would ask teachers to leave their school buildings when they were finished teaching. We did not call for strike action, nor did we ask teachers to slough off in their duties with the students. It was harmless, and yet a message to the Board that all the extras that teachers did would not be done unless we were treated fairly. The principals balked and reported the 'trouble makers' to the personnel department. Our action was a disaster, and many of us were harassed for years after.

But, it was the beginning of the end for having administrators in our Association. Burt Stephens was a teacher who had come from New York City, and had been a member of the American Federation of Teachers.

He called me and about six or seven of the people who received letters of reprimand, and suggested we meet in his home for informal discussion of what had just transpired.

Ten of us braved a wintery, snowy night and joined Burt and his wife for the first discussions about our plight. We quickly established our purpose which was to find a way to separate from the administration. One of the participants was a member of the Industrial Workers of the World, a Wobbly. I thought that they had disbanded after World War I, but I was wrong.

He was a special education teacher at a school for severely disturbed children and a bit of a hot-head. His stance was that there was absolutely nothing in common between the employer and the employed. I think that Claire was somewhat intimidated by his radical views, although she liked him.

Two or three of the group were people who had worked tirelessly in the anti- war effort during the Vietnam War. They had some training in San Francisco in some Communist offshoot group and stressed discipline in every move we made. Manfred and our Wobbly clashed on just about everything except the need to rid the Association of the administrators. We often found ourselves mediating between the two of them over substantial differences of tactics as well as strategy."

Gerald stopped typing and reread what he'd just written. He remembered how Manfred became so frustrated with Nick, the WOB, and accused him of obstructionism, radicalism and every other anarchist, screwy idea he could think of. Nick, for his part, accused Manfred of being a Marxist, dictator, and inflexible. There was probably truth on both sides. But, we loved those men and their zeal.

Gerald began to type again. "The Association elected a president who was mild-mannered and highly respected by the Administration and teachers alike. He was a lay minister and on the surface a pacifist. But, we learned that he was not happy with the attempts of the principals and, through them, the superintendent to manipulate him and sabotage his presidency.

Three or four months after we started the group, we received a message that he wanted to meet with us in private at his home. He suggested that some of our little insurrectionist faction come over for a chat. It was the beginning of the end for the administrators running the local association. There were teachers who shivered with fear, particularly women of the old school who depended on the platitudes of the principals. I would imagine that some of that attitude still prevails especially among elementary school spinster women who get some psychological needs met by the good will of their father and mother-like principals. Paternalism was ripe back then. It probably still is.

A year later after emotional and hair-pulling rhetoric on both sides, it was put to a vote, and the administrators were told to leave the local Association. They did with anger and spitefulness, but eventually they started their own bargaining unit, and elected one of their own as the first president. There are probably no principals left from those days. They are all retired or deceased, but for all the years I was in the local National Education Association, many of them shunned me and the others, and held a lasting grudge. If the truth be known, many of the teachers hated us as well."

Gerald thought about what he'd just written and the battles with the Board of Education and with other members of the bargaining unit over priorities. Claire and he served many terms on the Board of Directors and fought unsuccessfully for the State to pass the same articles to their charter. But the State presidents and the smaller counties would not hear of their principals and other administrators being asked to leave the bargaining units in their counties. Even in the national conventions while Gerald was still a teacher, unionism was tantamount to vileness. Only in the waning years of his career had the NEA joined forces with the American Federation of Teachers. Gerald assumed this was a move for financial gain, and wondered who had given up the most to join with the other.

This was the reason that Gerald wanted to write an essay on the work of the great writer and socialist, Upton Sinclair. Back in the 1920's, Upton had seen the NEA for what it was, a tool of the textbook industry and government corruption. Gerald did his research and determined to be as scholarly as he could in copying Sinclair's words, and also the words of some who disagreed with him. He began to type again.

"*The Goslings,* long before I was alive and involved, portrays the horrors of the school systems throughout the United States and tells a tale of betrayal, corruption and malfeasance. The muckraker who wrote *The Jungle* does a meticulous job of proving how the NEA played a major role in demeaning the teaching profession and destroying public education in his day. I quote:

'The effect of official tyranny such as we have been observing is to reinforce and intensify the occupational diseases of the teaching profession, which are timidity and aloofness from real life. The teacher lives in a little world of her own; she spends many hours every day with her children, and other hours in reading their themes, and marking their examination papers, and making out complicated reports. For the rest, she knows only her colleagues, whose life is as narrow as her own. And this is the way her superiors want it. Said the superintendent in Agra, Kansas to a young lady graduate of Wellesley College: "You ought to have gone to a normal school instead of college. There they teach the teachers just what they ought to know, and not anything else."'

Gerald considered what he'd copied. He read more of the book, and realized that Sinclair was condemning more than just the NEA here. Gerald decided that he wanted to concentrate on the areas of the book concerned with the NEA.

"In a chapter titled, *A Plot against Democracy,* Sinclair writes: 'The National Education Association is a very old institution predating the Civil War. It has always been controlled entirely by the supervising force: in other words, it has been an employers' organization. During several decades of it s history no classroom teacher was ever elected to any office. At the present time some well- trained teacher is occasionally admitted to office for the sake of appearances. It required many years of struggle to get the NEA to give any consideration whatever to the living and working conditions of the classroom teacher, or to recognize salaries, pensions, and tenure as legitimate subjects for discussion. It required a revolution in the organization to secure in the year 1903 the appointment of a committee on salaries, tenure, and pensions; and this committee made a report which was full of misrepresentations. Not until 1911 was action taken even to gather the real figures of these questions.

I will give you a glimpse of the organization in those early days, just to let you see how these things remain the same. At the 1901 convention in Detroit, the United States Commissioner of Education gave a paper outline of the progress of the schools. He was an aged dotard; as an eyewitness said to me, "In the educational system we don't bury the dead. We let them walk around to save funeral expenses." The speaker congratulated the country upon the growing number of school pupils, but said not a word of the need for school money. An orator who rose to applaud him declared that the educational sky was without a cloud, and his only regret was that the American public schools had not been able to get a donation from Rockefeller.

But suddenly a cloud rose upon the educational sky. A thing happened which had never before happened in the history of the NEA- a classroom teacher rose up from the floor of the convention and asked to speak! To make matters worse, it was a woman teacher. This female rebel declared that she for one was glad that the American public schools had not got any money from Rockefeller, and she hoped they would keep clear of all corporation influence. If the rich wanted to help the schools, let them pay their taxes; let the railroads, for example, pay taxes on their franchise valuations, which they were everywhere evading.

You may not need to be told that this was Margaret Haley, making her debut to the NEA twenty-three years ago. The great assemblage was stunned; to attack the railroads, the NEA's main source of revenue! At that time, you see, when you bought your ticket to the convention, the ticket included your dues, and the NEA got the rake-off.'"

Gerald grew tired after copying so much into his essay, but he was exhilarated as well, because he was finally writing what had been on his mind for years. Granted, the NEA had finally admitted Negroes into its ranks and the need for a separate Black Teacher's Association ceased to be, but throughout his career he struggled with the fact that Black and White teachers alike were more interested in having their picture taken with public figures than in leading teachers to better pay, hours, and working conditions. The NEA leadership promoted the idea of caucuses which stressed identity as a Black, Hispanic, Gay/Lesbian, Veteran, Peace,

Conservationist- all issues of importance Gerald sensed, but totally meant to dull the spirit of unity for the purpose of building better lives for teachers and other educational workers. It reminded Gerald of a line that the Reverend Jesse Jackson had made famous, "I am somebody." The NEA cleverly massaged the egos of the teachers, while constraining anything resembling standing up for their economic needs.

If any part of the Sinclair rant was correct, that is, if the NEA was truly a tool of the monied interests and tasked with keeping the classroom teacher in his place, how far, even now, had the organization really come? Was it possible that, even though there had been articulate and brilliant minorities elected by the representative bodies to the presidency of the Goliath organization, underlying the twenty-first century façade was a cabal to promote public education servitude?

Gerald recognized that a favorite scapegoat of the political right and even blue dog Democrats was teacher unions. Massive amounts of money were spent almost every political election cycle to decry the state of the public education system. Blame fell on the teachers for the poor quality of education and the dismal results of standardized examinations given to students each year. In his opinion, the NEA and AFT did little to defend the teachers against the onslaught. Yet, back in the early part of the twenty-first century, governors showed their contempt for teachers and their unions by trying to write out their paltry gains.

The NEA was still a conglomerate of people beating their breasts in mea culpa hair shirts who joined the administrators to blame the system for the poor performance of the inner city and rural sad state of affairs. Fearful of reprisal, teachers got the blame instead of placing responsibility on the parents and the apathy of the business community to better the existing educational systems. This practice became the rule, not the exception. Gerald believed that the schools had the children for eight hours a day and the parents had them for sixteen. Rarely did he read of any politician attacking the parents for their malfeasance. Rather, it was the "teachers' fault" and the hacks of the NEA would often lick their proverbial wounds to avoid taking the offense. The NEA feared strikes as much as the Board of Education, because it meant that the Association would have to support and supplement loss of wages by its members. Gerald believed that the teachers really had two adversaries: the Administrations and the professional staffs of the NEA itself. When he thought about it, he felt bile rising in his throat and he gagged.

Gerald boiled when he received ballots from his local Association office asking him to vote for contracts which gave the teachers no raises or at best a mere pittance. He remembered a year during the great recession when the Congress gave itself a three percent pay raise, and the local government cried because they had no money. He wondered what deals were made under the table to exclude the teachers at the expense of local politicians and other government workers. Being fair-minded, he realized that he didn't have many facts and since his hip fracture, he really had been out of touch with what was happening back East where he had taught.

He reread his material and decided that he wanted to tap into Sinclair's work again before he put it aside. He found a chapter entitled: *Bread and Circuses* and thought it of interest in light of what he remembered during his own tenure in the Association. The NEA used to have their conventions in big cities where thousands of representatives would be elected by their local and state representatives to attend these huge conventions. They were like circuses and Sinclair wrote:

'We have followed closely the business and politics of the NEA conventions; let us now consider them in their educational social aspects. They are imposing assemblages, and of course loom colossal to the cities in which they occur. To have thirty or forty thousand visitors spend a week in the city inspires the local merchants with a deep respect for culture, and the local boosters get busy to show the teachers a good time. The NEA politicians naturally make this a condition in the placing of the convention; they want to have the delegates occupied with scenery and entertainments, so as to distract their minds from political controversies. This wisdom has come down to us from the Roman Empire; then it was bread and circuses, now it is boat rides, auto rides, luncheons, and telephone calls.' "

Gerald considered the places he'd gone to for national conventions. Teachers and their families made summer vacations of the event. Usually the halls were so large that business could only be conducted after many closed door decisions were made and then voted by the Assembly. In essence, Sinclair's observations were the way Gerald saw it. Gerald decided to end there, and be prepared to present elements of his essay to the group on the following Thursday.

The collective had been opened for about a month and a half and it was time to consider who would be elected to take on the role of house manager and chair of the meetings. Pauline was doing a great job in every aspect of her duties, but the guidelines specifically spoke to diversification of leadership and for good reason. Ben deplored dynasties.

Lee and Pauline were alone n the workroom and each wanted to chat a bit before they began to work. "You know my time as house manager is over in two weeks. I do not mind having fewer responsibilities and more time for my classes at the Reuter Center."

"I know you want to do more with the Unitarians." Lee stole a glance at Pauline and went on, "Are you and Gerald planning to go to the church again?"

"Maybe, maybe not. Oh, Lee, I do not know. All the women there think he's so dashing and charming. He is so tall and debonair. What is a poor girl to do?" Her face turned a crimson red.

"Are you telling me that you are falling for him? I mean that's fine, but don't rush into anything, Pauline. I don't want you to be hurt."

"No, I do not want to be hurt either, and I think that he is still in love with his wife. Lord knows, I understand that. I miss Max too. But Claire is such a powerful force to deal with even in death, maybe more so in death."

"How do you mean, Pauline?"

"Well, we all tend to idolize our dead spouses, and forget that they were human beings with the foibles and human qualities which could drive us to distraction. Even you do it when you talk about Sandy, your third husband."

Pauline realized that she had brought up a sore subject by reminding Lee she'd been married three times with two divorces and children she only saw on rare occasions. She was mortified by her comment and looked furtively at Lee to see if she took offense.

"Pauline, I'm not offended by the reminder that I've been married three times. I remember years ago I was at a dance in Oregon, and one of the women there told me that I was a loser because I was divorced twice. That was before I met Sandy. It was at a Catholic Church and I guess she was a widow. It hurt me at first, and then I began to wonder why she had the need to be so abrasive. Oh well, life doesn't always offer an easy path to travel."

"Lee, I am sorry that I brought that up. There were times in my marriage to Max that I wondered what I was getting out of the marriage. I was always living in his shadow, always meeting his needs, not necessarily my own. But, I never considered leaving the marriage. Perhaps, I was frightened or fearful that I would not be able to care for myself."

Lee sighed and mused, "And now here I am living in a commune and finding myself attracted to Gerald. How bizarre!"

The women laughed, and returned to their own thoughts. Lee decided that she would write a short story, that maybe short story would be her genre. She considered a group of short stories which she'd written over the years and always kept with her. She still had them, and decided she would remove them from their musty file folder, and reread them. Some had been written years ago when she was still a school girl. She would volunteer to read in two weeks during the writers' group.

The weekend was busy. It was so beautiful and warm that the commune members decided to have a picnic in a place they'd heard of called Max Patch or something like it. It was reported to be in Madison County on the Appalachian Trail. Pauline did some research and decided to share it with the group while they traveled the hour and a half trip. Saturday they piled into the van, and Ben drove the group through Mars Hill, Marshall, the county seat and out into the lovely countryside.

Pauline read, "Max Patch is a 4,600 foot mountain near Hot Springs. It was used as a pasture in the 1800's. Today, it's a 350 acre tract of open land on a high knob with 360-degree views. On a clear day, you can see Mt. Mitchell on the east to the Great Smoky Mountains in the south. It's in the Pisgah National Forest. The Smoky Mountains, only 20 miles away, dominate the southwest horizon. To the west, the terrain drops over 3600 feet into the flatlands of eastern Tennessee. To the west, 50 miles distant, raises the dark ridge line of the Black Mountains. Endless ridges and peaks fill in the panorama everywhere else."

Max Patch was as enthralling as they'd read about, and everyone lolled about and ate a hearty lunch prepared by Hazel the day before. The walk up to the actual trail was somewhat stressful, but the men decided to hoof it. Ben huffed and puffed his way to the top with Gerald and David following his lead ever so slowly. What would take youngsters about twenty minutes took the trio two hours, and they whooped and shouted in glee upon reaching the crest. Unbeknown to them, Pauline had absented herself from the group and no one noticed.

"Where have you been, boys? I've already had my cup of tea up here." Pauline laughed uncontrollably at their dismay that a woman beat them to the top.

The party returned to the house exhausted, totally at peace, and ready for a quiet evening and a long night's sleep. Everyone was beginning to realize how beautiful and wonderful their new surroundings were.

On Sunday, Pauline and Gerald set out for the UU Congregation, while Hazel took Sadie to the Baha'i Center to show her what they did there. Sadie was nervous and wondered whether this would be similar to the experience she'd had when she went to her first service of the Messianic Jewish movement. Would these Baha'is talk in tongues, praise Jesus incessantly, want her to kneel and beg for forgiveness? Would they try to exorcize the devil from her as her son had done to Jennie, her sister before her death? Who were these people who believed in world citizenry, the unity of all mankind? Were they Christians? Were they some crazy spiritual holy rollers? So many questions bothered Sadie as she drove along Tunnel Road, through the tunnel, on to Sawyer Street, and the Baha'i Center.

It was not an imposing building, being stuck between large parking lots on both sides. Hazel decided to drive to the back of the building where there was handicap parking and close to the entrance for the elevator, which would be easier for Sadie to manage, as meeting rooms were on the second floor. The elevator opened to a large auditorium room which was dark and empty. Sadie wondered if they had arrived too early.

Hazel said, "No, we're not too early. This room is used for large gatherings, special events and such. We'll go through here, across a small hallway and into the Tucker Room where the Sunday morning devotions are held."

Upon entering the Tucker Room with its many high windows and light streaming in, everyone smiled at Hazel, who introduced her guest. Sadie felt that everyone welcomed her warmly. They began with some announcements, then prayers for healing and for the departed. The wording of the prayers reminded Sadie of her beloved Psalms. Then a young lady gave out copies of the readings for the day for everyone to follow as it was read aloud. The topic was on the love of God for mankind. After that there was open discussion. Sadie felt comforted, and thanked Hazel for taking her.

CHAPTER SIXTEEN

On Wednesday the communal members met for their weekly meeting. It appeared that the portable commodes were working well, because Pauline had received no negative feedback from the men. They readily handled the cleanup details every morning, and for that Hazel was grateful. Next week the new compost treatment system would be installed in the corner of the workroom which thrilled everyone to no end. No longer would there have to be a mad rush to the rail to take someone up to the first floor bathroom before he or she wet their pants.

"I still think that we ought to pay for the compost toilet system. It just isn't fair for Ben to be burdened with all the costs here. I, for one, think we could cover that cost." David seemed adamant and had the ear of the others. Pauline asked if there was a motion to be put before the group.

"I move that the commune members who use the workroom be financially responsible for the toilet installment." Britt waited for a second and got it from David.

"All in favor. It's unanimous. All hands were raised. I should think that $200.00 from each of us would cover the cost of buying and installing the commode. If it is a little more, I will be most happy to pick up the difference," said Pauline.

"Good and Welfare is next. Does anyone have anything to say?"

Pauline told the group that they would soon be voting for a new house manager and group leader. She made it clear that she would not do it again until everyone else had a chance, if they wished to assume the duties. There was a gentle ripple of protest from the group, but it quickly died down. They began to look around and to begin the process of deciding for whom they would vote.

Ben grumbled about the members taking the cost of the compost toilet, but he understood pride, and that the members didn't want to be charity cases. He was gratified, even if a little perturbed at their independence. Ben knew that they each showed a spirit which was not present in any of them except for Pauline when he first met them in Florida at the nursing home.

It was amazing to Ben that the members were actually appearing to reverse their aging processes, if that was possible. What had been five people ready to die, and at least four of them showing signs of preparing for the act of dying, was now a complete turnaround. It was time, in his opinion, to call Jane at the rehab facility and report on the activities of the group as soon as the meeting adjourned.

"Jane, Ben here in Asheville. How are you? I'm happy to hear that. You sound great. How is your family? Good..... And that boss of yours, Cohen, is he still happy that he cooperated with us? Really... Wow, that's great. People do change sometimes..."

Ben gave her a report on each of the members, their health, psychological state of mind as far as he knew, and what they were doing with their writing. Jane was pleased to hear that they seemed to be in such a positive state of mind, and thanked Ben for his part in making the change. She told him that her journal submission had been accepted, and that they were in fact interested in follow-up reports. She also told Ben that she'd started a new group and that they were beginning to write some of their autobiographical material for the group therapy sessions. Volunteers were on board to help, but unfortunately she did not anticipate another Ben appearing to whisk the writers away.

What Ben didn't tell Jane was that he'd taken up with Britt, and that Gerald and Pauline might have something going, too. Perhaps he was a little unsure.

On Thursday Gerald and Sadie presented. Gerald made it clear that he'd chosen the essay as a genre, and decided that he would compose and collect several compositions of importance to him. Over the years, he wrote short pieces on education, religion, politics, and topics of interest of the moment. He stated that he would put them together in book form and see if anyone was interested in what he had to say. He began to read. The group sat and listened in silence, some of the writers shaking their heads in dismay from time to time.

"I never knew that the NEA was made up of businessmen and run by such tyrants. Gerald's information is astounding."

"I agree, David. What an eye opener. I mean the part about the docile women teachers is amazing," Britt said and shook her head in disbelief.

"I would be cautious that he could be accused of libel. I know that it's been many years ago and things are changed, but if any of the corrupted officials are still around or anyone from that era reads anything Gerald writes, will he need a lawyer to defend himself?" Pauline seemed deeply concerned for Gerald's welfare.

The discussion continued for another twenty minutes before the group turned to Gerald for his comments.

"Thank you all for your words of wisdom and criticism. However, I did not hear any comments about the mechanics of the writing style, nor do I have a clear picture as to whether you believe that what I have written will be of interest to anyone outside of this room."

"Gerald, your command of the English language is beyond reproach. You were, after all, an English teacher as was your dear wife, Claire. As for interest, if we are any example of the reading audience you may expect, it is clear that some of us were more interested than others, but that would apply to all our writing. Some readers will be amazed, just as David is, while others will not be interested."

Again Pauline was on target. She knew that all art of any kind was in the eye of the beholder. She imagined that writing, painting, sculpture, any art form was interesting to some and not to others based on their baggage, their interests, and their intelligence to grasp the meaning that the artist meant to convey. This was also true of music, as far as she could tell.

Sadie began to read her work. She read slowly and had to hold back tears when she read about her sister and brother. She didn't look up from her reading because she feared that she would lose her place. Sadie did not see that all of the writers were tied to her story emotionally, and that some had tears in their eyes. When she talked about her friend and her husband, and the antics of the two young husbands, there was a sense of amusement in the group. She finished and looked up.

"I have a feeling that Sadie's work is the stuff that movies are made of. I mean it. Such emotional and powerful imagery cries for a screenwriter and actors to portray the characters."

"I feel the same, Pauline. Her writing comes alive for me, makes me sad and then happy, all at once. I think she has such a fine style of writing. Really, I mean those characters couldn't be fictional. They're too real, too alive."

"Right, Britt. I think you've expressed what all of us feel," David said earnestly.

"I, for one, will look forward to her analysis of the Messianic movement. I just hope that she can do so with as much emotion as we have just heard. I think that she may need to have someone help her with some of the syntax and grammar, but that will come in editing and preparing the manuscript for publication. I am impressed!" Gerald said, and his comments summarized what each writer was thinking. Sadie beamed.

Lee realized that she was the only one of the original writers who had not presented, and offered to be ready with Pauline's help next week. David agreed to be second, and the meeting concluded with Hazel's sugar-free cookies, coffee, and tea. Everyone relaxed and didn't seem in any hurry to leave.

"So who would be willing to become house manager for two months? I think two months isn't long enough." Britt announced, and Pauline eyed her, realizing that this was a ploy to get her to extend her time. She wanted no part of that.

"If the group believes that two months is not long enough, make a motion next week, and we can discuss it for new business, but it will not apply to me. I want my freedom to do the things I want to do at the Reuters, and maybe take classes at other places."

"I understand your concerns, Pauline, and this may be something that Ben will want to get involved with. I think that a three month tour of duty would be in order." Gerald had been considering the issue for a week or two.

"Pauline, will you talk to Ben and get his feedback on this idea. It may conflict with some of the guidelines which he wrote and we agreed to."

David didn't want to vote for any new guidelines without Ben's approval.

Gerald turned to David. "There is a breakfast group at the UU Congregation which meets once a month on a Saturday. It's for men only. It's going to be coming up soon, and I was wondering if you, and maybe Ben, would like to go with me. You do not have to be a member of the congregation to attend. I hear that the discussion can be quite interesting, and even somewhat provocative. The group has been meeting for twenty years or so, or at least that is what I was told. We would have to bring something to feed about five or six people, and then they have a discussion lasting about two hours."

"Sounds interesting. What do they talk about?"

Britt eavesdropped and asked David, "David, what do you think? Women, sex and other macho subjects. What do men always talk about?" The girls giggled and shook their heads in approval at Britt's feigning disgust. She had a twinkle in her eye.

"No, no, no Britt. I do not believe that for a moment. Some of the men told me that the subjects are philosophical, profound, and anything but macho."

"Like what for instance, David?" Britt looked skeptical.

"Well, for instance, death and dying, aging, children, tragedies in their lives, marriage vs. single-hood, things like that. These are heady subjects, and I imagine there are many points of view shared. It is all confidential, of course, but the subject matter is not, just who says what."

"Do the women have a group too,"asked Sadie?

"Yes, Sadie, on the next Saturday morning after the men's group."

"Some of the woman told me the same thing that the men told Gerald. However, they meet in private homes and have a slightly different format," David answered.

Lee became interested, "Pauline, do you plan to go to one to see what it's like?"

"Yes, Lee, in about three or four weeks. Do you think that you would like to come?"

"Yes, I think so. You know, my mother and my aunt used to go to the Unitarian Church a long time ago. They felt welcomed there. It was one of the only churches which opened their doors to gay and lesbian people. Now, it's sort of fashionable to do so, but the UU was the first as far as I know. Maybe some Christian churches did, too, but it was always a ploy to spread their ideas about the sinfulness of lesbianism, and how God meant for them to be like everyone else," Lee recalled, and smiled at the memory.

"I will ask Ben and Stephen whether they would like to go with us, David. Maybe they will be interested. Some of the men are older, our age, you know what I mean, but some are young, perhaps in their forties or maybe late thirties. Stephen might be interested. Funny, the fellow who told me about the group referred to the meeting as the men's room. He thought it was so funny calling the all male group the men's room," Gerald laughed.

"Maybe he was referring to graffiti, but I don't see anything like that from what you've told us. Who knows?" David raised his eyebrows in cartoon fashion.

Gerald looked at David and smiled, "It might make a good title, if someone wanted to write about the group, its history, some of the personalities. I gather that many of the group members have passed on, and from what I have heard, some very interesting people. Anyway, it would be my pleasure to bring the three of you to the group the next time it meets, which I think is in two weeks."

Lee made her way to the workroom. She, too, wanted to use the new transcriber that the group had bought for David. She would speak into the microphone, and Pauline could transcribe her work. She began.

"My mother was something of a genius. She belonged to MENSA! She wrote a book on how to win at poker using all sorts of statistical analysis and made her own classical guitars and canoes. Mom had a great job as an economist for the federal government, and I guess that's where she met Elizabeth.

I don't know much about my biological father because Mom rarely spoke about him. He was a journalist, I think. How he and my mother took up with one another is still a mystery to me. I was born in Chicago when my dad was working for a newspaper, and mom was working on a master's degree at the University of Chicago in economics.

She had short, cropped hair, a raspy voice, and little patience for anything feminine. Mom was very masculine. I think today she would be called a dyke or some other horrible name like that. She wore drab and unimaginative clothing and rarely wore any sort of make up or rouge. I remember as a little girl I would dress up, and chide my mother that she was more like a man than a woman. I don't remember Mom getting angry about that. I think she sort of liked being thought of as a manly person. When Aunt Elizabeth came to live with us, she was more like a mom than Mom. Mom was more like a dad, or what I thought a dad should be like."

Lee sat back and reflected on what she was saying. She hoped that she was not maligning her mother or Elizabeth, but that was the way it was back then. She flipped the switch and continued.

"We all moved to a house in northwest Washington D.C. So many years ago, but I remember it was a long semi-circular street with one end coming out on the elementary school and the other joining another street which ultimately ended on a main thoroughfare into Rock Creek Park. Our backyard looked out into the park full of high trees and shallow streams. Some nights we could hear lions, elephants, and other animals from the National Zoo. Their sounds would drift in on clear nights. I was so scared, I hid under the covers.

I remember seeing a couple addresses with one half addresses, like 1883 and a half. That struck me as so funny. I never understood why they needed to have an address with a half. Mom would tell me, 'Because the city planners made a mistake'.

On Christmas, Elizabeth would give me dolls, dresses, girl stuff. Mom would buy me baseball gloves, basketballs, compasses. She was disappointed when I wanted the dolls and dresses, and ignored the boy presents. I know that she would have been happy had I followed in her footsteps, but it wasn't to be. I never had any doubts about my being a girl and when I got older, I wanted the attention of the boys, never the girls. Strange, I even became a dress designer. I never fit into her image of what a son, I mean a daughter, should be.

We didn't have many friends on the block. I didn't know why people wanted to keep their distance from us, except for one family who had a son who I played with and loved like the brother that I never had. They used to come over on Christmas Eve and other holidays and we'd all have dinner together and sing Christmas carols. I think they were Jewish. But they were the only friends my mom and Elizabeth had on the block. Elizabeth was Jewish too, but she wasn't an observant Jew, but from the beginning she was very nurturing and loving, not like Mom. Poor Elizabeth, I always wondered what her family thought of her lesbianism. I guess they weren't Orthodox. Elizabeth's relationship with my mom would have killed them if they were."

Lee sighed and murmured, "I wonder if they ever knew or suspected."

"Mom bought a cottage on the Chesapeake Bay, and we all spent a lot of time there. She made her canoes and guitars, Elizabeth cooked, cleaned, and washed clothes. We were a perfect family- maybe 'Same, Same but Different'. I bought a T-shirt once that said that." Lee smiled to herself, and took a breather. She went upstairs for a cup of tea and to chat with Hazel.

"You know, Hazel, the time is passing so quickly. I never thought that I would say that ever again. In Florida, time crept along, and all I could think of was why me, why did Sandy have to die, why not me? Why did I have to get Parkinson's? Why did I get breast cancer? Why didn't I have the nerve to just die? It was always a burden that I didn't want to have to cope with any longer."

"Well, I think that I understand, but I can't really be sure. No one can walk in someone else's shoes. I'm happy that you feel better now, and that you are writing and doing a great job as a commune member."

"Thanks, Hazel. I needed that encouragement. I mean Pauline is always heaping praise on me, but she's a little prejudiced in my favor. I'd better get back to work."

Lee returned to her work in the workroom, and turned on the transcriber.

"When I began to develop, Mom made rules that I wasn't to have any boys in the house without her or Elizabeth being present. That meant that my friend from down the block couldn't come in either. She liked Aaron, but she may have thought we'd be doing things we shouldn't. It was OK if my girlfriends came over, but no boys.

I went to junior high school about three miles from the house. I could walk through the park to get there, but soon Mom decided that it was too dangerous for a young girl to be in the park alone, so I took the H4 bus to Georgia Avenue and then the streetcar. I can't believe I still remember the number of the bus. Sometimes, with this Parkinson's I can't remember my name, but here I am recalling the bus number." Lee shook her head in wonderment.

"I had three best girlfriends, and we were inseparable. One was a girl from Lithuania whose father was a giant or so it seemed to me. He was a librarian in the Library of Congress, an expert in Lithuanian literature and history. Her name was Grazyna and she was Catholic. She was beautiful with golden hair in two long braids. She developed early and the boys went crazy with their new found testosterone hormones raging. Graz, that's what we called her, had a sixth sense about the boys and took great pride in keeping them at a distance. I think that the boys were afraid of her dad, so they stayed away from their apartment. The boys were like hungry wolves licking their chops. Aaron was the only one who could come near the house because he was madly in love with another of my friends, and Mr. Lukošius wasn't threatened that his daughter's virginity would be in danger.

Gloria was a cherubic-faced southerner from rural Virginia, who was a Baptist, and grew up a few blocks away from my house. Her grandmother and mother raised her and her little brother. She was so pale, her skin was almost translucent. Gloria never had a bad word to say about anyone and was everyone's friend. She was the shortest of us all. I think she never grew beyond four feet, seven or maybe four feet, eight. We all loved Gloria, and would talk to her about everything, particularly boys. She spoke in that sweet, southern drawl that melted like sugar in your tea.

Cindy lived in a big hotel on Sixteenth Street, downtown. We've been friends the longest. Even when I was first diagnosed with Parkinson's disease, she would come out to the west coast to see me and that lasted a long time. She was widowed early, and left well-off by her husband who was a great deal older than she was. I never quite knew who her father was, or for that matter, much about her mother. Her mom was always pleasant enough, but I think that I remember several men who lived there, and Cindy always referred to them as Dad.

She was so sweet, always smiling and patient with us girls. She seemed to be like an angel. Funny, sometimes I thought she had a halo over her head, and her skin reminded me of those Japanese actors who painted their face calcium white. For a while she dated Aaron, and seemed to like his parents more than him. Maybe they provided some tranquility that she never got at home. I still don't know, and Cindy and I have never discussed it in all these years. She held my hand when I fell in love for the first time with the best looking, tall, muscular boy in high school. He was my Adonis. All the girls were happy for me, and cried with me when he broke it off. They were my best friends. Even Aaron stroked my ego."

Lee switched off the transcriber and replayed what she'd written. It would make for the beginning of her memoir about her life. To be sure, Lee wanted to insert some short stories that she had in mind, but that would come later. Now, if Pauline was still willing to transcribe her work, she would be ready to present to the group next Thursday.

Ben sat down with Pauline, and she outlined the concern about whether a house manager and group leader, which was really the same person, should be in those positions for three months rather than two. Ben's initial reaction was to object. It was well known that he favored anarchy rather than someone being in charge. Now the group was asking for someone to be in charge longer, not shorter, as he was hoping to hear.

"I assure you that I had nothing to do with this idea. I made it clear to the communal members that I was anxious for my tenure to be over so that I could do the things I want to do, and help David and Lee with their writing."

"I know Pauline. Maybe they're right. Maybe two months isn't enough time to institute new ideas and create different ways to operate the commune. I have no problem with going to three months, so long as no one becomes a despot. Years ago I watched benevolent and well-meaning people placed in positions of high power only to become dictators. You remember Orwell's *Animal Farm.* I just don't want that to become the model for Kelly House." He laughed, studied his belly, and smiled weakly.

Pauline understood and had seen similar takeovers herself with Max when he traveled to developing countries and took her with him. She agreed in principle with Ben, and felt quite certain that it wouldn't happen in Kelly House.

On Wednesday, the group presented Pauline with roses and a card of thanks. Ben applauded her for fine work as the first house manager. A bottle of champagne without alcohol or sugar was liberated, and all drank a toast to Pauline and themselves for surviving the first two months. A motion was made and seconded that the position of House Manager and Chair of the Meetings be raised from two months to three. Discussion centered on the theme of the person being able to institute their ideas with approval of the membership, of course.

Hazel spoke to the fact that she felt better about having an employer to work with for a longer time than just two months. Stephen had nothing to add, but indicated he'd be happy either way.

Pauline called for a vote and it passed unanimously. Nominations were called, and Gerald and Britt's name were put into the hopper. Britt begged the group to vote for Gerald because she didn't feel ready to assume that kind of leadership- yet. Gerald, embarrassed by the fact that he was the only name on the ballot, implored others to step up. They didn't, and he was elected. Gerald did not vote. He assumed his office the next day.

During Good and Welfare, Ben spoke, "I am extremely pleased with the way things are going here. It seems to me that everyone is doing their share of keeping Kelly House going smoothly. Everyone seems to be in good health, and don't worry about meeting any deadlines for me concerning your writing. I realize that this experiment isn't just about producing creative works; it's about changing lives."

Ben stopped talking. Everyone was listening intently and when he mentioned the writing and purpose, there was a decided sense of relief on the part of the members.

Sadie was the first to speak, "I know that I'm slow, and that I don't always have my thoughts in order. I was beginning to worry that I wasn't able to do my part, and would let you down."

Ben shook his head and went over to hug Sadie. "Never, never think that, my dear Sadie. You do more for me, and I think for everyone here, by being who you are. Don't worry about not producing whatever you are writing."

A quiet murmur indicated that he spoke for all including Stephen and Hazel.

"Look folks, let me be honest with you. I don't expect you to produce great works of fiction or whatever else you're writing. If you can write and we can get you published, great, but this experiment isn't about writing. It's about all of us living together in harmony and deciding that life is worth living."

"Thank you Ben. I think that I can speak for us all. We are dedicated to completing what we have started here, and that includes our work as writers or whatever creative enterprise we may aspire to do. But, I doubt that in one year's time we can do enough to actually be published. Perhaps, one or two of us, will finish, but certainly not everyone." The group appreciated Gerald's comment.

"I know, Gerald, and what I am trying to say in my bumbling way is, don't worry about it. Have fun and live life to its fullest. That's all. If you want to sit at the computer all day and night, fine- But, if not, don't sweat it."

Ben's grin consumed the entire room. "I'm not. I love you guys."

The members and staff formed a circle and hugged each other. The love was palpable.

CHAPTER SEVENTEEN

Hazel answered the phone on the third ring. "Ben Zangwell, please." The voice was gruff and yet not unkindly.

"May I tell him who's calling?"

"Tell him, it's an old friend from the company." Hazel handed the phone to Ben..

"Hello, this is Ben Zangwell." Ben's hairs on his neck stood erect. His voice was strained and his hand trembled slightly. Hazel couldn't help seeing his reaction to the voice on the other end.

"Ben, is this a secure line?"

"No, of course not. Who is this?"

"Leonard Wiley. Do you remember me?" "Z" relaxed a bit.

"Yes, how are you Leonard? Long time since we talked. I thought you'd be retired." Ben relaxed his grip on the telephone and smiled slightly.

"I am sort of retired, but sometimes the Company brings me in on something off the wall. You know, weird or kind of out of their line of work. You get my drift?"

Ben laughed a little and said, "Yeah, I remember the drill. Something off the record so to speak. I was involved once in a while in some of those little drills."

"Yeah, well, we got a little problem up here in Virginia, and was wondering whether you'd come up and see what you think."

"Leonard, do you realize that you're talking to an 82 year old overweight senior citizen? Do they want me to play Santa Claus this coming Christmas or something like that?"

"No, Ben. It's a lot more serious than that. But I can't discuss it on a non-secure line. You know that."

"Why me? I haven't done any" Ben looked at Hazel who hadn't moved from her spot since the call came in. He motioned that he needed to speak privately. She broke her trance and smiled before returning to her duties.

"Sorry, a good friend of mine was standing nearby. As I was saying, why me? I haven't been involved in an ops in years. I'm out of touch with anything I ever did, and I'm so out of shape I'd be of no value to you."

"Maybe, maybe not. We'll pay you to come up from Asheville for a day or two. We'll even get you a room in the Motel 6." He laughed, "We're even cheaper now than when you worked. Could you come up Tuesday? We've already booked you on the 10:30 flight out of Asheville on Tuesday morning. Please don't say no to your Uncle."

Ben laughed and then agreed to come up, but told Leonard that he thought they were crazy, wacko to think he could do anything for them. But, he agreed and would see them on Tuesday. "Oh, who do I report to?"

"Jim Westerman. You don't know him. He has a desk in the Americas Department." Leonard hung up before he would tell Ben too much on an unsecured line.

Ben wondered how the hell they knew where he was, but realized that the Company could find anyone they wanted without much trouble. Modern technology kept them informed around the world. They had sort of made peace with NASA under a new president.

He went to Gerald who was now the house manager, and told him he had to go to Washington on business. Gerald asked no questions because he had Ben's cell phone number. In a real emergency, he could contact Juan and Maria if needed.

Ben spent the weekend with Britt and took her to Chimney Rock. They took the elevator that opened into the usual crowded gift shop, got through that, and then on a boardwalk and steps up to the security fenced plateau at the top of the singular, huge column called Chimney Rock.

They were stunned at the raw beauty and vastness of the mountain ranges from their vantage point. Britt agreed to a short hike on the side of the mountain adjoining the Chimney, and viewed more Blue Ridges from another direction.

Later, over dinner, he told her that he had to go to Washington on business and would return on Wednesday or Thursday the latest. She didn't probe for information because she knew that there were things about Ben's past that were left unsaid. But her curiosity peaked.

Most of the writers spent time on Saturday and Sunday at their computers or with their transcription machines.

David was having some trouble with his ability to walk. His balance was giving him a problem, and he told Stephen, who made a note to call for an appointment for David. It was almost too good to be true. Not only was David's health going well, but everyone appeared to be as healthy as they could, considering their problems.

Sadie's sugar levels were within normal range; her prosthesis worked well, and she had no wounds to watch over. Gerald complained of some residual arthritic pain in the hip joint area, but over-the-counter ibuprofen was keeping the pain tolerable. Lee had good days and not so good ones when she seemed a little stressed. That was to be expected when one suffered from Parkinson's disease. Stephen watched his brood like a mother bear, and that may have had something to do with their well being. He kept his fingers crossed, and adorned his room with dream catchers.

David turned on the transcriber and began, "TOK Junction is at the crossroads of the Alaskan Highway and the Glennallen. Going west takes one to Anchorage, going north to Fairbanks and the town of North Pole. I rode the bus to Fairbanks. That may have been the last year that Greyhound operated in Alaska. I never saw them again in all the years that I went there.

Tired, still achy from the long hike with my backpack weighing me down, I limped into city and headed directly for the Fairbanks Hotel, a square building of about three or four stories. It was on Second Avenue which was full of tourists, drunks, and obnoxious music blaring from saloons up and down the street. A few all night dives which served hamburgers and hotdogs was all I saw. My first night I slept through all that noise and the banging of doors and the yelling of people too drunk to be civilized to each other. In the morning my leg hurt, but nothing would stop me from exploring.

I was across the street from the visitor's center located on the Chena River. Women and men dressed in early twentieth century garb worked at the center, and answered hundreds of questions from the tourists who'd been bused on private Holland Line buses to Fairbanks from Anchorage. Some of the tourists had come up on the Alaska Railroad, a full day trip from Anchorage through Denali Park.

Second Street also had assay shops which were like pawn shops. The gold pokes were sold to the shops as were furs, native art work such as beaded hair barrettes, scrimshaw ivory pieces, and a host of other ornaments made by the Athabascan Indians and the Inuit. The word Inuit means "people." White people call these people Eskimo, but I'm told that the Inuit don't like that word. The Inuit are in the North, the Yupik down near Bethel. But, they are all Inuit anyway. In the North, the Inuit are Inupiak.

I wandered around for about three days and the pain in my leg subsided, but really that leg has been a problem for me since then. Not that it hurts every day or is weak, but I have leg cramps from time to time, and now that I've had this stroke, I wonder when I'll collapse because the leg won't hold me up.

The city bus depot was about a block or two from the hotel. One day I got on and went up to the University of Alaska. I wandered around, and saw a bunch of people who were teachers looking for jobs in the Bush. They were in the student union building overlooking a wide valley with mountains in the distance. Mt. McKinley, over 20,000 feet was one of them, the highest mountain in North America. There are actually three mountains. Mount Foraker is a 17,400-foot mountain in the central Alaska Range while Mount Hunter, or Begguya in the Dena'ina language, is approximately eight miles south of Denali, "Begguya" means child of Denali. Mount Hunter is the third highest major peak in the Alaskan Range. Of course Mt. McKinley is named for a president. Denali is the Native word for the mountain.

The students were from all over the United States, some young, just graduated, and others middle-aged and having taught elsewhere before. Some told me that every summer teachers would come up to the University, stay cheaply in empty dorm rooms and go through interviews with human resource personnel from all the school systems throughout the State of Alaska. Their stories were interesting, and I had the feeling that many of them left out a whole lot about their situation. If there was a common denominator, it was that Alaska paid better than any other state, and these people wanted a piece of that action.

All the interviews were held in one of the halls dedicated to some Alaskan pioneer or politician. The students dressed up in their finest for the interviews only to change to jeans and sweaters afterwards. They attended a class in one of the other buildings for perspective Bush teachers. They could take the class for credit or just audit it. They had assignments if they wanted three credits toward a master's degree. I made up my mind that I would come back next summer and take the class.

I trained down to Anchorage through Denali Park, but didn't get a glimpse of Denali. The train meandered slowly through breathtaking gorges, mountain roads with drops of thousands of feet. I can't imagine how the tracks could have been laid in such treacherous terrain. Once in a while, someone would whoop and holler as they looked out of the window. We'd all run to see what they were excited about. It was usually a moose, elk or some other wild animal. I think we may have seen two or three black bear with their cubs. Eagles flew overhead as did ravens. They were the biggest damned black birds I ever saw. The Tglinket Indians have a Klan named for the raven.

Anchorage is the largest city in Alaska. To me, it's not so different than any other large city except that it's surrounded by huge, imposing mountains and an inlet which is called Cook's Inlet. It's named after Captain James Cook, the famous explorer.

I found a hotel to stay in, a run-down, flea trap with locals who all seemed to be down and out. I loved it because some of those people graciously told me about their lives and many of the stories weren't pretty. Almost all of them were from 'outside' which is the term used for the rest of the United States. They'd all come to the Last Frontier looking to turn their lives around, to strike it rich, and to find peace of mind. Unfortunately, they brought a lot of bad habits with them, and found that Alaska was even harder than where they came from in the first place.

I made friends with a woman who came out of Nevada somewhere. She'd been beaten up by her last boyfriend, and escaped within an inch of her life. She had a married daughter in Anchorage who was deaf. The daughter and her husband worked for the local social service agency challenged with helping the deaf population in Alaska. Their children were born with hearing, and did a lot of communicating with the outside world on their parents' behalf. My friend signed to her daughter and son-in-law. So for the two weeks I was in and out of Anchorage, I spent a great deal of time with Jean and her family.

I decided to go to Nome to see the Bering Sea. The airline ticket wasn't too expensive back then, but it's astronomical now. Alaskan Airline has a big picture of an Inuit on its tail section. Back then American airlines fed people and treated customers better than today. I've come to hate flying in the United States because it's all about profit, not service to the customer. I cannot understand why the government doesn't nationalize the airline industry."

He turned off the machine, and realized that he was on a soapbox again, and laughed. Like his good friend Gerald, he had trouble with the American mindset which was so against the word Socialism. People seemed to love Capitalism even though he believed that Capitalism was responsible for so many people sinking into an economic quagmire. David smiled as he thought of the vast number of Americans who were so committed to Capitalism. He thought about the adage, "We have met the enemy, and it is we." David felt a momentary sense of despair.

He returned to the machine. "Nome is like being in no man's land. Front Street borders the Bering Sea and I walked about five miles on the sand. Pup tents lined the water's edge in which gold miners slept. They all had sluice boxes and worked the waters for the shiny slivers of the yellow element. Further up the beach, I saw walrus heads severed from their bodies with the tusks still attached to their heads. There were hundreds of them. The smell was odorous and the sight grotesque. Later I found out that the Inuits killed the walrus and planned to take the ivory tusks to craft scrimshaw scenes on the tusks. Whites and Blacks weren't allowed to touch the tusks. They belonged to the Natives only. What a horrible thing to do to those walrus was all I could think of. Cultures are different.

I stayed a night at the Polaris Hotel, and surveyed the walls full of newspaper clippings dating back to the nineteenth century. There were articles about the Wobblies coming there to organize miners, lumberjacks and other laborers. Those articles would make for excellent research on the history of the labor movement in Alaska. A few years later I revisited Nome during the drab winter and later during breakup when the ice melted. I was astounded at what the ice could do to buildings and streets as it careened over the banks of the sea wall. The deafening noise and gigantic waves reminded me of a horror movie where natural forces wiped out everything in their way. The only thing missing was the giant octopus with an ominous personality.

That summer I met a woman on the plane who was in her seventies and she invited me to come to her home and visit with her and her husband. She was a pioneer, born and reared in Nome. Her Swedish parents came to Alaska in search of gold and shipped up to Nome to strike it rich. When I arrived at her little cottage, there was a garage with a narrow gauged steam engine inside. Her dad had barged the engine up to transport gold from his mine to Nome. The engine was a monstrosity. My friend thought I might want to buy it as a memento of Nome. She would give it to me for nothing if I would pay to have it transported to Seattle in the summer. I begged off, thanked her, and changed the subject. Scuttlebutt has it that she finally got rid of the engine by giving it to a railroad museum in Seattle. They paid to have it transported by sea."

David thought about his experiences in Nome and then Kotzebue, an authentic Native village. The plane returned to Anchorage with a stop in the Eskimo village. It was the first time that David had stepped on Native owned land. He remembered being awed by the thought of being so far away from his surroundings in Maryland. It was the heart of the summer, and yet the temperature was in the thirties and would drop to the twenties at night. Dogs yelped and pulled at their ropes, screaming to be free to run and mate wherever they could. In the summer, women wore kuspuks, the Eskimo dresses with hoods to carry little ones.

The plane remained just long enough for him to deplane and go into the hanger used as a passenger holding pen. His was the only white face there. But it was enough for David to realize that he wanted more, much more, and that he would return again and again.

CHAPTER EIGHTEEN

Ben's flight was an hour late. Waiting at Reagan National was a black Chevy SUV and a driver to whisk him to Langley. Ben was annoyed. Why the hell were they still using these gas guzzlers? Then he thought about how uncomfort-able it would have been had they sent one of those little electric toys that people ride around in.

He entered the all too familiar building, signed in, and was escorted to an office without windows. A young, curvaceous Afro-Asian woman asked about his flight and offered him a cup of Starbuck's best. The wait was all of ten minutes.

Jim Westerman looked to be in his forties, shorter than Ben, wiry and fit. His dark reddish hair was beginning to thin and he had a high forehead which glistened. His handshake was firm, but not bearish, and he smiled with a sincere look of concern.

"Ben, good to meet the legend. I've heard so much about you, and I believe there's even a plaque somewhere in this building for your service to your country."

"That was a long time ago. I'm curious as hell as to why you were willing to use our Uncle's money to get me up here to Langley."

"In due time. We're waiting for Sam Thompson to get here from the FBI. Also Cynthia Lewis is coming over from State for this meeting. I just wanted to meet you before the fun starts. You know, get the measure of the man and all that."

"You a veteran? You're too young for Nam."

"As a matter of fact, I am. Two tours in Afghanistan, and some UN stuff in Kosovo. Why do you ask?"

"Well, Jim, I kind of judge people in this line of work by their credentials. I heard that the Company was hiring a lot of college kids with no experience except degrees on the wall."

"That's true, but some of them are geniuses and have helped America remain strong. I think that the mantra used to be warrior, but not so much anymore. I guess the best of all worlds is a combination of both."

Ben admired the man. Jim didn't try to butter him up, and at the same time held his own with the bearish elder. Ben liked that. Fifteen minutes into their introductions, a Latina woman and a black man came into the room. Coffee was served.

Westerman began, "Ben, about six months ago, the State Department began to get information that elderly Americans were being bilked in Colombia. Some of them disappeared, and we still haven't located their bodies."

Westerman turned to the woman. Cynthia Lopez was a striking middle-aged woman, nearly six feet tall, a rich brownish skin tone which was obviously well taken care of. Her body was athletic and yet alluringly sexy, or so Ben thought.

"We began to receive communiques from a small island resort in the south of Colombia that some of our senior citizens were either complaining of being swindled out of their life savings, or at least on two occasions we were notified by the Colombian Police that three couples had gone out on fishing vessels with locals and the boats haven't been heard of since. We began to advise our citizens not to go to the island, not to become involved with deals too good to be true."

Cynthia turned to her FBI colleague, "Sam, would you fill Ben in on your involvement, please?"

Ben recognized Sam Thompson now. He knew the name but couldn't place it until he actually set eyes on him.

"Are you the football player?" Ben asked, eyes wide with anticipation.

Sam Thompson was a giant of a man and made his name on the

gridiron at Notre Dame and then the NFL where he was named all pro linebacker at least twelve times.

"Guilty as charged, Ben. But, I'm trying to hide the past," Sam laughed and stuck out his hand in a gesture of friendship.

"I saw you play for Chicago and the Jets. You were incredible. Wow, meeting Sam Thompson. Thanks, Jim, for bringing me to Langley. I didn't realize that I was going to meet one of my all time heroes."

Thompson was embarrassed. He'd read "Z"s personnel file and felt humbled by being in Ben's presence. There was instant mutual admiration.

"When the Colombian police contacted the State Department, they contacted us because if a crime had been committed against our citizens, then the FBI usually gets involved. No bodies, ten or fifteen elderly folks admitting that they'd fallen for a scam, and pissed as hell. You can imagine what that was like.

We sent down some of our people to investigate but they stuck out like sore thumbs. You know, crew cuts, straight backs, young, bulges in their jackets. They didn't do more than consult with the police. No boats, no bodies, no leads. We sent agents to talk to all of the elderly who'd lost their money. They were in the States licking their wounds, and promising to tell us all they knew, but it wasn't much. They'd been contacted on their computers with a sales pitch."

Sam reviewed his notes, a notebook lost in his huge hands. Sam was easily over six feet, seven, and probably tipped the scales at over 280 pounds. Ben, too, was huge, but that's where the comparison ended. That was one persona. The other was that he had his law degree with top honors from Yale Law plus a doctorate in Criminal Justice. He earned all that while beating the hell out of other pro ball players.

His desire was to be a Federal Bureau of Investigation's agent from the day he was a sand lot ruffian growing up in Detroit. He knew the streets, and had more dead friends than living ones by the time he was twenty years old. Bu his size and his brains made the difference, and scholarships flowed like milk and honey. He left Detroit, and didn't look back until he joined the Bears in Chicago. From then on he was a hero in Detroit and Chicago by giving millions to the non-governmental agencies tasked with helping the poor and homeless. His exploits on the football field were almost secondary to his philanthropy.

"Where was I? Anyway, the only thing we could come up with was that for a few hundred dollars up front, the couples were wined and dined like royalty at this resort in Colombia. But, before they could leave the island paradise, they had to sign away their earnings. For this they were promised a beautiful condo, excellent medical care, deep sea sport fishing beyond their wildest imagination and everything that they'd always wanted. Oh, and they were promised tickets every year to anywhere in South America they wanted to go for free once a year. Too good to be true, right- but at least five couples bought the package, and gave up two, three hundred thousand each."

Ben began to feel uncomfortable. He knew where this was going.

"So what about the others, the ones who went fishing and didn't come back?"

Sam said, "We think, but we don't know for sure, that three couples may have balked and were fed to the fish rather than catching them. We don't know for sure. Our people were too obvious. We don't have anyone who fits in or fits the profile."

Jim Westerman spoke. "Ben, the FBI and State Department looked everywhere for someone who would fit in, speak Spanish, know something about investigation, and be able to assess the situation, and let them know what was going on. That's when they called the Director. You know the drill. Here we are. You're the only one who fits all the categories. You're old, I'm sorry, I mean experienced. You aren't being asked to do anything that you didn't used to do back in the day."

Ben hated to admit it, but he was getting excited.

"But, I don't have a wife. You said that couples were involved. Right?"

Sam leaned forward, "We know about the commune, the others and that you have a lady friend." He opened the notebook again, "What's her name? Britt Manning, right."

Ben's ire rose, and he was about to say something nasty when he realized that he'd be saying it to his hero. "Are you suggesting that Britt go with me as my wife?"

"Now that you mention it, not a bad idea. She would make a great cover."

"I don't want to put her in any danger. She's got a respiratory ailment and she's old. I mean she's 81 years old, for God-sake."

Cynthia chimed in, "We owe it to our citizens to find them one way or another. By the way, two of the men who disappeared were Viet Nam vets. One lost an arm. I don't have his name with me, but we owe them."

"I don't think Britt has a passport. She's not a strong woman. But, if I do take this job, and by the way I would do it for no salary, just pay our way and expenses. Just for the sake of argument, what if I do find out what happened to them, then what? What if I find the bastards who are doing these things, then what? I'm not in any shape to do anything about it. I'm not strong like you, Sam, and Britt's not a good looker like you, Cynthia. No disrespect mind you. Just telling you like it is."

"That's quite a mouthful, Ben. Let's take it one step at a time. Cynthia, can you arrange for a passport for Britt and falsify her last name. Or does that take an act of Congress?"

"No, we can do it and we'll go one step further. If she goes with you, the government will have a new passport with her real name waiting for her when you return. I think we should make this passport with her real name. People often keep their names anyway."

"Ben, neither CIA nor FBI want you to do anything but be our eyes and ears for a week or two. That's it. No sanctions, no action, nothing. That's from the director's own mouth. So help me God."

"Sam, if we say yes, will you give me an autograph?"

Sam laughed, put his arm around Ben and said, "I'll give you an autographed photograph, and a NFL football with the entire Bears team to sign it. That's a promise."

"Well, I have to go home to the commune and talk to Britt. I'll do it, but I don't know what she'll do. I can't speak for her. Can you give me a week?"

"Sorry, Ben. We have to know in two days from the time you get back to Asheville. It takes a little time to put an ops like this in place. You know what I mean?"

"Yes. Well, I'd better get back then."

"Right. We have a plane waiting to fly you to Asheville now. It's our Lear. I think you've flown in one before, right? They have some K-rations on board," Jim laughed.

"You're serious. What a waste of government money."

"We're very serious, Ben. We want these bastards and we need you to do the recon."

Everyone got up from the table and shook hands. Twenty minutes later Ben was on the tarmac waiting for the Lear to take off for Asheville Regional.

Stephen picked Ben up at the airport, and while they were driving told him that Sadie's fasting blood work returned showing that she was not doing well on her blood sugar levels. Stephen feared that if she continued to have ups and downs it could be dangerous to all her organ systems. He was visibly worried.

"What do we have to do, Stephen?"

"I don't know, Boss."

Ben noticed that Stephen used the word 'boss'. He wanted to be sure that it was used as an endearing term and not as a slur as many former prisoners used it to refer to their jailers. He always suspected that someone who'd been in jail or prison referred to the 'man' or 'boss' in a negative and pejorative way.

"Stephen, you called me boss. Why?"

"I don't know. It just seems right. I just think of you that way and it fits you."

Ben relaxed and smiled. Juan Morales called him boss, too, and they had a father, son relationship.

"I thought maybe you'd been in the Joint or something like that, and saw me as a Screw, you know one of those corrections guys."

"No, no nothing like that Ben. The closest I ever got to trouble was when I was a kid and stole some candy from the store. Lucky, my uncle owned it, and I had to listen to twenty hours of sermons before that little fiasco was over. He was the lay preacher in the Baptist Church. I can still hear him threatening me with going to hell for stealing five tootsie rolls. Stephen thought to himself, "No way, man, I ain't going to hell for tootsie rolls," and laughed.

When they arrived at home, the members greeted Ben as though he'd been gone for two weeks. He had such a sense of well-being, one that he'd never had before in all his 82 years. Britt unabashedly gave him a long and passionate kiss on his cheek. His face flushed, but he loved it.

That evening Ben took Britt aside, and they went outside to the little gazebo where they couldn't be overheard. He decided to lay the whole thing out to her, and get her reaction to such a dangerous and wild mission.

"Britt, what I'm about to tell you has to stay here between us. It's confidential and important. Can you agree to secrecy, even from the others?"

"You're scaring me a little. I hope you're not leaving us or something like that."

"No, no, nothing like that, but it involves you, possibly, and my trip to Washington."

"Go on then, tell me. I'm dying to know, and I'm full of curiosity. So were the others, Ben."

"OK, how would you like a little trip to the south of Colombia, South America?"

Britt wasn't sure she'd heard him correctly. "What did you say?"

"South America. Colombia. You heard right. My trip to Washington was to the CIA in Virginia. You need to know some things about me which I haven't shared with too many people. I used to be a spook, you know, a spy or whatever you want to call it for Uncle Sam."

Britt wanted to remain calm, but her eyes widened, and her breathing quickened. She was obviously captivated.

"Anyway, years ago I worked for the Company, and I speak several languages as a result of training I've had, and living in so many places - I can't even count them anymore."

"What about South America, Ben?"

"OK, I was just trying to give you some background. Anyway,

apparently a bunch of old people like us have been going down to this place in Colombia, getting ripped off in some sort of scam, and some of them may have been killed for their troubles. The agency wants me to go down, and investigate what's happening to our citizens."

"Do they know that you are retired? Do they know that you're an old man?"

Britt's eyes widened, her flash of anger passed and she said, "Ben, I love you. I don't want to lose you. I don't want them to risk getting you killed, too."

"I know, I know, but they've sent people to investigate and they've gotten nowhere. They want me to go down as a potential mark. I mean, you know, as a possible buyer of this land and resort that they have down there. Actually, they want us to go as a couple for two weeks or so, look things over and report back to them."

"Are you saying what I think you're saying?"

"Yes, you and me as a couple. We wouldn't be suspected of anything except two old fools that they can swindle."

"I don't have a passport and I haven't taken any shots. The last time I had a passport was thirty or more years ago when I was in the Peace Corps."

Ben laughed, "It was a hell of a lot longer than that, my love. But don't worry, we'd be working for the FBI, CIA and the State Department. They can arrange a passport in a day, get you whatever shots you need, but I doubt that you'll need any. You'd be a great spy. Who'd ever suspect someone with an oxygen canister slung on their shoulder? Now me, a dashing, older man with a youngster on his arm like you would be a different story."

Now it was Britt's turn to laugh, and she punched him in the arm. He pretended to cry, and rubbed his arm.

"I want to do it. I'd go anywhere with you, Ben, anywhere. Would we go as a married couple or as friends? She had a sly, gleam in her eye.

"Well, a lot of people just live together rather than marry. Depends on who you talk to. Maybe it would be better to go down as a couple planning to marry some day. Our story could be that we aren't married because we both have our own money and children and grandchildren, etc. The bad guys might figure two fish instead of one. I don't know."

"What would we tell the others?"

Ben hadn't considered that angle yet, and said, "Well, I don't know. I can't tell them the truth. There might be people checking up on us to verify where we live. We could tell the truth, and they might think Kelly House is some kind of independent living facility or something like that. But the others would only know that we've gone to South America to vacation. I haven't thought it out yet. The first issue was asking you what you thought. I just thought of something, Britt. This might be another episode in your memoirs."

"If we live through it, two octogenarian sleuths working a case would be a best seller. Can I take my cameras?"

"Sure, that would be even more authentic."

"Count me in, Sherlock. I'll be your female Watson, big boy."

CHAPTER NINETEEN

Gerald rose early on Wednesday, went into the bathroom, and surveyed what greeted him in the mirror. He saw a tall elderly man, a bit stooped over, lean Polish aristocratic face with a mane of hair that reminded him of the Lion King. His hair was almost all white with shades of black around the edges. He opened his mouth wide and saw his own teeth gleaming at him. His dentists were always proud of his mouth because Gerald followed their prophylactic advice to the letter. To this day he'd only had two cavities in his entire life. He knew that he had little to do with this good fortune. Genetics did.

He thought back to the day that he slipped on a wet floor in his kitchen, and had to be taken by ambulance to the hospital, the surgery to repair his hip, and then Greentree Rehabilitation and Nursing Home. Claire's death, loneliness, a sense of despair made his rehabilitation a matter of no importance to him until he met the writers and Ben. Depression, for Gerald, was acute, but limited by the involvement with Jane Finestein and these marvelous people. He considered that they saved his life, and for that he came to be most grateful.

Today would be the first meeting that Gerald led, and he was worried that he could never equal Pauline's skillful management style. He knew intuitively that he did not have to compete with her or anyone, but force of habit is difficult to conquer. All he now wanted to do with the rest of his natural life was to give to his new family, and if there was any anger left in him, to correct the wrongs he described in his essays.

He prepared a sheet of paper with the order of business, reviewed his well earmarked Robert's Rules book, and felt ready to go. He wondered whether there would be any new business today, and went outside to meet with Ben.

Ben sat with Gerald in the gazebo, and told him that he and Britt would once again be gone from the commune, that this time it could be for an extended period of time. He couldn't tell Gerald the truth about the assignment. At the same time he wanted him to be aware of the potential danger involved.

"Gerald, for reasons that I hope you will understand, what I am about to tell you cannot go any further than this meeting. Do I have your word?"

"Of course, Ben." Gerald's curiosity was peaked.

"A long time ago, I used to work for some people tasked with looking out for the U.S. You know, I was in the military during the war."

Ben noticed Gerald cock an eye, and knew that Gerald had been an anti-war activist. Ben was actually proud of him and the war resistors.

Ben continued, "After my military service I joined a civilian government agency which the country has hammered and loved from time to time. You probably know what I'm talking about."

Gerald knew, and kept his counsel.

"Well, I've been retired a long time, and a few days ago they called me and that's why I went to Washington. There's a problem, and they think that I can be of help. Lord knows why, but I've agreed to do some investigating. I've asked Britt to go with me because I need a cover of being an old retired fart with a wife and some assets."

"Ben, you don't have to go any further. I know that you wouldn't do this unless you felt it was important. Will Britt be safe?"

"I hope so. I certainly plan to keep her safe, but I need you to be sure that if anyone tries to check up on where we are, telephone calls, the like, that you tell them that we're on vacation. It's very important that no one knows anything about us except that we're living here with a bunch of other old people, and that we've gone off somewhere. The less anyone knows, the better. Will you handle that, Gerald?"

"Of course, I will. I think we should tell the others that you and Britt have decided to take a vacation. It will not be entirely untrue from what you tell me."

"That's right. Now if you need anything, anyone gets sick, or anything else, call Juan and Maria. I will tell them about this, and they will know what to do. Don't panic, just call them. Live life as though nothing unusual is going on, but call them if you need them. I think that you should mention that we're going away at the meeting. If they have any questions, I'll answer them, but at least you know what the truth is."

They concluded their meeting and went in for breakfast.

The meeting progressed well. Gerald guided the members through the order of business. There were no old or new business items. Good and welfare was next.

"I would like the community to consider getting a dog from the shelter. Everyone knows that pets are good for old people, as well as for kids."

Lee rarely spoke in the meetings. She hadn't discussed this idea with anyone before. Pauline cocked her head, and wondered why Lee hadn't broached the subject with her.

"When I was a child, we had a cocker spaniel and I loved him. He was there when my mother and my aunt didn't have much time for me. Ricky went everywhere with me."

"I think that's a great idea, Lee," said David. "I was so damned angry with the condo association for not allowing any dogs or cats to live in our apartments. I would be happy to look after our dog, walk him or her, feed it. Wow, I'm excited."

Gerald asked whether there were any other thoughts about a pet. The only question was about the age of the animal.

"Should we get a puppy or an older dog?"

"What about a cat or kitten?" Sadie purred and made cat like noises.

"Hazel, how do you feel about a pet in the house?"

"I love dogs, Pauline. I always had a pet when I was raising my children. But, who's going to clean up after it? I know you said you would, David, but can you really do it?"

"I think so," answered David and looked at Stephen who sat impassively.

"There were times on the reservation when hunger was so great that there was no place for a pet. Most of the dogs and cats were strays, and they were always suspected of spreading disease and even rabies. His people even talked in a disgusted way about other tribes that ate dog.

"Do we need a vote on this?" asked Gerald.

He sensed that not everyone was enthusiastic about a pet. He, himself, had not owned a pet as a youth, but Claire, her son, and a little Lhasa Apso were part of a package. She used to say, "You marry me, you get three for one." He laughed aloud. Gerald motioned to Ben to jump in if he desired, but Ben sat quietly.

And then he said, "I've heard that having animals gives people comfort and love. Why not have one?"

The group didn't need to vote, and it was decided that a committee would go to the shelter and save some poor pooch from the needle.

Gerald told the group that Ben and Britt had decided to take a vacation together. Everyone was surprised, but wished them well. Without much fanfare, he told them that if anyone called for either of them, they should tell whoever called that Ben and Britt had gone fishing.

Ben smiled and thought, "How true." And then he grimaced.

On Thursday, Stephen drove Ben and Britt to the airport, bade them happy holiday, and saw the plane off. They were off to Washington Reagan near the city center on the Potomac River.

David gave each of the writers and Pauline a copy of his work that he'd completed. Pauline continued transcribing for him and Sadie.

The gentle criticism was overshadowed by the admiration the writers felt for David's exploits. They saw his work as non-fiction adventure, and encouraged him to continue to write. They were anxious to read his memories of village life and his attempts to make a life in Alaska.

Britt was to have presented, but her vacation with Ben preempted her participation. Sadie and Lee promised to have something to contribute next Thursday to the group, and Pauline told them about the classes she attended at the Reuter Center.

"I have signed up for three classes, and I am so excited. One is a studio oil painting class workshop. The teacher is a world recognized artist, and studied in some of the most prestigious schools in America. Another course is a beginning watercolor workshop taught by a delightful woman from the Deerfield Senior Community. Just for kicks, I am taking a Tai Chi class as well. There's something for all of us there. Next semester there will be courses in writing, self-publishing and editing.

It was agreed that the writers would invest money in becoming members of the Reuter Center which was also called the North Carolina Center for Creative Retirement. Pauline brought them copies of the fall schedule for their perusal. Each would pay a small sum of fifty dollars for a year's registration.

Ben and Britt were met at the airport by the same young man who'd picked up Ben the first time. He was especially polite to Britt, and carried her bags and an additional tank of oxygen.

Once at Langley, Jim Westerman, Cynthia Lewis and Sam Thompson were seated and ready to go as soon as the pair arrived. Ben introduced Britt to the three. Then Britt and Ben were finger-printed, photos taken for passports which would be rushed through and ready in two hours. A nurse came into the room and did a quick vital signs check on the two, frowned and peered at Westerman in consternation. He shrugged and nodded. Hepatitis A shots were administered to the couple, and the briefing began.

No new cases of fraud had been reported, and there were still no signs of the missing Americans. Britt would answer an advertisement posted on a website in an hour and ask to see the resort. The story given would be that she and her fiancé were in Costa Rica looking for a retirement home to spend their remaining years. They liked what they saw in Costa Rica but heard about Puerto Sonomo from other couples, and wanted to come down right away to see it. They would be arriving in three days, and would like to be met at the Hotel Nationale for a tour, if it could be arranged with such short notice.

"By the way, they raved about the fishing down there. Y'all think that we could get out for an hour or two on such short notice?" She was assured that a fishing boat would be at their disposal. The woman on the other end had a Midwest accent.

In fact, they would be met by Jorge Munoz, an agent in Bogotá, who would see to their flight to the resort town. He also was tasked with finding them a hotel room in Bogotá and helping them with their cover story.

Britt was tired from her flight, and slightly dizzy from all the attention and whirlwind activities. Ben worried about her and whether she could handle another six or seven hours of airtime to Colombia, and then all the stress of carrying out the assignment. Westerman made it clear that although Ben was to receive no pay, Britt was now on the government payroll and would be making $450.00 a day and her expenses were to be paid by Uncle Sam.

"I have to wait until I'm 81 years old to earn decent money. I can't believe it. I've waited all my life for something like this- at least the money, and now when I'm an old broken down woman and I can't spend it for a good time, I get it. Go figure!" Everyone laughed and tea and cookies were served.

Ben asked some technical questions, such as would he be armed, how would he make contact, and with whom, if he found something. Jorge Munoz would be the point man, but from Bogotá, not the resort. Westerman didn't want any complications. If Ben sensed that they were in any danger, he wanted them out quickly.

"No heroics. Do you get that Ben?"

Ben nodded, and took him seriously because he didn't want Britt's safety compromised in any way.

In two hours, a courier appeared with two passports that had been doctored. The documents were three years old and stamped with entrances and exits to and from countries in Europe, Asia, and Australia. Someone had spilled coffee on the passports to give them authenticity and proper visas pasted into the passports. Unless the papers were scrutinized thoroughly, they would pass for well-used and worn covers. Each was given an International Immunization yellow form which showed routine shots. Everything seemed in order.

The next day they met again, the script rehearsed, went to dinner, and were driven to Dulles for a flight to Colombia on an Argentinean Airline. They had tickets showing that they had been in Costa Rica with receipts from hotels and restaurants. Agents in Costa Rica had attended to this piece of the story.

Britt felt amazingly alive. She couldn't believe her fortune, and on top of that, she was with Ben, not as a mistress, but as an operative for the CIA. If she believed in a God, she would have thanked him, or her, or it profusely. All she could think of was writing about this experience in her memoirs back home at the commune. She wished she had her camera with her.

The couple was met by Munoz as planned, and whisked to a hotel for a good night's sleep. Britt wondered whether the government paid her to sleep or just when she was awake. Making money, so much money was so new to her that she kept tallying how much she was earning by the hour, the minute, and if possible, the second.

Ben laughed when she told him what she was doing. While they were briefed by Munoz, the wheels were turning preparing them for their drop into the resort. As expected, someone called Kelly House, and pretended to be looking for Britt. They told Hazel that they were a long lost friend who'd just happened to be in the city of Asheville, and wanted to get together. The voice was that of a female with a Midwest accent.

Hazel dutifully told the caller that Britt and Ben, her financé, were traveling somewhere in Central or South America and weren't expected home for three or four weeks. Hazel went a little further than she had been told by Gerald to say, and told the caller that maybe the couple would go fishing because Ben loved to fish and Britt loved to gamble. Hazel asked the caller for her name, and was told that it didn't matter. The caller thanked Hazel for the information and hung up. The cover was successful.

Back at the commune, Stephen got word that he was wanted for a festival which would take place the next week. His chief wanted him to drum with the men for the dancers. It would be on Saturday and Sunday in Cherokee, and it was expected the attendance would be in the thousands. He knew that the organizers were being optimistic because they were always excited to see people from other nations as well as Cherokee. Stephen decided that he would ask Gerald whether the entire commune would like to go as his honored guests. Elders were always welcomed and treated well.

"You've heard Stephen speak about his invitation to us for the powwow. Are there any questions from anyone?"

"Are there places to go if we get tired? I've heard that it goes on and on because there are so many dancers and songs," asked Sadie.

Stephen reassured her, "Of course, Sadie. This is being held at the agriculture center and there's plenty of chairs, cover in case it rains, and food venders hawking their fry bread, corn on the cob, arts and crafts. You can't go wrong. If there are any problems, there's paramedics, a couple of ambulances and some Indian Health Center nurses. You won't have to worry about anything. My family and all my cousins will treat you like family. It'll be fun. You'll love it and they will love you. The powwow is two days, but we'll only stay for one.

"Any chance that we can go over to the casino? I've heard lot about it. You know, shows and big names a lot of the time."

"Maybe David, maybe. I can't promise that because I'll be drumming five or six hours, but who knows, maybe my aunts or uncles will take you. I can ask for you."

"I don't know about the rest of you, but I consider it an honor that Stephen invited us to his home and to his gathering. I would love to go," Pauline affirmed.

Gerald acknowledged Pauline's sentiments, and asked the rest what they thought about the idea. Everyone was excited, and it was decided to leave on Saturday morning at 8:00 for Cherokee and the festivities.

Pauline decided that she would do some research on the history of the Cherokee Nation. The first reference she found related to the horrendous history perpetrated against the Cherokee by the White government in Washington. She started by recording two statements by heroes of the Cherokee Nation.

"I believe it is in the power of the Indians unassisted, but united and determined, to hold their country. We cannot expect to do this without serious losses and many privations, but we possess the spirit of our fathers, and are resolved never to be enslaved by an inferior race, and trodden under the feet of an ignorant and insolent foe, we, the Creeks, Choctaws, Chickasaws, Seminoles, and Tsalagi (Cherokees), never can be conquered..."

Confederate General Stand Waitie, Tsalagi (Cherokee)

"We are now about to take our leave and kind farewell to our native land, the country that the Great Spirit gave our Fathers, we are on the eve of leaving that country that gave us birth...it is with sorrow we are forced by the white man to quit the scenes of our childhood... we bid farewell to it and all we hold dear."

Charles Hicks, Tsalagi (Cherokee) Vice Chief on the Trail of Tears

Pauline wiped away tears as she reread these words and felt a pang of guilt.

Then she went to Wikipedia. She remembered the horrors and tragedy which befell the proud Cherokees and their allies on the Trail of Tears, but she wanted more information. Her intent was to share information in the van while they traveled to Cherokee. Stephen would undoubtedly add his own take on what she discovered.

She reread what she'd written: "The Cherokee people historically settled in the Southeastern United States, principally Georgia, the Carolinas and Southeastern Tennessee. Linguistically, they are part of the Iroquoian-language family. In the 19th century, historians and ethnographers recorded their oral tradition that told of the tribe having migrated south in ancient times from the Great Lakes region, where other Iroquoian-speaking peoples were located.

In the 19th century, white settlers in the United States called the Cherokees one of the "Five Civilized Tribes", because they had assimilated numerous cultural and technological practices of European-American settlers. According to the 2000 U.S. Census, the Cherokee Nation has more than 300,000 members, the largest of the 563 federally recognized Native American tribes in the United States.

Of the three federally recognized Cherokee tribes, the Cherokee Nation and the United Keetoowah Band of Cherokee Indians have headquarters in Tahlequah, Oklahoma. They were forcibly relocated there in the 1830s. The Eastern Band of the Cherokee is located in Cherokee, North Carolina."

She asked Stephen to listen to what she'd typed. He did intently, and nodded his approval of the information Pauline gathered. What wasn't said was that his people chafed under the Bureau of Indian Affairs, the various treaties made and broken by the white man, and the horrors of drugs and particularly alcohol that decimated his people. As he had pointed out to Ben when he hired Stephen, Stephen knew more dead braves than living ones.

But this was a festive and deeply religious and spiritual time for his people to don their customary tribal garb, to dance and drum unabashedly to honor their ancestors and their way of life. His people did not hold grudges for long, and the group looked forward to meeting the people Stephen talked about on his trips home.

The trip to Cherokee took about two and a half hours with a stop in Sylva for coffee and a bathroom break. The group stopped in a small diner and everyone observed the elders as they meandered their way to the bathrooms. Some patrons shook their heads in disbelief seeing the wheelchairs and walkers. It was assumed by the town folk that they were just some old sorrowful elders going to the gambling halls in Cherokee to lose their money. Stephen recognized the looks and had a moment of joy. The Natives all over the country got their revenge in the long run by owning the casinos and getting rich off the non-Natives who spent their money freely. This was different, though. This was his family and he knew that they were going to join him in a joyous activity.

Stephen's friends were welcomed with open arms. The seats given them at the wide open arena where the dances were held was VIP seating. A welcome dance and then dances by brave warriors, hunters, and dances by only women provided each of the writers and their friends with a plethora of colorful costumes, gyrating rhythms, headdresses made for warriors and women alike with hundreds of bird feathers unequaled elsewhere. The costumes were exceptionally beautiful.

Children plied the commune members with fry bread, puddings and other delicacies made by the women of the reservation. The visitors were honored with a gift of beaded bracelets for the women and beautiful necklaces for the men. For each new dance, after the master of ceremonies announced what would happen next, a teenager embellished upon the story for the group.

After the powwow the writers were treated to a show of alligator wrestling by hearty young men and some of the group purchased baskets and bead work sold by the tribal artists. When it was close to dark the group began their trip home. They were exhausted, and felt they were honored by and had honored the Natives. They would have to wait for another visit to sleep over.

CHAPTER TWENTY

The first realization that Ben had upon entering the resort town of Puerto Sonomo was that this place was hotter than Florida in the middle of summer. The heat was brutal, and if it weren't for the ocean breeze that floated lazily by the pool at the hotel, Ben would have hung it up right there and then.

Britt loved it. Her frail, thin body soaked up the heat, and found strength from it. She still couldn't believe her new found riches, and thought about sitting by the pool drinking a glass of raspberry ice tea, and getting paid for it. The heat did have a negative effect on her weakened lungs though. It seemed that she could hear some wheezes emitted from her bronchi, but she hoped not.

"I love it here. Maybe when we're through with this year, I'll move down here and settle in. Have you ever seen such lovely bodies? I'm not talking about mine, mind you. But, such beautiful tans and muscles on the young men." She drooled.

Ben couldn't bring himself to wear swim trunks. He had on his lavender shorts with a triple X t-shirt with Asheville Opera written on it and a picture of Pack Square in the middle. His suspenders held his pants up and he looked the part of a tourist par excellence.

Across the pool veranda in a hooch bar were a man and woman watching Britt and Ben. They sat at a table obscured by a bandstand but with a view of the old couple. They looked for anything that would dissuade them from making contact with the couple, anything out of the ordinary. But these two old fools looked like their next paycheck, and appeared to be wading in money.

From a hotel room window, overlooking the pool area, two swarthy men observed the scene. Any sight of the police or anyone who seemed out of the ordinary- anything unusual, and they would call off the white haired man and pretty strawberry blond before they could approach the marks. They were the muscle in the organization, and were there to protect the middle-aged couple from trouble. Three times before, they had to deal with old fools who wanted their money and passports back. They didn't want to have to kill this fat hombre and his skinny, sickly old woman.

Ben and Britt lazed at poolside for an hour, enjoyed idle chatter and passed for vacationers. Ben sensed that they were being watched. He saw the couple in the bar, but not the men watching the scene from the hotel. His skills weren't entirely gone and he trusted the hairs on his neck when they were erect. He mused to himself, "Why can't my thing stand up like the hair on my neck?" Then he laughed out loud, and Britt awoke from a nap. She purred and gave Ben a hug and a kiss on the cheek. He responded with a smile and grabbed her leg.

This seemed to please the couple in the bar. They grabbed their drinks, wandered outside, and over to Ben and Britt.

"Hello, you must be Ben Zangwell and Britt Manning". Britt was startled, but Ben spoke quickly.

"Howdy, sure are, and you might be?"

"Bob Feathers, and this is Amanda. Amanda spoke to you when you were in Panama."

"Well, you got the right names, but we were never in Panama. We were in Costa Rica, friend."

"Right, my mistake. We get a lot of tourists here to see the resort. Amanda, I thought you said they were in Panama when they called."

"My mistake, Bobby. It's so nice to meet you both." Her accent was Chicago, maybe Detroit or even Wisconsin. No doubt about it, it was Midwest for sure.

Bobby gave Ben a raised card with gold trim. It had his name, title of broker and the name of the resort- Tropicana Linda, with a symbol of a palm tree and some kind of fish smiling on the card. Amanda didn't offer a card, but smiled benignly at the couple.

"Well, we're excited about seeing your place. We've been searching for a place where we can soak up the sun, fish everyday and drink lots of this good raspberry tea." Britt's head bobbed up and down with a look of a fawn hanging on every word Ben uttered.

"Well, now that's Tropicana Linda for sure. You must be tired from the trip. You're our guests for dinner tonight. The hotel has a fine seafood buffet, and we want you to be our guests."

Ben smiled, squeezed Britt's leg, and accepted the offer for dinner for 7:00 in the restaurant.

As Bobby and Amanda got up to go, Bobby said, "Oh, I almost forgot. Do you have your passports? The city has a rule that you must sign in at the police station with them. They make a copy and keep it until you leave. They do it for all foreigners. I'd be happy to take them over for you and return them at dinner- unless you want to do it yourself."

"Britt, what do you think? Should we trust these two young people? Oh hell, we may be buying a place from them. Honey, you have the passports in your beach bag. Let them have them. See you at din-din."

Ben knew that they wanted to see the passports to check their story and that he wouldn't get them back at dinner. He doubted that they would be taking the documents to any police station.

At 7:15 Ben and Britt, after having a nice warm shower where they played around for a while, came down to the restaurant. Britt wore a long yellow dress with a light sweater with roses on it. Ben, still in shorts, but having changed his shirt to a short sleeved blue polo shirt, was jubilant when he saw the couple. So far the cover seemed to be working.

There were about twenty-five people in the restaurant. All of them seemed to be Colombians, and spoke in cordial tones. Ben could make out some talk about the weather, fishing, and world news. He didn't let on that he knew any Spanish, and the evening went peacefully. The food was plentiful and scrumptious. Bobby didn't offer to give back the passports, and Ben didn't ask for them.

Ben noticed two dark skinned men watching the four of them.. He figured them for mestizo, probably Indian and a little European somewhere in their gene pool. Both looked like they could ruin a pleasant night if they wanted to do so. Ben decided to stay clear of them- for the moment anyway.

"So, when can we see your beautiful resort, Bobby?'

"How about tomorrow? Amanda and I will pick you up here at the hotel around 10:00 and take a ride out. You up for that?"

"You bet. We'll be ready. Right, honey?"

Britt smiled broadly. Once again Ben realized how beautiful she must have been as a young woman. He sighed.

When they returned to the room, Ben once again checked for bugs just in case someone at the hotel was in this with Bobby and Amanda. He found none, but put his finger up to his lips so that Britt would know not to discuss their real identities. They went out onto the veranda and pretended to be young sweethearts.

In the morning, Ben and Britt ate their breakfast in the hotel restaurant, and were sitting in the lobby when the scam artists arrived. Ben asked Bobby for his passport and was told that the copy machine was acting up again,

"The humidity, I think. As soon as it's fixed, they'll let me know, and I'll give them to you."

That seemed to satisfy the couple and they were off in Bobby's Jaguar. He was unhappy that he had to have them in it because he knew that Ben's weight and girth was too much for the seats. He tried to forget this little inconvenience and thought of the money.

Puerto Sonomo was gated. The security guard looked familiar. He wore shorts and a flowery chartreuse sports shirt. He smiled through a thick mustache which was coal black and well kept.

"You won't see too many people around. They're off fishing or shopping in the market. Today the natives have a big vegetable and fruit market in a small village not far from here."

"It's beautiful, Ben. Look at those mimosa trees and the palms. We don't have anything like these in North Carolina."

Britt was playing her part like a pro; Ben was impressed. He winked at her, and enveloped her hand in his huge paw.

"We have a golf course about a mile from here. I'd show it to you, but the boys are working on the road right now. It's really beautiful."

They wandered around a bit, and Bobby showed them a villa which he said was unoccupied and wouldn't it be just great for them. Ben began to sense that maybe this sales pitch was probably the same others had been given. When he asked to see the restaurant and dining room, he was given one excuse after another why they were not available at the moment, but assurances were made that as soon as they got back to the office, he could see a DVD of the entire compound and all the amenities. Bobby checked his watch and hustled the old couple away.

Back at the hotel, Amanda suggested that the couple take a siesta for a couple of hours, and then meet again to go over some of the documents for a sale or rental agreement for a month's stay. Ben and Britt cooperated, and bid the sales people adieu for their much needed siesta.

They waited fifteen minutes, and then left the hotel to go to a small bar for a drink and a sandwich. Ben motioned to Britt not to say anything until they were on the veranda.

"So, what do you think?"

Britt cocked her head, sat for a moment and said, "Well, I don't think they're on to us. From their point of view, we're just a couple of old fools who bought their story and they see dollar signs."

"Right. I agree. What we experienced was pretty much what we were told happened to the others who somehow managed to leave. I wonder what happened to the three other couples, or better yet, what did they do differently than the ones who got away?"

"So are you going to write them a check or give them a credit card? How are you going to get our passports back?"

"All in good time, Britt. Don't be so impatient. Let's see what happens this afternoon. They'll pitch their spiel this afternoon, and try to get our money. I have to keep them interested. I have an idea."

"I'm listening."

"OK. We act gullible, and you keep talking about how beautiful it is and the trees and all that. I act like it's just what we've been dying for, but I ask to go out fishing once before I make any financial commitments. We tell them that we need a good night's sleep. Tomorrow you start having trouble with your breathing and complaining of headaches and the like. When they get to the hotel to take us fishing, I'll say that we have to go by the hospital to have the doctor check your blood pressure and check your oxygen tank, etc. What are they going to do? They have to take us over there. I'll insist that you stay in the hospital for a night just for observation, but I'll go with them. They won't suspect anything because I will go with them, and they can see you have a breathing problem."

"You mean you want me to stay here while you go out with them? Are you crazy? That's what happened to the others."

"I'll be safe because you'll be here in the hospital. I'll find a way to contact Jorge in Bogotá. He'll talk to the doctor ahead of time. You'll be out of harm's way, and I'll be able to investigate knowing that you are OK. I might even get in some good fishing."

Ben laughed and smiled warmly at Britt. She wasn't sold on this plan.

They ate in silence and returned to the hotel. At two Bobby and Amanda returned with a DVD player and nearly a ream of paper. They played a DVD which showed people enjoying themselves dancing, playing golf, swimming and waving at the camera from a yacht docked in a marina. The people were all in the age range of seventies and eighties. If Ben and Britt didn't know better, they would easily have marveled at the sheer delight of the people on camera. But, they reacted they way Bobby and Amanda expected and hoped for.

When the DVD was finished, Bobby beamed and said, "Well, there you have it. Everything you could possibly dream about for a retirement and more."

"It's beautiful, just beautiful," said Britt, who then began to cough and seemed to gag. She was faking an episode of respiratory distress, but it was so real that even Ben became alarmed. Ben took Britt's hand, played with the dials on the oxygen tank, readjusted her nasal cannula and seemed highly stressed.

"I think I need to take her over to the emergency room at the hospital."

Bobby was annoyed, but couldn't show it. and said that he would be happy to take them over in his car. Ten minutes later Ben and Britt entered the door to the ER, were met by a nurse who spoke no English, but had been told by the attending physician to expect two Americans. She had Britt lie down on a gurney, took her vitals, and within twenty minutes Doctor Suarez was by her bedside. He spoke broken English and whispered that he'd been in touch with their man in Bogotá. He would help them, and told the nurse to admit Britt to the female ward in a room for herself.

When Ben came back to the waiting room, Bobby and Amanda were sitting there, and visibly distressed themselves. This had never happened to one of the unsuspecting marks, and they weren't sure what to do about it.

"They're going to keep her overnight for observation. You know she has chronic lung disease. They call it COPD back in the States. But, this is pretty typical when she gets excited. She begged me to tell you not to worry, and wants me to go out fishing with you or play golf, and not to worry about her. I don't know what I should do." Ben wrung his hands.

"Well, I guess we can go fishing for a few hours tomorrow if you like. I brought the papers for you to check over. What we have here, Ben, is kind of a time share. You know, you don't have to commit to anything until you've spent some time with us. It would save you a hunk of change instead of buying outright. Of course, buying a villa or condo would be much cheaper if you did it now rather than waiting. Every year the villas and the condos sell like hot cakes. So we suggest that you not wait."

"I don't know what to do. I'm so confused with Britt in the hospital. Do you mind if I look over the papers tonight, and tomorrow we can go out on the water. That always settles my mind, you know, being on the water and all that."

Bobby and Amanda knew that they couldn't close the deal now. They'd have to wait until the old lady got out of the hospital or croaked. They didn't want her to die; that would screw everything up. They drove Ben back to the hotel, and told him to be ready for fishing tomorrow at 7:30, "mañana por la mañana."

Once in the hotel, Ben placed a call to Bogotá and Jorge who was ready to move when Ben gave him the word. Apparently, Bobby and Amanda were not the same couple that the others remembered as being the swindlers. The ring, or whatever it was, had more than just one couple to trap the oldsters. Ben peeled fingerprints off the wine glasses from the night before, sent them to Jorge, who would transmit them to the FBI lab back in the States. Jorge told Ben that the two might be using. Ben assumed that they were probably wanted in the States for other crimes.

A task force was being convened by the U.S. and the Colombian Federal Police to take them all down, but they still needed Ben and Britt to investigate what happened to the missing couples. Ben knew that tomorrow might be interesting.

He read the papers handed to him. They were in double talk, and the print was so small that he would need a magnifying glass just to read. All he could understand was that he would have to pay $50,000 up front in order to stake out a condo and $100,000 if he wanted a whole villa. If he didn't accept the deal, he would have to pay his own way back to Bogotá, and then the U.S. Some of the writing was in Spanish and there were clauses in the language which were out- and-out illegal in the United States. He doubted that any of the people who lost their money could read any Spanish. Ben was so angry he gnashed his teeth. He felt his blood pressure rising. His eyes hurt from the small print and the poor lighting in the room.

The next day Ben met Bobby down by the pool. Ben was drinking thick, rich Colombian coffee, a stronger dose of caffeine than usual. He knew that this was the day that things could get ugly, and he wanted to be wide awake after a restless night of tossing and turning. He couldn't remember his dreams, but knew that they weren't pleasant. These slimy, slick, sleaze balls were not only his enemies, but the worst of the lot in Ben's opinion, because they preyed upon his cohort. He wanted blood, and would get it one way or another.

Bobby introduced Ben to one of the two men who had been tailing Ben and Britt.

"This is Tomas Martino, who will be taking you out fishing. He doesn't speak much English, but you can get your needs across with hand gestures and a little English."

Tomas wasn't smiling, and seemed to bore into Ben's skull with his pitch black small eyes. Ben instantly disliked the man, and knew that he might be the muscle to get at Ben's money, or the money that Bobby thought he had. Tomas wore shorts and a t-shirt, and there were no bulges anywhere that Ben could see. So, at least for the present there were no hints of a weapon.

Back at Langley, Jim Westerman was on the telephone with his contact in Bogotá.

"Damn it, Jorge, nothing must happen to Zangwell. Have you talked to the Federales?"

"Yes, yes of course. They want this garbage as much as we do, but right now Señor Zangwell is our best resource. I've sent down three of our agents, but they have to stay out of sight. If they're spotted, it could be dangerous for Ms. Manning and Mr. Zangwell."

"I thought she was hospitalized to keep her out of trouble, Jorge."

"Yes, yes, she's in the medical unit and is being watched for trouble breathing. But, who knows maybe the slime have people working there, too. We just don't know. Don't worry. I have a civilian guard watching her. Nobody will finger her. I thought it best to use a female."

"Good work, Jorge. Do your best. I know you'll be careful. Ben Zangwell was one of our best ever. He knew five, maybe six directors personally and if he hadn't been so radical, he'd have gone places. Still one hell of an agent in his time. Buena suerte, mi amigo."

Westerman thought to himself, "It isn't Jorge who needs the luck; it's Ben and Britt. "Doing government work in their eighties. Can you beat that?" The line was already dead. Westerman was talking to himself. Then he had a thought. Would they have to pay Social Security and benefits for the octogenarians? He laughed to himself.

Bobby was concerned that he couldn't get to the old hag. Maybe she'll die in the hospital, he thought to himself. "Shit, that's no good," he grumbled under his breath. "Then the fat son of a bitch won't give us a dime. He wouldn't want to stay here, then."

Britt was annoyed that Ben had placed her in the hospital. She'd lived with breathing problems for a long time, and it hadn't killed her yet. Sure, she was slower, more forgetful, a little unsteady on her feet, but that was because she had to carry around the damned oxygen tank, as far as she was concerned.

But the real reason that she was annoyed was that she was worried, and more than a little frightened, that something would happen to Ben. She admitted to herself that she loved him, and couldn't bear to lose him or have anything happen to him. The feeling of loving someone made her feel like a schoolgirl, and she felt a warmth inside her that she hadn't experienced for a long, long time.

But what to do? Some young uniformed, lanky gun-carrying soldier was always present outside the hospital room where she'd been placed, and nurses were always coming in to check on her vitals. How could she get out of the room and find her way to her man? She dismissed a fleeting thought that her presence could be dangerous for her. She had an image of hitting that young peroxide blond with her oxygen tank, and Britt smiled.

She needed a plan. She had the cell phone that Ben had given her to use in an emergency to get hold of him. She called the number, and Ben answered on the second ring.

"Are you OK? They feeding you OK? How's the bed?" He spoke quickly, and in spurts.

"Yes, everything's fine, but I'm worried about you, and not being there with you. I love you Ben!" There was a moment of silence before either spoke. Britt worried that she'd spoken foolishly.

"I love you too, Darling."

Ben's heart was racing, and he glanced at a mirror to see whether he was blushing. He was beet red with joy. He'd not said anything like this to anyone since he'd laid his fiancée to rest on the terrace behind the commune so many years ago. What a hell of a place to talk about love.

"Ben I want to get out of here, and be with you. No matter what happens, I want to be with you, by your side - forever."

"I've got to think straight, Sweetheart. I'm going out with them fishing. I need to know where those couples disappeared to, and this is the only way. If I have you here, I'll just have more to worry about. You understand, Britt?"

"But, with me in the hospital, they won't do anything, because I'm a loose end to them. They need me either way this thing goes."

She made sense. What will they do if he's alone? On one hand, if he doesn't sign the papers today, they will try to kidnap Britt from the hospital. On the other hand, if he does sign them, he may never find out what happened to the others. He knew that his thinking might be a little screwy. He'd read somewhere that as one ages something called fluid intelligence wanes. Was he thinking straight? Was he figuring all the angles correctly? Were his emotional feelings for Britt getting in the way?

He didn't have a lot of time to think, and that, too, worried him. He wasn't as fast as he used to be.

"OK, darling. Maybe you're right. Maybe whatever happens we should be together. Tell you what. When they get here, I'll tell them that the hospital called, and that they are releasing you. I'll get them to swing by the hospital, pick you up and we'll all go out fishing. I have a tracking device that Jorge gave me. You won't believe where I wear it. It's like a ring that I wear around my – you know what I mean."

Britt couldn't help herself. She began to laugh and choke at the same time. The nurse came running. She was actually working for Jorge, and was tasked with the well-being of her patient in more ways than one. "Señora Manning, are you OK?"

"Yes, yes, don't worry. My fiancé just told me a funny joke."

She held her hand over the phone mouthpiece, and had a fleeting thought that it was like piercing his tongue or nipple. She wondered what that would feel like.

"OK Ben, Whatever you say. See you in an hour or two. I'll be ready."

A quick call to Jorge with the change in plans, and instructions to have the doctor release Britt, and Ben made ready for what he hoped would be the last day of adventure. His world changed, and he didn't want any more excitement of this kind anyway. No more assignments, no more excitement. He longed for the commune and to hold Britt for the rest of his life. His last thought before he dressed was whether he was experiencing some sort of old age fantasy.

The next morning Ben didn't wait for Bobby and Amanda to come to his room. He was sitting in the lobby waiting for them and beaming with joy.

"They're releasing Britt from the hospital this morning. Great news. She wants to go fishing with us."

"Wonderful news." Bobby thought, "There is a God."

"She'll be waiting for us when we get there. You two had breakfast yet? I'm buying."

"No, but if we want to get some fishing in, we'd better hurry. I think we have enough time for a coffee and rolls."

Bobby and Amanda hadn't brought the papers with them because Britt was in the hospital. They thought they'd wait until the boat for that. It would scare the old fool if he couldn't see land. He'd either sign on with a check which they could collect on electronically, or they'd take him to the island house where they kept the prisoners who'd screwed everything up for themselves. The island was about fifteen miles off shore behind a group of rocks. The house was converted into a prison where the rest of the gang held them. The idea was to work on them to sign checks which could be cashed electronically. It was up to the bozo to sign and shut up, or face trouble with the gang. They had no idea what they were about to experience.

Britt was ready when they arrived in the lobby of the hospital. She thanked the nurse who wheeled her down from the ward. Seriously shocked at the turn of events, the nurse was more than perplexed to see Ben with the men who, sooner or later, she would be arresting and placing in handcuffs. José was on his way with a squad of Colombian commandos who were trained at Ft. Benning in Georgia. Celeste knew that they would take no prisoners if the gringos gave them any trouble. José thought it better that Britt not know who Celeste really was, but Celeste developed a feeling of simpatico for the old woman, and worried that she might be going into a danger zone. When she saw Ben, her anxiety only worsened. She wondered whether the "Company" was loco.

Dark clouds hovered on the horizon and perhaps foretold of the horrors which awaited Ben and Britt. They didn't know it, but soon they would be in great danger, and close to something they couldn't get out of – at least not on their own. Luckily, "Z" stuck the transmitter in his jockey shorts, figuring that no one would want what he had in there anyway.

Down at the dock, a small fishing boat just about big enough for two deckhands and the four gringos awaited them. Introductions were made, and the lines drawn to set sail. Bait was on board as was the fishing gear. Everything looked kosher as far as Ben could tell, but he knew the two thieves only waited to make their play for his money as soon as they left port. It didn't take them long.

"Let's get those lines baited. I can hardly wait to take pictures of my marlin or whatever I catch." Ben seemed so excited, and Bobby could hardly wait to stick it to the old fool.

"Ben, before we do any fishing, I think we should do some business."

He glanced at Britt and Amanda. His deckhands were ready for any trouble because they'd been on the boat when the old gringos paid up or were taken by force to the island and locked up.

"Can't it wait until I catch me a big one?" He laughed and his belly shook like jelly. Britt feigned innocent joy, too. Actually, she was not prepared for what happened next.

"No, we can't wait really, Ben. We need to talk business now. I have bankers waiting for this transaction." Bobby maintained a ready smile, but felt on edge. "Look, we need your check now. I mean, we told our people that you would give us the money for the down payment on the condo. They're not very patient people. You know, put your money where your mouth is." He laughed without mirth.

Britt began to feel a little queasy from the rocking of the boat. The water was a little rough and she'd just been in the hospital. She wasn't expecting Bobby's mournful stare. She turned to Amanda with a pale smile. Amanda appeared anxious, and a little bit like someone who Britt remembered from a movie. But she couldn't place who it was. She had a sickly feeling that what was going on here wasn't good.

"Oh, come on, Bobby, where's your spirit? We're here to have fun, and we can talk business when I've caught a big fish. I need to have a fish story to tell all my old buddies when I return home." He winked at Bobby, and could feel Bobby's anger shaded by his sunglasses and Panama straw hat.

"No Ben, it's not going to work that way. Business first, and then you can fish all you want to, but not now. Give me the money so we can call it in on the boat's radio. Now!"

Ben felt the hairs on his neck stand erect. This was the moment he'd anticipated. It wouldn't be long now before two helicopters would be swooping down to end this whole nasty business. He still needed to get to the island and find those people. That was the mission, not just save Britt and his own ass.

"Wow, you really mean it, don't you? Jeez, I don't know, Bobby. What's the big rush? I mean, Britt and I are good for the dough. We just want to have a little fun before business."

Ben noticed that Bobby had given a nod to the two deckhands who weren't getting ready for any fishing. They looked grim and fingered their shirt tails. It appeared that they had something under their shirts. They did. Each carried small barrel 38's with silencers on them. They didn't draw them, but Ben knew what was happening.

"I want to see your money now, old man, or you'll regret it. I'm not kidding. Show me your money." Bobby was almost growling, and Amanda had stepped behind Britt in a threatening manner.

"I left it in the hotel safe for safety reasons. I mean AARP always warns its members not to carry cash with them. It's dangerous. Why are you acting this way?"

"What did you say?" Bobby seemed perplexed, and began to sway a bit, his face was turning crimson red. The two Colombians knew something was wrong as Amanda grabbed Britt's wrist and gave her a pull. Britt grimaced and whimpered.

"Now, wait just one minute! I thought you two were upright business people. You're scaring Britt and acting mighty ugly. Why?"

Ben felt apprehension mingled with anger now and just a little fear- not for himself, but for Britt, and what he would do to these three men if Britt weren't there to see his fury in action.

The deckhands drew their pistols and waved them toward Ben and Britt. Ben thought, "Well, now it begins." Immediately, he wished that he'd left Britt in the hospital. If things got ugly, he didn't want her catching a bullet meant for him.

"OK, OK. Why the guns? What's this all about anyway? We're old people who just wanted to have some fun and catch some rays. I don't want no trouble!"

Bobby relaxed a bit, feeling that he had the situation well in hand. These old fools would have to join the others at the house, and that would mean their death, but not until the crew had their money.

"Dammit, why couldn't you have cooperated, given us the money, and enjoyed your fishing trip? Now you got to go to the house and kiss your fat ass goodbye."

"What house? What are you talking about? I thought you were a real estate agent who wanted us to look at some property for our retirement." Ben began to sweat, and Bobby assumed it was due to fear. He was wrong!

Bobby yelled something to one of the deckhands in Spanish, thinking that Ben wouldn't understand what he was saying. Ben knew that he had given orders to go to the gang's hideout. The plan was working. So much for fishing.

Britt played her role like a star, but in truth she was scared, and more than a little sick to her stomach from the rolling of the waves. "Do you have any sea sickness pills? I think that I'm going to be sick."

"Old woman, you're going to be sick alright. Your fool of a fiancé is playing us for chumps. But he's the jerk chump, and so are you. Now be quiet or we'll feed you to the sharks."

"Young man, you are rude, disgusting, and I resent your tone of voice." She turned to Amanda. "Are you in this with this sicko?"

"You'd better be quiet, old woman. He means it, and if he doesn't throw you in the water, those two will." She nodded in the direction of the dark mestizos who wearily watched the scene between Ben and Bobby.

"Why are you doing this, Bobby. I was just going to go out for some fishing, and now you've gone and spoiled everything."

"Shut the hell up, you old fool." Bobby lunged forward and grabbed Ben's shoulder. Ben spun around, surprising Bobby. Shock crossed Bobby's face as he slipped on the wet deck.

"Shit, shit, shit." Bobby sprang up and his face was a dark crimson. "I ought to shoot you now, you old bastard. Fuck, Watch this guy!" Bobby was livid.

José sauntered forward with a 38 snub nose in his hand. He didn't plan to be as stupid as the gringo. He laughed to himself, thinking how funny the punk was when he fell. Who would have thought that he would see the punk fall down? Nodding at Michel, his buddy, he said, "I no fall down, fat man. You do anything stupid and you no live long. Comprende, hombre?"

Ben knew that he'd shoot him without any remorse. These two mestizos were barrios boys for sure. Life was cheap, and Ben knew they probably hated Bobby and his white woman as much as they hated him. He made a small gesture of supplication to them, and feigned fear and horror.

"Sientese ahora, anciano!" (Sit down now, old one), ordered José.

Ben didn't let on that he understood all too well. He stood glumly as though his world was crumbling. José snarled at Britt, who was genuinely afraid, and guessed correctly that she was going to cry, which she began to do silently.

Amanda didn't feel comfortable with the turn of events. She'd not felt so uneasy before, but for some reason this was different. Britt reminded her of someone, someone from her past long ago. She'd been close to a woman very much like Britt, but where? She looked at Britt's eyes, her gray hair, her frail body, and all of a sudden she knew. It was her grandmother. It was the farm again, and her grandmother calling her to come out of the tall corn fields for dinner. That was more than thirty years ago, and she began to have a flood of memories which caused her to want to cry and long for the old woman again. Grandma protected her from her uncles' abuses when she could, but too many times when they were liquored up, they'd done her bad, real bad. What could the old woman do? She feared them and yet, didn't run away. Those were bad days, and they left Amanda filled with anger and hatred toward men and the world in general.

Bobby sensed something wrong with Amanda. He knew very little about her, but had always suspected something dark in her past. He'd made passes at her, slept with her, but found her cold, unwilling to let go. She knew the right things to say, but her heart wasn't in it. He'd never seen her react this way before, and wondered what was going on.

For her part, Amanda regretted being harsh with Britt, but she had no feeling for the fat man. He was just another predator as far as she was concerned, another sleazy old man who'd have his way with her if he could.

"Sit down over there on the chair. Don't do anything wrong. Those two will kill you for sure." She nodded in the deck hands direction.

"Head for the island now. We'll get their money the hard way, and then kill them both."

Ben was thankful that they were doing what he wanted them to do. The transmitter ring around his penis was already signaling the Colombians where to look for them. For a brief moment, he thought about killing them all there on the boat, but gave the idea up for the necessity of having to find their hideout so the others could be saved. It never occurred to Ben that he wasn't as young as he once was, and would probably die before he accomplished his mission. "Once a Marine, always a Marine. Semper Fi."

Twenty minutes later, the boat looped around a cove out of sight of the ocean. Ben could see an island in the distance. He hoped the cavalry would find the prison quickly once they were on land. Acting completely lost and beaten he allowed himself to be led on shore with Britt being helped over the edge of the boat by Amanda.

Three swarthy Colombian men met the boat as it docked, each with a kalashnikov slung over one shoulder and each had blood shot eyes. They'd been drinking the night before. Two grabbed Ben by the arms and dragged him up the hill. He allowed them to manhandle him. Amanda brushed the other man aside and helped Britt. Britt was terrified, and Amanda tried to think of ways to save the old woman should things get messy. Britt's body sagged as she was escorted up the hill and into the house. Even the oxygen tank carried by Amanda was close to empty, and showed only about five or six liters left.

Ben had no idea how the commandos would arrive. The Colombians wanted to handle everything, but unbeknown to them was the fact that a detachment of SEALS was dispatched to bring home the Americans at any cost. Ben wasn't informed that the SEALS would be there to do the work instead of the Colombians. It was the way that CIA worked. "Need to know" was still the mantra and that included the Colombians even though it was their country, and Ben's major function was to lead them to the quarry.

Ben was not surprised to see seven frightened, bewildered, and forlorn elderly people, each tied loosely to cots bolted to the floor. Four women and three men looked up listlessly as they entered. One had no left arm. He wondered where the other man was. He'd been briefed with their names, what they looked like, and their approximate age. They were all haggard and beaten. He'd done his job, and now it was just a matter of time before they'd be freed- or so he hoped.

Patted down and thrown roughly on a ratty couch, the two newcomers huddled together, Britt in fear, Ben in anger and yet fearful for Britt and the others. His first inclination was to ask where the other man was. But, he thought better of that idea because it would throw suspicion upon him and Britt that they were more than two new old fools who wouldn't cooperate and open their bank accounts to the thieves.

"Tie them up good. The old fool thinks he's Superman. Tried to jump me in the boat. The old woman is sick. Give them some water and food. Then we'll work them over to electronically wire the money to the account," Bobby ordered as he looked at all the old people, and felt sick of the whole thing.

"What happened to her husband?" Amanda noticed the missing husband and was alarmed.

"He in other room, Señora. I think maybe dead. Last night he was not so good, so Enrique and José, they move him to back room. He not wake up yet."

Amanda became startled. No one had died yet. She gave Bobby a concerned look and ran to the other room throwing open the curtain that separated the two rooms. "Bobby, come quick. He looks dead."

A shriek suddenly erupted from a woman sitting across the room with a rope around her waist. Ben lied and said he was a trained paramedic a long time ago and could help.

Bobby raced to the room, and saw that the old man was ashen and looked dead. He turned in anger at Ben and screamed, "See what you caused, you old fool." Ben bolted to the room and felt for a pulse. There was no carotid pulse, and the body was beginning to get cold.

Ben knew from pictures that this was Harvey Paxton. He'd memorized the photos and bios of each person unaccounted for so far. His brain was racing. He motioned Bobby to shut the curtain, and bid him to say nothing.

In a whisper, he spoke. "He's dead, probably a cardiac. Don't say anything, or the woman out there will go into shock. Is he her husband?"

Bobby nodded his head in affirmation, and began to sweat.

"It wasn't supposed to happen like this, god dammit. Enrique, venga aquí! Que pasé, amigo?"

Enrique entered, looked down, and shrugged. "No sé que pasé. He dead?"

Bobby looked at Ben, and then back at Enrique, and nodded his head. He held up a finger to his lips to warn the Colombian to say nothing. He didn't want the wife and the others going crazy on him. Ben knew that the wife's name was Merle, and that they were both around his age. Ben covered the body. It was murder now and that upped the ante.

Merle Paxton was crying and yelled for Harvey. Ben went to her and offered her his shoulder to cry on. Britt realized that something was dreadfully wrong and wept for herself, Harvey, and everyone involved.

Meanwhile the other couples, all in their seventies began to whimper and hold each other as best they could, although tied to the cots. In a show of emotion, the Colombians crossed themselves, as did one of the couples. They began to say a prayer in Latin, while the other couple began to chant the prayer for the dead, the Kaddish in Aramaic. Ben knew that they were the Cohens, and the other couple, the Ryan's. Merle and Harvey's dossier had no mention of religious preference. All of them simply wanted to find a retirement villa to spend the rest of their days in peace. Some peace!

Ben knew more than he could say to relieve their anxieties, but with the death of Harvey he doubted that he could do anything to make them feel better. He also knew that the Colombians didn't kill Paxton. Three heart attacks before venturing out to Colombia had, but he didn't want to lighten their spirits in any way.

Poor Merle was beside herself, and cried for her children and grandchildren. She began to talk about her family that they would be crushed by their father's death. Nothing said or done would pacify her grief. She was in denial and already beginning to go through the stages of bereavement.

"He can't be dead. He's so strong, and he takes such good care of himself."

Ben knew that she was wrong about Harvey's health, but said nothing. For the rest of the day, the thieves huddled outside mostly, and reverted to their alcohol, perhaps as a means of dealing with this new development. It left the prisoners to themselves in the front room.

Ben considered telling them that they were going to be saved, but had to hold his tongue. He was not sure whether they would give away his news in some manner. As dusk began to fall, he wondered whether the Colombian forces would land soon, and how they might do so.

Amanda prepared beans, rice, and a beef dish on a portable stove. With all the excitement, Ben and Britt hadn't eaten in ten hours, and were beginning to experience hunger and thirst. The others picked at their food listlessly while Merle sat rocking herself in grief.

While the prisoners and their captors were spending the day knowing that one of the old people had died, the Commander, Detachment Leader of Seal Team Bravo was going over last minute details with his men. Insertion was planned for 2:00 in the morning under the cover of darkness. A medical evacuation ship off the coast would be the take-off and return vessel. Already on board, a small hospital unit was readied to administer first aid to the elderly couples, and to any of the gang that might be still alive, as well.

Bravo Team prepared for this mission, and went over the plans until everyone knew his role, and the jobs of his team members as well. The

SEALS were well trained in fast insertions, mission completion, and exiting with all due speed. Having to be responsible for senior citizens was a new twist, and each member was cautioned about the health and well being of the old folks. It was hard to tell what was on their minds. Perhaps they thought of their grandparents, and wanted to protect these people as though they were their own. The trained paramedic with surgical technical training before he went SEAL was totally familiar with medical records of all concerned. He knew about Harvey Paxton's heart condition, about the colon cancer in Silvia Cohen's records, the transient ischemic attacks that Mr. Ryan had suffered in his sixties. He was loaded down with portable oxygen tanks figuring that the woman by the name of Britt, the chronic obstructive pulmonary disease patient would need O2 immediately.

The team leader was an E-7, Nelson Devor. He'd seen action in five continents, was loaded down with commendations, and would be retiring in a year. His men were tough, younger, stronger, and more pumped than their leader, but he was their mentor and each loved him as a father. They would die for him, and he for each of them.

CIA Headquarters was alive, and tuned into everything going on in Colombia. It had taken some doing to get the Colombians to back away from using their own forces to extradite the Americans. State Department, FBI, and Department of Defense were all involved with the President being kept informed in a regular briefing by the National Security Adviser. President Simon conferred with her counterpart in Colombia, and assured him that the team would not kill any civilians including the gang of Colombians unless it was unavoidable. There would be no collateral damages.

Ben and Britt huddled together and she buried her head in his massive chest, smelling his manly sweat, and raw anger and fear for her safety. She knew that were she not there, Ben would probably try save the others by himself. Her fear and sorrow for Merle was at moments overwhelming, and the oxygen tank was drained of its life-saving gas.

Night brought a cool breeze, and the sky was overcast. There would be no moonlight this night. Outside, the five Mestizos and the two Americans smoked and drank from bottles of Colombian wine. They grumbled about their new problems with the death of Paxton and two new captives. Bobby knew that sooner or later he'd have to eliminate the old fools, and maybe even some of these blood- thirsty cannibals he had to deal with. He considered his options, and was not happy with any of them. He lamented again on his bad luck. The more he drank, the more morose he became.

Amanda excused herself and went in to feed her unwanted guests. She grabbed some tortillas, some canned ground beef, seasoning, and brought the oldsters food.

"Eat up and tomorrow, if all goes well, we'll take you all back to the mainland."

She looked at Merle who only seemed more shrunken and lost. For a moment Amanda felt pity for the old woman, and wished that she'd never gotten into this mess. She knew that she'd always be running from the law from now on. She felt fear, anger, and despair all at once.

"How the fuck did I get into this mess?" As usual she had no answer to how life had been so unkind.

Around midnight the deck hands and the other three Colombians were sleeping, snoring peacefully, and dreaming of their women. Bobby tried to find a place to get comfortable, but could only bemoan his situation. Sleep would not come. He left the group to relieve himself, and thought he heard the faint sounds of a plane in the distance. But the waves were lapping the shore, and in the darkness he dismissed the thought. Returning to the others, he saw Amanda sitting with her back against a rock. He went to her and sat down.

"I'm scared Bobby, real scared," she whimpered.

"About what? Tomorrow we'll get them to transfer the money to our account in the Caymans, and then kill them all. We'll be rich! Come over here, baby, and rub my back a little." He wanted a lot more than a back rub.

At 2:01 AM precisely, with an overhead cloud bank, lines were dropped from a helicopter, and six black hooded figures slid down the ropes in quick succession. Using infrared glasses, the team assembled three miles from the hideout on the backside of the island. Only the whine of the engines could be heard, and as soon as the men dropped to the ground, the transport rose effortlessly and disappeared. Radio contact was minimal and the pilots knew not to stray too far away.

Making sure that his men were in order, Nelson gave hand signs to fall in, and move with speed toward their quarry. Forty-five minutes later they broke through a clearing, and saw the silhouette of the house. Using his binoculars he could make out five bodies sleeping on the ground, but couldn't determine how many more were there. He assumed the Americans were inside. Two of the men slid off their backpacks, shouldered their assault rifles, and moved slowly through the brush to get a better look. They were to make no contact, just reconnoiter.

Seeing the sleeping thugs and empty wine bottles strewn about relieved the warriors. Their weapons lay by their sides. There wouldn't be a problem with subduing them. But where were the others? In the briefing, Bobby and Amanda were described by the elders who'd already lost their money to the thieves. Where were they now? No lights were on in the house, no noise came from that direction. The scouts using hand signals reported five sleeping bandits, probably drunk.

"OK. On my count. Teddy, Ivan - around back. John, Will - subdue the five of them. No noise, no shooting. Sam,with me. Through the door. Any bad guys, kill them if they resist. Don't hurt the captives. Check your watches. Two twenty-two, we go. Make it happen, SEALS."

The team dispersed. It was over before it began. The five Colombians tried to get up, were knocked unconscious before they could sit. Meanwhile, the team members simultaneously charged the house. Bobby went for his gun, and felt a sharp sting as a bullet lodged into his right arm. No noise, just a silent slam into his right humerus. Amanda, wide-eyed and alert, tried to shout something, but was quickly knocked unconscious by an unknown assailant.

Nelson spoke first, "Secured."

The seven hostages were more fearful of what greeted them than they were of their predicament before. Hooded giants with huge guns were as frightening as were the gang, until Nelson spoke.

"Hello, thought we'd drop by, and take you folks home to America." His voice was gentle, yet exuded authority.

Ben knew what had happened. "Well, you're not Marines. But you'll do. My name is Ben Zangwell. Thanks for joining our party."

"Chief Devor, Sir. Bravo Team. Glad we could help." He pulled a radio from his vest. "Clear. Land at will."

"Roger that, enroute." The pilot radioed the ship and the commander of the navy vessel radioed back to his command.

The five Colombians were secured, each bewildered by what had just happened to them, and had no fight left to resist. Bobby's wound was superficial, quickly cleaned, and bandaged by the medical team member. Britt's oxygen was changed out, and she began to get her two liters which made breathing easier. Harvey Paxton's body was placed in a body bag by the men before they administered to the captives.

Tired, bedraggled, and relieved after hot showers and bed rest on the ship, all of the hostages were able to move about. Medical attention revealed no one was seriously hurt. For Britt, it seemed like a blur. Everything happened so fast, and then it was over. The SEALS had saved almost all of the victims except for Harvey Paxton. Ben had to admit that he was glad that he hadn't had to act.

CHAPTER TWENTY-ONE

T he President addressed the senior citizens over the loud speaker. She congratulated them, and praised their heroism. The last thing she said before signing off was that she wanted all of the couples, including Ben and Britt, to come to see her in the White House, and that when they returned to the States it would be arranged. Even Merle Paxton, in her sorrow, was excited.

"I can't believe it. The President wants you and Britt to visit her," beamed Sadie. Britt and Ben were in every newspaper in the country. The rescue was international news. Ben called Maria and Juan, and asked them to handle their new found notoriety. He was both happy and saddened. This was not part of the agreement with the CIA. Ben had always stayed under the radar away from prying eyes, and for good reason. He didn't want Colombian drug lords or anyone else jeopardizing the well-being of those nearest him.

They'd been home for three weeks when the call came in from the Press Secretary's office at the White House. The President and her husband wanted to greet the elderly hostages with members of the Congressional Caucus, especially those interested in international intrigue. The entire North Carolina congressional caucus would be, and the President planned to award Ben and Britt with medals of honor for their bravery. All Ben could think of was that he wouldn't be able to work again.

Excitement reigned. The telephone rang incessantly. David's family shook their heads in wonderment, as did Sadie's children who thanked God for his intercession on behalf of Britt and Ben. Kelly House took on notoriety. It seemed that every senior citizen wanted to know how they could become part of the commune. MNBC sent a graying Rachel Maddow to interview Britt and Ben. She was so intrigued with Kelly House that she did two more pieces on the Commune and each of the women who lived there. ABC, NBC, CNN, BBC and even FOX wanted interviews. Spivak of Fox commented on his theme of This is What Good Americans are all about. When Ben heard about that, he nearly threw the TV across the room. All the anchors wanted their pictures on the screen with Ben and the rest of the commune. It was an avalanche.

Ben and Britt were flown on a jet sent by Washington to get them. A Navy nurse was dispatched, just in case. For Britt, all was a wash of excitement. She'd finally been recognized; not for her photography, but for heroism and patriotism. Her son called and told her how proud he was of her, and maybe she could send him a few bucks- if she had it.

Ben and Britt hugged and kissed the hostages when they met in the Rose Room in the White House. The ceremony would be in the garden. Press Corps representatives were everywhere, and the President and her husband presented their three little ones to the elderly couples and Merle, the widow. The children were shy, being only five, seven and nine. President Simon and her husband, Timothy, were in their mid-forties, and started having children late in life. She'd served in the Senate for two terms; he practiced law for a homeless advocacy group in Oregon before she was swept into office as the first woman to be elected to the presidency. It was a presidency following on the heels of the difficult Obama years.

As a moderate Republican who stood by capitalism, but had a sense of what it was like not to be part of those who had made it, she offered sound economic goals to the electorate with a safety net for those less fortunate. She gave the country a taste of humble Lincoln-like leadership. She promised an end to the wars in the Middle East, and kept her promise, bringing to an end a tragic pair of wars. She managed to bring all sides to the table and created meaningful legislature to end tax loopholes for employers who exported their businesses off- shore. Employment picked up because entrepreneurs came home and tried again. Loretta Simon was doing well in the White House and people gave her a seventy-three percent approval rating, but she didn't let it go to her head because she knew that the electorate was fickle. The White House was alive with children, dogs, and cats racing about like it was rumpus room. The staff had to adjust and loved it.

The guest list for the ceremony was small. President Simon went to Merle Paxton first, felt a pang of sorrow, and kissed her on the cheek. No one could remember a president of the United States every allowing emotion to flow so freely. Merle, herself, was surprised and more than a little touched. The President wiped a tear from her cheek, and whispered something in Merle's ear. The women locked eyes and sealed something that only women can do. Little Charly, the President's youngest, saw Mommy crying, went up to her and took her hand, tears dotting his cheeks. It was a moment for the history archives and a photo journalist delight.

"So, you're the guy who made this happen." The President was lost in the presence of the walrus mustachioed bulk of the man. Ben blushed, lowered his head and said nothing. Then she whispered something to him which no one could hear. Later he told Britt what she'd said.

"She asked me what I did with the device that brought in the SEALS. She winked at me. I felt smaller than – you know what."

Britt laughed until she began to cough.

The White House kitchen staff prepared a lunch for the visitors with the President and her family. Everyone thoroughly enjoyed the festivities and was given an autographed picture of the first family before they left. No one would forget this glorious day.

On the flight home, Ben decided, then and there, never to get involved in an operation again. It was time to get on with Kelly House business.

CHAPTER TWENTY-TWO

Pauline wandered the streets in Montfort. She loved the old houses which seemed Baroque to her. She loved the assortment of people who floated by on bicycles or roller blades. Often she stopped at the Fresh Food store and drank thick coffee, and just gazed at the men and women who seemed so self-absorbed in their private worlds.

She saw bedraggled older people stop at trash cans and emptied tables. Some devoured cakes and food left by people who'd gone. It was the same men and women who showed up on a daily basis, and she wondered if they were homeless. Too shy to approach them, she watched and felt like an eavesdropper on their solitary lives. Tears welled in her eyes.

"I've seen poverty, Lee. Max and I traveled through India. The poor are everywhere, just everywhere. I think David said, 'In your face.' He's right, you know. But what I saw at the store made me so sad. I could not get my mind around it here, here in Asheville! I saw it in Florida too. So very sad! In this land of milk and honey- or is it?" Pauline shook her head in perplexity.

"I am not sure who said it, but somewhere I read that people see the homeless in one of two ways."

"One of two ways, Lee? What do you mean?"

"Well, Pauline, as I remember it some people say 'I have mine. Tough luck you get your own. It's your own damn fault.'" Lee lowered her head in shame that she used a bad word in front of Pauline. "Excuse my French."

Pauline smiled, "I have heard a lot worse than that, my friend. Are you saying that people dismiss the sorrows of others without concern, Lee?"

"I'm just telling you what I read in the New York Times. One of those writers who writes on Sundays said that there's those people and another type; those who do care, those who think they are responsible for their brothers and sisters."

"It's so sad, Lee. We live in a land of plenty, and yet so many are in poverty. I do not understand! In India it is overwhelming. But, here in our country it is a disgrace."

Pauline and Lee were lost in their own thoughts, each thinking about their own demons. Pauline was the first to speak.

"I think we need to build hundreds of senior centers for elderly homeless. So many, how do you call them, baby boomers. I read about one in Seattle, Washington, called a senior center. But I read that most of the participants are either literally homeless or living so close to the poverty level that they are within a few dollars of utter homelessness."

"So depressing, so sad. I wish I could do something." Lee answered, then began to drool and shake.

"Rest, Lee. We can talk later," Pauline said and tried to sooth Lee, but had a sudden sense of despondency. She looked at Lee and despair engulfed. It was palpable. Lee seemed to be doing well---- but now?

"Shall I ask Stephen to visit you?"

Lee did not answer, she was snoring softly. Pauline's thoughts shifted to Gerald. She could not help herself. He was charming, gallant, and oh-so- knowledgeable. She wondered what it would be like to kiss him, to be kissed by him, and she felt the warmth of her thoughts engulf her being. She had not felt this way since the first year or two with Max. "Oh my, what is happening to me?" she thought.

Lee stirred and her body shuddered, bringing Pauline out of her reverie. For a brief moment Pauline realized she'd felt young, alive and reborn.

Gerald was having similar feelings, but each time Pauline's image crossed his mind, he felt pangs of guilt. How could this be? How could he think of another woman? Claire was his life. And she's been dead for only four years! He winced.

He thought of Sadie always saying "May he rest in peace" when she talked of her husband. Gerald wanted to say the same words, but couldn't bring himself to utter religious words. He'd been an atheist for so long since his childhood and anger at the Catholic Church. But now the words seemed soothing, and he did not fight them. Claire, his beloved Claire! Would he ever find love again? He chuckled and said to himself, "I sound like something from a TV soap opera."

For some unfathomable reason, he remembered his Polish grandmother who wore nothing but long, black, ugly dresses as long as he could remember. She always had a room in his parent's house with a crucifix hanging on the wall, along with several pictures of a silver haired, debonair gentleman in a black suit wearing a red tie. Grandfather was a man who came from the old country, a place somewhere near Warsaw.

People said that Gerald favored him, especially as he aged. Grandmother spent hours every day praying before the crucifix at St. Pious Church in the Polish neighborhood on the near Northwest side of Chicago. The priests still used Polish. It was between the pews that he first fondled little what-was-her- name, anyway. They both thought that they would go to hell, but it felt so good and she loved it, too. At least, Gerald thought so. He heard she was sent to a convent in River Forest in the western suburbs. He wondered if that incident was the reason so many, many years ago.

Gerald fell asleep and dreamed of Claire, but awoke with a start. How could Pauline's face be on Claire's body, and what's-her-name be looking at Gerald and Pauline or Claire, or whoever she was. His forehead was drenched with moisture. Max and Pauline, Pauline and himself, a blurred sense of couples, then and now, mixed in the sophomoric metaphor, what was this all about?

CHAPTER TWENTY-THREE

For the last four months Kelly House had a visitor who showed up at odd times. He called himself Cody Watkins, and always seemed to enjoy the surprise on everyone's face. Cody appeared to be in his 70's, but who could tell. His teeth were rotted away except for two in the front which were stained brown. If the stains were from cigarettes, it was hard to tell, because no one saw him smoke. Lean, almost gaunt, about 5'10", white curly locks surrounding a bald circular spot made him look like an aesthetic monk. His eyes were deep in their sockets and spoke of living a rough life. He didn't say much for a long time, politely accepted any food offered him by Hazel with a gracious "Thank ya Ma'am." After a month, comfort set in as he sat on the porch and talked about Asheville. He seemed to know a lot about its history and the Civil War.

One day David, Gerald, and Cody were chatting about Asheville's part in the war. Cody sat up straight, and over some hot coffee given him by Stephen, began to talk about Shelton Laurel's massacre. David and Gerald were mesmerized by the story.

"Back in them days, the folks around here, mostly in Madison County wanted to be left alone. They didn't want no part of the Yankees or Rebs. Fact is they wanted to feed their families and stay out of it. You know we didn't have any slavery round these parts, what with the mountains and short growing season, and all that. So around 1863 or 4, I'm not sure which, some men and their boys rode over to Marshall- that was the county seat then, still is, and broke into a armory full of stores for the Rebs. Those folks back in the hollers in Shelton Laurel, they were hungry you know, their families starving. So they stole some food and went back to their places. Sure as hell, a group of Reb soldiers followed them there, and killed the men and their sons. Shot them dead in front of their kin folk. Bad blood even now. Those Madison folks don't forget or forgive."

David was the first to speak. "Are they that backwards that they'd hang on to something for over a hundred years?"

"I don't know about backward, but yep, they still talk about it, and don't like any strangers coming round them much. I know, I was born there."

"Why did you leave?" asked Gerald.

"Long story, Gerald. Long story." Cody's eyes clouded over, and he slouched down in his wicker chair. He seemed to be in deep contemplation and consternation.

"I did some bad things in my life, and I would understand it if you all told me to move on, but I paid my dues, and I even went to school and got my degree in drafting. Worked for ten or fifteen years until I screwed up, and lost it all. My wife and kids didn't want no more to do with me, and I haven't seen them for a long time. I know my language is not acceptable. Being on the street makes me want to blend in, and not be thought of as a snob. Sometimes I forget where I am."

David and Gerald stole glances at each other.

"Cody, are you homeless, my friend?" David immediately regretted asking.

"Yes and no. I mean I have a tent on the river, and get some money from my days drafting. I get Social Security. For how long, I'm not so sure."

David and Gerald smiled in agreement. Obama was out of office, and the Republican Congress was on the verge of stripping away the little safety net that existed. Even the Tee Party stalwarts were wishing that they had not been so gullible. The President would not let Congress, even members of her own party destroy everything that elders and poor people needed. It seemed to be a matter of time before everyone would be on their own with just a little Social Security for however long that lasted. President Simon had to juggle her conservative economic policies with a sense of justice and commitment to attending to the needs of the most vulnerable and marginalized. She sought counsel in her husband, they both knew that if Loretta hadn't been his wife, he would have become a Socialist long ago.

"Cody, I have been wondering why you like to come here, and sit with us so much." Gerald said and eyed Cody intensely.

"Well, you folks are all writers, and interested in communal life. I believe in what you're doing. It's a lifestyle that I'm convinced all older people should have in our society. It isn't like the old days when there were extended families, and kids took care of their parents and grandparents. I think that this lifestyle is the best one for all of us."

"You know our history, right? We met in the hospital, and have a year here to see if we like communal living," said David. "Oh, and we are all supposed to create artistic materials like stories, novels, art work, and the like."

"Would memoirs constitute something creative?" Cody leaned forward in his chair.

"Memoirs, surely if they are original, and you are interested in selling them," said David.

"What do you mean?"

David told Cody the agreement they had with Ben. Cody never talked to the big man before, and didn't know the history or circumstances.

"How long you all been here"?

Gerald spoke. "It's coming up on eight months. We have four months more. No one has sold anything yet, but we are writing, and we meet every week and read to each other. Ben hasn't pushed us to publish, but it is always on the back of our minds to be productive."

Cody thought a while and said, "Fubar County is one interesting place I've written some stuff about which might be interesting. Matter of fact, some folks might say it would blow the lid off of some of the things that went on there. Did you know that a social worker from DSS was killed because some idiot thought she was a revenuer?"

"You're kidding, Cody!" David looked stunned.

"I swear it's true. Some of those people are plain crazy. Like out of a horror story. I'm not joking. The woman who ran DSS for years was a frightful looking woman. Looked like that fella who ran for president on the Green ticket. What was his name? Some other people thought she looked like that Dr. Death from Michigan. All I knew is she smoked a pack a day, ran some real shady deals in that DSS, and hired some real kooks who had more problems than the clients."

"You've told us about Madison County, but never Fubar County. Where is that," asked David?

"Well it's near here, and between Madison County and Buncombe County. Nestled in between the two you might say. Back in the Civil War days they wanted to make it East Tennessee or West Carolina, I heard, but obviously that never happened. Territorial rights, you know."

"So how do you know so much about this county's problems?"

"Jerry, sorry - Gerald, I used to live over there for a couple of years. I got a job with the local Department of Social Services for about six months until the witch fired me. They were right though. I'd sit around during staff meetings and the workers would gossip about the clients. They were all kinfolk to each other, and there wasn't any objectivity. One day I blurted out that they all sounded inbred, or something like that, and sure enough, it wasn't long before I got canned." David smiled remembering some of his own fiascoes with employers.

Cody continued, "One of the supervisors had mental problems which were from her own days in foster care, and people had to listen to her woes over and over. She was probably in her fifties then. I guess she'd be about my age now, maybe older. It was a sorry office. A bit of a Peyton Place," Cody laughed uncomfortably.

"So you've written about all of this, and what else?" asked David.

"I've done some writing about some of the women I've known, if you know what I mean."

"Really, love stories, Cody?" Gerald smiled and gave him a wink.

"Well, I've known some real interesting ladies, let me tell you."

"Come on in and have dinner with us. You haven't met everyone, especially Ben. He's the owner of the commune, that is the house here. You'll find him incredibly interesting." David smiled widely.

"Well, I don't have any other clothes to wear for dinner. I left my good clothes in my foot locker at a place in town."

"Don't worry about your clothes. Ben isn't about what people wear, or how dressed up they are," beamed David. "He doesn't pass judgment on people if they're honest and straight forward. You'll fit right in, I'm sure of it." David and Gerald exchanged looks in agreement. It was getting dark. The men went into the house.

Hazel had made a baked chicken dish with rice, corn on the cob, and iceberg lettuce salad. Dessert was left in the fridge. It was blueberry cobbler. Everyone was home for dinner, and slowly meandered into the dining area. Sadie and Britt were the first to arrive. They'd been napping after a day of doing some gardening in the back of the house. A small vegetable garden and perennials were about all they could manage. Sitting in the living room, reading to each other, were Lee and Pauline. They'd gotten into the habit of sort of pushing each other to create something every other day, so that on the off days they could share their creations. They joined the others at the table.

Ben was sitting at his desk going over some of the bills and statements. He hated this part of communal living. He paid all the bills anyway, and saw no reason to check the statements, but Maria insisted that he go over all the papers whether he liked it or not. So dutifully, he spent two days a month reviewing paperwork. He lumbered down the stairs and came into the room. For Britt, her heart seemed to miss a beat every time she saw him come into a room. She was so in love with her hero, and he with her. They were going to make an announcement tonight at dinner and not wait for the weekly meeting. It was a bit of a surprise that all saw another place set for Cody.

Although everyone had seen Cody with the guys on the porch before, even said hello to him, and exchanged pleasantries, no one could remember him ever coming in for more than a visit to the bathroom once or twice. Seeing Ben and Cody juxtaposed against each other made Ben seem even larger than usual next to the thin strip of a man.

David spoke first, "I want to introduce Cody Watkins to you all. He's a friend of Gerald's and mine. Cody's a writer from time to time, and we've invited him to meet you all."

All eyes focused on their guest and Ben at the same time. Ben turned to Cody, grabbed his hand in his two paws, and said, "Any friend of David's and Gerald's a friend of mine. Welcome to Kelly House, Cody. I guess formal introductions are in order."

Sadie was the first to speak. "My oh my, you're so thin, young man. We have to fatten you up." She beamed at him, and Cody immediately liked the woman who seemed so motherly.

Cody had to stoop a little to hear Lee whisper, "I'm Lee Lansing, Cody, and I am pleased that the boys," she looked to David and Gerald, "invited you to meet us. You must be very special. They haven't done this before."

Pauline and Britt spoke at the same time, and Britt gestured to Pauline to go first. "I, too, am happy to meet you Cody. Maybe some time soon you'll tell us about yourself."

"My name is Britt Manning, and you must be sent from above because tonight Ben and I have an announcement to make, and you'll be the first outsider to hear it." Cody's face went white, as if all the blood had run out of it.

"I didn't mean 'outsider.' I meant the first person we didn't know before to become a part of our excitement."

Cody looked at the petite, frail woman and felt pity for her embarrassment.

"I'm honored to be invited to share your food with you all. And don't be embarrassed, Britt, about calling me an outsider. I am an outsider, and it's been a long time since I have felt so welcomed and accepted."

The rest of the dinner was spirited and everyone ate with a good appetite, especially Cody. He kept remarking how great everything was. He couldn't remember a time when he felt so full and happy.

"OK, we're full, fat and happy. So without a lot of tears and fanfare, I want you to know that I've asked Britt to marry me."

Ben had rehearsed a speech, but when he spoke the speech went out the window. He grabbed Britt's hand as he rose from the table. He broke out in tears, and scooped her up from the table in a big bear hug, and kissed her passionately in front of all. The gasps around the table were audible. When the kiss ended, he looked sheepishly around the table and said, "I guess I ought to ask her for her hand, right? Britt Manning,will you be my wife?"

"Yes, yes, yes, my love. I love you, Ben," Britt replied emotionally and cried as tear streaks caressed her cheeks. She could barely get the words out.

Sadie was the first to speak, "Mazel tov, mazel tov. I am so happy for you both."

The room exploded in a cacophony offering love, joy, happiness, and good wishes. Cody was overwhelmed with a joy he'd not felt in over fifty years. He didn't know why, but he had tears rolling down his cheeks.

CHAPTER TWENTY-FOUR

David and Gerald sat in the study, each going over their writing for the week, and contemplating the same thing without the other knowing so. In the afternoon the weekly meeting would be held, and they wanted to present an idea.

Cody Watkins would be discussed as a possible candidate for joining the commune. True, there were only four months to go before the year was up, but four months was four months, and thinking of Cody living by the river in a tent, or under a bridge somewhere with winter coming on was a thought that made David and Gerald uneasy.

"I think that we should talk to Ben about asking Cody to live here," said David.

"Yes, yes, definitely. I think that he would fit in perfectly and contribute. I have talked to Pauline about it, and she likes him. This is between us, David. She told me that she had never met a homeless person in person before. Even on her trips to India, and other countries where she saw horrendous conditions, she never actually spoke with someone who lived in garbage dumps, or anything like that. Cody has made an impression on her and the others, as well."

"When do you want to talk to Ben about him, Gerald?"

"Now, if he and Britt are not busy." Gerald raised an eyebrow.

They agreed to go to Ben' s room, and made their way to his room. David knocked. They heard something like a shuffling and smothered giggle. David couldn't stifle a wide grin.

"Coming. Hang on a minute."

"Hello, Britt, planning your wedding, my dear?"

Britt smiled mischievously at Gerald and David, and pretended to be caught in a compromising act. It was amazing how this frail, small, elf-like woman seemed to have been transformed into a happy, beaming, and adorable child. Seeing her standing next to the hulk of a man never ceased to amuse the two men. They loved the two as if they were their own flesh and blood.

"Excuse us for barging in on you two love birds, Ben," beamed David.

"Could we have a word with you, Ben? We don't mind if Britt remains," Gerald inquired, and David shook his head in agreement.

"I have to get downstairs and help Sadie and Hazel in the kitchen. You boys have a good talk." She gave Ben a peck on the cheek, which was quite a feat because she could barely reach his shoulder, but anticipating her movement, he bent down to her.

"Lucky you guys didn't catch us doing something we shouldn't be doing," Ben winked at the two. "What can I do for you?"

"It's about Cody, Cody Watkins," David cleared his throat and went on. "How would you feel about asking Cody to live here, at least until the year is up?"

Ben wasn't surprised that this would come up. He'd anticipated that he'd be asked about the idea.

"Have you thought about what that would mean? I mean, he's homeless. You don't really know much about him, do you?"

Gerald answered, "No, but considering what he has been through, and his wealth of knowledge, I would say he is one of the most erudite fellows I have met in many years. How he has been able to maintain his incredible encyclopedic memory is a wonder."

"I've been thinking about where he'd sleep. He could sleep in the storeroom next to the workroom downstairs, or upstairs in one of the spare rooms. We always knew that there might be others who'd move in here. I think that he would be a great addition to our group." David was obviously excited. "He doesn't eat much, and I'd be happy to help pay for his food and the like. He's on food stamps, and that would help."

Ben nodded and smiled, "Do you want to bring it up at the meeting, and see what the others think?"

That was it. No more discussion was needed. The duo was elated.

That night after dinner the weekly meeting began. Hazel and Stephen were always invited to stay and join in as equal contributors. Sadie was now the elected leader and took her job quite seriously. She asked for any new business to be brought to the group. David indicated that he had something to say.

"Gerald and I would like to make a proposal. We'd like to nominate Cody Watkins for membership, if that's the appropriate word, to join our commune."

No one was surprised. He'd met everyone when he was invited to dinner, and during his visits with David and Gerald. Hazel and Stephen were impressed with him, and liked his matter-of-fact demeanor. Stephen even suspected that Cody might have some Cherokee in him, but when asked, Cody denied any knowledge of having Native blood, but he admitted that he didn't know all his ancestors, or where or with whom they slept. His wry sense of humor pleased Stephen.

A few questions from Pauline and Sadie centered on background and whether Cody was a wholesome person. Was he a jailbird? Where had he been living? Do we know enough about him? Answers from both David or Gerald seemed to satisfy their curiosity. Sadie examined her planned agenda and her notes on how to run a meeting.

"Are there anymore questions"? No one raised their hand. "OK, let's vote. All those in favor."

Five hands raised. Hazel and Stephen chose not to vote.

"Anyone voting no?" One hand rose.

"Well, it's not unanimous, but our by-laws say we can accept a majority. Who wants to tell Cody we want him to live here?"

David and Gerald raised their hands simultaneously, and everyone agreed that they would be the ones to ask him whether he wanted to live in the community. In fact, it was not at all certain that he would want to live in a house, or sleep in a regular bed. About twenty percent of the homeless were chronically homeless, and did not want to live under a roof for a lot of reasons. Would Cody decide he liked his situation just as it was, and opt out of the invitation to join the commune?

The next day, Thursday, was cold and damp. Temperatures fell to the forties, and Hazel told Sadie that her bones told her snow was on the way. Sadie had her own thermometer. When cold or rain was in the air her missing leg ached. Doctors told her that the phantom limb might cause her problems for a long time. David and Gerald, wearing their heavy jackets and having blankets over their laps, sat on the porch and waited for Cody to arrive. Would he come today? Would the cold keep him away?

At 2:00 p.m. Cody appeared wearing a ragged sweater that hung on his slight frame and a pair of torn jeans over obviously thin legs. He looked slightly blue around the lips, the tip of his nose was pink, and his teeth chattering made an odd, whistling noise. His smile belied his muscle cramps and aching neck. Hazel appeared at the door with a tray of sandwiches, hot cocoa, and two blankets tucked under her arm for Cody to regain some of his normal body temperature.

David began the conversation, "Cody, Gerald and I went to a meeting with the rest of the commune. You know, we told you how we operate. Everything that we do here is by consensus when possible."

Cody was listening and nodded his head.

"Well, we didn't tell you we were going to do this, but Gerald and I have gotten to know you a bit, and we were wondering whether you'd be interested in joining the commune- you know, living here and being part of everything we do?"

Gerald began to speak, "You have a gift for memoir, my friend, and your stories have kept us spellbound and in stitches. We would be delighted if you would agree to give communal life a chance- at least for four months during this winter until April when our year concludes."

"You want me to live with you all here in this house, with everyone here? I don't have no money to live here. I mean, you know I'm living on the street, rough you know. I mean, what you see is what I am."

"We know, we know, but none of us pay anything really. Ben's gift to us is for this first year to pay all expenses. We add a little, but he wants Kelly House to be his experiment in communal living, and he handles everything. We talked to him, and he is in complete agreement about your coming here. Of course, it's up to you."

"Well I don't know what to say. I mean, what if I have a drink or two or whatever?"

"We take everything up as a group. We support each other in anything that happens. You'd be part of us, and we'd try to support you, too."

"No one," Cory gulped, "ever offered me anything like this before!"

"We know. You want to think it over?"

"Yeah, maybe I'd better do that before I say anything else."

"OK, sure, you do that, and let us know when you come back." David said, and hoped that Cody would agree immediately, but understood and admired Cody for not jumping on being housed without thinking about it.

The rest of the afternoon was spent on talking about writing and common-place conversation. Cody talked about some of the problems which the homeless were experiencing on the street. He mentioned that the organization which used to be sort of a day shelter closed down most their services because they had a new definition to be an agency committed to solely finding housing for the homeless. Cody worried that the cold would claim the lives of some of his homeless friends who drank and would freeze to death on the streets or under a bridge somewhere. At least one person seemed to freeze to death or die of drinking methanol alcohol every year. This was nothing compared to deaths from hypothermia which occurred in Washington D.C., Chicago, New York City and all large cities in the north throughout winter.

Cody's voice softened, taking on a loving tone as he spoke highly of two women who ran a house for the homeless.

"If ever a book needed writing, it would be about Betty and Toni. They ain't got nothing, but share whatever they got with anyone who walks through their door. Black, white, brown, straight, gay, it don't matter to them. Everyone's equal, all the same. I love those two ladies. That's what love is all about. Those people who make their living on us poor folk, they don't have any heart. It's like we're there for them to kick around unless we bow down and kiss their shoes. I really meant to use another word, you know what I mean," Cody commented and changed the subject, "So if I were to move in here, would I have to think about publishing my stuff?"

David and Gerald traded glances. David was the first to speak. "Well, none of us have published anything yet. I don't think that Ben really meant that to be important. He just wanted us to feel productive. But, yes, that's the idea, Cody."

Hazel invited the men to come in out of the winter weather and warm up. She had cups of tea and homemade cookies for them. Cody felt warm and wanted. His brain wandered back to the last time he felt so good. He couldn't recall such a time and he immediately felt depressed. It was usually when he was feeling depressed that he sought solace in the bottle, or not so long ago, the needle. But this was different. For the first time, he could find consolation in having an invitation to live with these good people. The ambivalence was scary. He wanted to blurt out "Yessss, I want to live with you all," but his natural inclination to be cautious stopped him. The street taught him to be mistrustful.

Cody spotted Ben coming down the stairs. He never failed to be in awe of the grandiosity of the man.

"Ben, could I have a few words?"

Ben saw David, Gerald and Cody, and gave them a jolly greeting. "Sure Cody. You want to talk alone or with these two pundits?" There was a twinkle in his eye.

"Alone, if you got a minute."

David and Gerald excused themselves, realizing that Cody needed time with Ben.

"You know David and Gerald invited me to live here with you all." Ben smiled in agreement. "I was wondering how you felt about me. You know I'm on the street

living rough, and ain't got much money or much of anything." Ben tilted his head in acknowledgment and Cody continued, "Well, I mean no one ever invited me to live with them like this. You know I've been in jail, right? I ain't been the best of citizens, you know what I mean? Are you OK with all that?"

Ben removed his hat and stroked the end of his mustache for minutes that seemed like hours to Cody before he finally gave his opinion. When he did the confidence in his voice was unmistakable.

"Cody, I don't know how much David and Gerald told you about us. Do you know how Kelly House got its name? I mean about Ted Kelly. This place is named after him. He died in Florida. He hated human beings, but loved humanity. No one knows how many people he helped without anyone knowing he did it. I think that he would really approve of your coming to live with us. He was a son of a bitch on the surface, but a real human being under it all. He'd probably say, 'Cody, is real people, my people. Bring him in.' So, there you are, my friend. We want you if you want us."

CHAPTER TWENTY-FIVE

Cody didn't have much to do to move to Kelly House. He rolled up his bedroll which he hid during the day beneath some rocks near the river. Once before, his site was invaded by some mean-spirited police who accused him of defecating in a scrub of bushes. He tried to convince them that it wasn't his doing, but to no avail. He lived next to the river for three months with half a sleeping bag for cover.

One day while he was panhandling a nice lady gave him enough money for a used sleeping bag at the Goodwill on Patton. A black trash bag full of stuff from the day shelter, and he was ready to say goodbye to his site. He didn't tell anyone that he was going to live at the commune. It wouldn't have been safe. He didn't want any drunks showing up and getting nasty. He sighed, whistled softly to himself and expected to be back if something went wrong at the commune. Life had taught him that nothing ever lasts, at least anything good. Anyway, he rationalized that he only had four months before he'd be back on the street. Cody saw it as parole or a break from the cold. Already three of his friends lost toes due to the cold.

Hazel served a turkey dinner as a welcome festivity for Cody, and everyone made a little speech of greeting.

"Thank y'all so much. I just don't know what to say. I mean no, I mean no one has ever treated me so good."

His first night in the little make-shift bedroom was a dream come true. Yet, he missed the smell of the trees, the weeds, and wild flowers. It was hard for him to get out of a real bed to take a leak and find the small bathroom near the workroom. He was used to using Mother Nature's gifts of shrubs and grasses to relieve himself. Even sheets on the bed were unfamiliar. For that matter so was a bed. First he was cold and then too hot and he slept fitfully.

His first full day at the commune was spent walking around the house. David and Gerald were writing at their desks most of the day. Once in a while they spoke to each other in hushed tones, and then returned to their work. Sadie spent most of her time with Hazel in the kitchen, sitting at a long table drinking tea.

"Cody, would you like a cup of hot tea?"

"Sure would, Hazel. It's cold outside. My insides are always kind of cold, if you know what I mean."

Hazel and Sadie exchanged glances.

"Have you thought about what you want to write about, Cody?"

"I think I'll stick to writing some more about my life," Cody laughed uncomfortably. "I guess it's almost like fiction- I mean all the street life and stuff I've been through."

The women smiled benignly.

"A few years back, I remember a bunch of folks put up tents under the bridge over on Lexington. Something to do with overhaul or overtake Asheville. I don't think that's what they called it, though." Cody seemed to be fighting a memory lapse.

"You mean 'Occupy,' I think. I remember those tents, too. Many people were very unhappy with everything in this country, as I remember it. Those people, mostly kids I think, but a lot of older people also were everywhere." Hazel was contemplative. "Veterans from that group, Veterans for Peace, who still stand up there at Pack Place, peace groups from everywhere were involved. I was proud of them."

"Yeah, well, I was staying over there in their tent city under the bridge until the cops chased us out of there. I mean, it was awesome. Some street punks and bums ruined it for everyone, but while we were there, they fed us, had a medical tent, clothes, and blankets. It was great. I even helped out a bit by doing some time as a security guard at night. I felt good about being a part of something, and being trusted to watch over the folks in the tents while they slept. I didn't get to do much of that when I was on the street alone."

While the three talked, David stood in the doorway listening.

"You know, what you're talking about reminds me of a man by the name of Abraham Maslow who came up with something called the Hierarchy of Needs theory. He talked about people needing to meet their basic and security needs first. Then they needed to feel nurtured, that they belonged to some group, and to feel a sense of self worth. I don't think I know anyone who has reached it, but he said that the highest need was to be self-actualized. I think that he meant something like that sign with Uncle Sam pointing a finger and saying, 'Be all you can be.'"

"I don't know about that fella, but some of us street folks felt really good in that tent city. I know some who stopped drinking and doing dope there and really became part of it all. They saw themselves in what was being talked about in all those meetings. They had so many meetings day and night, everywhere. Course, when the cops threw us out, most of them went back to drinking and whatever".

"I remember that the Occupy movement was everywhere. Whatever happened to it?" asked Sadie "Maybe it's still going on in some cities. You don't read much about it, though. Didn't Ben tell us that he originally bought this house for the purpose of creating a school for dissidents?"

"Yes, he did. You're right, Sadie. Let's ask him about Occupy Asheville when he comes in," suggested Hazel and everyone agreed.

Cody fit in well, and began to do some writing. He was intent on telling his story about his time with those Occupiers.

"Them fellas and girls slept out on the street next to the government building on Patton Avenue. Rain, shine, cold – It didn't stop them. I bunked with them for a while until I just had to get out of the cold so I went to the Mission."

He thought about the Mission and having to pray with them in order to eat or stay there, and to not fall asleep during the sermon. If he did they would escort him back to the street.

"I went to some of the Occupy meetings at Pritchard Park where they had drummers on Friday nights, and a sickly looking guy who fed the poor every Sunday. Poor guy died suddenly in his sleep. Smart as a whip, but smoked and drank just like the rest of us. He always looked like he was on his death bed, and sure enough, he must have been because I heard one day he just didn't wake up. Nice guy, no lie about that, and smart as hell, and dumb as hell about taking care of himself. Some old fat guy used to try to help him, but Rick was stubborn and didn't listen to no one." Cody thought about Pritchard Park and the breakfast.

Cody sat back, and pictured Rick in his mind. Stooped over like he had that old peoples' disease. Osteoporosis, that was it. Couldn't have been more than fifty something when he died. Cody shook his head and shuddered. So many of his friends and others on the street dead, just like that. Cody's throat tightened, and he felt a pang of intense sorrow.

He lifted himself out of his sadness and continued, "Every night those occupiers had meetings. They called them GA's for general assemblies. They'd stand in a circle or sit on the steps over at Pritchard, and each night they took turns running them. Funny hand signals, too. They'd wiggle their fingers to show they liked what they heard, and if they didn't like something they covered their chest to show nothing doing. They called it consensus which meant that everyone had to agree or nothing happened. I remember thinking that they couldn't get nothing done that way, but those people really loved their consensus. That's for sure."

Cody reflected on his experience with them. Some of the occupiers had tats all over their bodies, and he heard some of the guys talking about something they called out of body experiences. They'd do all sorts of horrible things to their bodies, like piercing their tongues, nipples, and putting hooks through their skin. He shuddered. He had a couple of tattoos, but nothing like them fellas and girls had. Once he heard that it made them more sexy. He never got to find out, though.

"Cody, are you OK. I've been watching you at the desk writing there. So lost in your thoughts."

Gerald was mesmerized by watching Cody. Consternation and grief engulfed his features. Gerald couldn't imagine what was going through his new friend's mind, but sensed that it was profound somehow.

"Tonight we have a meeting, and it's Sadie's last night as head of the commune. We have one more house manager to vote for before the year is up. Three more months to go before it is over, and we go back to Florida or whatever we decide."

"Have I been here a month already? I suspect this has been the fastest month of my life. It feels like just yesterday that I started living here," Cody remarked.

Gerald could understand because he'd felt the same way after a month in the commune. Time flew by without as much as a warning of how fast it was going.

"Do you have any ideas about who should be our coordinator for the last three months, Cody?"

Cody thought about the question for a while before he asked, "How do you choose?"

"Democracy, with one exception. If someone has already done it, like Pauline and myself, we are exempt. That way, it gives everyone else a chance. That leaves David, Britt, you, and Lee. Ben told us that he refused to be a leader here because he felt it was taking undue advantage of his position. Lee feels she should not assume any additional responsibilities because it seems to have an adverse effect upon her Parkinson's disease. Any ideas?"

"I don't know. I mean no one ever asked my opinion about something like this before. Street folks just get told what to do, and when to do it, or else we ain't got a bed for the night, or any food. We don't usually get any vote on it. Do it or get lost!" Cody laughed, and Gerald had a moment of remorse.

He wished he had he money to get Cody some teeth where they'd rotted away over the years.

"I suppose any one of us would do well, 'cept for me. I don't think that I've been here long enough for that job."

After dinner the plates and rest of the service was cleaned away by the commune members as was the custom, so Hazel wouldn't have to do everything. Chairs were placed in a circle, and Sadie opened the meeting.

"'Blessed are thou, our Lord and our God, who has given us life and each other.' I wanted to say that especially with today being my last day as house mother," Sadie's smile was infectious.

Britt saw a radiance emanate from Sadie, and felt once again the strong sense of sisterly love. Britt had never before experienced this love for any woman.

"You all know that I didn't write a lot, and I didn't spend a lot of time trying to examine my children's religion. I wanted to do so much, but the time got away from me. My son is still preaching his religion, and one day I was walking around Haywood Street by the library and saw a sign with his name on it. He was giving a speech in Boone and some people were looking at the sign. They told me that they were Messianic Jews here for a day before they went to listen to him. They really love him. I love him, too, but not for the same reasons. I never told them I was his mother. I think in some ways I'm ashamed."

"It's not too late to write something, Sadie. We still have three months to go," said Britt.

"I know, I know. Maybe I will." She changed the subject. "So who's going to take my place, and shouldn't we start talking about electing someone now?"

"What do we have to do to elect someone? I haven't voted in any election like for president in twenty-five years or more," Cody said with a little apprehension.

"Ben, do you have any ideas about who should run the commune for the last few months?"

Ben smiled wisely at Sadie, "I think you did a fine job, Sadie, really a great job. You even began to write about Messianic Judaism. I never understood any of the stuff about why Jews didn't accept Jesus as the Son of God. You cleared that up for me, anyway,"

Ben looked around the room and winked at Britt.

"Yes, yes, I did, didn't I? I guess either here or later when I return to Florida, I'll continue with my writing. Of course, without any duties as house manager I will have some time, won't I? Well, so who wants this job?" Sadie laughed and broke the seriousness of pondering the meaning of such weighty issues.

"I think that David would make a fine house manager to bring a close to this wonderful experience."

Everyone turned to Gerald as he spoke, "He has given a great deal of himself to the commune, and it seems to me he would be a most appropriate communal member to bring this glorious experiment to its conclusion."

Gerald's mane of white hair and his aristocratic demeanor seemed to stand out at this moment.

"I agree with you, Gerald. From the very beginning even back at Greentree, he's provided us with so much strength and love," Britt said.

David smiled at Britt whose face radiated a loveliness borne of her adoration of Ben, and her new found love for all of the commune members. It was a transformation rarely seen in the life of anyone.

"I agree with both of you. David will provide us with a fine management style and a beautiful fulfillment to what we have shared. But, in truth, any of us could provide management equally," Pauline added.

"Is there anyone else who would wish to take on this role? I am not the only one here who could do this job," David replied. No one raised a hand.

"So then," asked Sadie, "can we vote, and make this a decision by all? All those for David to be our house manager, raise your hand."

Everyone's hand rose. It was settled. David was humbled by the vote of acceptance by the members.

CHAPTER TWENTY-SIX

Snow began to fall. Hazel prepared a scrumptious Christmas dinner. Gerald and Pauline wrote a short prayer service leaving out denominational connotation.

The members decided to bring food to the weekly Sunday morning breakfast at Pritchard Park, a service to the homeless and hungry. They volunteered to help serve the homeless and anyone else who showed up for the meal. Unitarians and Quakers were already there with the food, and they had small holiday gifts for the homeless. Children had prepared little stockings with candy, wool socks, and other small articles of clothing in them. The Baha'is brought more food, and after a short prayer by the Unitarian minister, the homeless began to move through the line. It was cold, but people felt warm in spirit. The children began to sing Christmas carols, and all in attendance joined in. Cody wondered why this spirit could not be maintained all year, and quickly realized that when you have nothing but the clothes on your back good feelings were few and far between.

Communal members rotated between the guests, and offered handshakes and glad tidings. Cody knew many of the homeless, and talked with some of them in hushed tones. Picking and choosing wisely, he introduced some of the men and women to his new friends. As always, there were many new faces, but the majority was familiar. The entire day would be spent in going from one place to another, mostly churches where meals would be served, and people from the congregations would give up part of their day to share nourishment and good cheer with the less fortunate.

Ben and Britt spent the week before Christmas buying gifts for everyone at the commune. They didn't wish to make anyone uncomfortable by spending lots of money so the gifts were modest. Wool scarves, gloves, and hats to cover their ears when it got cold were the ticket. For Ben, this was the time to splurge on Hazel and Stephen. He decided to give each of them money so they could buy something that they wanted. He did the same for Maria and Juan, their children and grandchildren.

Sadie suggested that a holiday card with a photograph of everyone at the commune would be a good idea, and since she was still house manager, she organized it. A collection was taken. Cody threw in a couple of dollar and felt good that he could contribute. The group decided that the words on the card should be simple, yet a statement of sorts. It was agreed that it should read: *To all of you: peace, love and dreams come true.* Everyone signed the card, and copies were printed in time to be sent to all the friends at Greentree and individual family members. Ben even sent one to the people he and Britt worked for when they went to Colombia. The CIA obviously didn't print a holiday card with their workers' picture on it.

New Year's Eve was cheery, and everyone decided to go out for dinner to celebrate the New Year and their time together. They chose a Nepalese restaurant downtown which specialized in a most exotic cuisine. This year, New Year's Eve fell on a Friday night and after dinner they wandered over to Pritchard Park where a small number of hearty drummers were beating away on their jambays. It was cold, but for the drummers their blood rushed to their fingers and warmth exuded from their hearts. David and Britt owned African drums, and joined the group of drummers. Keeping up was all but impossible for the duo, but they loved to drum and it didn't matter to them that they were out of rhythm with the others. Everyone had a great time, and Ben invited them to join him at a wine shop for some fruit of the vine. Sadie offered a prayer for the Sabbath for the drinking of wine.

"*Baruch atah adonoi, ellohenu, melech o'olom, prea, prie hagoven.*" She smiled with an inner peace she had not felt since Morris and the children sat at the dinner table for a special Sabbath dinner each Friday.

"What does the prayer mean, Sadie?" Cody asked. She grabbed his hand, and gave him a peck on the cheek.

"'Blessed are thou, oh Lord our God, who brings forth fruit from the vine.' In every Jewish home where the Sabbath is kept holy, this prayer has been said with the blessing of the wine for centuries, Cody."

Cody had never experienced the sense of awe that he felt at that moment. It was poignant. A tear came to his eye and he had a sense of déjà vu as though he had been in the presence of a party of love and superb peacefulness before. But when he tried to remember an earlier experience like that, he could not.

They returned to Kelly House about 10:30, and sat around the living room watching the scene in New York as many of them had done for so many years. Sadie snored peacefully in her chair as did David while Gerald and Pauline held hands on the sofa. Ben cuddled Britt on their love seat, and Lee and Cody watched as the ball descended. They were the only two who knew that a new year was upon them. But the others sensed a New Year and awoke to Ben's loud "Happy New Year to one and all." A rather poor rendition of Auld Lang Syne followed as no one could remember the words.

January 1st was David's first day as house manager. For a few days he'd been contemplating a grand finale for the year in Asheville. They were writers, and yet very little writing and no publishing took place. Probably the most writing was done by himself and Gerald, but nothing was done to publish. His idea was a simple one, really. What if they could put on a show of sorts, kind of like an art show, but instead a writer's show, somehow? He wondered to himself whether some sort of a commune finale or an evening of works by Kelly House residents could be put together. The germ of the idea began to take shape. He did not discuss it with anyone, not even with Gerald, because it was too fuzzy.

Could they put on something worthwhile which would lend a sense of credibility to this grand experiment? There was no doubt that many of the writers, and now even Cody, were doing so much better physically and emotionally. Everyone was a different person than before the commune began. Ben and Britt had already announced their intention to marry and remain in Asheville. Their marriage would take place sometime in March. Pauline and Gerald were leaning in the direction of sharing a home probably back in Pauline's apartment in Oakland Park, Florida, or maybe getting a place here in the mountains.

Sadie wasn't sure what she wanted to do when the year was up, but she talked of trying to spend more time near her children even if it meant that they would be Christians and she would be a Jew. She no longer fooled herself into thinking that Messianic Jews were simply misguided Jews. Her son and daughter were Christians, pure and simple, and she loved them and their children despite it all. Morris wouldn't have agreed, may he rest in peace, but he was dead, wasn't he?

Cody, for his part, knew that he didn't want to return to the streets. His time in the commune brought him more happiness than he'd experienced for as long as he could remember. He talked to Ben more than a few times, and Ben offered to help him stay off the streets somehow. But Cody didn't want a hand out. He wanted to find something to do which would supplement the small amount of Social Security he received each month. Cody knew that he didn't want to return to the streets. He was beginning to feel better, but when he was outside the cold really got to his bones, muscles cramped, and he felt chilled most of the time.

"You wedded to this place, I mean Asheville? Could you see yourself moving on, if you had something to go to, Cody?" Ben asked.

"What do you mean, Ben?"

"Well, you hate the cold, the snow and dampness. Right? So what if, and I don't know anything for certain, but what if we could find work and a place for you to live in Florida? I mean, could you deal with leaving everything that you know, Cody?"

Cody felt a moment of apprehension. "Leave Asheville, leave the streets? But wait a minute. I'm not on the streets now, maybe never again. Thoughts flooded his brain. Me, a life, a real life. I mean OK, I'm here now, but I always reckoned I'd go back to the shelters and the river. Leave it behind. Wow, I never thought about that!" he mused silently..

Ben could read the consternation on Cody's face, see his muscles twitching as he was trying to absorb what Ben was saying. Could Cody shake the past, start again in a new life with a future? Or was the street the only thing he knew, and when the commune came to an end, were the streets the only possibility as far as Cody was concerned? These were Ben's inward thoughts and doubts.

"Cody, I don't want to rattle you, partner. Just think about it, and if you decide you want to give a different life a chance, let me know. I know people who might be happy to meet you, and possibly offer you a job doing something you like, and in a place which is a lot healthier for you than what you've been through. Just think about. No decisions need to be made now."

Cody retired to his room full of anticipation. Could it be that he might turn his whole life around at this point? He couldn't sleep and when he finally did, he had dreams of falling into an abyss and not being able to escape a well. It scared him and he awoke in a sweat. Cody tried to figure out what it all meant. He remembered having similar dreams when he slept under a bridge and almost fell off a siding just below a beam which was both a protection and a hindrance to his balance. Could he be going through a similar experience of feeling unsafe? Could Ben's offer be a blessing and a danger of sorts? One night David told him that sometimes the fear of staying where he was had to be more pronounced than the fear of change. Cody wasn't quite sure what that meant, but he didn't want to seem stupid so he didn't question the theory. But, now, in the middle of the night having just awakened from this nightmare, he thought he understood. Street life was terrifying at times, especially for older men and women. Muggings, especially from young homeless kids or punks, were not uncommon, and Cody had more than one close call.

But the notion of changing his whole life around, that was scary, too. The street or a "respectable life" with a job and a future? Maybe meeting a nice widow down in Florida, relaxing at the ocean, new friends like Pauline and Gerald who were talking of going back to someplace called Oakland Park, and Sadie, beautiful, motherly Sadie. The thoughts flooded his brain and both tantalized and scared him. He fell into a troubled sleep.

Lee began to have significantly more difficulty with her breathing and swallowing. Stephen was concerned, and called the specialist for a consult. Gagging when she ate, saturation levels lower than desired, constriction in the use of her vocal cords was worrisome. She'd written about her mom and her Aunt Elizabeth who wasn't really her aunt, but rather her mother's lover. Surely being raised by two lesbians who conducted their lives as though they were a married couple, rather than some secret, forbidden relationship, played a role in how she dealt with life.

But with the death of Sandy, her despair with her life, and readiness to end it all before she met the writers, and decided to give the commune a chance to help cheer her up, she was once again beginning to show more signs of Parkinson's symptoms, and they were worsening. The communal members were acutely aware of her problems, and feared the worst without knowing much about the progressive nature of the disease. Stephen decided to inform them so that they would be more prepared for anything. He had to do some research.

Lee still wanted to write about her beautiful life with Sandy in the glorious northern Californian retreat home that he brought her to when they married. She wished to make Sandy come alive in her pages so the reader could love him as she had. His love and understanding was such a rich and bountiful gift that she could never find the words to describe it.

They'd met at a Unitarian church in San Francisco. Tall, elegant in her eyes, retired as a forest ranger and supervisor in the Park Service for the Department of Interior, he'd spent his life in almost all of the nation's glorious outdoors making parks safe and pristine for tourists and wildlife lovers. He told her that he had been an educator on board the Alaskan Marine Ferry System for a summer. He loved talking about the flora and fauna of the forty-ninth state. He'd been married once before without any children. It just didn't work out because she loved the city and he, the wilderness.

Two weeks after they met, they went to city hall in San Francisco and married. They had to borrow a couple who were also there to get married as witnesses, and they in turn witnessed their marriage. The four went out for a drink and that was it. Not very ceremonious, but at their age what did it matter. Besides, Lee thought that this, her third marriage, didn't require a white dress and brides- maids. She laughed. For ten years they lived in Sandy's home in the mountains with a view of the 14,000 foot peak of Mt. Shasta and thick forests. Their marriage was comfortable- that is, until Lee was diagnosed with Parkinson's disease and then later cancer in both breasts. Mastectomies and a prayer that there was no movement of the tortuous cells throughout her body plus having to learn to live with the Parkinson's seemed to consume all of their energy. Sandy would spend every penny he had to get his Lee healthy again.

First one remedy for the Parkinson's and then another with travel to Mexico, and then the National Institute of Health in Bethesda, Maryland, as a member of a protocol team for surgery to quell the neurological issues, took up a great deal of their time. Lee began to wonder whether she could endure any more poking and prodding of her body. It was heartbreaking, and yet Sandy stayed with her and even showed more loving kindness and tenderness. Her illnesses seemed to bring out a side of his which would have made Mother Theresa proud. And then without so much as a warning, it was over. Sandy died peacefully in his sleep, the victim of what the paramedics called "the big one." Her children came to her side and tried in vain to console their mother, cried with her, and spread Sandy's ashes on a hill overlooking their property. For a week all she could say was, "It was supposed to be me, not Sandy. Why, why, why did he die?" There were no answers. The children returned to their lives after the perfunctory offer to take their mother with them to which she adamantly declined. At first Lee wrote short pieces to try to answer her questions about elusive moments, existence, and dead dreams. She read them over and over, looking for help. Looking at the words she repeated them to herself.

The Elusive Now
What is real and what is dreaming?
There is no difference in the meaning
There is no real; 'tis only seeming.
In the past and in the future
The moment of now can never last.
At its only attempt to stay and live,
Robber time walls it up in the past.

Non-Existence

Present moment-what a fool!
Claiming to have importance
But you have no substance.
Your existence is less than
That of a shadow in the crevice
Between past imponderable
And future unknowable.

Dead Dreams

The past is the graveyard of dreams, thwarted
By the press and rush of practical matters.
The future's a coffin awaiting dreams aborted
By life spent on practical matters.

The three poems didn't solve anything. As the weeks passed to months, her grief did not subside, and she considered ending her life with an overdose of pills. The Parkinson's symptoms increased, and were it not for a neighbor who had a key and often dropped by to make sure that Lee was eating, she would have died. To add to her suffering, the hospital treated her as deranged after they attended to the poison in her system, placed her in a ward for troubled women, and then finally released her. This act of charity, as she thought of it, only produced more depression and sadness, and she tried to commit suicide again.

For some reason, though, she called the medics herself. Again, they transported her to the hospital. Her niece, Selma from Florida, was called, who packed up Lee and flew with her to Florida, and prevailed upon Greentree nursing staff and the new physiatrist to accept her aunt as a patient even though her biggest problem concerned her mental health, not her physical health at the time.

Stephen began to read as much as he could about Parkinson's. He called in the physiatrist whom he used as a consultant. The progression of the illness was disheartening. The doctor recommended a nursing home rather than Stephen trying to administer his skills to Lee. Lee was having trouble swallowing and her tremors increased almost every day. A neurologist examined her at Mission and found that what had already been done in California and NIH could not be improved upon.

The doctor pointed out to Ben and Stephen that the Parkinson's was not considered fatal but complications which might arise could shorten her life. Any respiratory complication such as pneumonia, even severe bronchitis, could be aggravated by the Parkinson's which could in turn kill her. Lee was beginning to become depressed again. Seeing the on-call doctor produced a diagnosis of clinical depression brought about probably by her physical condition. Lee's mental status deteriorated rapidly. All of the commune members were in fear of losing her. It brought back the painful memory of losing Ted Kelly in Florida. Lee was not capable of making decisions for herself, so Ben called Selma in Canada where she lived with her new husband.

"I hate to call you like this, Selma. It's Lee. She's had a turn for the worse with her Parkinson's. She's -- well, she's failing, and we wanted to call you because you're the one on her sheet to call in emergency. We don't have access to her children. We're so sorry."

Selma turned to her new husband, Fred, and he knew immediately that there was trouble with her Aunt Lee. With tears in her eyes, she managed to ask whether she should notify Lee's son in Oregon. She was pretty certain he'd know how to contact the girls, his sisters.

"Do you think that I should come to Asheville now, Ben?"

Ben thought about it for a moment and put his hand over the cell phone.

"She wants to know whether she should come immediately. What do you think Stephen?"

"I don't know, really. She could recover briefly according to the doctor. They're treating her pneumonia symptoms now. I think the doctor changed her meds slightly with the hope that it would turn things around. I don't know what to tell her."

Ben handed him the phone and whispered, "You talk to her."

"Selma, this is Stephen. I'm the practical nurse here at Kelly House. I've been watching over your aunt for nearly nine months. She was doing

OK before now, but this Parkinson's has hit her hard now. The doctor says she might pull through this episode. I don't know what to tell you about your coming now. It's kind of up to you."

They agreed that Selma would contact the son and stay close to a phone should there be any changes- good or bad. She would give Ben's private number to Lee's son, and wait to hear more. Lee remained in intensive care at Mission.

At first, her lungs seemed to clear on the x-rays, but then it was discovered that the lungs had become infected with a serious bacterial infection. The nurses began administering massive dosages of antibiotics. This seemed to hold the infection in check, but still Lee was being fed intravenously and showed no signs of coming out of her comma. Ben and the others rotated sitting by Lee's bedside. Pauline seemed the most distraught and wanted to be with her constantly. Gerald prevailed upon her to let the others take turns because they, too, loved Lee. For two weeks Lee remained in intensive care, and then died peacefully in the presence of Pauline. The doctors said that her heart had had enough and just gave out. Tragically, she never woke up to see Selma and her three children by her bedside. The hospital social worker made arrangements for all to be present with Lee. The staff was most kind and arranged for food to be delivered to the family so that they could remain with their mom.

Lee's body was cremated as she had written in a will which her son brought with him from Oregon. He would be responsible for taking the ashes back to Sandy's house, and with his sisters spreading the ashes in front of the looming Mt. Shasta. The communal members held a service and Sadie read the Kaddish, a prayer for the dead. Lee's children were in attendance and this service was for them. David prepared a eulogy and included anyone who wished to say something. Pauline's anguish kept her from speaking, but everyone understood.

At the commune everyone was in deep sorrow, and mourned the death of their sister. After the children were on the way back to their homes and families, and had taken their mother's possessions from her room which were all that she owned in Florida and now here in North Carolina, the writers decided to hold a memorial service for their dear Lee. They knew

Lee had been raised a Unitarian and that she was not very religious, but was indeed spiritual. Ben went over to the Unitarian-Universalist Congregation on Edwin, and asked if he could borrow a prayer book or whatever they called it. He wanted to read from it for Lee.

Each of the house members who wanted could read something they'd written, or find something they liked in the book. Hazel prepared some of Lee's favorite foods, and Sadie provided a little wine to share as a blessing in Lee's honor. She also decided to share the Kaddish Prayer again, the prayer for the dead, said for more than two millennia by the Jewish people. Sadie told Cody that the prayer actually admonished the Jewish people in the prayer to choose life, and that the prayer was about living not death, per se. Cody questioned this concept, but held his own counsel.

For a month Pauline felt the anguish of Lee's death more than the others. She and Lee shared the room together and bonded as sisters. Pauline felt lonely and thought her loss unbearable at times. Gerald tried to console her, but she was inconsolable. Time took its effect, and slowly the house returned to its purpose and cheerful existence. Selma arranged for Lee's clothing to be given to the homeless shelter in Asheville, her other belongings were taken by her children for their children to have as a means of remembering Grandma. Selma stayed a little longer than Lee's children, but her husband needed her, and she responded. Ben drove her to the airport for a flight to Detroit and on to her new Canadian home. Misty-eyed and still feeling the loss of Lee, she cried silently on Ben's massive chest. He understood and held her gently. Then she was gone, and he returned to Kelly House.

David went to town to talk to Malaprop's owner about a night with Kelly House writers. Malaprops often held open house at times for poetry and writers from the area. She knew of the commune, and wondered whether she'd ever get a chance to entertain them or at least hear some of their writing. When David came in to talk, she was pleased. The decision was made to hold the soirée in March in the middle of the month. She decided to do the publicity, and take a loss because there would be no books ready to be sold. It would be a night just to give the writers an opportunity to be heard. Leaflets, media attention would be handled by the staff, and the only money to be earned would be generated from what could be sold in the coffee shop and the selling of books by other authors. She was happy to do it. Malaprops was well-known for the kindness they bestowed upon authors.

In the next meeting, David announced their upcoming debut at a bookstore, and all manner of questions barraged him. Lee had been dead three weeks, and normalcy was beginning to be seen. This idea of impending notoriety was just the charge needed to activate each writer's batteries. David fielded the barrage of questions with ease.

"Do we have to read our stuff?" asked Cody. "I don't know about reading any of what I've written so far." He seemed to be sweating a bit.

"Not if you do not wish to be famous, Cody," quipped Gerald. "I think anything that you write would be incredibly interesting to anyone listening. Just think about it. Your time with the Asheville Occupiers in their tents on Lexington Street, or your life on the street is bound to attract attention."

Everyone agreed that Cody's life would probably be of great interest to Malaprop's clientele.

"Of course we would have to publicize his work in the newspapers and probably television stations as well. We need a publicist." Gerald stated and the writers agreed. "What do you think Ben?"

"I agree that all of you will do great at the bookstore, and maybe we can even invite Jane or even Cohen, the guy who owns Greentree, to come up for the reading." Ben said, and inwardly reflected upon how he had held the owner, Sid Cohen, in such disdain originally while he was working with Ted Kelly on his memoirs. Things change, he reflected to himself. Britt wasn't the only one whose personality seemed to mellow. Maybe love can do funny things to people, Ben wondered.

"I'll call the center and talk to Jane and Cohen, ask them to come up to see Kelly House, spend time with us, and come to the reading, if you'd like," offered Ben.

Everyone seemed to be in agreement. Cody was the only one who didn't know either of the people they were talking about and didn't have the history the others had.

"Oh yeah, I'll call Juan and Maria, too. They'd have a fit if I didn't invite them."

It was agreed that David and Gerald would contact the Asheville papers and Channel 13 to see if they would like to do a story on the event. A reporter from the major paper and the free Mountain Express was dispatched by the city editors for the next week. They would come out to the house for interviews and pictures. Everyone was excited, if not a little fearful. Now they had to produce at least for their night on stage.

Everyone except for Cody remembered all the hoopla upon leaving Greentree and preparing to come to the commune. They remembered the Sunshine Express reporters, too, and the press they received for coming here to live together. It seemed they were going to be celebrities again. They were famous in Florida and now again in Asheville.

Gerald decided that he would read some of his memoirs about Upton Sinclair and his life as a writer. while David decided to put together some of his writing on living on the Arctic Circle in Alaska in a small Indian, interior Eskimo village. He would work on it again and again until he felt this was his masterpiece to be shared with the others at Malaprops. He reread everything that he'd written both at Greentree and in Kelly House. He realized that his writing was not the stuff of great novels or even non-fiction prose. But he could not *not* write.

He rationalized that just as most artists do their work for recreation and personal satisfaction, so too the communal writers were in the same boat. Most writing would never be touted as 'must reads' by book clubs or in the great literature classrooms. He laughed to himself remembering an incident in his undergraduate speech class eons ago. He wrote what he believed to be a fantastic speech, one that would rock the class and instructor. He couldn't remember the content but it was sometime around the Bay of Pigs event in the Kennedy administration, and he had the audacity to recommend to the woman who was instructing the class that she submit his speech to *Vital Speeches,* a magazine which the students had to read for class. She laughed, and in not so gentle admonishment, told him his speech was good, not vital. This in turn reminded him of an incident when he wrote a love poem to a co-ed studying to be an English teacher. She sent it back to him with his errors red-lined.

"I shouldn't have written anything to her. I was married at the time. What a schmuck. Served me right!" He laughed at himself, and returned to his work about living in little Huslia near the Arctic Circle.

"Cold unlike anything I ever felt before in my life. For at least six months the temperatures never rose above 40 below, and in that cold the kids and young men in the village played basketball in the gym, raced outside in t-shirts to cool off and smoke cigarettes. I couldn't stop them from smoking on school grounds, but I tried to keep beer and hard liquor away from the school. When the thermometer could not be read, it was assumed that 70 below had been reached, and then and only then, did the kids wear sweaters. The snow crunched and the dogs howled. Tied to their little houses in the dog yards, shivering with only some hay for bedding and some mush to eat, it was a wonder they did not freeze to death. Once in a while, some kindly musher would let his dogs into the house, but not often. Mushers fed the dogs frozen stiff cod fish. Most of the dogs appeared emaciated, but that was not the case. They were muscular and fit, eager to run and pull a sled. Dog yards had from three to fifty dogs, depending on the financial situation of their masters.

Some of the mushers worked on the "slope," a name for Prudhoe Bay, on the Arctic Ocean. BP and Chevron had massive programs there and all manner of employment was found. The Athabascans and Inuit made their small fortunes in the oil fields and came home to build log cabins, raise and run dogs, and drink hooch when flown into the village. For years, since pipeline days in the seventies, oil was king of Alaska. Anchorage corporate buildings attested to the part that oil interests played in economics, politics and the social fabric of Alaska. The environmentalists cringed at every new attempt to deface the land and change the migratory patterns of the wildlife in the 'Last Frontier.'"

David wanted to tell his story to the people at Malaprops and hoped they'd not be bored with all his narrative. He didn't want to talk about his personal life, his marriages and problems, so much as his experiences. In his mind this was the meat of his writing anyway, not his screw-ups and feelings of total failure as a husband.

"Hello Gerald, I've been writing about Alaska. Do you have a little time to listen to some of the stuff I've written?"

"Surely, I have some time for you, my dear friend." Gerald seemed a bit disheveled, at least for him. He rarely was publicly seen without a tie and sports jacket, handkerchief, three pointed at that. But today he wore jeans, a sports shirt opened at the neck, and his white hair was unkempt.

"Pauline and I have been walking in the neighborhood. She is attempting to pull together some of her poetry which she has written here and in the past for her contribution to the soirée. I think she is a little intimidated by the thought of sharing her work with others."

"Understood. I can identify with her. But, we're all in the same boat. I've never read aloud to anyone but you, Gerald. Maybe we all could do a practice of sorts before our night at Malaprops. What do you think? Sort of a dress rehearsal."

"That's a splendid idea, David. Ben, Hazel and Stephen could be our audience, and make suggestions about what we write, or how we project our voices. Would you ask them for us,and bring it up in our weekly meeting?"

"Of course."

The two returned to their efforts.

CHAPTER TWENTY-SEVEN

Some of the commune members worried about catching colds due to the chilly weather. Each received their flu shots, albeit cringing at Stephen's insistence that the shot was less to worry about than getting sick. He administered the serum, and only Ben hid from him, but Stephen was relentless. So when Sadie, Gerald, and Pauline developed cold like symptoms with low grade temperatures and sniffles, Stephen didn't assume that they were in immediate need of a doctor. He was right and soon Gerald and Pauline were themselves again, but Sadie seemed to lack the immunity needed to fight the illness. Her fever spiked at 101 and she was achy all over. A trip to her endocrinologist who handled her diabetes was in order. Antibiotic treatment was ordered by mouth, and Stephen watched over Sadie for a week with concern. She moaned and prayed, asked for the ancient remedy to be made by Hazel. Chicken soup seemed to do the trick as she slowly regained her strength and exuberance. She was certain that Hazel's chicken soup saved her from destruction. Stephen suspected otherwise, but growing up with healing herbs in Cherokee, he knew that the Shaman had awesome powers using herbs.

"I feel like getting back to my writing for our night at Malaprops. You know, Britt, we could do more than one thing. I mean, I have a few poems from when I was a girl which I wrote at Greentree and also here, being so much older. I don't think they're so good, but with some help from you and maybe Gerald they might be fun for our night there."

"Great idea, Sadie. Why don't you find them, and we'll look at them together. It was all Sadie had to hear. Like a little girl with a curl, she reached under her desk in their bedroom and opened a drawer from which she pulled out two or three sheets of paper. Her nightgown was freshly washed by Hazel and the smell of sickness all but gone. She pulled herself up onto her bed, tucked her good leg under the blankets and began to read.

"This one is called *A Woman in Transition.*"

I am older and wiser now.
I have climbed to the peak of Transition Mountain
where the footing is rocky and sharp
and the downward view is perilous and real.
Courage, my heart, as you scan the lonely panorama of aging.
Make the careful descent
from denial to acceptance,
aware of the wild flowers peeping from the crevices.
Adjustment is the order of the day and the long nights."

Sadie looked up at Britt in anticipation. She started to speak, but Britt held up her hand.

"Sadie, sweet, fun loving Sadie- You wrote that? Let me read it to myself. It's so profound." Britt shook her head in wonderment as Sadie handed her the crumpled piece of paper. Britt read it again and then again, shaking her head.

"I never would have known that you had such a serious and deep side to you. I don't mean that I thought you were empty-headed or anything like that, just that ---"

"Don't worry your head about it, Britt. No one knew I could do many of the things I can do. Just like when you told me that women can handle financial matters. You were right. I just always thought that men were smarter than women in all matters. That's what I was taught at home by my mother, may she rest in peace, and all my relatives. But, yes, sometimes I feel very different and that's when I write poetry and even some journals which I think I lost a long time ago. Want to hear another, or do you have one to read to me?"

"As a matter of fact I do. I wrote some short poems and I have one here. It's called, *Infinity*. See if you think I should read it at Malaprops."

Britt read,

> *"Imagine the numbers*
> *Of all the leaves*
> *Of all the trees*
> *In all the world.*
> *Millions of seasons*
> *From the first tree.*
> *Unattainable number*
> *Does not touch infinity."*

"Well what do you think?" Britt asked, and found Sadie snoring lightly.

She found herself irritated, and a moment of anger swept across her face, then softened and she thought, "Poor dear, too much for her to grasp all at once."

Britt reread her poems and smiled to herself. Life does have a way of changing, and what is important one moment isn't the next. She wondered about her future with Ben, the future unknowable. She, too, fell asleep for her afternoon nap.

CHAPTER TWENTY-EIGHT

David, Gerald, and Cody worked in the workroom. David and Gerald sat at their desks while Cody draped himself in the huge, blue, velvet Lazy-boy, pondering over his creation.

"You think that I could use a poem that I found on the street once?" asked Cody.

David looked at Cody with puzzlement. He sneaked a peak at Gerald and inquired, "Where did you find it? Do you know who wrote it?"

Gerald also seemed perplexed. "Do you mean to pass it off as your own writing, or simply recite it and give credit to another street person?" Gerald's face reddened.

"I am sorry Cody. I do not know whether to say 'street person' or 'homeless.' Which is less offensive, or is there another word which I should use which is politically correct?" He seemed troubled.

"Gerald, don't worry your head about it. We answer to anything." Cody laughed and winked at Gerald.

"Funny you should ask though. I remember some of those Occupiers really got torqued out of shape when people who weren't street people had trouble with the word 'homeless' and would get pissed off at anyone who said anything they didn't agree with. They preached non-violence and peace and all that good stuff, but some of them really had bad tempers." Cody laughed half-heartedly. "Maybe the reason they was there was because they had a lot of problems."

Gerald was mindful of Cody's bad grammar at times, but said nothing.

"All those years on the street and sitting in the library, sometimes I would write stuff, you know poems, short stories and what have you. They've all turned yellow by now, but when I got my stuff from that shelter, they were at the bottom of my bag. I'm going to look them over, and see if anything I wrote might be better than the poem I found on the street. What do you think?"

"I believe that your contribution at Malaprops would be more legitimate were the writings composed by you rather than someone else you don't know," opined Gerald.

David wagged his head in agreement.

"Well I found this one. Want to hear it?" asked Cody.

The men turned their chairs toward him.

"I wrote this one when I felt pretty good about the streets. Course, I might have been a little drunk. Here it is. I call it 'Free.'"

Free

Who gives you the right to walk with snubbed nose
And pass judgment and assume an air of self-elevated pose?
Am I not good enough to walk by your side?
Must my conscience repeat over and over, 'You have lied?'
No, rather be I dead and isolated from your kind
So that my way may be clear and honest for what I seek.
I am human, I am being, I am free!

Cody looked up at the other men. They sat silently in contemplation. For Cody it seemed an eternity.

"So, what do you think?" He craned his neck in anticipation.

David was the first to speak, "It surely comes from your heart. I guess people do sit in judgment of those who are on the street. I hope that I don't come across that way when I'm walking near Pritchard Park or Vance Monument. As for the poem, wow, that's all I can say. I hope you use it at Malaprops."

Gerald nodded his head in agreement.

"Let's see, there are five of us, and Stephen and Hazel who might wish to read, too. If the whole reading takes about two and a half hours that gives us each about twenty minutes. I would like to add something by Lee, and explain that she is not with us any longer. Ben might be willing to read it. He probably won't have anything of his own to read."

"Yes, that would be about right, I should imagine, David. We do not wish to bore the attendees with too much, but neither do we wish to deny anyone their moment of fame at the microphone. What do you think about a dry run here at the house a couple of days before the soirée?" Cody and David agreed with Gerald.

The three returned to their writing. Later that night, David called the meeting to order for the weekly communal house meeting. The writers, Hazel and Stephen were present.

"Well, we have guests this evening. This is Lila Wilson from the Citizen Times and Maggie Jones from the Mountain Express. They wanted to see a meeting of the commune and write articles about us, our night at Malaprops, and our return to Florida- for those of us returning." He studied the others.

"A few short announcements before we go into the session tonight. Malaprops has given us March 15th for the soirée, It's a Saturday night. We start at 7:30 and have roughly three hours, but we can stay until 11:00 if we wish. So I guess we have about a month before the big night. Any questions?"

The reporters were scribbling furiously on pads of paper. Each brought photographers with them who were taking pictures from all angles.

Ben was the first to speak. "I've invited Jane and Cohen to come for the weekend if they can get away."

He could never muster the respect to call Sid Cohen "Mister." Everyone except for Stephen, Hazel and Cody beamed at the thought of seeing Jane again. Maggie Jones asked who they were, and David explained about the two. The reporters exchanged glances and saw a possible angle, another facet to the story.

"Do you think that we ought to invite those two youngsters from the

Sunshine Journal? I mean they did write us up, and came out to see us at our apartments," offered David.

"Brilliant idea, David. The paper might even send a photographer with them and pay the entire bill if they thought that they could sell more papers with pictures." Gerald beamed.

"Let's ask Jane to call them. For all we know, they aren't even working at the paper anymore. Those jobs are hard to come by and easy to lose," lamented Britt. She spoke from experience. All agreed with her, and David as house manager was empowered to make the calls.

Pauline began slowly to speak. Her eyes misted.

"You know, we have not even begun to discuss our time here in Kelly House, and why some of us have decided to return to Florida. I mean, I believe that we need to begin to find closure or something akin to it."

She looked around the room at the other members. A sense of melancholy seemed to descend upon the room as though someone had just died.

"All of my life, I believed that the best way for elderly people to live their final days was to enjoy a communal lifestyle. For me it was a matter of coffee brewing 24/7 and a chess board set up and ready for anyone who loved the game. That was my answer to waiting for death to descend upon me and..." David sighed.

The two reporters were mesmerized and yet uncomfortable as though they were invading something very private. Their eyes exchanged a sense of wishing to disappear so that the others could speak more openly. David, sensing their discomfort, let out and awkward laugh.

"I didn't mean to become so macabre and scare you two."

Britt changed the subject, "I suggest that we continue the meeting and schedule two or three sessions, whatever we need to begin the process of concluding our year here at Kelly House."

"Good idea, Britt. What do the rest of you think?"

Heads wagged in unison, and there was general agreement that separate sessions rather than during a house meeting and with strangers present was in order.

"OK, then, let's continue with the meeting." David was happy to return to business.

Ben was the first to speak, "I think that we ought to think about how we are going to return to Florida for those of you who have decided to go back. Also you might want to talk to people back there and prepare them for your return. I'm not talking about the emotional stuff." He looked uncomfortably around the room.

"I think that this is still about the feelings and emotions which we are all going through, Ben. I realize you're talking logistics, not feelings, but are not the two intertwined?" Gerald posed the question to the entire group.

There was agreement and Cody, forgetting himself, raised his hands and wagged his fingers.

He explained, "Wow, I forgot y'all may not know that when you agree with something said in the Occupy Movement you show your liking it by raising your hands and wiggling your fingers. Sorry about that."

The others seemed interested and encouraged him to continue about hand signs in Occupy.

"Well, OK then. If you don't like somethin' you drop your hands to your waist and wiggle your fingers down, showing 'No way.' And if you really hate something you make fists, cross your arms in front of your chest, and that means that if the others agree with the idea, you're finished and will walk out of the movement. Then someone runs over to you and tries to explain why something passed. They called it consensus, not like here where if something passes by majority, it passes. There the idea was that everyone or nearly everyone had to agree or it didn't go nowhere."

"I doubt that we could do without majority rule and the Roberts Rules of Order," said David. "I was never in an organization that demanded unanimity."

"Did it work, Cody?" asked Britt.

"It was slow, real slow at times. People got real frustrated with not getting anything done, but they really loved their consensus, that's for sure. It was all about feeling good about decision making. Lot of us street people never got to give their opinions about nothing in those shelters. Like I said before, 'You don't like it hit the door'. Hey, I just made a rhyme, " Cody shook his head and smiled.

"Bravo, Longfellow. You're a poet now, my friend," David smiled at

Cody and gave him a high five which Cody taught him when they first met. "Well, let's get back to business, shall we?"

"I want to invite my son and his wife to visit us here before we leave Asheville. He wants to come to Asheville to meet with that Graham evangelist. You know, he's the son of that man, Billy Graham, who died a few years ago. I can't promise that he won't try to convert you all when he comes, but I will ask him not to do that if you want," said Sadie.

"When does he want to come to Asheville, Sadie?"

"In two weeks, Gerald. I would like to ask them to stay in one of the rooms upstairs, if it's all right with everyone."

"Do we need to vote on it as a community?" David wasn't sure about this finer point, and could remember nothing within the document that Ben had written.

He turned to Ben who said, "I have nothing to say about guests. How long would they stay, Sadie?"

"Just a couple of days, but you know he feels that he needs to tell everyone about his religion, and it's hard for him to just let things be."

Cody was the first to respond, "So I know from what you said that he is Jewish or what did you call it--- A messy something "

People snickered and were immediately sorry for it.

"A messianic Jew, Cody. They believe that Jesus was the Messiah while the Jewish people do not accept Jesus as a messiah."

Sadie's phantom leg hurt her. She realized that when she felt stress or sorrow, it still hurt even if the doctor said that the pain would go away eventually. She felt tremendous stress now.

"I won't ask them to come if anyone will be uncomfortable."

Perhaps she was projecting her own doubts.

"Do we need to vote on this, Ben?" asked David.

"Up to you, David. I don't have a problem with it. If he tries to convert me, I'll be honest with him, but I won't go ballistic or anything like that--- I promise Sadie."

The group laughed and without a vote David knew that there were no problems with Sadie inviting her son to come and see the commune, and maybe even stay with them.

"See Cody, we have consensus."

All hands went up and fingers wiggled gleefully. Laughter broke out and Sadie's pain stopped. There was no other business to discuss and the group dispersed.

With only four weeks to prepare for the finale, the soirée at Malaprops, the group worked feverishly to get ready. Britt reread her letters which she had written to her friend about her time in Alaska living with her Korean War veteran husband who came home with what was then called shell shock. She considered writing a short story for the soirée about this period of her life, but she developed writers block and could not construct anything that made sense. Maybe it had something to do with being madly in love with Ben and her new sense of feeling good about herself and the others. She wasn't sure. So, instead of dealing with the letters, she found a story that she wrote for a magazine years ago concerning a young girl who almost died in a plane crash in the Last Frontier. She liked her story although three rejection slips were attached to the yellow parchment. She asked Ben for his opinion of the story. Not being much of a reader, he made a valiant attempt to stick with it and heaped praise upon it because it was the love of his life who wrote it.

She reread the title, *It Wasn't Her Time*. Britt began to read it aloud knowing that Ben may have missed some of it in his perusal.

"*She turned and started unsteadily across the road, holding one hand out for balance. Hunger and thirst wrapped themselves around Susan and would surely kill her if she didn't find some food and clean drinking water somewhere. How many days had she wandered on the tundra trying vainly to follow the meandering brackish waters of the river? There was no darkness to measure her days as it was still summer and she was somewhere south of the Arctic Circle. She didn't exactly know where she was and that was part of the problem.*

She felt like sleeping and would allow herself a brief moment to rest, but she knew better than to give in and succumb to the bliss of sleep and eventual death at the hands of the elements and lean vultures that hovered above her waiting for her to give it up. She screamed curses at them and in the same breath asked God to be found by anyone. From time to time she heard and saw a plane or was it just auditory tricks or a mirage in the flat, dry bed creek of her imagination?

She read somewhere that people lost in the wilds of the Last Frontier usually died if they stopped moving, but there was a twist to that. If they didn't move in a straight line and follow a river, they would simply move in circles and that had to be avoided. The rivers in Alaska didn't know that they were supposed to move in a straight line. She found herself laughing aloud at the thought of moving in circles and getting nowhere fast. She feared hallucinating.

The first couple of days she recounted over and over how the pilot had tried vainly to glide the Cessna 172 into a field. He missed and landed in a rock strewn river bed and died upon impact while she somehow lived with only contusions and a nasty bump on the head. Joe had over one thousand hours as a Bush pilot and had flown this route before, many times. He went over his plane with a fine tooth comb, but in Alaska that didn't seem to mean much.

"God, that weather came out of nowhere and poor Joe lost his way," that was all Susan knew. She had only flown to Platinum once before and there had been no warning of weather shifts. The coast was always unpredictable, though, always a mystery to Native and White alike. One minute they were able to see for miles and the next everything was gray and foreboding. If it had been winter it would have been a severe white-out. Could it have been a squall? It was too early for white-outs, but it looked like one anyway.

At first her efforts were directed at getting out of the tiny plane. Once she thought she heard Joe moaning and she wanted to get him out too, but it was only the gurgles of the blood escaping from the gaping hole in his left temple. His eyes wide in the pangs of death, his pupils dilated. Susan wished, as she had so many times before, that she had medical training but she never seemed to have enough time to take the survival training courses offered by the regional medical office. Her job as a social worker with the Department of Family and Youth kept her going without let up. There were so many cases, and she was deeply involved in each one.

Somehow covered with her own and Joe's blood, she managed to extricate herself from the seat belt and release the hatch on the door. Pain in her legs made her scream out, but she found the strength to pull herself out and over the edge of the wing. She slid to the ground in a heap. Susan was barely able to see around her as there was a fog which enveloped everything. It wasn't cold yet, being in July, and that was good because Susan had not brought *her winter gear with her. She was only going to visit the Noonak family and check on the welfare of the children, talk to the Indian Welfare Worker, and see whether the father and mother were attending their sobriety classes. As a child welfare worker with the department, she had to fly to the villages at least monthly to see her families court ordered to stop drinking or face the loss of their children. Even her closest village of thirty or forty people was a ten minute flight. Sometimes she could catch a ride on a boat in the summer or a dog sled in the winter. In July flying was the means of getting around to the villages if they didn't connect to a river from Bethel.*

She forced herself to think, to reason, not to fall prey to the animals that she imagined would be hungry and eat her alive. Her fear could destroy her. Luckily, she had mosquito repellant in her jacket because she knew that the mosquitoes would eat her alive. Platinum was famous for mosquito stories. She feared them because she knew of moose that had been driven crazy by the little predators.

Was it her imagination or did she see "A" frames and a school? The fog had lifted and everything was flat without vegetation save the tumble weed and lusty, tough grasses that thrived on the nearly barren tundra. She moved closer fearing this was a mirage as well. No, the village school was always the first building to be seen from air or ground. It always loomed out of nowhere, a monument to the school system's rural education Molly Hootch Act. Hell, it was the only way that pilots often knew what village they were flying into most of the time. The villages were often so similar, but the schools unique.

Weakness prevented her from moving quickly and she fell several times. In a last act of super strength and determination, she crawled on her hands and knees to the edge of the village.

The road was nothing more than a plowed dirt lane, the main thoroughfare of tiny Gooseneck, a village of maybe seventy Yupik Natives and two hundred dogs. But she made it and lived to talk about her ordeal. Old women who had not gone away to fish camps found her sprawled on the road and carried her unconscious body to the health aide's clinic. The health aide, an elderly woman, radioed to Bethel for a medical evacuation unit which was dispatched immediately with a paramedic and flight nurse. There aren't many who walk away from the almost daily flight mishaps in the Last Frontier and fewer who walk away and live to tell their tale. Susan figured it just wasn't her time-yet."

Britt stopped reading and asked, "So what do you think? Should I read this at Malaprops, Ben? Do you think that anyone will find it interesting. Look at these rejection slips. The magazines didn't think so."

Ben was an auditory learner and listened to the story intensely. He immediately wondered whether this was autobiographical, and asked Britt if she was Susan.

"No, no, God no. If it had been me, I probably would have died alongside the pilot or been eaten alive by some hungry bear or something like it. No, it's just a story which I wrote while at one of those teacher meetings in Fairbanks when I was trying to get a job teaching English and Journalism in some village."

Ben wondered whether this was before or after Britt married the Korean War veteran who once held her captive during one of his flare-ups due to his shell shock.

"Maybe after the others leave and we're married you will have time to reread your letters we got when we went to New York. You might become inspired to do some writing about them," Ben suggested.

She stared at him. "Well, you haven't answered my question. Do you think it's good enough for the soirée?"

"Good enough? It'll knock their socks off. It's great, as far as I'm concerned. Use it as part of your contribution. I think those magazines were crazy for not buying your story, sweetheart."

Britt was overjoyed that someone finally appreciated the story enough to have others enjoy it too. She kissed him on the forehead and hugged the bear. A fleeting thought went through her head. This was one bear she wanted to have eat her up. She felt embarrassed that she had such wicked thoughts.

David, Gerald and Cody spent more time in the workshop now that it was almost time for the big finale. Each worked feverishly to complete their work and test it out on the others before deciding for sure that they wanted to present the work to strangers. "I found something that I wrote when I was in the army," David laughed, "If the paper doesn't crumble in my hands from antiquity, I'd like to share it with you guys and see what you think." Gerald and Cody looked up and smiled at David bidding him to continue.

"It's about a man that I knew when I was enlisted over in Germany. He was one of the strangest men I ever knew. I remember thinking that he was like Abraham Lincoln without a beard. I call my story *A Recluse*. See what you think."

"He was ingenious at finding places where a ray of light from the sun, a desk and his books were his only companions. One day I climbed the three flights of stairs to the battery day room to find Painter on his flight from reality into his storehouse of wisdom. "Painter, Painter, it's me Stern. You in there?"

A voice tired and calm beckoned to me from the far end of the room. Old Harold had pulled three wall lockers away from an alcove with a window and placed his desk and chair in. After sliding in, he pulled the lockers back into place and no one could see him. He did this six days a week.

"What is it this time? Russian—Why, will you use it? Will they promote you? Aren't you tired of being a fifty year old private first class?" I hated to hurt him, to spit out sadistic questions, but I had to. I had to know. I was uneasy like slipping on wet grass.

That goddamned smile, long, peaceful; I felt like throwing up. He's not real. Why didn't he tell me to mind my own business? Day after day, just sweeping the day room and cleaning latrine bowls, then nine or ten hours of study. Philosophy, Greek, Russian, history, geography, religion- for what- to draw $99 a month? I wanted to run, to tear down the barricade of lockers that separated him from the herd. He's a fuck-off, a good brick, lazy. It was hard to escape my past.

But, I stayed and listened to the Thoreau of the Hill, and I kept coming back for more. He was peaceful and radiated that inner calm.

Even in the mess hall, he was different. He ate no meat, but devoured ten boxes of cereal and two quarts of milk for breakfast day after day, six or seven helpings of vegetables at each meal, a loaf of bread a day and yet a body like Lincoln long and graceful shoulders aching with the weight of the world. The eyes of the ocean deep blue, the nose of a Roman aristocrat, the hair of Father Time and the mind of a Dorian had this giant of a man.

In a shakedown inspection, the captain had found a straight edge razor that old Painter still used, his underwear given to him when he felled huge trees in California during the Conservation Corps days. His fatigues and military drab green was all he owned.

A member of the Seventh Day Adventist Church, he took Saturdays for his day of rest. Pedaling religiously to a German Seventh Day church some forty kilometers away in any weather was another one of Painter's idiosyncratic behaviors. He was ridiculed by the soldiers in our battalion who saw him as an odd ball and asked me time and again why I hung around him. Sometimes I could not answer, but I knew that he was the shining light of wisdom that I found nowhere else.

Walks with him were like walks along a meandering river, peaceful, quiet, deep. An inner calm would overcome us, quieting the hard, materialistic corrosion of my embittered being. I cried not for blood, but for peace, not for hate, but for love in his presence. He was as a Zen monk might be, but I knew no Zen monks.

What hope had this quiet man of becoming a specialist fourth class? None—out of sight, out of mind—but this obscure woodsman, by his very need for solitude, seemed to have promoted himself to the ranks of the –found, the self- actualized.

It's been a task, now that I'm away from Painter, for me to keep his light burning in me. I'm more demanding than he, always wanting, always taking, but still a part of him is in me. God, help me."

David looked up from his pages. Cody and Gerald had listened intently. From time to time it appeared that each had a moment of recognition from their own past, a fleeting thought of someone they had known themselves. For Cody, the streets were full of highly spiritual men and women who came upon hard times, yet in moments of clarity seemed as if they were seers or prophets. For some it might have been mental anguish, but for others it seemed as though they knew and felt things that others did not. Both recognized that David had captured a mood, a sense of the man, Painter, which was powerful. They told David as much.

"Will you read this story at Malaprops ?"

"Yes, if you both feel it's worthy of doing so."

"It is your story and it is a powerful one at that. I think it will be well received by any audience," said Gerald.

The three returned to their own work and thoughts.

CHAPTER TWENTY-NINE

Stories appeared in the Citizen Times and the Mountain Express. A picture of the entire household was featured on the front page of the Times. The upcoming night at Malaprops was highlighted and Channel 13 sent their anchors and producers to do a piece on the commune and their stories. A producer from the local public news channel wanted to interview Ben and the others. He sent a crew to do so with cameramen. Malaprops put out fliers and enlarged pictures of the commune members posted in other bookstores, places, and restaurants. If the attendance was standing room only, they were prepared to ask the writers for a second night soirée if they wished. For the bookstore, the business would be good in the coffee shop, and hopefully people would browse and buy books. Jars would be on each table and by each seat for donations to the elderly writers if people cared to give them some money for their efforts.

Jane and Seymour, her husband decided to come to Asheville for the event, but the two reporters from the Sunshine Journal were not given funds to make the journey. They were disappointed and discussed going on their own dime. Mr. Cohen begged off, citing poor health and meetings as an excuse. But he asked Jane to present to the commune a check for $1,000.00 for whatever they wished. Jane was visibly touched by his generosity. They planned to make the presentation of the money at Malaprops if possible.

On Tuesday night instead of the meeting, the rehearsal was planned. Each of the writers and Hazel and Stephen were present. Hazel agreed to introduce each of the performers and to begin with a very short introduction of what the commune was all about, how it came to be. She wanted to start with a short Baha'i prayer for the well-being of humankind. She also began with one of her own poems.

"This is a poem about love and God. I wrote it when I tried to understand what they meant. I hope you like it."

What is Love?
I do not know what Love is.
It is a tired, old over-used word.
In one language
Love has thirty-one meanings.
And I was asked,
"What is Love?"
And I answered,
"I do not know.
Love is a mystery."
Some have said,
"God is Love."
And I said,
"I do not know what God is.
God is a mystery."
So Love and God
Are mysteries to me.

Hazel looked up from her reading, thanked the audience for their attention and began to read again. She had never shared her love of the environment with anyone, not even Sadie, and so all were surprised by this next piece. She read from a notebook.

Death Knell of a Mighty Tree
I ask who tolls the bell for thee?
Strong guardian of the mountain side,
Majestic branching monarch tree,

a perch where singing birds reside.
In Spring the wild flowers hurry up
And flaunt their beauty 'neath your shade
To bloom before they're covered up
To bide till winter's snow is laid.
You purify the air we breathe
While reaching high into the sky,
and I profoundly do believe
that man and nature form a tie.
Kudzu, you earn disdain from me
for the death knell of this mighty tree.

Hazel, usually quiet, unassuming, and demure searched the group for reaction. They sat stunned, without words looking from one another and then to Hazel. She could stand the silence no longer, prayed to Baha'u'llah for strength, and in almost a hushed tone asked, "Well, what do you think?" She wasn't looking at anyone in particular.

"It's beyond beautiful. It's exquisite. Thank you for writing this and thank you for sharing it with us," Pauline beamed and took Gerald's hand in her own.

Hazel smiled benignly. Pauline was in tears. She did not know why she cried but somehow this poem struck a chord in her that she rarely experienced. Taking Gerald's hand, too, was unusual and particularly in the presence of others, even those people for whom she felt love. Gerald, a little surprised by Pauline's behavior, felt a stirring of something he had not experienced since sharing life with Claire, his wife. But this time it was different. Gone were the pangs of guilt which he felt before.

"I hope this is an omen of things to come. Could it possibly be that I will get a second chance to become one in mind and spirit with Pauline?" Gerald thought silently. He smiled at her and felt a deep satisfaction.

Hazel introduced David next. She talked about David's life giving an abbreviated synopsis of his involvement in the commune, his biographical sketch.

He in turn began by speaking, "I wish to read you a short story that I wrote many, many years ago."

David read his short story, *The Recluse*, straight through to the end without stopping before he looked up.

The audience clapped politely and thought about their own lives. Gerald thought about the work of Erik Erikson on experiencing the seventh of the eight stages of change in human development. Generativity versus stagnation dealt with a person's sense of giving something of himself back to community versus being caught in a stagnation without purpose. He pictured himself as Painter, the character in David's story, and wondered whether in another situation, he might have sought an alcove to retreat to for peace of mind and self study.

For Ben, the story made him somewhat uncomfortable because he might have also seen Painter as a goldbrick when he was a young Marine officer. Now, he wondered about his own life and whether it made a difference and if so how. Stephen saw Painter as a shaman or one of the elders of the tribe who often took young braves under their wing. He wondered whether Painter had Native blood in him.

David changed the mood, "And now for something lighter. This is a poem I wrote while here in Asheville at the commune. It flows from my days as a waiter on Bourbon Street in New Orleans. I call it *Jazz Notes.*"

"Poems 'n jazz
Like fish 'n chips
Or steak 'n French fries
Or po'boy san'wiches
In N'aw Leans---
Some likes 'em hot
Some likes 'em cold
Some likes'em
Full o' pot
Nine days cold.
I heard Miles playing
Come to Jesus

On his mello phone
What's with this cat?
He don't believe in Jesus
Or the mello phone
Yet He keeps putting us on-
Like fish n' chips
Or steak 'n French fries
And po'boy san'wiches
In N'aw Leans.

David bowed and almost toppled to the floor, caught himself and held on to his walker. He smiled, raised his head, and winked at the crowd in an exaggerated pose which brought first a gasp and then applause from the audience.

Sadie was the next to rise. "I haven't done much more than I did in Florida about what I went through with my late husband, may he rest in peace, and my children's religious beliefs, but I did write this crazy little limerick and I think it's pretty funny." She began to read.

There once was an alien from Mars
He frequently frequented bars
He drank himself silly
He went willy nilly
The ground was so hilly
And now he has earthy scars.

Sadie displayed a broad smile across her face. The others froze in their seats. Stephen was the first to speak,.

"I like it Sadie, but I wouldn't have thought you'd be the type of person to write it."

The others were as puzzled as Stephen. Sadie's first sense was one of joy, but seeing the others not responding caused her to feel a moment of apprehension.

"Well, perhaps it wouldn't be good for the night at Malaprops, but I had fun writing it."

"No, no, Sadie. I like it too. It's just, it's just what can I say? Not you, until now, I mean," Britt felt herself blushing. She didn't want to hurt her precious Sadie, but her words had blurted out.

"I mean, I didn't know you liked limericks," Britt said, uncomfortable about being surprised at Sadie.

Gerald, sensing that the others were still in a sort of shock, said, "Sadie, it is a fine limerick, and I believe that the audience will love it."

Turning to the others, he said, "I believe that our evening at Malaprops would not be complete without Sadie's limerick!"

In a moment of release of tension, everyone smiled and readily endorsed Gerald's remarks. It was settled and clapped their approval. Cody raised his hands in the Occupy fashion and wiggled his fingers in agreement.

"Well then, why don't we take a break and continue the rehearsal tomorrow." The writers felt a sense of relief and adjourned to their rooms for some much needed rest.

CHAPTER THIRTY

On Tuesday, less than a week from the big event, the Citizen Times and Channel 13 returned to Kelly House with reporters, an anchorwomen from the channel, and photographers. Interviews with the elders, staff, and Ben were concluded, to be aired on Friday. The newspaper also interviewed the members, and the reporter was especially interested in what Cody had to say about the plight of the homeless in Asheville. He promised to run his exact words.

In two days Jane and Seymour would be arriving in Asheville; Juan and Maria were due later the same day. Sadie's children, somewhat apprehensive about what she would say, came down from their summer home in Boone with some trepidation, but more curiosity than angst. David's son and his wife came up from their home in Rats Mouth (Boca Raton) Florida. Stephen invited his cousin and her husband to come to Asheville from Cherokee where they lived on the reservation. Hazel's married daughter, to Hazel's delight, brought her twelve year old daughter who was the only child present.

Other grandchildren were mostly grown by now and away in college so they would not be coming. It was pandemonium with the coming and going of so many people. Cries of joy greeted Maria, Juan, and Jane. Seymour wondered why all the commotion. The only one who knew no one was Cody, and yet he felt so much a part of the house and having heard so much about Maria, Juan and Jane, he felt like he knew them for years.

Ben basked in the glory of knowing that he was responsible for so many happy people joining together for this festivity.

That night the Moose Café was delighted to close off a section of the restaurant for Ben and his family as they came to be known by the waiters and waitresses in the restaurant. Ben suggested that he order for everyone which he did in his take-over fashion. Everyone ate until they could barely stand. The food was scrumptious. Knowing that the walrus of a man would leave a gigantic tip made the two wait staff assigned to the party joyous. By this time everyone knew that Ben had asked Britt to stay with him as his wife, and that Pauline and Gerald were slated to try out Pauline's apartment as a couple. Hazel was asked to present a Baha'i prayer before dinner and she picked a beautiful testament to the power of God. Even Ben, an avowed atheist, closed his eyes and visualized Britt as he thanked whatever there was to thank for this year.

One more rehearsal was needed, and in between visits with guests, touring of the city for those who'd never been to Asheville, and tours of the big house, the rehearsal was held. On Friday, the Citizen Times ran a major article on Kelly House with an advertisement paid for by Malaprops for the soirée plus an additional open house to be Sunday afternoon. What had originally been planned as a one night affair soon took on the need for additional time to accommodate everyone who wanted to come. It was decided that in addition to Saturday night, the writers would perform again on Sunday afternoon for those who could not come on Saturday night.

Stephen's grandmother and his uncle, her only living son, came to the afternoon rehearsal. They rarely left the reservation for any reason. There was not much outside the reservation that interested them but for the sake of Stephen, Big Steve, his uncle, agreed to drive his mother to Asheville. She was nearly 90 years old, and this was her second visit to the city in her entire life. Big Steve was about 6'4", wore a long braid of silver hair down his back, and dressed in jeans and a plaid shirt. He wore a Cherokee four-strand necklace of beads and porcupine quills. His baseball cap had a picture of a white girl drinking a brew. She was blond, had plenty of cleavage and a sailor suit cap on her head angled to one side. Some of Big

Steve's buddies wanted that hat bad, but they didn't dare take it from him or steal it. They valued their lives.

Grandmother wore her best long multicolored dress with tassels spun from the mills near Cherokee by young girls in that school those preachers set up about ten years ago. Grandmother hated the old BIA schools and figured that the girls needed some good moral training. At least, they wouldn't let those young bucks get those pretty girls in any trouble, Grandmother figured. Stephen, her son Brian's boy was a good boy. He went to school and made something of himself. He didn't get drunk and laze around the reservation like so many of the young braves. Brian, her oldest- well, she was happy that he couldn't do any more damage. She hated to admit it, but she thanked God that he took her son when he did. The doctors called it pancreatitis. Stephen was a good boy, she repeated to herself. She, too, had her gray hair braided and beautifully pinned around her perfectly shaped head. Her hazel eyes were like a library full of the brutal history of the Trail of Tears.

Stephen wondered whether this poem would upset Uncle Steve who he'd been named for.

"I wrote this poem when I lived in Cherokee. I hope you like it."

He was uncomfortable, but determined to go on, "It's called *Incongruity*.

> *On the Qualla reservation*
> *I saw a Cherokee sitting on a low rock wall*
> *Staring vacantly into space*
> *across the smoky mountainside.*
> *His classic Indian face*
> *was the color of oil sludge.*
> *He smoked no pipe of peace*
> *But held a cigarette*
> *And puffed round rings of smoke*
> *between his sips of bottled beer.*
> *His "veil of tears"*
> *still watered the swift Oconoluftee.*
> *His humiliated heart*
> *was buried not at Wounded Knee*

but in his grim, aloof, defiant face.
He viewed the crowded carnival
with nauseous disdain.
Then with grudging resignation,
he donned his chieftain headdress
and bravely crossed his warpath
to the tawdry roadside stand.
To pose there for a dollar
beside a painted tepee
with a grinning woman tourist
who was eating cotton candy."

Stephen looked up from the poem, studied his Uncle Steve's face, searched for a sign from his grandmother. Seeing impassivity on both their faces, he lowered his head, and a tear fell from his eye. Grandmother wiped her brow with a small handkerchief. Steve simply stared into space.

David spoke quietly and all had to strain to hear him, "Stephen, it's so powerful." He wanted to say more, but couldn't.

Cody felt a sense of déjà vu. "I've been there and I"ll tell ya. It's the same for us- I mean, the street. No one sees us for who we are. Or they pity us and give us a dollar if we're panhandling."

Stephen shook his head in agreement.

"I wrote another short one. I think it's pretty simple. It's called *A Thousand Tears."* Stephen began to read,

"How heavy
A thousand petals
Scattered over tombs withdrawing.
No longer shared
But swallowed
Into seas.
No longer scattered
But seas
Made by a thousand tears."

"Absolutely profound," whispered Gerald. Everyone felt the same.

Sadie turned to her son and said, "See, I told you so."

No one was aware, but Sammy felt a sudden pang of guilt that he had tried to get his mother not to go to the commune for fear that she would write something about his life as a Christian. No longer did he try to cover up the truth. He was a Jew in name only. His life as a Messianic Jew was, he knew, not Jewish at all. He was a Christian, same as his wife and daughter. All his adult life he rationalized that if he used the word Jew or Jewish, he'd still be a Jew. He looked back on his life over the years and realized what a hypocrite he'd been. This poem, a thousand tears into seas meant something deep inside of him, but it was in a place that he could grasp. For the first time, he felt a sense of pride in his mother. He wasn't quite sure why, but something about these people reminded him of his youth at Grandpa's house, and he felt the sting in his eyes from the salt of his own tears.

The rehearsal ended with David reading a short story for use at Malaprops, and then Ben making a short speech thanking all the guests, the families, and friends of writers. He launched into a short history of the birth of the commune, and opened the floor for questions. There was one from Jane. She asked whether those returning to Florida would be willing to come to Greentree and talk to her current group of elders who were writing their stories. Everyone agreed to be in contact when they got settled in once again in Florida.

Hazel decided to make a brunch for everyone on Saturday. The house was in a state of energy unsurpassed in the past. Even Sadie didn't want to eat too much. Everyone reminded each other not to forget their writing and to speak slowly, loudly, and with good diction. Even Cody swore to himself to remember not to say "ain't."

At six in the evening, everyone piled into the van. Sammy and his wife drove their own vehicle, as did Seymour and Jane, so that the van wouldn't be overcrowded and uncomfortable. Big Steve and Grandmother rode in the house van with the others and Stephen drove. Ben and Britt rode with Juan and Maria. In all there were thirteen excited people in a state of exaltation on their way to Malaprops. The unknown was would anyone else be there?

Ben found himself praying for a good turnout, not for himself, but for the others. He mused as he found himself talking to God. He couldn't remember the last time he even thought about something called God. Not even in Nam. It must have been when he was a little child and said the Shema. What was it? "Hear, Oh Israel, the lord our God, the lord is One." He smiled and touched Britt's hair and smiled.

Parking was horrible. Stephen decided to let everyone off at the door on Haywood Street. There was a throng of people standing in a line and he couldn't understand what was going on. His first inclination was to think they were waiting for some performance at the US Cellular Center, formerly known as the Asheville Civic Center, just up the street, but they weren't moving toward the Cellular Auditorium. As the writers and guests prepared themselves to go into the bookstore a cacophony erupted. Old, middle aged, and young people greeted the writers with thunderous applause.

"Oh my God, can you believe this? There must be two hundred people here," David yelled over the applause.

"Make room for them. Let them through."

A woman from the bookstore was trying to muster some order in the crowd. Malaprop employees, seeing what was happening, hastily called a meeting and decided that they needed to rearrange the space. They rigged a podium of sorts and placed chairs all over the store with a sound system used only two or three times before for world-renowned writers with best sellers. This amazed them. Somehow they managed to put up fifty chairs, and hoped the rest of the people would come back the next day. The manager saw dollar signs at the coffee bar and book sales. Interestingly, none of the writers had any books to sell.

"Truly amazing," said the young store manager to the older woman standing next to her. She was the owner who rarely came into the store unless there was an issue to be solved.

The rest of the evening was a blur. There were baskets strewn around the room for donations to the commune. When the night was over, exhausted writers, barristers, and Ben couldn't believe how much money had been placed in the baskets which were emptied after the first hour only to be filled again and then again. Ben tipped the wiped-out staff and announced to the writers that they had amassed $8,673 and change. The store manager was astonished that the amount of money made at the coffee bar and in book sales far exceeded her wildest dreams.

The van was filled and everyone exhausted, deliriously happy, and beyond tired, returned to Kelly House to sleep. Tired as they were, Hazel and the rest of the visiting women went into the kitchen to make tea, coffee, and bring out a huge cake which had been ordered three days before from City Bakery.

Britt was so excited by the night's activities that she went into a coughing seizure that lasted three minutes. Stephen took her into her bedroom for a short respite from the party and happy people. She would not stand for being left out of anything and willed herself to stop the coughing, smoothed her dress, and returned to a relieved Ben. They hung on to each other for the rest of the night. Like two young lovebirds, they cooed and kissed all night long. The others were pleased and made cute remarks like teenagers do.

On Sunday, Cody awoke around 8 am, went upstairs thinking everyone else was sound asleep. He wanted to say goodbye to his old street friends, and have breakfast with them at Pritchard Park one last time. Ben had found him a job as a greeter at a restaurant near Ft. Lauderdale. It was still cool outside and he had to wear his heavy jacket. The rest of the house was as quiet as a cemetery. He thought to himself that 'cemetery' was a bad analogy.

Pritchard Park was full of people waiting patiently for the church to show up and feed them. Cody knew some of the old-timers and chatted comfortably with them. But it was different. He thought about that writer who said "you can't go home again," and wondered whether that was what he was feeling. Sure, he was happy to see all of them, like Razor who he'd shared many a bottle of hooch with in tents and even under the bridge on Lexington. Big Dog was there too, still smelling like a garbage dump but smiling as though the world was his oyster. Mother Mary was in line. She was as beautiful as ever with her dreads piled high upon her head. She never seemed to age, but then she looked old enough as it was. Everyone was curious as to where he'd disappeared to and kept asking the same questions. But Cody felt that he needed to hide where he'd been. What with some of these guys ready to cut you for a dollar and who knew what all they'd done in their lives. So many covered with prison tats up and down their necks and arms. Tattoos were like a badge of honor for cons. No, he wasn't going to tell them much about his whereabouts. Course some of them were in Malaprops last night and they could tell the rest if they wanted to. Cody couldn't stop that.

That Congregational Church on Oak Street was still feeding the folks. Incredible people they were in Cody's mind. So many years doing good works. Every week, rain or snow, it didn't matter. They were always there. He looked at John at the coffee urn pouring like he did for years now. Cody heard that his wife had some sort of back trouble, couldn't be there anymore especially in this cold spell, but John was always there. "Now that's a good Christian," as far as Cody was concerned.

Twenty minutes into the breakfast the school bus pulled up and fifteen or so men and a couple women piled off to eat breakfast with the others. Mostly blacks, but a few whites too. The driver was that preacher from the little Baptist church who always brought them and invited everyone to come pray with them. Cody went with them a few times because they served a pretty good lunch. Course you had to pray a lot and hear all that stuff about sin. He remembered that most of these churches who did stuff for the homeless made them sit and listen to sermons and go to Bible study before they could eat or sleep. He shuddered thinking about some of those babbling idiots who said God didn't have no favorites. Oh well, he was finished with all that street stuff now, thanks to the commune and Ben.

Sunday afternoon the writers went back to Malaprops for their second performance. This time there were only about fifty people waiting in line. These were mostly elderly people who felt a kinship with the writers. Some of them actually thought about becoming part of the commune themselves after they read the articles and saw the pictures in the paper. The performance went well and the communal members were less worried. Gone was the stage fright and the great crowd of last evening. After the readings and Ben's final remarks, some of the guests and patrons surrounded the group and four or five talked about their own writing or art work, and how lonely they were living alone after their husband or wife died. It was becoming all too familiar a story. Ben worried that the commune was actually disbanding. What would that mean to these good people? At the end he invited them to visit Kelly House, and see what it was all about for themselves.

On Monday morning Jane asked Ben whether she could talk with the writers and included him in the pending conversation.

"I think that I want to sit down with everyone and just get an idea what people are thinking about now that a year is coming to an end."

Her husband and Cody decided to take a ride to see Fubar and Madison Counties. Hearing Cody's story about the counties over the weekend, his interest peaked.

Early on Monday before breakfast, Big Steve and Grandmother bid everyone goodbye and thanked Ben for inviting them. Big Steve pulled Stephen aside and told him that his poems were good and he thought Stephen really understood what was going on. Big Steve took his nephew's arms, held them firmly in his huge hands, looked him in the eyes and shook his head up and down. It was a sign of respect and caring from the older man to his nephew. Stephen kissed Grandmother on the cheek and uttered something in their native tongue to which she hugged him and patted his cheek. Then they were off.

For Sadie, it was the same thing only within her culture. Sammy and his wife, Pat, kissed Sadie and Sammy said a prayer in Aramaic, the Kaddish for his father. He asked his mom whether she thought that dad would know that he loved him and was sorry that they had not understood each other. Pat wondered whether her husband was feeling the loss of his father or the religion of his roots or both. She took his hand and he smiled weakly at her.

"Anyway, Mom, we still want you to come to visit us on the island. It's not so bad in the winter and you would enjoy the breezes. We love you and it's not about religion. You're my mother and we want to spend the rest of our lives close to you and try to make up for some of the time we've lost. Think about it, Mom."

Sadie said she would, and then they were off in their Lincoln convertible. The house seemed empty with so many guests gone.

"So, then we are finally able to talk. Wasn't it wonderful, this whole weekend, I mean, and I really love it here in Asheville. So beautiful, Ben. I think I know what you see in this town."

"Jane, we have this whole year to thank you for in a way. If you hadn't invited us to the group, some of us wouldn't be alive today."

David looked around at the others, and they sadly agreed with him. Some thought of Ted Kelly and Lee who were no longer with them.

"Yes, it seems that way to me also. I have struggled with Claire's death for so long and this horrible hip problem," Gerald said and looked at Pauline.

He continued, "I may have still been alive living like a hermit or worse. My sorrow would have probably eaten away any desire to live at all. Now with my desire to make a home with Pauline and continue my research into Upton Sinclair's works, my life is once again worth living."

He took Pauline's hand and smiled down at her. Gerald felt enormous content.

"What about the idea of staying on at the commune. Why have so many of you decided that this life style isn't what you really want. I don't understand that," Jane inquired.

"Jane, it isn't the commune or the wonderful year we've had. I want something special with one person, with Ben," Britt smiled up at her hero. "I fell in love, really in love, and I love the rest of you too, but it's not the same thing."

Jane's training came to the fore. She remembered Erikson and his eight stages of development. She wondered whether Britt was really saying that her life was now one of integrity, not of despair. All of the writers, including Ted and Lee, had lived lives of despair when they first came to Greentree. But now something new was in their being. They seemed to have made peace with themselves, to find, what Erikson called it, 'integrity.' She wondered whether he meant integration, wholeness. It could even have something to do with Maslow's self-actualization.

Each of the writers seemed to have found a peace they didn't have while at the rehabilitation center. She saw them as morphing into butterflies, wonderfully beautiful butterflies.

"So David, Sadie and Cory, too, are coming back to Florida. I can understand Cory wanting to start a new life, but what about you and David?" Jane asked and looked at Sadie for answers.

"Well, I miss the temperatures, really I do. I know it gets unbearably hot in the summer, but that's what air conditioning is for. I miss Dilly and the small condo I have in Hollywood. You know, going to the thrift stores on Hallandale Boulevard, the food (she turned red with embarrassment and laughed), canasta. What can I say? I miss my people, my Jews. I love you all, but it's different. I have my son and his wife, Pat, that I want to get to know again. Maybe I can talk them out of their their craziness," Sadie beamed.

"How much longer do any of us have? Three, four years, maybe a little longer. Asheville is beautiful, but it's not Hollywood, Florida and the boardwalk"

Sadie thought awhile, her face lit up and she said, "In Florida, at least I know where things are, and who my friends are, and that's important. I mean you're not just friends. I mean you're my family."

Her words seemed confusing, but Sadie knew exactly what she meant.

David spoke next, "I'm going to find a friend who likes to travel with a disabled person. Maybe I'll get one of those service dogs. You know, a traveling companion. I can get him on the Greyhound, aboard a plane. They can't say 'no.' I don't really think I'm a writer. I'll always be a wannabe. No, I see myself getting a big service dog that can help me when I'm down. Old man with dog. Will travel. That's what I want."

Jane listened to David intently.

"What a year. I'll never forget any of you. You are my family, but it's time to get on with my life and see parts of the world I've never seen before. I want to go to Rashistan in India. Nothing like the desert to make you wish for snow," David's joke broke the solemnity.

Ben spoke, "It was a grand plan, wasn't it? I mean, how was I to know I would fall in love at my age and with my problems? It just happened and now I think that I just want to spend the remaining years with Britt, here in Asheville. At least you'll all have a place to come in winter next year."

Jane and Seymour packed their car and left for Florida that afternoon. Tears and an unwillingness to separate permeated the departure. Britt was the saddest because she wondered whether she'd ever see Jane again. Over and over she begged Jane to tell everyone in rehab and nursing that she was so sorry that she gave everyone such a hard time. Jane assured her that all was forgiven. And then they, too, were gone.

CHAPTER THIRTY-ONE

On Tuesday, just three days before the grand experiment was to end, there was a call from Malaprops. The store owner wanted to meet with Ben and the writers.

"Can I come over. I have some news for you, great news for you. We didn't talk much about this, but you know I recorded both sessions. I've had about a hundred calls from the people who came to hear you and others who couldn't make it, like disabled and people without cars. You know, people in nursing homes and too far away to travel. They want to buy a CD of the stories and poems. I need to talk to you soon."

"Sure, whenever you want. Tonight would be fine. Why don't you come to dinner at our place?"

The bookstore owner readily agreed. Ben informed the others that a guest would be arriving from Malaprops with some sort of an idea. The writers, Hazel, and Stephen were intrigued. Were they going to be famous? There was a peaked curiosity. Small talk about the possibilities abounded. Rumors were started that the writers were being invited to make a movie about the commune. Another was that the owner wanted to start a traveling show with the writers going coast to coast doing what they did at Malaprops. Someone suggested that a national magazine wanted to do an in-depth article on the idea of communal living for older people. Ben was amused by the rumors flying.

Hazel and Stephen were invited to remain for dinner because they'd contributed to the night's activities also. Sonnie Bliss, the owner of Malaprops, ate with gusto. She enjoyed the banter at the dinner table, and knew from Ben that everyone was very interested in what she had to say. Britt had trouble holding her tongue. She wanted to ask Bliss questions about her soon to be fame- or so she thought.

"So thanks for showing me Kelly House, and feeding me so much great food. I guess everyone is wondering why I want to speak to you. Well, I recorded everything at the soirée and Sunday afternoon, and with some editing I want to combine them into one CD, and sell them to people who are calling us for copies. If we do this we want a small percentage for the work we do, and taking care of all the administration, et cetera. You brought us so much business that we want just ten percent per copy. I think that $15.00 should be a fair price and we can get it judging by all the calls we're getting. That means that the commune would get somewhere around $13.50 for each CD sold."

David was the first to speak, "Wow, that's great Sonnie. I never dreamt that we would be worth anything financially, never."

The others shook their heads in agreement.

"Well, I guess we all are surprised, but that's what's happening," Bliss chuckled.

"Our agreement with Ben was that he would receive fifty percent of any money that came in due to our productivity. So, we are thrilled that he will receive some gratuity from our efforts," Gerald explained and everyone including Cody agreed with him.

Sonnie opened her backpack and fished for a sheaf of paper. It was a contract for royalties. She told the group that if they were in agreement, she would have her public relations, artistic and other staff members begin work on the CD immediately. She saw the possibility of not only selling it locally, but the chance of it taking off nationally and who knows where. She appeared to be very optimistic, even mentioning that NPR might possibly use parts of it on *All Things Considered*.

Ben scratched his head and looked at Britt. If the truth be known, he never expected to make any money on the communal members' output of writing or anything else they might create. He did this as an act of love for them without any thoughts that he'd turn a profit. He wasn't quite sure what to make of this new twist to what he thought was coming to an end – the commune.

"Sonnie, thanks for this incredible offer! Do you think that we could talk about it for a while before we say OK"? Ben countered.

Sonnie looked surprised but quickly recovered.

"Sure, sure, talk it over. When can you let me know?

David was the house administrator and spoke, "I think that if you would give us about a half hour we could discuss it and give you an answer."

He looked to the others for confirmation, and again all the members indicated their agreement.

"Right, no problem. Why don't I wait on the porch? It's not too cold," Sonnie offered

Everyone began to talk at once. Sensing a need to grasp what was happening, David suggested that everyone quiet down and be given their chance to express their thoughts.

Twenty minutes later, Ben spoke, "Look, you don't have to do this for me. I'm happy that you are finally getting some recognition for all of the work you did all year, but if you agree to this contract for the CD and whatever else might happen, don't do it so that you can repay me. It *ain't* necessary, I assure you. So, let's not keep Sonnie waiting. What'll it be?

"I move that we accept the offer and sign the contract," said Britt.

Cody seconded the motion and everyone including Stephen and Hazel raised their hand in agreement. Cody wiggled his fingers. Sonnie was called in, and smiling broadly, accepted the good news. Malaprops was in business with the communal members.

Each person signed the agreement and since Ben, Britt and the two employees were remaining in Asheville, it was agreed that they would handle all the business issues for the others.

Sonnie left with the last word, "I am so very happy that we are doing this. Not for the business, but for so many people who will now share in your experiences and works. I have someone in mind to do an introduction to the commune. This is a first for us as it is for you."

On March 31ˢᵗ, a Thursday, two vans appeared to remove furniture belonging to David, Gerald, Pauline and Sadie. Cody decided that he would carry his duffel bag. He had all his clothing, three shirts, a couple pairs of pants, some books and his personal items, all packed away in his bag. The vans would unload their cargo at each of the writer's apartments, and that would be handled by Maria who had driven back with Jane and Seymour on Monday.

Juan's plan was to return to Florida with Gerald, David, Pauline, Sadie, and Cody the next day, and deliver everyone except Cody to their homes. Juan and Maria would host Cody for a week or until he could find a place of his own. Ben gave Cody a loan to get him started, with Cody swearing that he wasn't taking "no handouts." He promised to pay every penny back as soon as he got his first paycheck from the restaurant in Pompano Beach. No amount of talking by Ben to assure Cody that he wasn't worried about the money was acceptable to Cody.

"You'll get this money back as soon as I get paid."

Ben even tried to encourage Cody to give it to someone who needed it rather than himself, but his pleas went unheard. Ben asked Juan to make sure that Cody started a bank account, and that he would put a couple of thousand dollars in to start him off.

For everyone, it was two days of mixed sadness and joy. Leaving Asheville, leaving friends, leaving family was awkward and brought lots of ambivalence. Ben decided that the last dinner should be at a restaurant, and of course Moose Café was the favorite. Everyone prepared a speech to give, but no one was able to mouth the words. Tears mixed with anticipation of their move back to Florida created a sense of emptiness.

When they returned to Kelly House, the talk was muffled by sounds of whimpering and low laughter when someone said something about the year in the commune. For everyone aches and pains seemed to hit all at once. But Stephen expected as much. He spent the night at the house mothering everyone and telling them that they were going through separation pangs and that they would be okay. Physical aches often accompanied emotional turmoil.

Sleeping on sofas and made up cots where once was their furniture was difficult, but somehow insomnia gave way to sleep and some understandably uncomfortable dreams. And then it was morning, the last day.

The van was loaded the night before and ready to go east to Interstate 95. Juan had made arrangements to spend the night in Georgia between Savannah and Brunswick. This way the elders wouldn't be too tired on the trip. Hazel prepared a breakfast of oatmeal, scrambled eggs and plenty of coffee and tea. She realized that her work at Kelly House was also coming to an end. She wondered where she'd work next, but her concern didn't last long. Ben took care of everything and arranged for Hazel to work for a nursing home where she would be the head cook with a salary commensurate with her talents. She, too, would be getting some of the royalties for the CD, and would stay in touch with Ben indefinitely.

Stephen mulled over his future and decided that he wanted to go back to school and to medical school eventually. He would finish his classes in the sciences at UNCA and then apply to medical school at Duke or North Carolina State. Ben offered to give him a fine reference and assured him that if finances got tough or anything needed doing, Stephen should simply call him. Stephen thought back to the poem and his Uncle Steve and wanted to somehow make a difference on the reservation. They always needed good doctors and especially Native doctors.

Putting off the moment of departure finally came to an end. Everybody teary, clinging to each other, finally separated, and the doors to the nine passenger van closed. Ben held Britt close and they both had tears careening down their cheeks. Hazel said a Baha'i prayer asking for health and a safe journey. She and Stephen felt the emotion of the moment. The time was all too short. Juan started the engine. The sun was shining and the mountains radiated the warmth of the moment. All too soon the writers were gone.

As Ben, Britt. and the other two went inside, the phone rang.

Hazel answered it. "Who did you say is calling? Yes, hold the line, Mr. Langley, hold on. It's for you, Ben. I think he said a Mr. Langley."

"Hello, who is this?" Ben felt the hairs on his neck bristle.

"Ben, it's Langley. We need to talk!"